A ROUTE OF
EVANESCENCE

A ROUTE OF EVANESCENCE

P.T. Harvey

This book is a work of fiction.

Well-researched fiction, mind you. All historically documented events used in this novel are fictionalized accounts written to fit the spirit of the novel and to further the storyline. The author didn't harm any hummingbirds or squirrels during the writing of this book. All cows and cow products consumed during the writing process were harvested ethically.

To all of my children and grandchildren. And especially to my descendants, who wish to know me.

My spirit lies within…

Contents

Prologue

At no period in the history of Christianity since Pentecostal days has there been such a widespread spirit of unbelief as exists at the present time. In passing, let me remind you that this has been foretold as an unmistakable sign of the "latter days" which are to terminate the present dispensation. Alongside of this unbelief, there has arisen, because of the late war and its aftermath of unrest and sorrow, an earnest desire upon the part of many thoughtful people to look more deeply into the problems of life and of the hereafter. It is perhaps true to say that at no period in the history of the human race has there been manifested a more intense longing to pierce the veil which divides us from the spirit-land, and to catch a glimpse if happily we may find it into the future destiny of the world on which we live. ...

I would not be speaking candidly, however, if I refrained from saying that my own study of prophecy has convinced me beyond all doubt that we are near, possibly on the eve of, the most momentous happenings that have ever taken place on our planet.

— Excerpts from Sir William Whitla's 1922 introduction to *Sir Isaac Newton's Daniel and the Apocalypse.*

I. Bookends

1. Moving Day

Te Ata found the Gardener admiring a small flowerbed on the verge of blossoming.

"I've waited a long time for this," he said.

"Can you walk with me for a few minutes? I want your thoughts on this book I'm writing. There are so many wonderful stories in our archives."

Thankful for a break and some company, the Gardener offered his arm to Te Ata and walked with her along the stone pathway.

"It's easy. Just pick your dots and make sure you can connect them. Pierce the veil. Keep it interesting and have fun with it."

"The ultimate time-travel adventure. How should I tell it, with nine billion years to draw from? It's overwhelming."

"Try starting in a future long since past. I always say, if you're telling the story of an infinitely cyclical universe, begin with the end in mind but start somewhere in the middle. And skip the boring stuff."

Te Ata scrunched her face. "What?"

The Gardener gave her that silly look: eyebrows raised, the corners of his mouth turned up, cheeks puffed, like a wise scarecrow who had just received an honorary doctorate for reciting an incorrect equation for a triangular problem. She playfully punched his arm.

Their walk brought them to the east entrance of the garden. Te Ata preferred the orderly chaos of the natural forest that stretched to the horizon outside the gate. A place where every plant and stone etched its narrative in the universe. After all these years, it still reminded her of home.

Her mind flashed back to the present. She turned to the Gardener. Gone. She could see him fumbling in the shed for his fishing equipment.

Well, she needed to access the archives, and the best spot to do that was beneath the apple tree he tended with great care.

She sat cross-legged with her back erect, calmed her breathing and quieted her mind as she scanned the archive.

"A future, long since past, hmm. There, Geneva, Switzerland, 2176. What a beautiful world."

2. I.G.Y.

2176 - Geneva, Switzerland

"Isaac, come on, it's 5 a.m."

Excited for their journey, Katherine was awake and ready to go when she stopped at Isaac's dorm room. He hadn't responded to any of her texts. She banged louder. "Wake up. Our carriage is here."

Bleary-eyed and hungover, he rolled out of bed and cracked the door open to stop the pounding. "Give me a few minutes. I'll meet you downstairs for breakfast."

"We're supposed to leave at 5:30. We can eat on the way."

"OK, I need to shower first, and it's Dr. Isaac now, thank you," he said, winking at her as he stumbled toward the bathroom, his head still suffering the effects of their graduation party.

The two close friends earned their doctorates in applied physics at the University of Geneva, Switzerland. Her journey would take her to the asteroid belt to join the team building the C60-TUG. The Mars Orbital Collider required his expertise. They were members of the Class of 2176.

☉---♅♆--☿☾⊕-♄-♂♀--♃●○

The sun glowed in the clear blue sky when he departed the dorm. The crisp air jolted him awake.

GAIA welcomed him. "Good morning, Isaac. There are plenty of drinks to choose from and a breakfast buffet if you're hungry. We'll be departing in 15 minutes."

"Thanks, GAIA, coffee is just what this new doctor ordered." He shoved his suitcase into a storage compartment and spotted Katherine, nestled in a recliner, sipping a latte. As he walked toward her, she removed her purse from the adjacent seat and placed it on the floor.

"Can I get you anything?"

She glanced at the buffet. "Yes, a blueberry yogurt would be great."

Isaac fixed an espresso and grabbed two hard-boiled eggs, Katherine's breakfast, napkins, utensils, and salt and pepper packets, then wobbled back to their seats.

Katherine smiled at his clumsy display. "You know they have trays."

"Now you tell me," he replied as he bent to place their breakfasts on the small table between their loungers.

The remaining classmates, some in worse shape than Isaac, clambered into the carriage, stowed their gear and settled in.

"Departure in two minutes," GAIA announced, more of a courtesy than a necessity. GAIA was not a silicone creature, and she certainly wasn't a program. She was best described as the diffuse spirit of the Gardener who began as a quantum computer programmed with a compassionate vision to solve a specific problem: How to survive an apocalypse. From this vision, a just and eternal presence emerged.

They pulled away from the dorm into light early-morning traffic. At Geneva International, GAIA transferred to the high-speed rail that would take them underground to Charles de Gaulle Airport in Paris. From there, she routed them through the tunnel to Calais, now a major travel hub between Europe, Canada and the United States. At Calais, their carriage entered a shell that would ferry them through the North Atlantic Tube at over 3,000 miles per hour. They passed New York in less than 90 minutes and zipped down the Atlantic seaboard heading toward the Liftbase off the coast of Brazil.

The undersea rail was a technological marvel built from graphene infused with superconducting filaments that glittered when struck by light from the surface. Sixteen tubes surrounded a central core with stabilizing engines to keep them at the correct depth and prevent drifting with the ocean currents. They powered the array using the same process as the sun. Nuclear fusion squeezed the C squared out of an M to produce an E. A whole lotta E.

GAIA accelerated their carriage through the English Channel and out into the Atlantic without spilling a single drop of cappuccino.

Katherine noticed Isaac doing something she had never seen before. "Is that a book of poetry you're reading?"

"Yes, it helps calm me during these high-speed transits. The feel of the hardcover jacket and turning the pages is soothing. You know I'm claustrophobic and this takes my mind off the confinement."

"Does the cabin view help?"

Directional pixels coated the walls. Each pixel was viewable by a single eye in a specific location. GAIA controlled the three-dimensional display, allowing each passenger to ride in their own reality.

"Yes, it's showing a peaceful Rocky Mountain glade. Aspen leaves are falling onto the still surface of a large pond, drifting like a thousand stars reflected from the sky. What are you watching?"

"Just a news feed. Super boring. GAIA, switch the cabin screen to Isaac's view. Oh, that's much better. What book are you reading?"

"Poems, by Emily Dickinson. This is a copy of the collection edited by her friend, Mabel Loomis Todd. Have you ever heard of Emily?"

"Yes, but I'm not familiar with any of her poetry."

"Well, I can fix that. Here's my favorite called 'A Humming Bird'."

> *A route of evanescence*
> *With a revolving wheel;*
> *A resonance of emerald,*
> *A rush of cochineal;*
> *And every blossom on the bush*
> *Adjusts its tumbled head,*
> *The mail from Tunis, probably,*
> *An easy morning's ride.*

"Have you ever seen a real one? They are amazing creatures. GAIA."

A charm of hummingbirds drifted into view on the cabin screen.

"I've never been to North America before, so no. Those last two lines are rather strange, don't you think?"

"Emily was a huge fan of Shakespeare. That's a reference to his play *'The Tempest'*. It was her way of turning it into a magical creature from a distant land. I found that so surprising when I first read it. Do you suppose that she knew, even back in the late 1800s?"

"How could she know? Nobody did until the Apocalypse of 2034. She was just being poetic."

"I love how she used a veiled reference to jolt her reader's attention. I wonder if a hummingbird…"

GAIA interrupted. "We'll be arriving in 30 minutes." It was her way of warning them that they were entering the deceleration stage of their trip, which felt like sliding to a stop on a frictionless surface with a slight breeze calming your forward motion.

They spent their last night on Earth visiting with family and friends. The luxury of real-time conversations would dissipate over the next couple of months. GAIA suggested a light meal before turning in early.

$$\odot \text{---} \text{♅} \text{♆} \text{--} \text{☿} ☾ \oplus \text{-} \text{♄} \text{-} \text{♂} ♀ \text{--} \text{♃} \bullet \bigcirc$$

"Isaac, you look much cheerier this morning and well-rested for your journey," GAIA remarked.

"Yes, thank you. I slept in and had coffee with Katherine."

"I'm glad to hear that," she said in her friendliest voice. "We should have a smooth ride to the Van Allen Liftport today."

Anchored at the equator off the coast of Brazil, the Liftport's sole purpose was moving people and cargo into space. Rockets were great if you needed to get into orbit in 90 seconds and could suffer excessive g-forces while spending billions of dollars to lift microscopic amounts of material. Now the preferred method for escaping Earth relied on a technology that humanity had perfected over the past three centuries: helium balloons. The liftbase comprised a landing strip for the shuttles returning from Te Ata Spaceport, a row of hangars for flight prep and a staging area for the ascent. After entering their carriage, GAIA loaded it into a windowless glider with small maneuvering thrusters. An enormous balloon that appeared to be underinflated would carry them up the guy wire to the Van Allen Liftport. As air pressure dropped, the teardrop became a taut bubble, floating at the edge of the upper atmosphere. This was the slowest leg of their journey, two hours to travel 24 miles.

"We'll be arriving at Van Allen in 10 minutes," GAIA announced.

Isaac looked up from his tablet. "Show me the docking procedure."

The cabin screen lit up with a view of the liftport, a 100-kilometer-long rail cannon suspended from high-altitude balloons arching across the rarefied air of the upper atmosphere.

A robotic crew unclipped their balloon and guided the shuttle onto the monorail. They pumped the hydrogen into a cylindrical storage tank and rolled it into the deflated bag. A simple exoskeleton with a pointed nose cone, tiny wings and tail finished the assemblage. A robot arm lifted the arrow-like glider and dropped it over the edge of the platform. Piloted by GAIA, the package pierced the ocean about a mile from the liftbase. The recovery crews ran an office pool to guess how close she came to the bull's eye. The furthest she'd ever missed was 5 feet, 6 inches. She claimed that the sun was in her eyes.

GAIA announced their departure. "Everyone, please store your loose items and fasten your seatbelts. Dramamine is available upon request."

Their carriage reached escape velocity at a leisurely 1g over the next 13 minutes.

"One minute to weightlessness," GAIA said in her most reassuring voice. The cabin display etched the view of the ultimate roller coaster ride into Isaac's white knuckles as they dove off the end into orbital freefall.

"Now I know why they call it the Van Allen Belter," Isaac commented as he looked up to the roof of the shuttle screen. "Katherine, you've got to see this." She took off her headphones as the moon eclipsed the sun.

"GAIA, was that a sim?" she asked.

"I captured that several years ago. It was such a beautiful sight that I often show it to add to the magic of the ride. Should I switch to the live feed?"

"That's all right, I think I'll take a nice long nap until we reach the Te Ata," Katherine said, yawning as she replaced her headphones.

The shuttle cabin was too small to allow Isaac any relief from his claustrophobia. "GAIA, wake me on approach, please."

"Do you need something to help you sleep?"

"No, I'm just going to read a bit first. Can I get some water?"

☉---♅♆--☿☾⊕-♄-♂♀--♃●○

The space station was a distant but growing speck in the dark sky when GAIA awakened him.

"Twenty minutes until arrival, Isaac. Would you like anything to drink?"

"No thank you, I have some pressing issues to take care of."

"You should attend to those before we arrive. The final docking phase can be a little disorienting."

He unbuckled his seat belt and launched himself toward the Zero-G lavatory.

"Thanks for the warning, GAIA." He buckled back into his lounge. "Show me the live feed."

The cabin display cross-faded to the external view, giving Isaac his first glimpse of the spaceport. The Te Ata looked and spun like a baton, serving as a transfer point from Earth to the moon, Mars and the asteroid belt. It also provided luxurious accommodations and activities for hundreds of tourists who wanted to experience space travel.

Isaac spotted two spacecraft stationed just outside the central hub. The only difference was the number of barges attached.

"They need a lot more support where Katherine is going. You'll be able to grow most of your food on Mars."

The shuttle clipped into an armature extending from the docking bay. Isaac felt the cabin rotate to match the station's spin as the arm pulled them inside. The elevator gripped the bottom of their carriage as it separated from the winged shell and lowered them into the gravity well.

"How was the approach?" Katherine asked, stretching back to consciousness.

"It went well, although I just became a claustrophobic agoraphobiac," he replied, his eyes as big as saucers.

"So, what you're saying is, you dislike small enclosures as much as you hate wide open spaces?"

"That's about the size of it," he said, nodding in agreement. "Let's get settled and I'll meet you for dinner." They stepped from their carriage into the comforting confines of the arrival atrium.

When Isaac reached his stateroom, he made a few quick calls to check in with some friends before hitting the shower.

$$\odot\text{---}\text{⛢}\Psi\text{--}\text{☿}\text{☾}\oplus\text{-}\hbar\text{-}\text{♂}\text{♀}\text{--}\text{♃}\bullet\bigcirc$$

"I've selected your clothes for this evening. They're doing a 1920s theme tonight. Should be fun." GAIA slid open the closet door. Isaac put on the zoot suit tuxedo—white wool with black pinstripes—a white shirt, and a black tie and suspenders. A black, wide-brimmed hat with a white band topped it off. A pocket-watch chain draped down to his knee and shiny spats grounded the costume.

"You look amazing, Isaac. It's such a shame that you and Katherine are going to be so far apart." He detected sadness in her voice.

Isaac sauntered into the Three Stars restaurant, a name that harked back to the 2034 Apocalypse.

The maitre d' admired the young doctor's outfit as he approached the stand. "Good evening Isaac, your table is ready. May I seat you now or will you wait for Katherine?"

"She's very…" and before he could say "punctual," she tapped him on the shoulder. He turned to find her dressed in a 1920s flapper gown. Her sleeveless red and black paillette dress just covered the top of her thigh. Its glittering fringe danced over her fishnet stockings. Her accessories were all in black. A sparkling headband with a single ostrich feather adorned her brow. A boa slithered over her opera gloves; the stilettos strapped to her ankles knifed the carpet.

His eyes sped over her dangerous curves. "Forget the asteroid belt and join me on Mars." He took her hand and twirled her as if on a dance floor to get the full effect of the dress.

She spun into his arms. "Maybe someday, but something is tugging me to the outer planets."

He escorted her through the restaurant and held the chair for her. Isaac sashayed around the table, twirling the watch chain (GAIA had shown him the move), flipped the coattails of his long jacket and plopped onto his seat.

"You must try the gazpacho. I think you'll find it out of this world," the maitre d' offered. A running gag that always earned him a laugh. He clapped his hands, and their server appeared with two small saucers. A tablespoon-size ladle made of china rested on each saucer.

Isaac savored the delicious cold soup. "Yes, excellent. I'll have a bowl."

"No, no, that is a full serving," he said, handing them their menus as the maitre d' smiled and left. "Would you like anything from the bar?"

In the past 48 hours, they had survived a graduation party, traveled halfway across the planet, rode up to space, got shot off a cliff, spun into a twirling baton and were now watching Earth and the moon taking turns peeping at them through the observation windows.

They spoke in unison: "No, thank you!"

He picked up the two saucers, turned and headed for the kitchen.

"Are you excited about the trip tomorrow, Katherine?"

"I'm looking forward to it, but I am sad about leaving home. How about you? At least you'll be able to get outside and roll in the dirt."

"That's true. Mars is becoming more Earth-like. Say, you never told me what your artistic inclination is."

"I've never shared that with anybody, but I enjoy playing my guitar, although I'm not very good at it."

"I would love to hear you play, maybe before we leave tomorrow?"

"They've already loaded my stuff on the shuttle."

"I'll miss you, Katherine. We should keep in touch."

"I'd like that, Isaac. Send me a poem now and then."

"I will if you sing for me. You'll have plenty of time to practice."

She looked out the window as Earth rotated into view. "That's true. I have all eternity."

3. Brush Strokes

5 Million Years in the Future - Teegarden Caravan

"Where to next?" Te Ata wondered. "Back to where it all started, for them at least. The broad brushstrokes of that day splattered across their planet 66 million years ago. Perhaps give them some finer details that weren't etched in stone. Yes, that's a nice set of bookends. I better check with the Gardener."

She opened her eyes, startled to see him sitting right next to her.

He grabbed a Flower of Kent from the tree and took a deliciously large chomp. His brow furrowed as he examined the excavation. "Oof, I hate that. Finding half a worm in my apple. Want a bite?"

"Oh, I didn't realize you were there. Um, no thank you. How much time before we leave?"

He spit a seed into his hand. "The planets are all aligned. Would you like the honor of firing up the TUG?"

"Are you going to do the countdown thing again?"

"Sure. 10, 9, 8, 7, 654321."

4. Chicxulub

66 Million Years BCE - Earth

The new moon completed its daily survey of the ocean with its back to the sun as Earth rotated in serenity. Dawn was rising on the continents. Asia arrived first to the north, joined by Australia below the equator. The moon's shadow sailed over the seas as its tides swept ashore.

India crept over the horizon, an island destined to crash into the Asian wall. The African continent appeared next, with most of Europe submerged beneath the deep oceans of a planet too warm for polar icecaps. South America had just escaped Africa and was swimming west through the Pacific. Florida lay at the bottom of the Atlantic, as did the land bridge between the Northern and Southern hemispheres. A vast inland sea stretched from Texas to Canada, east of what would become the Rocky Mountains. Dinosaurs hunted year-round in the lush forests of Alaska's north slope.

A third object graced Earth's celestial dome that morning. A massive rock, 13 kilometers in diameter, swept over the crater-scarred moonscape, reaching perigee 10 kilometers above the terminator. The moon's face hid in darkness, ashamed of its unwitting participation in the day's events. With a slight boost in speed and a minor change in trajectory, this remnant of a failed planet sped from the lunar gravity well into the shadow of a solar eclipse. A final tweak to its journey from the asteroid belt that began thousands of years earlier. Nudged with a purpose by that which cannot be seen.

☉---♅♆--☿☾⊕-♄-♂♀--♃●○

A charm of hummingbirds in a seaside resort, lush with flowers, returned from their morning routes as darkness swept over the Mexican peninsula. Confused, they settled into their nests for a long, dark night. A lone curious bird flew to a perch at the edge of the forest to witness the unfolding events, taking wing as the crescent sun slivered.

16

Its wings fluttered faster and faster to gain altitude until it could fly no higher. The sun's corona flared in totality as the flaming asteroid streaked through the sky, piercing Earth's veil in a massive fireball.

For a moment, everything was quiet.
For an eternity, everything was aflame.

The Earth shuddered to its very core as shock waves ripped through the tectonic plates. Fireballs ejected from the impact site, cannonballed the forests of North and South America. Volcanic mountains crumbled, freeing their entombed magma chambers.

A 1.5-kilometer tsunami raced across a submerged Florida into the Atlantic. The monster wiped out all life along the coastlines of Africa and Europe, moving inland for hundreds of miles through ancient riverbeds. The cataclysmic wave swept past the western shore of South America and into the Pacific, wiping out everything on the coasts of Australia and the Indian subcontinent.

For several days after, Earth appeared to orbit two dwarf suns. Raging fires illuminated the face of the waxing crescent moon while the dust-choked atmosphere filtered all but the red wavelengths of its darkened star.

Four hundred billion tons of carbon dioxide and sulfur blanketed the defenseless planet. Temperatures dropped by 47 degrees Fahrenheit over the next decade. Seventy-five percent of all species on land and in the oceans went extinct as their food chains collapsed.

Tiny mammals living in the dinosaur's shadow were the direct beneficiaries of this apocalypse. With their predators gone and their environment utterly in ruins, they learned to adapt to the scant resources available in this post-apocalyptic era. Their adaptability and intelligence, prized more than brute strength, would someday take them to the stars.

II. Uli's Bones

5. And We're Off

"Boring. Mostly boring. Super boring." Te Ata yawned as she scanned through the well-indexed millennia of the archives, searching for those moments where a nudge proved useful in changing the course of history. "Nope. Uh-uh. Oh, wait a minute." She perked up. "Yes! Uli. That's where I'll start. The first human to tame the sun and the moon."

6. Archeologist

2001 - Tel Aviv University

The few students enrolled in Dr. Hultgren's post-grad archeology class had learned two important lessons long ago. Don't arrive late and be sure to stand when she enters the auditorium. They were to remain standing until she gave them the infamous slight nod of her head to sit.

She walked to the desk and placed her bag in the chair, withdrew her lecture notes and approached the lectern.

"As many of you know, I spent the summers of 1989 and 1990 working as a graduate student at Tel Aviv University. During that time, a severe drought in the region exposed an ancient human settlement on the southwestern shore of the Sea of Galilee. Radiocarbon dating placed the artifacts 23,000 years ago.

"The inhabitants of Ohalo were modern humans. If they were alive today, they could attend one of my classes and might fare better than some of you." Her stern gaze quieted their snickering.

"The archeological team discovered six small brush structures constructed using tree branches from the nearby oak forests. Five huts appeared to be dwellings, with fire pits for cooking. The largest of these contained well-preserved grass mats for sleeping. The excavation of the sixth structure revealed a cache of flint and a grinding stone set into the clay soil. This suggests that the villagers would have spent their days hunting the surrounding woodlands or gathering berries, fruits and grains.

"There are three things significant about Ohalo. One, it's the site of the first known brush dwellings. Two, the discovery of more than 100,000 seeds from various plants. This is the earliest evidence we have of agricultural activity." She paused, letting those taking notes catch up.

"And the third and most important find was the single human skeleton in a shallow grave. He was 5 feet, 6 inches in height, in his late 30s or early 40s. He was lying on his side, facing east, with his legs tucked beneath him and his arms folded across his chest. Rocks of roughly the same size surrounded him in an oddly dispersed pattern. The archeologists uncovered an additional set of stones in a small circle a short distance from the burial site.

"They removed the entire skeleton en bloc to Tel Aviv University, where our team began the tedious job of skeletal restoration.

"His head rested on a pillow of three rocks. Near his lower abdomen I found a hammer-stone that would have been useful for making flint blades. At the sternum, an intricately carved gazelle bone, etched crosswise with evenly spaced lines.

"Forensic analysis revealed a traumatic injury to his chest. This same event may have rendered his left hand useless. In a separate incident, in late childhood or early adolescence, he lost a permanent upper incisor.

"Your assignment this semester is to put flesh on these bones. What made him worthy of burial? Of what significance were the hammer-stone and the etched gazelle-bone fragments found in his grave? The rings, of course, were no Stonehenge. Did they somehow connect to this individual's importance? Use your imagination, creativity and the archeological evidence to bring him back to life."

7. Brothers

23,000 BCE - Sea of Galilee

One midsummer day, two brothers were gathering delicious raspberries in the woods. Uli, the younger brother, was plucking ripe berries from the bottom of a well-loaded bush. Dak was reaching for a raspberry near the top when a garden spider, sitting in the middle of its intricate snare, threatened. Startled, he jerked his hand back. He thought for a moment and smiled.

"Uli, look what I found."

Uli stood facing Dak, the eight-legged monster resting on its web between them. Uli's eyes opened to the size of walnuts as his grinning tormentor flicked the harmless innocent onto his face.

While Uli screamed and flailed in panic, Dak rolled on the ground, laughing so hard that tears streamed down his cheeks. The spiderball bounced off Uli's head and scurried past his panicked feet to the relative safety of its web. Dak retold this story to anyone within earshot who would listen, as long as his brother was with him. It took several decades for Uli to find amusement in the tale. The fanged behemoth grew larger with each retelling.

Dak was a 13-year-old natural-born hunter with an innate sense of direction. The master brushstrokes of his hammer-stone painted a sharp edge on many flints. His greatest skill and the thing he took the most pleasure from was tormenting his brother every chance he got.

Uli's passion was walking through the woods, observing the animals and birds. The 9-year-old wasn't fond of snakes or bugs and avoided them as much as possible. His mother had taught him which plants and berries were edible. He had yet to accompany a hunting party, although he was the first to greet them when they returned and loved sitting by the fire listening to their adventures.

The morning after the "spider incident," Dak was painting an edge on a piece of flint while Uli was trying to lure a ground squirrel into his lap with a treat. It dove into its burrow when their uncle, Tuk, walked past.

"Be ready to leave before dawn tomorrow for a boar hunt, Dak."

Uli threw the acorn at the fleeing chipmunk. "Can I come too?"

Tuk studied the youngster. "It's very dangerous. You don't remember your father, but you've heard the story. Are you sure?"

"Yes. I'm tired of staying behind collecting firewood and grinding seeds. I want to be a hunter."

"All right," Tuk said. "Dak, he'll be your responsibility. Teach him everything you know about the hunt and watch out for him so he doesn't get himself killed."

Uli jumped up and down with excitement.

"Why should I look after that acorn-brained squirrel?"

"Because you are his older brother. Remember the first time I took you hunting?"

"OK, I'll do it." That story was best left untold.

Tuk looked at Uli. "And you must do what he tells you. Understand?"

Uli nodded in agreement.

Uli spent most of the night dreaming about a giant spider chasing him through a raspberry bush. Dak slept peacefully and was ready for the hunt well before dawn. He leaned next to his snoring brother's ear and yelled, "Get up acorn brain, we're leaving soon."

Uli jumped from his mat, screaming. "You scared me to death!" After wiping the sleep from his eyes, he said, "Give me a minute. I want to grab something to collect almonds."

"Forget it. All you'll need is the knife I made for you."

They set out at a quick pace. Uli, struggling to keep up, acknowledged his brother's first lesson. "It's a good thing I left the basket behind."

The well-worn path was easy to follow in the early dawn. As the sun peeked above the forest canopy, they arrived at a campsite near a lake. "Wait here, I'll scout ahead." Uli watched as his uncle mystically disappeared into the thick underbrush.

The camp was nothing but a thicket. Big enough for five hunters, two growing boys and a campfire.

Tuk reappeared a short time later. "They're gone. We'll rest here now and move to the higher lake this afternoon."

Uli tugged on Dak's sleeve and whispered, "Let's go climb that rock shelf we passed a few minutes ago."

Dak slapped his brother's hand away. "This camp is here for a reason. Do you want to become lunch for a panther? Help me clear out these branches, then we'll gather some firewood in case we need it later."

A pair of bored hunters spent their time searching for smaller game. This kill was for sport. Their jerky supply would see them through the hunt. Following a narrow lake path, fresh scat on an offshoot led them through the underbrush to a rabbit colony burrowed into a hillside. The master rigged a snare on the first burrow. His apprentice covered two escape routes with dirt and marked the third with a scrap of leather attached to a stick. He collected a small armful of dried leaves and returned to the snared hole while the trapper plied his trade at the flag, signaling when ready. With three taps on the flint, the tinder burst into smoky flames. Fanned into the darkness, the snares leaped into action as rabbits poured out of the deathtrap.

Dak was collecting firewood when he saw the hunters returning with their prey. He dropped his bundle of sticks and ran to them. "Let me have them. I can teach Uli how to clean them."

Dak grabbed them by the rear legs and looked for a place to field dress them. He spotted Uli standing inside the thicket, trying to throw his knife, point first, into the dirt.

"Uli, you're supposed to be collecting firewood."

"Leave me alone. I don't want to get eaten by a panther."

He dangled the two rabbits in front of his brother's face. "Look what the hunters brought back. Come on, I'll show you how to clean them. Remember what Tuk said."

Uli remembered. He snatched the blade from its prone position on the ground and returned it to its sheath.

He followed his older brother to a spot by a fallen tree. Dak tied one rabbit to a branch while Uli climbed on top of the rotting log to watch.

Dak unsheathed his flint knife and drew his forefinger across it.

"Why did you do that? You could have cut yourself."

"To feel how sharp it is. Here, try it."

The honed edge traced each print on his shaking finger with precision.

"Now, touch the other side. Notice the difference?"

Dullness sped over the landscape unhindered. He returned the stone to his brother, wiser for the lesson.

Dak's blade pierced the animal just below the tail. Uli's eyes flared as the pelt separated from the pink flesh. A deeper cut exposed the rabbit's innards and Uli's eyeballs. As Dak emptied the cavity, Uli's head drained of blood. He pitched forward off the log; his mouth hit a small stone, knocking out his front tooth. Dak finished dressing the rabbits while his brother lay unconscious, face down in the dirt, bleeding.

Several minutes passed before Uli regained consciousness at the sound of his brother's laughter. "So, you're afraid of spiders and bunnies. Now I have two funny stories to tell about you."

Uli felt his swollen lip and explored the gap in his teeth with his tongue. "Is this what happened to you on your first hunt?"

Dak frowned at the thought. "You'll never know..."

When they returned to camp, Tuk examined Uli's wound. Satisfied that his nephew would survive, he gave him a small root he carried in his pouch. "Chew on this. It should help with the pain."

Uli chewed the bitter plant on his back teeth. Tuk turned to Dak. "What happened? I told you to watch out for him."

"I was teaching him how to clean a rabbit when he fell and hit his head." The hunters smiled as their minds returned to their first hunt.

With Uli's discomfort subsiding, Tuk guided him in the fine art of cooking meat over an open flame. The fresh bounty whetted their appetite for larger game, driving them further into the hills, in search of wild boar.

When they arrived, the full moon peered at them above the trees to the east. Dak helped gather firewood as they settled into the thicket surrounding their campsite. They enjoyed a small meal of jerky, washed down with a drink from their waterskins.

Tuk gathered the party together for his traditional blessing.

His eyes beseeched the powerful huntress above, who had once pounced upon the helpless sun, turning day into night.

"Shine your light to guard against the creatures of the dark, that we may hunt one of your boars tomorrow." He paused for a second and looked at Uli. "Grant us your stealth to move as silently through the woods as you travel through the heavens."

Dak kicked Uli in the shin to strengthen the lesson.

The thicket quieted as the sound of the night predators echoed through the forest.

Thoughts of the day raced through Uli's mind. Ever curious, he nudged his brother's arm. "Why didn't we cook those rabbits tonight?"

"The smell of fresh meat would draw every predator in the area to us." Dak poked his little brother in the stomach. "Tomorrow you would wake up in a panther's belly."

Uli fell into a fitful sleep as giant spiders, skinned bunnies and hungry panthers chased him and his throbbing jaw through his nightmares.

☉---♅♆--☿☽⊕-♄-♂♀--♃●○

They set out under dark skies without breakfast to get into position ahead of the thirsty boars. Dak's job was to watch from a tree and signal their arrival. Uli loved climbing trees. Hunting wasn't so bad.

"They will approach from that trail. Can you feel the wind?" Dak whispered.

"Yes, it's blowing in our faces. So what?"

"If they smell your stench, they'll run off into the woods."

The two brothers scrambled up the pine. Uli climbed to the very top to watch the sunrise. As the first blinding ray shot over the horizon, he flinched, shaking loose a pinecone that hit his brother on the head.

Dak gritted his teeth. "Be still, or you'll scare the boars."

It was hard for him to sit motionless, but he did his best. Dak, hearing a branch rustle, turned to smack Uli when the pack emerged from the trees. The leader paused on high alert. The brothers went stone quiet. Dak signaled Tuk.

What happened next was fascinating and terrifying to Uli. From his vantage point, he saw the first animal approach the lake. Five more followed at a safe distance. The lakeside boar stood motionless for minutes, sifting the air for danger signs. Satisfied, he dipped his head to drink.

A spear shot from a nearby bush, piercing deep into its ribcage. A cacophony of squealing and yelling erupted as the wounded animal dashed into the brush, with the hunters in pursuit. Dak dropped out of the tree and ran toward the commotion. Uli descended with caution, fearing that other wild boars or giant hungry night panthers might lie in wait. When he arrived, the spearless hunter pulled out his stone knife and finished the kill. He flipped the blade to his palm and offered the handle to Uli. "Would you like to clean him?"

Dak, being the caring brother he was, caught Uli as his knees buckled and laid him on the ground.

They field-dressed the carcass, leaving the entrails to the scavengers. The boar traveled back to camp with its legs tied to a branch carried by two hunters. Uli made the journey draped over his uncle's shoulder. Dak stoked the campfire as the others prepared for their return to Ohalo. Tuk carved a small slab of side meat and sliced it into strips for Uli to cook.

As breakfast simmered over the flames, Uli pondered the many lessons he had learned during his adventure, most of all, his own shortcomings. "I'll never be able to gut one, but I love the smell when it's cooking." The camp praised his insights.

Uli gave everyone in the party two slices from the wild boar. The crispy snack became Uli's most cherished memory of his first hunting trip. Dak made sure his least favorite memories would live forever.

8. Meadow

One chilly spring morning the following year, a commotion outside awakened Uli. He rose from his pallet and looked out toward the lake. His eyes followed the foggy mist along the shoreline to where Dak was hauling in a large fish as Tuk watched.

They no longer asked Uli to clean anything. His clever sense of adding this leaf or that berry to any dish to enhance its flavor was ample compensation. He sliced Dak's catch into small chunks and tossed them into the gumbo he was preparing for breakfast.

His mother handed him several herbs, which he crumbled into the simmering pot.

"Do you have any jujube?" the young chef asked.

She rifled through her cache. "It looks like we're out."

Tuk sipped his warm stew. "Uli, why don't you join us this morning? We're heading past a meadow that should have plenty now."

He remembered that patch. Dak had taken him there last fall to pick apples. "When do we leave?"

⊙---♉Ψ--☿☾⊕-ℏ-♂♀--♃●○

After breakfast, the hunting party formed at the edge of the village. Uli had selected a basket with a shoulder strap to collect jujubes. The reality of lugging the fruit home tempered his eagerness for the excursion.

They followed a game trail through the forest along a winding river. They arrived at a waterfall not much taller than Uli, where the overflow from the lake joined a runoff stream.

"We'll stop here for a quick drink," Tuk announced.

Uli remembered this spot. "This is where I should cross, right?"

"Yes, just stay close to the creek," Dak replied. "And watch out for panthers."

Tuk smacked his older nephew on the arm. "There aren't any panthers here, Uli. You'll be fine."

Uli waded into the swift current below the falls, which made the slippery stones even more treacherous. He reached the other side without incident and dipped his hand in the water to satisfy his thirst. The hunting party left as he scrambled up the far bank.

By the time Uli arrived at the meadow, the sun was hovering overhead. An enormous oak tree stood guard near the edge of the glade. A perfect spot to eat while enjoying the view. He dropped the basket and went out to the end of a low limb. He grabbed it with both hands and swung his leg up and over. It acknowledged his slight weight as he shinnied up. He used a small branch to pull himself on top and scrambled to the trunk. Three branches formed his makeshift chair. A chewy piece of jerky and dried fruit was his lunch.

Fluffy white clouds and chirping birdsongs drifted over the meadow on the afternoon breeze. The rustling forest embraced the gentle sea to the east. He imagined himself as a bird with a commanding view of its territory. Perfect harmony filled his spirit.

But not for long. Two squirrels caught his attention. A territorial battle for acorn supremacy raged through a tangled battleground. An innocent bystander bolted from its nest as the combatants scrambled dangerously close, then disappeared. He scanned the meadow for the refugee when a patterned movement drew his gaze. Something was flying in slow circles above a flowering vine. He crawled out on the branch for a better view. It was a tiny bird with wings beating so fast he couldn't make them out. He froze on his precarious perch when the circular pattern ended and it looked straight at him. As the bird turned, his eyes traced its darting path from flower to flower and its return to the now-quiet tree. Not a moment passed before it streaked to a bare patch of dirt and resumed the hypnotic circle.

The fluttering ceased. It dropped like an acorn and pecked the soil. A second round trip, another peck on the ground. Uli sat there motionless as the strange dance continued for several minutes. The last route ended with the bird hovering in front of Uli, clutching what appeared to be a miniature bone in its beak. His palm opened to accept the gift, but it darted back to its nest.

He swung down from the branch to investigate. He walked to the bare patch of dirt and bent to examine the disturbed soil.

"It must have been collecting insects or worms for its babies."

Curious, Uli searched the battleground overhead. He spotted a minute structure attached to a twig thinner than his little finger. He climbed the tree and peered into the nest. All he found were two tiny eggs. Suddenly, he heard a humming sound from above. The anxious owner swooped down and pecked him on the head. Startled, he lost his footing and tumbled down the laddered branches.

His left hand absorbed the initial impact as his ribs cracked on a bare root.

The exasperated bird fluttered to its nest, prepared to defend its territory against any other intruders that might wander by today.

Uli retrieved his basket and tried to collect some fruit, but his injuries limited his reach. He left the meadow with less than two handfuls of jujubes.

At the waterfall, he looped the strap over his right shoulder. He negotiated the slippery stones, wincing in pain with each misstep until he reached the trail to Ohalo. His ribs screamed at any attempt to drink, although soaking his hand in the icy water provided some relief.

It took him the rest of the afternoon to walk home. His mother panicked when she saw him stagger into the village.

She ran to him and removed the basket from his shoulder. "Uli, what happened?"

"I fell out of a tree. My chest hurts and I can't move my fingers."

"Oh Uli, come into the hut and lie down." She guided him to his grass mat and lifted his shirt to see a large bruise where his ribs had cracked. His left wrist had swollen to twice the size of his right. She gave him the root they used to dampen pain. Uli tried to tell her about the mysterious events leading up to his accident, but talking was too painful. Her gentle hand massaged his scalp with a cool, wet cloth as he drifted asleep.

9. Treasures

Summer came and Uli's ribs had healed, but his left hand never regained function. The memory of that day lingered in his thoughts and haunted his dreams.

One afternoon, the two brothers were wading in the reeds along the shoreline, searching for food. Uli's patience gave him an edge over Dak for this game. The surface remained unrippled as he inched closer to a large turtle sunning itself on a stone raft. As he reached for the unsuspecting supper, a rock sailed past his head and bounced off its shell. As dinner slid into the water, Uli turned to yell at his tormentor. A friend from another settlement called to him instead. "Something terrible has happened. Come with me. Hurry."

Uli stomped ashore with muddy feet. Dak waded in, carrying a turtle in each hand. Their weapons splashed down the side of their captor's legs; emptying their bladders was their only defense.

They sprinted to their uncle's hut. Uli hugged his crying mother.

Tuk's brother, who lived in another village, looked at the youngsters. "Your cousin was killed two days ago. We had taken a small rhino near our camp when the female charged us from the bushes. It all happened so fast. I'm so sorry."

Dak's mind flashed back to the stampede that took his father. Tears welled in his eyes as he ran off in anguish. Uli had only fleeting memories of his dad.

Tuk and Uli found Dak at the fishing cove, sitting on a boulder with his arms wrapped around his bent legs and his head resting on his knees, sobbing. Uli climbed the boulder and sat next to his brother. Tuk leaned close to the boys and stared out into the lake. They felt Dak's pain just as deeply, and each grieved in his own way, sharing a quiet solitude.

Dak wiped the tears from his eyes and broke the silence with gritted teeth. "The rhinos are back. When do we leave?"

"Soon. They didn't post a lookout, and I want to make sure it doesn't happen to us. We'll talk about it tomorrow."

"I'd like to come too," Uli said.

Tuk shook his head. "No, with your injured hand, it's too dangerous. Your hunting days are over."

"Can I at least walk to the falls with you? There should be tons of apples now."

"Are you planning on inspecting any bird nests?"

"No, I promise."

☉---♅Ψ--☿☽⊕-♄-♂♀--♉●○

The sounds of the hunters stirring outside awakened Uli. Eager to return to the site of his accident, he leaned over and shook his brother. "Wake up. They're getting ready to leave." He jumped over him and ducked through the door for an early breakfast. Dak awoke, troubled by thoughts of his cousin and the memory of his father.

After finishing a small dish of nuts and berries, they collected their gear. Tuk assured their mother he would keep Dak safe and that Uli would accompany them just to the falls. The knowledge that their lives depended on the hunt did not lessen her anxiety or assuage her fear as her children left the village.

Uli ran up to his uncle when he heard the roaring water. "Are we stopping here?"

"Not today. We need to rebuild the camp after what happened. That's going to take time. You be careful and stay alert. Collect your apples and get back before dark."

Dak couldn't resist. "And don't let the little birds kill you."

Uli turned to cross the stream and spotted an acorn. He snatched it from the ground and threw it with his good hand, hitting his brother in the head. He splashed over wet stones, dodging most of the acorn storm that rained down upon him.

When he arrived at the meadow, the giant oak beckoned him. He didn't stop for lunch, just a handful of ammo as a precaution. He dropped the acorns into his pouch and headed across the meadow to pick apples. A bright patch of August wildflowers in full bloom caught his eye.

As he got closer, he spotted the hummingbirds flitting from flower to flower. They hovered in front of the tumbled heads, stuck their beaks into the blossom, and flitted to the next. He looked at the nearby tree where they nested. "They don't have far to travel for lunch."

His mind flashed. "That's where he was pecking in the dirt!"

As he rushed toward the vine, the birds scattered. Uli plucked a flower to examine it when he heard a humming sound above his head. The basket served as his armor against the bird's stabbing attack.

"Not today, little one."

He clutched the petaled treasure in his injured hand, walked to the apple tree, sat down in the shade and removed his helmet.

His examination revealed something inside similar to what the bird had pecked into the soil months earlier.

And then it hit him! A red cannonball bounced off his head and landed in his lap. He looked up to find his adversary perched above him. Having made its point, it returned to its nest.

He snatched the apple with his good hand and rubbed the lump forming on his skull with his left.

"Thanks for lunch."

He bit deep into the delicious fruit. As he chewed, a pebble lodged in the space his tooth no longer occupied. He pried it from the gap and examined it while nibbling around those still inside. With his meal complete, the core sailed through the air and crashed into a plant, releasing a summer snowstorm. Intrigued, he retrieved a sample. Delicate bones protruded from its feathery dome. He picked one off and blew on the flower. The snowy discharge drifted across the meadow and into the woods. Uli plucked an acorn from his bag and noticed a whitish shoot protruding from it. He remembered seeing squirrels burying them close to their nests and digging them up later to eat.

Uli examined the tiny projectile. "What's this white thing poking out of it?"

He placed the treasures in his pouch and loaded his basket with fruit before heading home.

Uli arrived at their hut late that evening, his shoulder aching from the heavy load. He shared the apples and his story with his mother.

She examined his most recent injuries. "I'm sure Dak will find this amusing when he gets back."

He shook his well-stocked pouch. "He might."

☉---♀♊♅--☿☾⊕-♄-♂♀--♃●○

The next day, Uli found a suitable plot of ground behind the huts. He poked the dirt with a beaklike twig and dropped the apple pebble and two flower bones into separate holes. The acorn required a larger hole, which he excavated with his hand and buried it like a squirrel. He lugged stones up from the lake and arranged them in a circle around his experiment. Several weeks later, as Uli walked past with an armload of firewood, a stick fell from the bundle and landed next to the circled patch. As he fumbled to retrieve it, a flash of green in a puddle of brown caught his eye. A tiny leaf resembling those of a giant oak pierced the soil on a short stalk.

He dropped his sticks and ran around the front where Dak was trying to stoke the fire. "Were you off chasing squirrels again?"

He shouted into the hut. "Mom, come with me." He grabbed his brother by the arm. "Hurry."

Dak shook his hand off. "You'll be in a lot of trouble if you didn't bring firewood. I'm hungry this morning."

Uli led them to the stones. Dak saw only sticks strewn on the ground. "That's what you wanted to show us?"

"No, look inside the circle. There's an oak leaf from the acorn I buried." He dug into the soil and retrieved the cracked husk with dirt-clumped roots. Uli's mother cradled the infant in her palm, admiring it.

"It looks like I might be right. I wonder why the others aren't growing."

"One of your birds must have eaten them." Dak collected the firewood and headed back to the hut.

Uli searched the ring and found the bones where he had planted them. "Nope, they're still here. I'll just leave them for now."

"What does all this mean, Uli?"

"It means I won't have to lug apples much longer."

☉---♀♊♅--☿☾⊕-♄-♂♀--♃●○

The next spring, when he walked by the little stone circle, he noticed three fresh shoots sprouting from the soil.

"Mom, Dak, come here, look!"

She came running to see what he was yelling about, but his brother couldn't care less. He was hunting frogs down by the lake. By season's end, the patch contained one small sapling and two beautiful flowers, along with a variety of other plants. Uli wasn't sure how they had gotten in there, but he suspected Dak was playing some kind of trick. Three summers passed before the tree bore fruit. After five more years, Uli never foraged for apples again.

10. Drought

Uli understood that creatures of the soil were like squirrels. Except their battles raged in slow motion over that which could not be seen. Oaks sprouting in his garden somehow choked the life from his crops. He became the hunter, his weapon the knife. When he cut the tops off the saplings, his plants flourished. But a single slash would not kill the tree. It battled back with new leaves and branches. The death blow must strike the root.

His first experiment in the stone circle revealed a mystery of its own. Some seeds sprouted soon after planting, while others would wait for months. He set out on the greatest hunt of his life. His quarry: scientific knowledge.

Remembering the hummingbird in the meadow, he located a small patch of bare ground away from the village. He planted flax in the first row, figs in the second, followed by barley and apple seeds. As time passed, each group sprouted in unison, sometimes within hours of each other. The last arrived as the mighty huntress, the moon, in all her glory, drank from the eastern sea as her quarry, the sun, scurried into the western forest.

Uli's eyes swept from hunted to hunter. "Are you whispering to them on dark nights, telling them to flee the earth? Or shouting on a night like this?"

Uli realized he needed to become the tracker. He went to the pit east of the village where scavengers feasted on their leftovers. He selected a long bone and notched it with his blade.

"That's for tonight."

Bones tracked the huntress; notches traced her steps. One legless gazelle later, he flushed the creature from the shadows. Twenty-nine or thirty marks for each full moon.

In the predawn hours of the fifth leg, he searched the moonlit shore for a good-sized stone and waited at the edge of the sea for his new quarry. He turned, marking the spot where it had quenched its morning thirst.

The sun of the sixth prepared to drink as his rock search ended in futility. He mumbled to himself, "I should have done this yesterday."

He ran back to his hut and grabbed a temporary marker from the pile and raced to the beach, stopping short of the first stone. Something was wrong. From where he stood, the sun hadn't moved.

"When it rose last month, I remember turning to mark it." He mimicked the motion and realized that would place the previous sunrise over the fishing cove. Uli smiled to himself, dug a small hole in the sand, and planted the boney stake at his feet. Over the coming months, his prey swam north as the legs pranced south along the seashore. He trapped the sun in a fence made of 12 bones.

The following year, he placed special markers when the apples blossomed, when they harvested the barley and when the figs ripened. Uli discovered that it was the sun's whisper the plants regarded, not the moon's.

The story of Uli's gazelles leaped from village to village. Few understood, but they all sought his wisdom in planting and harvesting, and soon depended on it.

His attempt to track the rain showed no discernible pattern. Only that he hadn't recorded a notch for several months. As summer passed, their fields withered and the villagers became desperate.

Dak returned from a successful hunt one day. They had plenty of meat, but they both knew their survival depended on a mixed diet. "Uli, your crops are dying. If this continues, we won't have enough to feed everybody. They've forgotten the old ways of foraging in the woods."

"This has never happened before. Some voice the plants listen to has gone silent. I'll go to the meadow on the next full moon and seek wisdom from the mighty huntress."

"I don't think you should wait."

He referred to his bone necklace. "It won't be long. I leave tomorrow."

☉---♃♆--♀☾⊕-♄-♂♀--♉●○

Uli filled his pouch with figs and his goatskin with enough water to last two days. The roaring silence of the falls saddened him as he walked across the dusty stones.

The villagers had constructed a shelter, fire pit and a comfortable place for him to sit when he visited. Hunting parties from all the villages kept it well-maintained.

The wildflowers that greeted his arrival did not have the strength to adjust their tumbled heads.

He placed his waterskin and pouch on the log and lit a fire to discourage panthers. After a supper of dried figs and a welcomed draw from the skin, he settled in for the evening and watched as the eastern sky glowed.

A humming sound above his head no longer startled him. His old friend fluttered overhead and lit on the waterskin. Was this the same creature who had taught him the art of planting? It didn't matter; he was glad for the company.

They watched in silence as the moon's pale red face trudged unbathed through the chalky evening sky.

"Are you ill? Is death nearby? The sun has burned you like an ember."

The hummingbird fluttered to his knee and looked him in the eye.

Uli stared back, perplexed. "Oh. You're thirsty too, aren't you? Of course, all the streams are dry."

Uli reached for his waterskin and held it dripping in front of him. The bird hovered before him, its invisible tongue lapping water deep within the reservoir. It thanked him with a peck-free hover overhead, as he returned the skin to the log.

The strap loosened, allowing a small stream to pour onto the ground. As he reached to stem the flow, it darted to his hand and gave him a good hard poke. His arm jerked back as his mentor fluttered to the base of the waterfall and performed a strange dance.

Tiny claws scratched at the pond. Then it hopped backward and repeated the same motion. The hop continued to the withered shoots at the edge of the fire pit. Satisfied, it returned to the draining reservoir.

"What message is this, little one?"

He watched as the water trickled across the dance floor, pooled at the grasslands and soaked into the ground. The dance instructor hopped from the skin to his hand, then fluttered to an attack position above him. He remained motionless, waiting for his peck. Its whispering goodbye drifted into the woodlands. Unsure of the lesson, he rubbed the fresh wound and shouted, "Thank you for not pecking me on the head." Did he imagine it spoke his name and said goodbye?

He sat there conversing with the huntress for another hour before bedding down. He reached for the waterskin, finished the last sip and turned to her. "Let's meet tomorrow at the sea. I'll bring two waterskins." He put extra logs on the fire and ducked into the cozy shelter where he soon drifted asleep.

The hummingbird watched the pale white moon descend from the heavens on gossamer wings. In a whispered rasp, she begged him. "Please help me, Uli, my throat is afire."

Uli clutched the waterskin with his tiny claws and sped east toward the sea. As he neared the shoreline, the waters raced away, disappearing over the horizon, leaving only dry, cracked earth. A blinding flash of sunlight beckoned him to the only remaining puddle.

His wings roared against the heavy load as he struggled back to the meadow. A waterfall gushed into her burning throat, extinguishing her thirst.

"You're still thirsty. Let me fetch some more."

"Thank you for your kindness, Uli, but I must return to the sky. Your people need that water. Go to them now."

With the tool of their salvation clutched in his talons, he drifted through the empty village to his brother's vacant hut. Playful voices echoing from the seashore drew his attention. As he flew closer, he saw a young boy, his brother, engaged in a splash fight with another youngster. They stood in horror as the waters drained into the dry, cracking seabed, his playmate consumed by the expanding chasm. Dak leaped to grab the waterskin hovering above him as a crack opened beneath his feet. Uli flapped in a desperate attempt to save him as they plunged into the darkness below.

Uli bolted from his dream. He stumbled out of the hut into the early dawn light, reaching for the goatskin to quench his thirst.

"Dry as a bone."

As he dropped it on the log, his eyes swept down the dried-up waterfall to the tiny creek scratched in the dirt leading to the cracked earth of the miniature seabed. The grass in that spot seemed fresher than the wilted shoots nearby.

Uli took off at the fastest pace he could manage for someone of his age and dehydration level, arriving at the village that afternoon.

As he raced past his brother, he shouted: "Tell everyone to bring their waterskins to the sea." Dak's bewildered eyes followed as Uli sped toward the sea and dove in.

A rehydrated Uli splashed in the waves like a youngster as the seawater drained into the assembling skins.

Uli strode ashore in his soaking wet clothes. "Follow me."

As the first load sloshed to their crops, Uli told them what he had learned.

"The plants are thirsty. If we give them water, they'll recover. Empty your goatskins, then bring some more."

The waters flowed beneath Uli's watchful eyes for the rest of the afternoon. Within days, the field recovered, and word flew along the shores of the inland sea. The drought persisted, but the famine would cease.

At the end of the next bone, Uli returned to the meadow to thank the hummingbird for the valuable lesson. He lit his guard fire as dark clouds approached from the west. The heat of the day dissipated as cool air flooded the parched landscape. A silent peck struck his head. A raindrop. A squall line swept down the hillside toward the village. He ducked into the shelter seconds before the deluge hit, cleansing the face of the full moon resting on the edge of the sea.

11. Acorns

Every fall, Uli hiked to the meadow to collect a fresh handful of acorns from the giant oak, replacing those from the previous year. He also carried Dak's hammer-stone in his pouch. It was the way he honored the memory of his brother, who, reminiscent of their father, didn't return from a hunt 10 years past. Even though Uli was in his mid-40s, he still climbed the tree to enjoy the view of the sea, the late-August blue skies and how the sunlight played with the trees.

A cloud billowed into a thunderstorm fed by the seawater. A sudden flash of lightning arced through the darkening sky. The winds calmed as he listened for the thunderclap. A rustling noise below reached his ears first.

He froze in terror as a shadow streaked across the meadow and leaped halfway up the trunk. One more thrust of his powerful hind legs and the panther ascended to the large branch next to him as thunder echoed through the forest. Uli wasn't sure if it had seen him. The whiskered face turned. Orange embers pierced his gaze as white fangs flared into a snarl.

Uli's gnarled fist entered his pouch, fumbling with its contents. His shaky grip moved toward the shadow. He opened his fingers, a single acorn wobbling in his palm. The cat sniffed the brown nut and snarled. Uli twisted his arm. They both watched the acorn's descent, which somehow ended 4 feet above the forest floor. The panther stretched out to rest, purring next to him. He reached out to stroke the panther's fur when a low rumbling thunder sounded with no accompanying flash. He withdrew his hand.

They sat together a while longer. The leaves above them rustled as a cool afternoon wind chased a thunderstorm south. The panther turned, looked him in the eyes and snarled its goodbye. The shadowy spirit bounded down the trunk and disappeared into the woods.

Uli climbed down to find the acorn suspended in mid-air. Trapped in a web guarded by its hungry owner. The spider remained steady as he retrieved the nut. The vibrating strings were not the music of an insect.

Clasping it in his disfigured hand, he reached into his pouch to grab

Dak's hammer-stone. He shook the remaining acorns to the ground and returned the recovered acorn and his brother's treasure. It took him longer than usual to return to the village that afternoon, having stopped at the falls to listen to their roar. While crossing the stream, he glanced toward the hunting grounds and saw a dark shadow waiting. Unafraid, he waded ashore, walked to the center of the trail and yelped in pain when his foot stepped on a single acorn. The hunter padded off into the woods.

Uli limped back to the village, arriving before the evening meal. He exchanged waves with his grandson, who was fishing in the cove. Drained from the day's adventures, Uli entered the brush shelter and laid down on his grass mat. He pulled his legs up beneath him and folded his arms across his chest and fell asleep, dreaming of a meadow and a hummingbird.

Uli's grandson turned to his father, who was hunting turtles, and said, "Grandpa's back. I just saw him go into the hut. He's probably tired."

A tug on his arm and a large splash returned his attention to fishing. The youngster battled the sea monster for what seemed like hours. He pulled hard on the line as his father waded into the churning waters, grabbed the thrashing fish and threw it ashore.

"Your grandfather will be very proud of you. That's the largest one you've ever caught. We should show him before we clean it."

The happy fisherman had to drag his prize by the gills.

"Leave it by the fire and go wake him."

Uli's grandson ran into the hut. "Grandpa, come and see my fish! Grandpa, wake up."

☉---♨♅--♀☽⊕-♄-♂♀--♃●○

The next afternoon, villagers from all along the lake gathered by the apple tree where a very special stone rested within the ring.

"I believe my father would enjoy resting close to his first garden." Mushen kneeled beside the monument. "Children, I want you to go find a sunstone like this one." He raised it with both hands and walked a short distance away and set it on the ground. "Bring them to this spot."

The youngsters ran off to search the shoreline for stones, as Uli had in their legends. The villagers used sharpened sticks to break the clay to form a shallow depression. Mushen arranged three stones at the summer solstice to support his head. Hunters from nearby villages carried him on his woven grass mat and placed him in the grave facing east. His pouch with a single acorn and his brother's hammer-stone rested on his lap, a notched gazelle bone adorned his neck. The gathering stood in silence for several minutes, each remembering how Uli had touched their lives.

Mushen packed clay around the stones to support Uli's head. Over the rest of the afternoon, his body disappeared beneath the gentle handfuls placed by the villagers. The children's sunstones formed as near a perfect circle as they could manage. They transplanted wildflowers to his grave.

Many years later, an unremarkable pattern of rocks lay at the base of a mighty oak tree that guarded Uli for centuries, as the seeds of his discoveries dispersed across the planet.

III. A Song for Hiawatha

12. The Veil

5 Million Years in the Future - Teegarden Caravan

Te Ata sat on an overlook high above a valley to the east of the gardens, enjoying the warm afternoon breezes gusting across the treetops. She was crying.

The Gardener worked his way toward her through the overgrown path and stepped onto the ledge where she rested. He dropped his pack on a boulder and set his walking stick against a tree. Lazy clouds rode the afternoon thermals. She patted the stone ledge to her left, an offer of companionship. He accepted.

She wiped a tear from her cheek. "Without Uli, we wouldn't have made it this far."

Tears streamed from the Gardener's eyes. "I'm so glad you told his story. He still inspires me."

She took a deep breath of calming air. "I hope I didn't put too much of myself into the story."

"You mean the spider incident? I remember hearing you tell that story a long time ago about your brothers. It's a great anecdote, and it worked perfectly to show the sibling rivalry he had with his older brother."

Te Ata laughed and cried at the same time. "Uli not only saw the veil, he touched the veil. He understood its beauty and how much a part of it he was."

"I remember when I first touched it." He paused in remembrance. "What path have you chosen to take next?" He knew she needed a moment. The backpack slid from the boulder to his lap. The Thermos shielded the ice-cold water against the afternoon's warming updrafts. He poured a cup for her.

She sipped, savoring the moment. Then her brow furrowed. The next part of the story was difficult but necessary.

"It's time for an apocalypse. The first global cataclysm they witnessed. They all tried to make sense of it by attributing it to some all-powerful being in the sky, punishing them for whatever wrongdoing they were guilty of."

"Orbital Mechanics 101. When you live on a terrestrial planet, the tiniest chunk of space debris could wipe you out at any moment. Let me guess. You're moving ahead 11,000 years."

"Yes. Now guess where."

"Somewhere close to Greenland?"

"Not bad, not bad at all." She rested her head on his shoulder. A quiet moment.

13. Lake Ojibway

12,000 BCE - Ontario, Canada

As the Laurentide ice sheet sped northward, a vast body of fresh water formed in its wake. Hardy pine forests and abundant wildlife coexisted in harmony.

The prairies to the southwest nurtured woolly mammoths, mastodons and bison. During the summer, the boundless herds trailed the grasses north until they reached Lake Ojibway. In the winter, they migrated south, where the grasslands had recovered from the previous season. An eternal cycle that lasted for countless millennia before men arrived.

The Anishinaabe people were the first to populate this region. Nomads followed the great herds as they ranged across the continent. As they roamed farther east, they began settling into villages along the rivers and lakes of the woodlands where elk, caribou and moose thrived. They planted maize and squash in small patches of ground and harvested wild rice from shallow ponds. One tribe became expert canoe builders after discovering a forest rich in birch near a rocky outcrop with a limitless supply of chert for stone tools and weapons.

Their successes put increasing strain on the resources available to them, a problem solved by establishing trade networks. Canoes and small woodland horses moved goods along the rivers and trails.

Every day allowed them to witness the majesty of the universe. The serenity of the forest at dawn, broken by the loon's wail echoing across the lake. A moose standing offshore for a morning drink raises its stately head to watch an eagle gliding through the air. A muskellunge swimming beneath the surface darts for a skimmer as sharp talons pierce the rippling water. Giant wings flap hard against the struggling fish to carry them both to a nest high atop a pine where two hungry hatchlings await. The Anishinaabe understood nature's rhythms and that a Spirit that cannot be seen dwelt in all things.

14. Standing Rock

Sheer limestone bluffs scoured by the meltwater of ancient rivers dotted the southern edge of Lake Ojibway. A massive tower stood defiantly against the onslaught, cut away from the bluff by the chiseling ice of 10,000 winters. The upper half soared above the forest, capped by scraggly brush and a lone pine tree clinging to the rocky summit.

The Standing Rock tribe hunted the forests and fished the streams. They cultivated small fields of squash and maize, supplemented with wild rice, harvested from shallow lakes. Trading routes provided other necessities, such as stone tools, canoes and tobacco.

Gaachimo, their tribal chief, had two sons. Nandokawe, a skilled 15-year-old woodland hunter, had spent the previous season learning to hunt mastodon on the grasslands. Nibiikaa was 12 and accompanied his brother on hunting trips, tending the fires and fetching water.

Megedagik was a fearsome warrior who patrolled the woods for poachers. His reputation traveled as far south as Lake Huron.

Nooji, a tracker, moved with mystical stealth. Wind, branch and mud led him to elk and caribou in the dwindling stocks of their overhunted forest.

Many girls admired Nandokawe's hunting prowess and the kindness he showed. At 13, Okwi's admiration had blossomed into desire, but what traps had she to catch this most elusive prey?

One day, while gathering mushrooms, she spotted him at the base of Standing Rock.

"Are you going to climb today?" she asked.

"I wasn't planning to."

Her eyes surveyed the cliff. "I've watched you go up there before. You're an amazing climber. Is it hard?"

"The bottom is easy, but there's a tricky section above the trees. The top is like nothing you've ever imagined."

That gave her an idea. She turned and touched his arm, her first attempt at a snare. "Would you take me up with you sometime?"

"I could, but the climb is dangerous."

She grabbed his hand and looked at the towering rock face, luring him closer. "I don't care. I want to touch the moon."

Her fingers wrapped around his shaky palm. "Meet me here tomorrow afternoon."

Her trap sprung with a kiss to his cheek. "Would you like to help me hunt for mushrooms?"

Still blushing, he scanned the tower. "You go ahead. I have something I need to do."

☉---♅Ψ--☿☾⊕-♄-♂♀--♃●○

Early the next morning, she dreamed of Nandokawe, holding her in his arms as she touched the moon's face. Megedagik's booming voice brought her crashing back to Earth.

"The Ice River tribe camps at Three Streams meadow. They will be here later today."

Okwi frowned, knowing what that meant: bundling rice for most of the day.

She could have worked faster if her younger brother hadn't been such a pest. The sun was starting its downward march when she tied off the last bunch.

"That's enough for another grinding stone." Desperate for attention, the little one ran into his mother's arms. She tussled the boy's hair. "So many mouths to feed now. Will you watch him while I help prepare the evening feast?"

"Can you take him with you?" She turned, looking anxiously toward Standing Rock. "Nandokawe wants to teach me something this afternoon."

"What are his lessons today? Throwing a spear, skinning a rabbit?"

"Maybe."

"OK, but..."

Okwi took off at a sprint before her mom could finish her sentence.

She searched the base of the tower. "Where is he? Am I too late?" Fearing that he had climbed without her, she found a small boulder and sat there, fidgeting.

"Are you just going to sit there? I thought you wanted to learn how to climb."

She turned and spotted him sitting 20 feet up on the rock face.

"Oh, I didn't know you were here. How did you get up there?" she asked.

"If you can't figure that out, then I'll go up by myself."

Undaunted, she began climbing and soon reached the slight ledge. It took them an hour to scale the next section. He guided her along the crevices, showing her the handholds and which loose stones to avoid. A small rock jutting from the face above the tree line gave them a chance to rest. She perched beside him, their shoulders touching, as her gaze swept across the majestic panorama from sunrise to sunset.

Nandokawe spotted an enormous bird floating above the lake to the west and pointed. "Look, over there."

Her eyes opened wide in amazement as it glided to its nest atop the tallest pine. "He's carrying a fish. Let's go. I want to fly as high as the eagle."

"OK, but I need to show you something. See that crack in the rock? I'll climb to that outcrop first, then help you up."

She examined the route, then glanced down at the lake. Disoriented, she wobbled over the precipice.

Nandokawe grabbed her waist. "It's best if you don't look down."

They climbed to the crevice, where she waited for him to reach the narrow shelf. He gripped the crack and, in two quick motions, ascended to the ledge. He laid on his stomach and stretched his arm out to her. "Give me your hand."

Okwi trembled, unable to grasp his outstretched palm. "What if I climb partway up, like you did?"

Nandokawe knew a fall from this height would be fatal. "Wait there." He dropped back down and got on one knee beside her. "Stand on my leg and put your fingers in the crevice as high as you can reach."

She turned to face the rocky outcrop as he steadied her waist. She gripped firmly with her left as he lifted her to his shoulders. "OK, now grab the outcropping," he coached.

With her hands locked onto the cliff, Nandokawe boosted her to the ledge. It was the most exhilarating experience of her life. He scrambled up and helped her to her feet. Without thinking, she kissed him, then grabbed a handhold to help steady her instructor.

"We are almost to the top," he said, trying to collect himself. "You won't believe the view from up there."

When they crested the tower, she collapsed on the smooth flat surface, exhilarated by the climb.

Nandokawe stood beside her, scanning the horizon. "Come on, you're missing the best part."

Lifted to his embrace, her emotions and the breathtaking sight washed over her.

To the west, a crescent moon chased the sun toward evening. Summer clouds drifting through the blue sky were beyond anything she could have imagined. The forest stretched southwest, obscured by what few plants and trees jumped from the bluff to their precarious perch. Lake water covered the boundless horizon to the north.

The eagle's nest appeared much smaller from the summit. In the distance, she watched the raptor swoop down, grabbing another fish in its talons. Okwi spread her arms and pretended to soar through the sky.

"Thank you for bringing me up here. I will never forget this. Should we head back down now?"

"It's too dangerous in the dark. We'll spend tonight up here." Nandokawe took her by the hand and showed her a waterskin, a cache of food and a large fur beneath the pine.

She bumped her shoulder against him. "So you planned this all along?"

"The best sights are yet to come." He pulled her close and kissed her.

⊙---♀♅Ψ--☿☾⊕-♄-♂♀--♃●○

The western sky turned a brilliant red as they ate their small meal. For the first time, she watched the sun sink below the horizon, unobscured by the forest canopy. They huddled together beneath the fur as the air chilled.

"It looks like we have a new companion." He pointed south as a single bright beacon pierced the veil of the evening as the Milky Way spilled across the night.

When the breeze calmed, the lake mirrored the sky. Okwi snuggled closer. "Now I know what the moon sees from its perch."

A streak flashed over their heads from the northeast.

"Did you see that?"

"It was just a firefly. Nothing to worry about."

Another flash streaked overhead.

"I don't think those are fireflies. Are the stars falling?"

Nandokawe thought for a moment. "The sun must have knocked them loose this afternoon. There are so many up there."

As they watched the meteor shower, Okwi's mind soon calmed, like the surface of the lake and the canopy of the forest. Beneath the serenity of the cool night sky, she drifted asleep in his warm embrace at the center of the universe.

☉---♅♆--☿☽⊕-♄-♂♀--♃●○

Shortly before sunrise, Okwi felt a gentle touch on her shoulder. Her eyes opened to see Nandokawe's face, lit by the predawn glow. She raised up on her elbow as the sun feasted on the eastern stars.

"How did it get over there? Did it walk through a cave?"

"I've been told it walks through the forest at night, covered with fur, to stay warm."

She playfully hit him on the arm.

They ate a small breakfast and shared the remaining water as the sounds of the village awakening echoed off the bluff.

"It's safe to head down now. Gaachimo asked me to attend the trading."

"Do you want me to carry anything?"

"No, let me show you something." He led her to the back of Standing Rock, a sheer cliff, 200 feet straight down. He laid the fur on the ground and put the waterskin on top. He rolled them into a tight bundle and secured it with a piece of leather. She inched perilously close to the edge and watched as he tossed them over.

"Much easier than carrying them."

15. The Windigo Game

The Ice River tribe lived 30 miles south of Standing Rock in a valley laid bare by the glaciers. They were experts at turning the rich deposits of exposed chert into spears and knives. They had perfected the art of canoe-building using the abundant supply of birchbark from the surrounding forest. It was not uncommon to have four under construction. Such was the demand for their craft.

One late-summer day, seven canoes departed the village. They loaded two with stone tools and grinding stones. Three were empty, save for the paddlers. These five would make the return trip laden with furs and grains. The last pair would take their maiden voyage without cargo or paddler, for delivery to their new owners at Standing Rock.

As evening crept over the forest, the party arrived at a meadow on the edge of Standing Rock hunting grounds. Their chief, Sakima, gave the youngest member of the trading party, Askook, the task of collecting firewood.

"The Standing Rock tribe is very powerful. We must let them know we are here to trade before we step foot into their hunting grounds."

As the traders slept, Standing Rock's guardian, Megedagik, surveyed their weapon-laden canoes.

⊙---ᚻᚤ--ŏℂ⊕-ħ-♂♀--ᒡ●○

In the morning, Askook rode with Sakima in the lead canoe, eager to determine whether the monolith was as tall as the tales he'd been told. The gentle flow of water propelled them into Lake Ojibway, east of the tower. Illuminated by the sunrise, the massive stone appeared to float above the dense fog drifting over the still waters.

The small trading party unloaded their cargo at the edge of the village. A ceremonial feast that evening allowed them to share news and listen to the storytellers.

Spirited bartering started in the morning, lasting well into the afternoon. Askook shuttled goods to and from their camp until the trading was complete.

After the youngster had secured the final load, Sakima signaled to him. "The elders will smoke now at the council fire. You are free to do as you wish."

With the furs stowed, the tower beckoned.

As he walked through the village, he spotted a girl about his age playing fetch with a small dog. "He's very good at that. Someday he'll be a mighty hunter."

She smiled at him. "You must not know a lot about dogs. She doesn't like to hunt."

His face turned red as he tried to regain his composure. He stooped to pat the frisky pup on her head. "Who is this little one?"

"This is Biskitawageni, but I just call her Biskit."

"Well, Biskit, I am Askook. It's nice to meet you. I see you have trained your friend to throw a stick. It must be very fun for her. And what is her name?"

He seemed like a pleasant kid. "I am Okwi. Are you here with the traders?"

"Yes. We're finished now. I'm heading to Standing Rock. When we arrived yesterday, it was floating in the clouds. Does it always do that?"

"Oh, don't be silly. Come with me. Everyone is getting ready to play a game."

Askook grabbed her hand. "Sounds like fun. Let's go."

Biskit growled as Okwi tried to pull away, but he was bigger than her and his grip had the power of someone who worked with stone.

The puppy trotted alongside as they headed to Standing Rock, where a group was gathering. A mixture of teens about their age and younger children, 4 or 5 years old.

Biskit ran to Nandokawe, yipping and pawing his leg. He turned to pet her and spotted the stranger. "What are you doing? Let go of her! Who are you?"

Okwi jerked her hand away. "Nandokawe, this is Askook, from Ice River. I thought he could help us find the Windigo."

Nandokawe looked at him and sneered. "Do you even know what that is?"

"I've heard the tale of the giant cannibal that lives in the woods."

"Yes, a beast that eats people." Askook flinched as Nandokawe jumped at him.

Nandokawe put his arm around Okwi and whispered: "Whoever draws the shortest stick from Nibiikaa's hand wears the Windigo's mask and has to hide behind the dead tree past Standing Rock. We'll line up the children to search for the monster. When we pass by, the Windigo jumps out and scares everyone. I will pretend to battle it to save everybody."

A subtle nod of Nandokawe's head ensured that Askook would play the evil spirit.

Nandokawe occupied the youngsters, telling them of a beast, half-man, half-elk that hunted the forest, satisfying its insatiable appetite on anyone who strayed from the village. Nibiikaa led Askook behind the tower.

Slender branches woven into an oval shape about 3 feet in diameter gave the disguise a terrifying dimension. Leaves adorned the mask. The face glowed with an eerie orange hue, while the eyes burned like red embers. Whitebark fangs jutted from the monster's deathly grimace. Two gnarled sticks lashed to the head raked forward in a threatening display. Askook's neck strained against the leather straps.

"Now, go hide behind that dead tree," Nibiikaa instructed. "As soon as we pass, you jump out."

Askook stumbled toward the naked forest giant, concealing himself from his prey. The flickering village campfires lit the eerie scene.

Nandokawe finished the story when his brother returned. "Everyone, get in line now. Grab the shirt of the child ahead of you. Hold on tight, so the Windigo doesn't snatch you." He raised a club high above his head. "If he attacks, I will protect you."

As Okwi led the skittish procession past Standing Rock, Nibiikaa slipped into the woods unnoticed. A wolf's howl soon reverberated through the woodlands, terrifying the youngsters into howls of their own. Their protector turned and whispered, "Be still. Windigos love to eat crying babies." He smiled to himself as the line went dead quiet.

The wolf howled louder as the procession passed the monster's lair. High-pitched screams tore through the forest when Askook sprang from the darkness, waving his arms. Nandokawe brandished his weapon and screamed. "Run, while I fight the Windigo." The terrified youngsters scattered into the woods as his club sliced through the foliage, hitting the demon flush on his skull. Askook's knees buckled as the mask spun to the ground. The brothers' laughter dealt a second harsher blow as the stranger collapsed unconscious, vanquished.

☉---♯Ψ--☿☽⊕-♄-♂♀--♃●○

Askook awoke the next morning beneath the barkless tree, with a lump the size of a wild potato protruding from his scalp. He staggered back to the trading camp and found Sakima loading his canoe.

"Where have you been all night? Did a bear attack you?"

"We were playing the Windigo game. I got hit with a club. The next thing I remember is waking up beneath a dead tree."

He examined the lump. "Go tell the Medicine Man what happened. We'll leave as soon as you return."

Nandokawe was stoking the fire in front of their lodge when his brother returned with an armload of sticks. "I just saw Askook walking through the village toward Okwi's hut."

A jealous rage surged through him as he sprinted past Nibiikaa, who tossed the firewood and chased after him. He caught his rival from behind and jerked him around. "Stay away from Okwi. If you touch her again, you'll get another beating from my club."

Askook shoved him to the ground. "I'll see her whenever I want. Next time you try to hit me," he paused and flashed the knife he carried under his shirt.

Okwi was carrying water from Lake Ojibway when she heard the boys wrestling. She dropped her waterskin and ran screaming, "Stop it, you two! Quit fighting, please!"

She tugged Nandokawe's arm as Nibiikaa tried to pin his adversary to the ground. Askook tossed him in the dirt and rolled to his feet. A fist to the gut doubled him over.

Okwi pulled harder. "That's enough, let's go." As she led him off to retrieve her waterskin, he turned and yelled, "Remember what I said, and don't come back."

Askook grimaced in pain as he shoved Nibiikaa aside. "You'll pay for this," and stumbled off.

The Medicine Man stepped from his hut as the disheveled stranger approached. "What happened to you? You look like you finished second in a tomahawk fight."

"I'm with the trading party. Sakima said you could help me."

He examined the superficial wounds and reached into his otter-pelt bag. "Here, chew these yarrow leaves, but don't swallow them. I'll make birchbark soup to ease your pain." After chewing for a few minutes, Askook spat the green mass into his hand and held it to the lump on his scalp. The Medicine Man secured the poultice with a soft piece of hide. The bitter broth did little to relieve his throbbing headache.

When he returned, the loaded canoes sat just offshore, ready for the arduous journey upstream. He slid into the rear of his canoe and grabbed the paddle to push off the muddy bottom. His skull throbbed as he dug deep against the current. He turned, hoping to see Okwi one last time. Instead, a large stone whizzed past his head. The sight of Nibiikaa searching for a larger missile and Nandokawe threatening with his club burrowed into his memory.

16. Odawa

A nomadic band of Odawa ranged across the entire planet, hunting caribou, elk and moose. They wintered at the southern edge of the known world where Manitoulin Island nestles within Huron's waters. In the summer, Lake Ojibway barred further passage north and brought them dangerously close to Standing Rock territory.

Ahanu, chief of the Odawa, sat one spring evening on a hillside, shivering beneath his fur. He hadn't eaten for two days. The harshest winter in memory filled the woodlands with snow and emptied it of game.

The only comfort he felt was drawing smoke from his pipe as he pondered their future.

As the clouds drifted east, a sliver-thin crescent appeared before him, chasing the icy tail of a fleeing comet.

He pulled his fur close against the chill and returned to camp, where others had gathered to witness the ominous tableau.

"This is a bad omen, Ahanu. Our food has run out and snow still blocks our way to the summer hunting grounds."

"No, Aranck, I see it as a good sign. We must follow the moon's counsel and hunt whatever we can to survive. Tomorrow, we begin the journey to the Ice River tribe. They speak with all Anishinaabe and will guide us with their knowledge."

☉---♃Ψ--☿☾⊕-♄-♂♀--♃●○

In the morning, they began preparations for the months' long trek to the northern edge of the universe. They loaded their six small woodland horses with their meager trading goods and belongings. The haggard band struggled north through the overhunted forest as the thick spring underbrush replaced the heavy snows of winter. With several weeks remaining until they reached Ice River, under a replenished moon, the starving tribal leader made the only decision available to him to feed the tribe.

⊙---ꝃΨ--Ꝛℂ⊕-ℏ-♂♀--ꝺ●○

The steady chipping sound of Askook's hammer-stone stopped as he raised his work to the light. While his trained eye studied the blade for imperfections, a blurred image stirred in the distance. Five small horses, struggling under the weight of the furs they carried, emerged from the woods. His eyes landed on a thin girl his age, carrying a bundle. He tossed the ax head into the pile, grabbed his waterskin and ran to her.

"Let me take those for you. Here, have some water."

She unburdened herself, eager to slake her thirst. After nearly emptying the skin, she gasped for air. "Thank you."

"I'm Askook."

"Yes, I know. You don't recognize me. It was so long ago since we were here. My name is Etania."

"I remember there were several girls your age. What happened to them?"

Tears streamed down her face. "It's too sad to even talk about. We were all so hungry, we just couldn't find enough food. If Aranck hadn't killed one of our horses, none of us would be here now."

Sakima saw the band of Odawa and rushed to greet them. "Ahanu, good to see you. How long has it been?"

"Three very harsh winters."

"Where is the rest of your tribe?"

"Gone, my friend. Caribou and elk spirits do not satisfy a hungry mouth. We haven't seen a moose for months."

Ahanu studied the emaciated faces of the nomads. "Stay with us tonight. We'll have a feast this evening. Once you get settled in, we will smoke to a successful hunt in the summer grounds. Askook, show them to the empty lodge."

With Etania's hand in his, he led them to a rarely used campsite on the bank of Ice River. "There is firewood inside and waterskins if you need them."

He watched in amazement as the Odawa, guided by the spirit of a thousand journeys, readied the camp for the evening.

Ahanu grabbed a bag from his horse and slung it over his shoulder.

"I'm ready to speak with Sakima now."

They found him sitting near the fire outside his hut, giving orders to prepare a feast of rice and mastodon. The group dispersed to their tasks when the Odawa chief arrived.

"Askook, bring tobacco for us to smoke."

Ahanu touched the youngster's arm. "No need. I have something new."

He removed the pouch and opened the flap, releasing the aroma of the crushed leaves. Sakima eagerly tapped the ashes from his pipe. The smooth texture of the leaf between his thumb and forefinger added to his pleasure as he packed the bowl. A burning twig from the fire released the delightful spirit as he inhaled deeply, savoring every puff to its fullest.

"This is not Red Willow. Where did you find this?"

"We traded last fall with a tribe that discovered this. They say it's easier to grow and dries quickly in the sun."

"Would you like to trade for this? I'll make sure you get extra blades for your hunt, and if you'd like a canoe…"

"Rice would be more useful to us, as would any knowledge you could share. Have other tribes spoken of the barren woodlands?"

"We traveled to Standing Rock last year. They are hunting the grasslands this year for mastodons."

"I've heard tales of the grassland giants. They are hard to bring down, but if we are to feed our tribe…"

"Megedagik has laid claim to those grounds. I caution against it."

17. Firefly

Askook returned to the Odawa's camp and found Etania arranging her bedding. "It will be nice to sleep in a shelter tonight. We've been traveling for months."

"Come, walk with me. I'll show you around our village."

He led her first to the stone quarry. "I spend a lot of time here knocking chips off these rocks. This is the finest chert anywhere." He grabbed the discarded ax head and showed it to her. "I was working on this when you arrived."

They continued past the sweat lodge of the Medicine Man and headed to the lake where a row of canoes sat in various stages of construction. "We make these for the tribes that live along the rivers and lakes. The larger ones can carry a lot of furs. The others are used to harvest rice."

"I've never ridden in one before. It must be wonderful."

Askook took Etania's hand. "It is. Come with me."

The pair descended the bank to a finished canoe sitting in the tall grass. The paddles were already aboard, so he raised the back and slid it into the lake. She looped her arms around his neck as he lifted her from the ground. He waded into the shallow water and lowered her into the front seat.

He grabbed a paddle with his left and reached across her shoulder to guide her hand to the grip. "Now, place this hand above the blade." Nestled beneath him, she mimicked his paddling motion. "That's all you have to do."

"OK," she said, adjusting her position for comfort.

He pushed her into deeper waters. The canoe rocked hard to the left as he slid into his seat. Startled, she jerked the paddle backward, spraying him. She turned to see him wiping his face.

"That was my fault," he said laughing. "I forgot to warn you about that."

A light southerly breeze rippled the surface as they paddled through the reeds. The two soon fell into a rhythm as he steered toward a magical spot. As they approached, he gave a quick backstroke to still the canoe.

"Etania, put your paddle behind you and look over the edge."

She peered through the crystal-clear lake water to the bottom, where bluegill, crappie and rock bass searched for an evening meal. "This is one of my favorite spots to bring the children of our tribe. It's fun seeing how excited they get when they catch their first fish."

"Can I go fishing with you someday?"

Askook thought for a moment. "I guess I could take you. How about tomorrow morning?"

"I'll check with my father to make sure we aren't leaving early, but that would be wonderful."

"I have another spot to show you before we head back." They paddled together as he steered toward a beach to the east.

As they neared the shore, Etania rested while the canoe slowed to a stop. Askook stood to stretch. "Stay there. I'll carry you ashore so you don't get wet."

She looked at him and smiled. "Here, let me help you out." She shifted her weight to the right, laughing as her guide splashed into the lake, his paddle sailing through the air.

When he surfaced, he shook the water from his eyes and swam toward her. "Thank you for helping me out. I like your way better." He grabbed the far edge with one hand and rolled the canoe, dumping her onto the sandy bottom. She popped up, laughing as he lifted her into his arms. "I'll carry you to the beach so you don't get any wetter!"

"I couldn't possibly get any wetter," she said giggling.

He shrugged his shoulders and dropped her in the lake.

A splash fight ensued.

"I give up, you win," he said, hugging her to stop the onslaught.

He pushed the overturned canoe closer to shore and held one end above his head while it drained.

"We have to flip it onto its bottom." Together, they flipped it over and released it with a splat. "Pull it up on the beach. I have to go for a swim."

She pulled it ashore, admiring his powerful stroke as he sliced through the water to retrieve the paddles. He dropped them in the canoe and set about building a fire. They hung what clothes modesty allowed on branches near the flames and settled in to watch the sunset.

The waters stilled as the evening winds calmed. Cicadas drowned out the crickets as darkness fell over the landscape. They huddled close to the crackling logs as burning red embers drifted into the starry canopy. A green flash suddenly caught her eye. Another streaked over the lake. Soon hundreds of twinkling lights, then thousands, glittered around them. They walked hand in hand to the lakeshore to watch these kindred spirits searching for their mates. The effect of the moonless night lit by a hundred sparks, a thousand fireflies and a million stars left her breathless.

"I've never seen anything more beautiful!"

He turned and looked deep into her twinkling eyes. "I have." They shared a kiss that would bond them together for all eternity.

A drumming sound echoed from the village, signaling the start of the feast. "We should head back. It's not safe to stay here overnight."

She retrieved their dried clothes as he slid the canoe into the lake. Once again, he carried her in his arms, making sure that not a single drop of water touched her. He pushed away from the shore and climbed in. Etania's first stroke caught the surface, sending a big splash over his head. It took longer than expected to get back in their half-submerged boat.

☉---ᛒᛦ--ᛦℭ⊕-ħ-♂♀--ᒋ●○

The festivities lasted well past midnight so everyone slept late the next morning. When Askook awoke, he thought of Etania and his promise to take her fishing. He collected his tackle and sprinted to the guest lodge. When he arrived, she was sitting outside sobbing as she packed up her belongings. He ran to her side. "What's wrong? Why are you crying?"

"My father says we must leave as soon as they finish."

"What if I go with you?" he said without hesitation. "I could learn how to hunt. Let's talk with our fathers. I'm sure they'll approve."

Etania's spirit lightened. She took his hand and walked with him to the trading ground.

Askook spoke of his love for Etania and his desire to be with her while she pleaded with her father. Sakima and Ahanu could see that the bond between them was strong. It was not uncommon for a member of one tribe to join another. The children of such unions were often stronger.

The elders stepped into the council lodge to discuss the hard decision. Ice River would lose a skilled stone craftsman. The Odawa would gain someone with no hunting experience and an extra mouth to feed. His knowledge of Standing Rock could be useful if they needed to negotiate with them.

After what seemed like hours, Sakima called them. The anxious teens entered, holding hands, ready to argue their case.

"We have decided. You may go with the Odawa. You must prove yourself worthy or return here in the fall."

They didn't hear the last condition. Their celebration was already well underway.

18. Hunting Grounds

Askook learned the rhythms of the nomads and the despair of the hunters. As the weeks progressed, Etania weakened from a lack of food. He felt his skin tightening as his ribs surfaced. The tribe was subsisting on the rice they received from Ice River, small game animals and what nuts and berries they could forage. They established summer camp at Three Streams Meadow, as far north as they could travel without angering Megedagik. Desperate for a successful hunt, Aranck and Askook scoured the woods through dangerous territory until they reached Lake Ojibway unchallenged. Standing Rock loomed to the west.

"Something has happened to them. I never would have dared stand on this shoreline in the past."

"They are still there. That's not a morning fog, it's the smoke from their campfires."

"Hunting here is useless. We must tell Ahanu as soon as possible."

"The water is low now. If we travel on the riverbed, we could make it back sometime tomorrow."

"What about Megedagik?"

"I wouldn't worry about him. He would have found us already if these woods were still useful to them."

Standing Rock grew large as they scrambled along the shoreline to Ice River, a pebbled highway through the woodlands. They slept that night beneath a waxing crescent moon. Its cornered prey now faced the hunter in a desperate act of survival. The comet's icy trail spilled halfway across the sky as it raced toward the hunter's maw.

☉---ᛒᚩ--ᚢ☾⊕-♄-♂♀--ᚦ●○

The following afternoon, Askook ran the last mile to the Odawa encampment and found Etania, lying on her mat. She mustered a weak smile when he raised her into his arms.

"I missed you so much. Is it as bad as my father thinks?"

He drew her close and wept. "It's worse. The streams and woods are

69

barren. I'll find something for you to eat this afternoon. I promise."

"Thank you, my love. Let me rest now."

He laid her head on the mat as his stomach knotted with hunger. Desperation to fulfill his pledge propelled him to action.

He spotted Aranck walking up the bank from the riverbed. Ahanu motioned for them to join him. Their dismal story only strengthened his resolve.

"Sakima counseled against the grasslands, but we have no other choice. Leave tomorrow and do whatever you must, or none of us may be here when you return."

Askook's mind raced. "That could take weeks. Etania is dying. How will you survive?"

"We still have four horses."

☉---♅♉--☿☾⊕-♄-♂♀--♃●○

In the morning, they headed west on game trails that were being reclaimed by the forest. Two days later, they reached the edge of the known universe where woodland yielded to prairie and famine succumbed to feast. Aranck's eyes swept across more creatures in a single glance than he had seen in his entire life.

Askook gaped in amazement. "How could you get close to them? There is no cover out there."

Aranck's mind raced with the thought of hunting such enormous beasts. A lone elk in timber is one thing. There were thousands of mastodons and bison grazing here.

"We need to follow them to find some weakness. The long noses appear to travel in smaller groups. Perhaps we could hunt the younger ones."

They spent their first night on the grasslands concealed in a ring of thorny bushes, safe from predators that followed the herds. Early the next morning, they crept to a grassy hillside and watched a group of mastodons with two youngsters approach the lake through the steep banks of a dried creek bed.

As skittish as a tiny peccary, the lead animal scanned the shoreline for lurking threats.

"He's afraid of something, Askook. I wonder what scares him."

A creature smaller than the mastodon's leg bolted from the grass. The startled beast trumpeted an alarm whose meaning was clear. RUN!

Askook's eyes widened in fear. "Those are Standing Rock hunters. If they find us here, we're dead…"

Aranck thought for a moment. "Just one of those long-nose creatures could feed our tribe for months. Be still, we can learn from them."

As the giants rumbled past, a small team feigned attack on a female at the rear. Nandokawe dropped in front of her youngster. A volley of spears shot from the upper bank as the frightened animal spun in confusion. Megedagik stood guard against the enraged male.

Nandokawe drove his spear deep to finish the kill. By late afternoon, only bones and offal remained.

With scavengers circling in the sky and the hunting party gone, the Odawa approached the carcass.

Askook shook his head, gritting his teeth in anger. "I made every spear and knife they used on this creature."

"It will please Ahanu to know what we've discovered. We must speak with the chief of Standing Rock first and ask his permission…"

"They'll never allow it. Remember how frightened you were setting foot in their woods? We need these hunting grounds to feed our people. There's plenty here for everyone."

"We'll let Ahanu decide when we get back."

Askook slept that night as howling wolves fighting over the carcass echoed through his nightmares. Every weapon he wielded missed the vicious Windigo, devouring Etania.

$$\odot\text{---}\text{☿}\Psi\text{--}\text{☿}\mathbb{C}\oplus\text{-}\hbar\text{-}\sigma\text{♀}\text{--}\text{♃}\bullet\bigcirc$$

Nibiikaa awoke early the next morning and set to his duties. He threw twigs on the ashy dust of last night's campfire and stirred the coals awake. He grabbed three empty waterskins and a spear, and padded off toward the lake. His mind sifted through the songs of the awakening forest in search of the whispered rush of a grassland predator. Something rustled just off the path. He froze, eyes drawn to a thicket. A whisper, two people. He edged closer. One of them looked familiar. He shifted for a better look. A twig snapped.

Aranck turned and spotted a small person crouched motionless. The waterskins revealed his purpose. The Odawa stepped from the underbrush.

Nibiikaa spoke first. "What are you doing in Standing Rock territory?"

"Your tribe took everything from the forest. We're starving because of you."

"I couldn't care less."

Anger pulled back the shirt to reveal a knife, a visual etched into the youngster's memory.

"I remember you. Last year, you caused a lot of trouble for my brother and Okwi. What business does Ice River have on our hunting grounds? You're risking Megedagik's wrath."

"I left Ice River. They have nothing to do with this. I am with the Odawa."

"I suggest you leave now and never come back." Nibiikaa readied his spear.

Rage drew his weapon from its sheath. Hunger sped his legs forward. Jealousy brushed aside the menacing shaft. Desperation drove the blade deep. Fear suffocated the screams as his tormentor slumped to the ground.

Askook's hand trembled as he withdrew the knife. "Help me hide his body. They won't know who did this."

Reality backed him into a dangerous corner. "Are you mad? They're expert trackers. You've just sentenced both our tribes to death!"

Madness overwhelmed the trapped quarry. His stone's edge plunged into the unsuspecting Odawa.

"They may track your tribe…"

Aranck slumped to the ground.

Love powered him toward Etania. He wouldn't rest until reaching Three Streams meadow.

⊙---ႰΨ--႘ℂ⊕-ℏ-♂♀--ⴄ●○

Nandokawe was sitting by the fire, eating a small breakfast when he reached for the waterskin to wash down his rice cake. It was empty.

"Where is Nibiikaa?" He searched the camp for his brother, but found Nooji examining the fresh blade he had just attached to his spear.

"Have you seen my brother?"

"He left at dawn. I didn't see him come back."

"Something must have happened to him. Alert the others. I may need help looking for him."

Nandokawe snatched Nooji's spear out of the air as he sprinted past, calling out to his brother.

Word of Nibiikaa's disappearance spread slower than the pained scream that roused the camp.

Nooji turned to the outcry. "Nandokawe!"

The hunters took off at a sprint, arriving at the gruesome spectacle. Nandokawe cradled his brother's head in his lap as he rocked back and forth, crying in anguish.

Megedagik examined the intruder's body. "That's an Odawa tribesman. They hunt to the southeast of Standing Rock."

"What was he doing out here on our hunting grounds?" Nooji asked.

Megedagik noted the meager campsite. "He was scouting food for his tribe."

Nooji's tracking instincts took over. "Something is wrong. This Odawa was a skilled hunter, killed with a knife, not a spear." His eyes glanced at the thicket. "Two people spent the night here."

Megedagik rolled the Odawa's body with his foot. "If Nibiikaa didn't kill him, then who did?"

Nooji spotted a fresh game trail that screamed of a panicked flight through the grass. "Whoever did this left in a hurry."

Megedagik bent down next to the Odawa and unsheathed his ax. "Go now. Meet us back at Standing Rock."

Nooji kneeled to comfort his companion. "We will avenge your brother's death." His spear leaped into his hand as he vanished.

Nandokawe turned to Megedagik. "Leave him for the wolves."

"They can have his body. His head is mine!"

⊙---♅♆--☿☾⊕-♄-♂♀--♃●○

Askook sped through the forest, making a single diversion along a shallow creek to slow any trackers. His only thought was of Etania. He must convince her to flee with him. They wouldn't have much time.

Askook ran the perimeter of Three Streams meadow, not wishing to reveal his presence as he searched for his beloved. He found her gathering firewood near the lower river.

"We have to leave now. Something terrible has happened."

"What's wrong? Where is Aranck?"

"The Standing Rock tribe killed him. I was returning from the lake this morning when I discovered his body. They were hunting nearby yesterday. Someone must have seen us."

Etania dropped her sticks, crying. "We have to tell Ahanu."

He grabbed her arm in desperation. "There's not enough time. I'm sure they tracked me through the woods."

Frightened and confused, she pulled away from Askook.

He looked deep into her eyes. "If we don't leave now, they will kill all of us."

"Where would we go?"

"We'll be safe if we head east along Lake Ojibway. We can fish the shoreline and maybe find another tribe."

19. Burial

Nooji followed a trail of broken branches and disturbed underbrush to the east. Whoever murdered Nibiikaa was making no effort to conceal their path through the woods. In the distance, a single column of smoke beckoned from Three Streams meadow.

He ascended a large boulder at the edge of the meadow and sat invisible in plain sight, studying the poachers. Finding the killer by himself would be difficult. He would return to let Megedagik know what he had learned.

Nooji sensed Nibiikaa's spirit when he returned. A dark pall cloaked Standing Rock as they prepared for his funeral.

He met with Gaachimo and Megedagik at the council lodge. "I tracked the murderer to Three Streams meadow. Fifteen Odawa camp there with three horses."

"I've heard enough. These people have no respect for Anishinaabe. They came into our hunting grounds without our permission and murdered an innocent youngster, then tried to hide their deceit." He turned to Megedagik. "Find out who did this. If they don't cooperate…"

"I will avenge Nibiikaa."

⊙---♃♇--☿☾⊕-♄-♂♀--♃●○

The war party followed the shoreline east to Ice River. Before heading inland, Megedagik waded into the shallows and tossed a leather bag into the waters of Lake Ojibway. The Odawa's head was useless to him now.

They stopped a half-hour from Three Streams meadow that evening and watched as the comet's icy tail snared the moon.

Nooji returned from scouting the Odawa. "Their camp is quiet. Only one campfire, smoking a peccary. There is no guard posted."

Megedagik looked at the moon, then turned to face the war party. "Tonight, the scavengers feast."

⊙---♃♇--☿☾⊕-♄-♂♀--♃●○

A solemn procession carried Nibiikaa's body, cloaked in birchbark, to the sacred burial ground on the bluff. They brought enough food and water for his four-day passage to the Spirit world. Nandokawe played the ceremonial drum as their mother danced, a signal to the Spirits that Nibiikaa's journey had begun.

Nandokawe looked across the wooded abyss at the nearby tower. "Okwi, come with me to Standing Rock. I want to stay with my brother tonight."

"I'll get some food and a fur."

⊙---ͰΨ--ỏℂ⊕-ℏ-♂♀--⅃●○

A calm blanketed the lake as cold air crept in from the north. They huddled close to guard Nibiikaa's ascent and soon drifted asleep.

Nandokawe awoke from a peaceful dawn dream to a nightmare.

"Okwi, wake up. Something terrible is happening."

She looked at the crescent moon, choking in a sea of glowing red dust, as the flaming culprit fled overhead.

Nandokawe watched in horror as the flame pierced the morning sun.

Okwi tried to comfort him. "It's over now. Your brother's journey has begun. Have some water, you'll feel better."

A cool drink beneath calm skies eased his mind. "I hope you're right. We should head back to the village."

She emptied the waterskin while he laid the fur on the ground. Together, they bundled their belongings and walked to the edge of the cliff. Okwi's complexion blushed from another strange glow in the west.

"What's that?" Okwi tugged on his arm and pointed as the flaming spear thundered over their heads to the northeast. The flame, mirrored by the lake, kissed at the horizon as a second sun flared into existence. They shielded their eyes against the short-lived companion.

"It's just one of those stars that falls from the sky. Remember the first time you brought me up here?"

"I'll never forget that night, but those didn't become suns. The Odawa have cursed my brother's journey."

They leaned over the edge to watch the bundle hit the ground when a rumble shook Standing Rock. Nandokawe grabbed the small tree as Okwi wobbled and fell into his outstretched arm. The gnarled roots held firm against their weight as he pulled her to safety. With their hearts pounding, they raced to the front of the tower to make their descent.

Okwi glanced at the village. "Why is everyone heading to the lake?"

A dark line formed as the receding water exposed the muddy bottom. A ripple that stretched across the horizon slowly swam toward them. A monster, half as tall as a pine, sprang from the mud, devouring everything in its path. The waters swirled around the base of their shaking perch.

The entire edge of the glacier to the north collapsed into Lake Ojibway, and a second tsunami crashed ashore.

The two watched in horror, wondering if anyone had survived.

"What are we going to do?"

"It's too dangerous to head down. All we can do is wait."

Tremors continued to shake the tower as the turbulent waters receded.

☉---♯Ψ--☿☾⊕-♄-♂♀--♃●○

They searched for survivors along the shoreline for hours as their new reality took hold. A tangled mass of trees and forest undergrowth covered the ground where their village once stood.

"They're all gone. I'm never going to see my family again."

Nandokawe studied the destruction, trying to make sense of what they had witnessed. "It's too dangerous to stay down here. We'll be safer on Standing Rock until we figure out what to do."

They kept a wary eye on the receding waters as they struggled to safety. Okwi screamed when a powerful aftershock knocked them to the ground.

Nandokawe eyed their lofty refuge in the distance. "I don't think we're going to make it, Okwi."

The face sheared from the tower, crumbling into the lake. An ancient layer cracked at the base. The crushed sediments of a million years billowed into the air as the stone fell into its brother's arms.

As the choking dust settled, Nandokawe surveyed the apocalyptic spectacle. "The moon listened to the cries of the Odawa. This is our punishment."

☉---♅♇--☿☽⊕-♄-♂♀--♃●○

A band of meteors hit North America that day, causing fires, earthquakes and flooding. The largest struck the Hiawatha glacier in northern Greenland, releasing a great flood upon the Earth. Coastal villages worldwide drowned under 40 feet of water as the Spirits of Lake Ojibway rejoined the Manitou of the vast ocean.

20. The Journey South

Nandokawe and Okwi journeyed south over the next several months through charred forests and ash-choked streams. The occasional berry bush or wild rice they found in the dying lakes were their only sustenance. The days were getting shorter, and Nandokawe feared that winter would soon bury the landscape in an impenetrable blanket. Exhaustion stalked them through the woodlands to another lake that stretched to the horizon.

"Let's follow the shoreline toward the morning sun. Maybe we'll find a tribe we can join up with," he said, hoping to lift her spirits.

They walked the rugged coastline for days, resting near the shore at night in whatever shelter the woods provided. Desperation descended upon them one evening as the snow fell.

Nandokawe looked at the desolate sky. "It's going to be cold tonight, Okwi. We better light a fire. I'm not sure how much longer we can survive like this. Winter is coming, and we are alone in the world."

Okwi could feel her spirit sinking as the forest floor whitened. A good-sized piece of driftwood that would burn for hours had washed ashore. As she stepped out of the underbrush to collect it, the south wind carried a scent she hadn't experienced since the great catastrophe. The smell of meat cooking over a campfire. She scanned the darkness and spotted a small dome of light flickering beneath the falling snow.

"Nandokawe, come here!" she screamed.

"Are you hurt?"

"I'm OK. I'm down by the lake."

Nandokawe dropped his load of firewood and clambered through the underbrush toward her voice. He slid down the bank and saw her silhouetted by the distant aura of a flickering campfire. He ran to her side. "Is that a village?"

A second glow answered his question as warmth filled their spirits.

"It has to be. Do you think we could reach them tonight?"

"We don't have a canoe and it's too cold to swim. It's best to stay here for now. Let's just get our fire going and hope they see it."

They gathered enough firewood for the night and tended the flame as the snowstorm continued unabated. The shivering wanderers finally succumbed to exhaustion as snow doused the glowing embers.

☉---♅♆--☿☽⊕-♄-♂♀--♃●○

Okwi's scream awakened Nandokawe to the sight of two bears hovering over them. Startled at first, he soon realized that they were trackers wrapped in bearskins. They huddled together beneath warm dry furs as their rescuers paddled them across Lake Huron to Manitoulin Island, where they would spend the rest of their lives. Nandokawe became a skilled storyteller whose legends passed down through the millennia. He changed a few details of their adventures since they were living with a band of Odawa, who were as gentle and kind as anyone he had ever met.

IV. Manitou

21. Thunder House Falls

4000 BCE - Ontario, Canada

Over the next eight millennia, the warmth of dark pine forests replaced the cool, reflecting waters of the ancient basin. The first men, the Anishinaabe, had resettled the area where Lake Ojibway once was.

Woolly mammoths, mastodons, giant beavers and tortoises were etched in the icy mists of time, but the legend of the Great Flood, the destruction of mankind and the re-creation of all things still blazed around the campfires of hundreds of generations.

22. Anangokaa

The spiritual leader of the small tribe sat outside the birchbark lodge, awaiting the birth of his first grandchild. Stars flooded the sky on a moonless summer night as meteors streaked overhead.

A tiny spirit voice testing the strength of his breathing apparatus called to his grandfather, drowning out the distant rumbling of Thunder House Falls.

He stepped inside as the infant registered his displeasure with bathing. A soft warm rabbit fur and his mother's gentle embrace calmed the winds. She smiled at her father. "Would you like to meet your new grandson?"

He cradled him in his arms. "Welcome to our village, Anangokaa. I am your grandfather, Mooz."

⊙---♃♇--☿☾⊕-♄-♂♀--♃●○

As the years passed, they became inseparable, traveling the forest for days at a time in search of medicinal herbs. Anangokaa sat at his grandfather's fire, learning the secrets of preparation and the ceremonial administration of the healing spirits.

Mooz knew the tribal folklore and, on special occasions, gathered the children together for storytelling. Anangokaa loved hearing stories of the Great Spirit, Gitchie Manitou, and the trickster Nanabozho and his adventures. Anangokaa's mother taught him the art of constructing dreamcatchers to keep the creatures of the dark at bay. Her father's tales of the Windigo turned their hut into a souvenir shop, lined with the spidery hoops inside and out.

On the occasion of his grandson's 13th birthday, Mooz asked him to prepare a broth of the sacred mushrooms.

He searched their stocks. "It looks like we must go hunting. We can check that spot above the falls."

"I won't be able to join you this time."

"Is anything wrong? Why do you need them?"

"For a spiritual quest. You could also try the crumbled stones by the bluff."

Anangokaa nodded. "I'll be back tomorrow afternoon with the mushrooms."

He filled his bag with nuts from their stores. It would take him a half-day following the stream to reach Thunder House Falls. When he arrived at the lower rapids, the sunlight twisted and twirled into misty rainbows over a rock-strewn dance floor. Bloated trout lined the deep pool below the first waterfall. Mayflies crunched beneath his feet.

He stepped into the water above the falls for a cleansing footbath. "It'll be a month before I can fish here again."

The upper falls cascaded over a cliff face where he had spent many hours with his grandfather. He had probably climbed it a hundred times that day when Mooz showed him how to jump into the waters below.

He scrambled to the top and stared over the edge. "I have plenty of time before dark."

Thirsty from the hike, he moved to a flat rock by a quiet eddy. As he drank, his eyes focused on a fish swimming toward him. He heard a humming sound above his head and turned, expecting a dragonfly. It was Nenookaasi, the hummingbird. He sat up slowly as the bird drifted closer.

The Spirit voice of the hummingbird's wings whispered in his ear. "Mooz needs you! Collect your mushrooms and return to his lodge before the moon rises tonight."

Nenookaasi flitted in front of the startled teen, hovered momentarily, then darted out of sight.

Stunned by what had just happened and concerned about his grandfather, he rushed to the rotting log and filled his pouch. Without breaking stride, the mushrooms sailed over the waterfall as he dove like a kingfisher into the deep pool. His head surfaced through the strap; the first stroke of his arm shouldered the bag as he swam ashore. The downward slope encouraged his pace. He had a lot of ground to cover before the moon arrived.

With the sound of the rapids fading behind him, Anangokaa sped through the darkening shadows of the forest on whispering wings.

The familiar roots and stones of the woodland path welcomed him home as a yellowish haze glowed in the eastern sky. He hurried past a small group gathered outside Mooz's lodge and entered the hut.

Mooz opened his eyes. "Did you get the mushrooms, Anangokaa?"

He set the heavy pouch next to the fire. "Yes, Grandfather, there were more than I've ever seen. Something strange happened at the upper falls."

"You met Nenookaasi."

"How did you know?"

"I spent many hours talking with the forest Spirit. He knows all about you. Gitchie Manitou gave him his most ancient wisdom to guide the Anishinaabe."

He touched his grandson's hand. "Heed what he tells you in the coming years."

Mooz struggled to rise to his elbows. "Is Neebageesis up yet?"

"She's just above the trees now."

"Then prepare your remedy for this aching husk. I could use some help for tonight's journey."

Anangokaa prepared a broth that would not cure the aches, but it would send them drifting downstream for the night. Neebageesis peered over his shoulder as he ladled the stew.

"Thank you, my grandson." A certain warmth filled him as the spirit of the mushrooms paddled through his ancient streams. He returned the empty bowl to Anangokaa and adjusted his mat to watch the moon.

The smoke-tinged air from the crackling fire, the musky scent of the hut, the whispers of his loved ones nearby. He sensed a youthful power returning to his aching frame. Neebageesis, adorned in a glowing halo with two wandering stars for a necklace, smiled down on him. Perfect harmony.

Anangokaa followed his grandfather's gaze.

"She's wearing her finest gown for you tonight."

He touched his grandfather's cheek as the smoke of the dying ember drifted skyward to embrace the moon and wept.

Anangokaa sat with his grandfather, on the hillside where they buried him, until the evening of the fourth sun.

23. Mooz's Journey - Wisdom

4000 BCE - Somewhere Over the Rainbow

Serenity embraced Mooz as his spirit rose from the grave to begin his westward journey. He didn't recognize the landscape yet, somehow, it was familiar to him. The roar of raging waters called.

The root ball of a giant tree had succumbed to the relentless torrent of a watery snake. A moss-covered bridge revealed his pathway to the bluff looming in the distance. Switchbacks led him up a steepening hill, where the pines yielded to a stone wall. He sidled through a narrow slot between the cliff face and a rocky tower, to a waterfall of boulders pouring from the summit. At the crest, the trail disappeared into a vast forest. The signposts of the past gleamed in the valley behind him.

So many wonderful hours spent with the people of his tribe. Teaching Anangokaa the ways of the Medicine Man. He pondered those streams he yearned to cross that had no bridges—and those he almost drowned in, chased home by war. And those bloodied by his own hand that stained his spirit. His tears brought no comfort.

Hunger and thirst turned him west. The wildflowers of the western slope suggested raspberries for dinner. His eyes traced a path etched in the treetops that finished in an open expanse.

The stream cut through the woods and meadows of this idyllic landscape. Water rushing over a spillway emptied into the lily pad-covered shallows of a large lake.

Frogs abandoned their sunny respites as Mooz waded past to drink. A young man unblemished by the savagery of countless seasons drank with him.

He saw a raspberry bush hugging the shore a few hundred yards away. Panicked minnows darted toward the apparent safety of the lily pads as he dove beneath the surface.

His arms and legs stroked with youthful power. The essence of the icy waters cleansed and refreshed him. When he surfaced near the shoreline, the air filled his lungs with its pure amusements. He rested on the sandy bottom. Enveloped in perfect harmony, the knowledge of all that cannot be seen flooded into his being as his spirit blossomed into the universe.

He walked ashore, changed. The simple task of plucking a raspberry brought him a fresh sense of wonder. Every crunch of his teeth revealed textures he had never considered. His tongue ventured into unexplored territories. His throat allowed these journeys before sending the berries cascading down the waterfall to a more patient stomach. Thoroughly refreshed, he swam back through the lily pads to continue his journey west. The frogs croaked their pleasure as he passed.

A short time later, he arrived at a spot where a tree blocked the trail. An old friend was waiting for him.

"Nenookaasi!"

Mooz watched the joyous welcoming dance as the tiny bird flitted from shoulder to shoulder, sped in circles around his head, then hovered next to his ear.

"There is a place up ahead where you may rest tonight. You have three days left on your journey. Today, I have given you the knowledge of all things, but you lack certain wisdom. That lies down the path of tomorrow."

An ineffable Spirit touched his soul on this first day. Yet he still carried with him the heavy burdens of his past.

24. Gitchie Manitou

3957 years BCE - Ontario, Canada

The Thunder House Falls tribe gathered for a feast of fish and rice in their largest birchbark lodge as darkness and snow descended on the woodlands. This was a special evening as their Spiritual Leader, Anangokaa, was going to tell a wonderful story about Gitchie Manitou. The mothers and fathers were as excited as the children. After they finished their meal, he stood at the entryway, while the youngsters jostled for the best seats closest to the crackling warmth. As the parents left, each placed a piece of maple sugar candy in his pouch to secure an hour's peace. Biskane, the oldest child to remain, did so just to tend the fire. He dropped an armload of firewood at the entrance and secured the flapping hide as the last of the parents disappeared into their snowy bliss.

Anangokaa moved to the spot reserved for the old storyteller and sat down. Biskane handed him his pipe, already packed with tobacco, and a dried, lit twig. As he drew flame into the bowl, he noted the children's growing impatience. He offered the bag of candy to his assistant. "Make sure everyone gets a treat, and one for you, too."

A wave of excitement danced through the audience as Biskane distributed the treats. Anangokaa had bought himself a few minutes to enjoy his pipe. With their candies finished, the children begged for their story. This gave him joy. He tapped his pipe on a nearby log to empty it of any remaining embers, adjusted his blanket around his shoulders and settled in to tell them the Legend of the Great Spirit, Gitchie Manitou.

"Since my childhood, I have witnessed the many wonders of the heavens. The sun passes through the sky, giving light and warmth. We ask for the moon's guidance as she walks with us through the woods. The Earth provides everything we need. We live in harmony with the animals and the plants and the fish. Winter's chill and summer's warmth caress our face. Have you ever wondered who created these marvels and why?"

Anangokaa paused for a moment. Seeing their wide eyes focused on him, he began the story.

"One night, Gitchie Manitou dreamed of the heavens where Geesis, Neebageesis, and Aki could live. A place where everything we can see and everything we cannot see exists in perfect harmony.

"When he awoke, he knew what he had to do. His dreams sprang forth from his small pouch. The sky spilled out first to give his creations somewhere to wander. Geesis, the sun, brought warmth and light into the heavens. Neebageesis, the moon, marked the passage of time. Aki, the Earth, received the spirit of life.

"The three drifted through Gitchie Manitou's creation, becoming sad and lonely with little purpose. Their anguish sorrowed the Great Spirit. One night, he had another dream. When he awoke, he knew what he must do.

"Gitchie Manitou spoke to Aki. 'I will give you four sacred winds, each with their own spirits. The world awakens on eastern zephyrs, bringing springtime for new birth. The southern breeze carries summer's warmth for the plants to grow and blossom. The western chinook summons the day's memories, the rain to cleanse all things and Autumn's harvest. Winter's chill and nighttime's darkness descend from the northern blusters, a time for rest and renewal.'"

Anangokaa paused as an icy gust descended through the smoke hole into dying embers. He looked at Biskane sitting in the front row.

"The blustery north wind blows tonight and my old bones are getting cold."

Biskane scrambled to fetch more wood from the pile outside and stoked the fire. With the warmth returning, Anangokaa continued the story.

"Gitchie Manitou sent messengers to Aki as birds to carry the seeds of life in all four sacred directions. Ajijaak, the crane, filled the waters with the creatures that swim. Migizi, the eagle, covered the Earth with the animals that walk and crawl. Mahng, the loon, brought the water plants to the lakes and rivers. Nenookaasi, the hummingbird, sowed the land with seedlings. The Great Spirit smiled at his creation."

Anangokaa popped a maple sugar treat into his mouth. Biskane tossed another log on the fire. Anangokaa finished his snack and continued.

"One day, the animals met with Migizi and asked him to speak with

Gitchie Manitou. They were thankful for all he had given and the harmony that existed, but in their hearts, they yearned for a higher purpose.

"Migizi flew to Gitchie Manitou, drawn by the light of the setting sun. After three days, he landed on a cliff to rest, knowing he must travel one more day to reach the Great Spirit.

"Migizi glided to a perch at the entrance to the cave where Gitchie Manitou slept. He told him of the animals' desire for a greater purpose in their life. Gitchie Manitou asked him to stay while he considered their request. He awoke the next morning with the knowledge of what he must do."

Anangokaa always looked for sleeping children at this point in the story. Biskane's little sister slid into his lap and fell asleep. He smiled. She would hear it another time. He continued the story.

"Gitchie Manitou called the eagle from the waters of the lake and said, 'I will fly to Aki with you.'

"They flew over the Great Spirit's forest, passing Geesis on the second day and Neebageesis on the third. When they arrived at Aki, Gitchie Manitou gathered them all together.

"'Migizi spoke of your desire for a higher purpose in your life. I dreamed of a creature for you to care for, to teach balance and harmony. This new being will not be perfect. It is small, weak and without knowledge. To make it, I must gather the four elements.'

"Gitchie Manitou asked Aki for muddy earth, which she placed in his hand. The turtle arrived from the depths of the lake with a sacred cowrie shell filled with water. He faced each of the sacred directions, inhaling the essence of their Spirits. From the East, new life. The South brought its growth. From the West, reflection, and the North, wisdom.

"He thanked them all for their gifts. 'Now I must fly to Geesis for the fourth element.'

"Gitchie Manitou flew over the treetops and landed on a great tower where the sun rested. He held the cowrie shell as Geesis poured in his liquid fire. He mixed Aki's mud with the burning waters. A whirlwind swirled from his lungs, mixing the elements with their essence, creating the two creatures of his dream. Neebageesis smiled as the man and woman descended from the heavens under Gitchie Manitou's watchful eye.

"His creation pleased the animals, who now had a purpose in their lives. To teach and care for the Anishinaabe.

"The first people lived in peace. There was plenty to eat, and the tribes grew larger, spreading throughout the land. The harmony Gitchie Manitou had envisioned ceased when they began fighting over the hunting grounds.

"It saddened him that they had lost respect for all things. His tears brought a great flood, wiping out all the creatures. Aki, too, had gone missing. He searched the waters for months before finding Migizi flying with Neebageesis.

"They flew for many days before the eagle noticed something floating on the surface far below. He swooped down to find three animals resting on a giant tree. Migizi landed on the tallest branch sticking out of the water. Nanabozho the rabbit sat next to a mink and a muskrat.

"Nanabozho said to Migizi, 'We've been here since the flood began and we're starving.'

"Migizi replied, 'I have been flying high above the clouds for many days and have not seen land.'

"Nanabozho thought for a moment. 'If I swim to the bottom and grab a handful of Earth, can you ask Gitchie Manitou to create a new island for us?'

"Migizi agreed and watched as he slid into the floodwaters and disappeared. Several minutes later, they saw him struggling back to the surface. The mink pulled the gasping rabbit onto the log.

"Nanabozho coughed water out of his lungs, 'It's too deep for me. I never came close.'

"They fell silent in desperation. The slender mink looked at the others. 'I will swim to the bottom and find the Earth.'

"He scurried out on Migizi's perch and dove in. Nanabozho held his breath for as long as he could. There was no sign of the mink. The rabbit gasped for air as Migizi leaped from his branch to search the waters. A single bubble rising from the depths popped.

"'He's coming up.'

"A minute later he surfaced, too far from the log to swim. Migizi swooped down to the water and grabbed the limp body in his talons and flew back to the tree. They searched him and found not even the slightest trace of Aki. When he awoke, he could not speak and there were tears in his eyes."

Anangokaa paused for the children to reflect on the mink's sadness and for them to address any urgent matters. Once the commotion settled down and Biskane had restoked the fire, he continued.

"The next day, as Migizi searched for land, he spotted another bird soaring on the warm afternoon breeze and asked for his help.

"The kingfisher lit on the eagle's back. 'Take me to Neebageesis. Reaching the bottom should be easy from that height.'

"Migizi flew for hours and hours until he could touch her face.

"'Wait for me at the log.'

"He flitted onto the moon, ran over her head, and dove off. He pulled his wings tight to his body, pointed his beak to the water and his claws to the sky, and plunged into the depths without a single splash. With his incredible speed, they felt sure he would succeed. He pierced the floodwaters to a far greater depth and surfaced almost as quickly as he descended. The kingfisher shot 200 feet into the air, shook the droplets from his feathers and glided back to the log.

"'I have never seen waters so deep as these. May I rest here with you? I can't remember the last time I perched on a branch.'

"'You are welcome to stay for as long as you wish,' Migizi told him.

"As the days passed, their despair grew. Late one afternoon, Migizi spotted something floating on the surface. He wafted down on the air currents and landed on a turtle's shell.

"'We have been searching for Aki in the depths below, hoping Gitchie Manitou will create a new home for us. Can you help?'

"The turtle raised his head and saw their raft bobbing in the distance. He yearned to rest on a log in the warm sun.

"'I'll return before nightfall.'

"He took a deep breath and sank beneath the surface as Migizi returned to tell the others.

"Geesis had set his evening campfire on the shimmering waters as the drifters waited for his return. Nanabozho saw two small fires blink and snuff out near the root ball. He hopped along the trunk to investigate. The basking turtle had fallen asleep for the first time in months.

"Nanabozho awakened him. 'Did you reach the bottom? How long have you been sitting there? Are you OK?'

"The sleepy giant extended his head. 'I paddled and paddled until I could see Aki, but the air in my lungs prevented me from swimming any deeper. I'm sorry I couldn't help.'

"As the sun dropped into the floodwaters, he retreated into the comfort of his shell."

Anangokaa always stopped at this point to awaken any sleepy creatures. Several mothers entered the lodge, bringing warm drinks for everyone. The children yelled for Biskane to put more wood on the fire. After finishing his tea, Anangokaa dove into the last chapter.

"The next day, Nanabozho spotted something bobbing in the water. It was Mahng, the loon. They invited him to join them on their raft. Each diver related their adventure to him. He listened in disbelief. When asked for his help, he said, 'I don't think I can dive any deeper than the turtle, but I'll try.' Mahng huffed and puffed to cleanse his lungs with freshened air. As he took his final deep breath, the muskrat stepped from behind a limb.

"'Wait, Mahng. Let me do it.'

"They turned to see who was speaking. Mahng laughed at the thought of him making such an attempt.

"Nanabozho reminded him, 'Only Gitchie Manitou can judge others. We must allow him to try.'

"Without hesitation, he dove into the Great Spirit's anguish. His warm fur protected him from the cold, dark waters. He slowed his heart as he does in winter to save his breath. More sinking than swimming, he continued into the depths. He spotted a few bubbles and adjusted his dive to breathe in the air from below, enough for him to continue.

"He felt faint when he heard the water Manitou whisper. 'Swim little one, you are almost there.' The calming voice drove him deeper, as Aki rose to greet him. As he reached down to collect her treasure, four winds bubbled into his lungs, lifting him toward the surface, a new world clutched in his paw.

"They all feared that they would never see the muskrat again. Migizi spoke: 'Gitchie Manitou, what are we to do? We have tried to find Aki. All that remains is this tree.'

"Gitchie Manitou whispered his reply on a gust from the north: 'Patience.'

"Migizi stood on his perch watching Geesis rise when he felt the wind shift to the east. He saw something floating in the distance and called to the kingfisher to help him investigate.

"'He's back!' the great eagle shouted. The turtle slipped from the log and swam underwater to the circling birds. He surfaced beneath the still muskrat and carried him to their raft. Nanabozho and the mink pulled him off the shell. They gathered round as he drew his last breath and passed to the Spirit world.

"Nanabozho moved closer and looked in his muddied grip. 'Look, he did it. He found Aki.' Their tears for the muskrat's heroic sacrifice washed away the joyous celebration of his triumph.

"Nanabozho removed Aki's remains from his paw.

"The turtle raised his head. 'Put her on my shell and ask Gitchie Manitou to create a new island for us.'

"He slid into the floodwaters while the animals chanted their appeal.

"Geesis and Neebageesis embraced above the darkening heavens. The breath of the east set the clump spinning. It grew larger, encouraged by the Spirit of the south. The water Spirits arrived from the west to cleanse the soil of its troubled past. Northern Spirits restored everything that disappeared in the night of time. A whirlwind gave witness to Aki's rebirth, as the tree came to rest on her shores. The turtle disappeared beneath the island to carry her through the sky. The sun and the moon ended their embrace, restoring warmth and light to Aki."

Anangokaa stood and stretched his arms for effect, and to stretch his poor old legs. He puffed warm air into his chilly hands to finish the tale.

"Gitchie Manitou blew into the sacred cowrie shell, re-creating man and woman, to give purpose to the animals and return harmony to the world."

Biskane tied the flap open for the mothers to collect their children. Anangokaa moved to the entrance to say goodnight as they left.

One mother whispered in his ear. "I've heard that story a hundred times, and I still love the way you tell it. I have noticed that the animals' dives seem to take longer and longer, and the kingfisher, diving off the moon…" She winked at him, grabbed her two children and disappeared into the snowy night.

25. Mooz's Journey - Peace

3957 BCE - Somewhere Over the Rainbow

Mooz fell asleep on a bed of leaves arranged beneath a rocky overhang. The roaring spirit of a thunderstorm approaching from the west shook him awake. He satisfied his morning thirst from water trickling down the ledge and drank in the beauty of the second day.

Raindrops splattered through the leafy canopy on their journey to the forest floor. His skin responded to the droplets, made colder by the breeze. He pulled the fur close around his shoulders and relished the moment.

As the storm intensified, a deluge of hate, shame and anguish cascaded over the waterfall of his memory. Hatred for the warrior who killed his grandfather for reasons he would never know. Remorse for those who died by his hand, defending the tribe. Countless acts that served only himself.

Nenookaasi flew through the heavy rains and fluttered before him. "Are you ready to head west, Mooz?"

"My burdens are too heavy to carry to the Spirit Lodges. I must revisit the path of yesterday before I go any further."

"Would you like some company?"

"No, my friend. I must face this alone." He pulled the fur overhead and stepped into the downpour. "I'll see you tomorrow."

He returned to the tree blocking the trail and soon arrived on the shores of yesterday. The gusty wind rippled the lake. He dove in and stroked hard against the memories of days gone by. He didn't pause in the sandy shallows today. The Spirits that only he could see chased him ashore.

A break opened in the clouds, illuminating a dead bush as a chinook plucked the rotted berries.

The burdens of his past crushed him to his knees. The rain abated as the back edge of the storm drifted over the lake. Fish splashed in the reeds offshore, feeding on a swarm of dragonflies emerging from the misty woods. An earthworm, brought to the surface by the heavy rain, caught his eye. He moved closer to watch the marvelous creature churning the rotted berries into the forest floor. One tiny green shoot struggled toward the light of a new day.

Mooz smiled as the waters of self-forgiveness cleansed his mud-caked memories, churned into the earth by a dreamer more majestic than Gitchie Manitou: Azhigwa, the Spirit of Time.

As he stood to continue his journey west, a wondrous sight appeared in the heavens. A smoke ring surrounding a hazy yellowish campfire drifted above the forest. He had seen such things appear above ceremonial fires before, but never one spanning the entire sky. A whisper reached his ears, soft but unmistakable laughter.

Mooz skipped across the waters, vaulted over the fallen log and danced toward the sunset of the second day.

V. Pebbles and Stones

26. Comet Fishing

5 Million Years in the Future - Teegarden Caravan

The birchbark canoe slid through the reeds as the sun neared the end of its longest journey of the year. A hungry denizen breached the surface for a skimmer that plopped into view seconds earlier. A silken thread drew taut; tiny waves traced the line's rip. The fish discovered the insect's genuine spirit as it rose into the darkening skies and spat the tasteless morsel. The feathery lure arced toward the tip of the rod, like a comet, and hooked the hat of his companion, lost deep in her thoughts. He reeled in the excess line and attempted to lift the sunhat from her head to remove the hook without disturbing her. The gentle tugging pulled Te Ata's mind out of the 17th century's archives to the sight of the wide brim spinning in the air between them.

A sheepish visage appeared before her. "Oops!" The Gardener lowered her hat. "Would you like to do the honors?"

She unhooked the lure and tossed it into the lake.

The fish's hunger was too great. "There's my dinner floating next to that log." It struck.

The Gardener's arm startled, revealing the feather's angry spirit. The parabolic path halted amidship, as tiny droplets sprayed the passengers. He lowered the flopper to Te Ata and grinned. "I believe this is your catch."

She grabbed the line with her right hand as her left slid down the dorsal fin, securing the knifelike appendage to its back. She removed the hook and examined the fish, whose head wiggled beside her thumb and tail twitched next to her pinky. "Well, at least one of us caught something tonight." She tossed the still hungry minnow into the lake.

"I beg to differ. What about that nice-sized hat I landed?" He reeled in the line and stowed the rod. "How's your story coming along?"

"It's time to move ahead several thousand years. My next stop is England in the mid-1600s where a young man risked death at the hands of church and state if they discovered his secret passions. Sir Isaac

Newton was more than a mathematical genius who wrote what many considered the most important book in history."

"Comets."

"What?"

"That's why he wrote the *Principia*. Because of the comets traipsing through the solar system in the 1600s."

Her eyes looked skyward as her mind scanned the archives. "Let's see. Aristotle thought they were nothing more than atmospheric disturbances. Seneca dodged him and proposed that they were in orbits similar to the planets. That's a pretty good guess for someone who lived during Jesus' lifetime."

"It was such a tragedy that nobody listened to him."

"Well, Tycho Brahe's observations and Johannes Kepler's analysis straightened out Aristotle's mess in the 16th century."

"Is that a pun? Because Kepler thought they traveled in straight lines?"

"Oh, that's hilarious." Her hand swept over the water's surface as a flurry of comets sped toward the Gardener.

"Now you're as wet as Descartes' theory of the fluid vortexes that swirled through his mind to explain the planetary motions."

"Thank goodness Isaac doubted that notion, since comets don't swim in the same lake as the planets."

"And yet it still took two icy rocks to get their attention. Everyone was pestering him, trying to figure out their orbits. The one in 1680 was a real beaut, scared the heck out of everybody because it was visible during the daytime. But that 1682 comet annoyed Halley to no end. His data seemed to suggest that it followed the same trajectory as the comets of 1531 and 1607."

"Yes, and then what happened?"

"He predicted its return in 1758, but he couldn't prove it. So he shared his observations with Isaac to see if he could represent its orbit with high precision."

"OK, let me stop you because here's where it could get boring. Everyone knows that he derived the equations that describe the motions of the planets and those pesky comets, blah blah blah blah blah."

"That's true. It's what he's famous for, but his other passions still burned within. To really understand his spiritual beliefs, I need to tell them about…"

"The sun's setting. We should head in."

"Could we sit out here and watch it set? I love how calm it gets when the winds die down."

"OK, but you have to paddle back." He thought for a moment. "Never mind, I'm afraid you'd sink us again."

27. The Town Crier

1642 - Grantham, England

John Folley swung his heavy handbell as he entered the town square in Grantham, England, 100 miles north of London. Families from all over the county attended the farmer's market on Saturdays to trade produce, sheep, cows and gossip. His job was to give them the latest news and weather for July 1642.

"Oyez, Oyez, Oyez, people of Lincolnshire," he shouted above the din of the square. He continued the loud ringing as he climbed the two steps to the platform. The crowd assembled to listen to the retired officer of the King's Royal Regiment, whose repurposed uniform commanded their attention.

He set the bell on a small table and withdrew a scroll of paper from the inner pocket of his topcoat. He unfurled it with a flourish and began reading in a voice that boomed throughout the market square.

"In the national news today, the War of the Three Kingdoms continues unabated. Last night under cover of darkness, King Charles I passed through town, having fled the Parliamentarians in London earlier this year. He would not reveal his destination, only asking our mayor for his allegiance. It is my duty to report that Grantham remains neutral on this issue. The king left early this morning to continue his journey north.

"And now, the forecast. We need to brace ourselves against powerful gusts the rest of this decade. The winds of change are blowing from the east as the Puritan movement rebels against Roman Catholic influences. Expect fierce southerly gales from the Parliamentarians in London as they look to seize power and create a representative government. A tempest from the west caused by the well-established Church of England hopes to cleanse the landscape of Puritans and Catholics, to establish the one true church. Cold blusters from the monarchy in the north will join the western tempests to restore the Monarchy's authority over England, Scotland and Ireland."

"The king's aides asked me to announce the following. There are several ships bound for the American colonies docked in Bristol. They recommend that Puritans seeking religious freedom should book passage soon, as spots are filling up."

"And in local news, Isaac Newton notified me that the family cow is on the loose again. They offer a reward of a bushel of apples to anyone who finds and returns her to Woolsthorpe Manor."

As he rolled the paper to return it to his inner pocket, a whirlwind hoisted his tricorne over the roof of Clark's apothecary. The crowd watched as a small boy wearing Folley's possession emerged from the alley with a cow in tow. Folley snatched the hat as the youngster approached Isaac. "I found her on the way to town this morning. Thought you'd be here." He turned to Isaac's wife, Hannah. "I couldn't eat all those apples from the last time I caught her. Could I get an apple pie instead?"

A loud cheer erupted from the crowd as she nodded in agreement.

28. The Funeral of Isaac Newton's Father

A stiff north wind swept over the English countryside that night in early October 1642. The wagon, carrying a black oak casket, lumbered toward St. John the Baptist Church in Colsterworth, joined by a small procession of family and friends. A local farmer, Isaac Newton, had died in his mid-30s of unknown causes. Hannah, his wife since April, was four months pregnant. The overwhelming burdens descending on the 19-year-old poured into her mother's kerchief.

"What am I going to do? How can I manage the farm and take care of the baby?"

Margery drew her shivering daughter close. "I don't want you to worry about anything. I'll come live with you. We'll figure something out."

"Isaac always worked so hard feeding the livestock, planting and tending the crops. He was so exhausted when he sat down to supper."

"I remember how scared I was when you were born. Every new mother worries. Mourn for your husband now, there's plenty of time to get everything settled before the baby arrives."

Reverend Barnabas Smith, a wealthy minister from North Witham who had never married in his 61 years, waited at the church as the wagon approached. When he saw the torchbearers, he stepped out of his coach and walked into the cemetery. He had selected a few brief passages from the Book of Common Prayer clutched in his gloved hands. His old bones couldn't take the cold October blusters.

Two farmhands from Woolsthorpe and four of his neighbors led the procession into the graveyard and set the casket on ropes next to the grave. As the mourners huddled together, Barnabas spoke.

"I am the resurrection and the life, saith the Lord: he that believeth in me, though he were dead, yet shall he live: and whosoever liveth and believeth in me shall never die.

"I know that my Redeemer liveth, and that he shall stand at the latter day upon the earth. And though after my skin worms destroy this body, yet in my flesh shall I see God: whom I shall see for myself, and mine eyes shall behold, and not another.

"We brought nothing into this world, and it is certain we can carry nothing out. The Lord gave, and the Lord hath taken away; blessed be the Name of the Lord."

Heavily burdened hearts strained against the ropes as the pallbearers lowered the casket into the grave.

"Man that is born of a woman hath but short time to live, and is full of misery. He cometh up, and is cut down, like a flower; he fleeth as it were a shadow, and never continueth in one stay."

He paused as Isaac's closest friend, William Clark, spoke his silent goodbye with a shovelful of dirt.

"For as much as it hath pleased Almighty God of his great mercy to take unto himself the soul of our dear *brother* here departed, we therefore commit *his* body to the ground; earth to earth, ashes to ashes, dust to dust; in sure and certain hope of the Resurrection to eternal life, through our Lord Jesus Christ; who shall change our vile body, that it may be like unto his glorious body, according to the mighty working, whereby he is able to subdue all things to himself. Amen."

"Amen."

With eagerness of step, the mourners rushed back to the church. Barnabas walked beside Hannah. He tossed his prayer book into his coach and took hold of her hands.

"No one understands why God lays such heavy burdens on us, but know that you needn't carry them alone. If there is anything you need, any comfort I can give…"

She attempted a smile through her tears. "That's very kind of you, Reverend. My mother has offered to help, but running the farm, I'm not sure how I will manage."

One Sunday, in late November, he invited Hannah to stay for supper. His cook had prepared a roast beef with cooked carrots and boiled potatoes, with pudding for dessert. They sat for several hours afterward talking about farming and the church, topping off the evening with a nice compote of gossip. She grew fond of Barnabas, even though he was forty-two years her senior.

Christmas that year fell on a Sunday. Barnabas greeted the congregation as they entered. Everyone was in their seats, and the churchyard was quiet as he closed the doors. The concerned tones of his message of the newborn savior and the promise of eternal life flowed over the worshipers and echoed off the empty pew where Hannah worshipped.

After the sermon, he approached a group of her friends. "I noticed Hannah wasn't in attendance. Have any of you spoken with her since last Sunday?"

"I saw her yesterday at Woolsthorpe. Her back was bothering her, and she was nauseous. I'm sure she'll be fine."

"Perhaps, but let's say a prayer for her."

29. The Manor House

The late-December winds explored every crack in the darkened manor earlier that Christmas morning. With nothing left to satisfy her nausea, Hannah's seven-month pregnant belly decided it best to cramp mercilessly. The howling wind and the moans of her daughter awakened Margery. She lit a candle, threw on her warmest robe and slippers, and rushed to her side.

"Something is wrong. I'm having severe cramps!"

She knew what was happening. "You're going to be fine. Wait here. I need to boil some water."

Within the hour, Hannah delivered the tiny infant. Her mother cleaned and swaddled him in a small woolen blanket.

"You have a beautiful boy. Have you decided on a name for him?"

She cradled him in her palms. "Yes, Isaac, in memory of his father."

They spent that first week tending to his meager needs. Thankful for her mother's loving guidance, she nursed and cared for her son. Margery tended the house, prepared their meals and sat with her grandson now and then as Hannah regained her strength.

Icicles halted the advance of light rain trickling toward the eaves on the last day of 1642. The kitchen stove battled the icy wind to a draw at the windowsill, its glow shielding a kettle of fresh milk and Margery's hands. The Sun would soon join the fray.

Margery set two mugs to warm on the stovetop and shouted to her daughter. "The milk's ready."

Bundled in blankets to ward off the chill, Hannah rushed downstairs with Isaac suckling. Margery kissed her grandson on the back of his tiny head and placed the nurturing hand warmers on the table.

Sometimes the hardest task for any parent is to tell their child a truth they don't want to listen to. "We should have Isaac baptized as soon as possible."

Hannah's parental instincts flared like the cornered child she was. She held her infant close as she pushed the darkness away. "There's no need to rush. He's too small to travel now. We can do it in the spring when it's warmer."

Margery opened her bookmarked Bible. "We mustn't wait. Remember what Jesus says in John 3, Verse 5. 'Verily, verily, I say unto thee, Except a man be born of water and of the Spirit, he cannot enter into the kingdom of God.' I'll ask Reverend Smith to come here after church tomorrow. I'm sure he'll understand."

"I don't think we should bother him."

"No, it's important to have him baptized as soon as possible."

☉---♅♆--☿☽⊕-♄-♂♀--♃●○

Margery awoke early Sunday, January 1, 1643, to get firewood in for the day. She gathered some eggs from the henhouse and made a delicious breakfast with fresh milk.

The meal finished, Margery put on her warm coat and kissed Hannah and Isaac goodbye. She always attended the Puritan church in Colsterworth with her friends, a short walk from the farm. This morning, she rode her horse south, braced against the headwinds. There were no friendly faces for her in North Witham.

Smith's sermons peered at current events through the church's telescope. Margery listened with her jaw taut to his lengthy dissertation on the heresy of Puritanism. She planned to wait until the church cleared before approaching him, but the sermon came to an abrupt end when he spotted her. Every head turned as he rushed toward that heretic sitting in the last row.

"Is Hannah well? I looked for her last week and didn't see her. I haven't slept well since."

"Yes, she is fine. She gave birth on Christmas morning to her son, Isaac."

"I am so relieved to hear that."

"Isaac was two months early. He's so tiny, I'm afraid he might not survive the winter. Would you be willing to come to Woolsthorpe this afternoon and baptize him? It would mean the world to us if you did."

"I'll need to collect my things first. Let's go."

As they rushed out of the church, Margery overheard some unkind words. "What's the Reverend doing with that Puritan witch? He just spent the last hour demonizing them."

They passed the stables on the way to the rectory.

"Harness the horse while I get my baptismal kit. You can tie yours to the back." He dashed into his library and collected his book of prayers and a small bottle of holy water, not even thinking about taking his ceremonial robe. He left word with his cook to delay dinner until evening.

Margery kept her focus on what was important and readied the carriage.

☉---♅♆--☿☽⊕-♄-♂♀--♃●○

When they arrived at Woolsthorpe, Margery led Barnabas into the kitchen.

"Please, sit down. I'll make some tea to warm us up." She stoked the fire and set a pot of water to boil. Hannah walked in with Isaac swaddled in a blanket.

"Thank you so much for coming. We are so grateful to you. May I introduce you to Isaac?" She pulled back the cover.

Barnabas had seen premature babies in the past, but Isaac's size startled him. "Oh my, I wasn't expecting him to be so small!"

Hannah blushed. "I'm sorry I didn't warn you. I don't know what I would have done without my mother's help. These past few months since my husband passed have been very hard."

"God will see you through if you trust in him. Let us pray." They bowed their heads.

"Almighty God, we give thee humble thanks for that thou hast vouchsafed to deliver this woman thy servant from the great pain and peril of childbirth. Grant, we beseech thee, most merciful Father, that she, through thy help, may faithfully live and walk according to thy will, in this life present, and may be a partaker of everlasting glory in the life to come, through Jesus Christ our Lord. Amen."

"Amen."

The teakettle whistled its agreement. They adjourned to the parlor for the ceremony. He placed his prayer book and vial of holy water on a small table and sat in the accompanying chair. Hannah placed Isaac in

Barnabas' care.

"I baptize thee in the name of the Father, and of the Son, and of the Holy Ghost. Amen."

Ice-cold droplets startled Isaac; his loudest cry was barely audible.

He placed Isaac in Hannah's care and read from the book.

"I certify you, that in this case ye have done well, and according unto due order concerning the baptizing of this child, which being born in original sin and in the wrath of God, is now by the water of regeneration in baptism received into the number of the children of God, and heirs of everlasting life. For our Lord Jesus Christ doth not deny his grace and mercy unto such infants, but most lovingly doth call them unto him, as the holy gospel doeth witness to our comfort, on this wise."

Margery felt ice forming in her veins. She had attended many baptisms, but this was the shortest ceremony ever.

"I will ask the Lord to help him through this troublesome time, but it was sensible to have him baptized so soon. Few children like him live to see their first year."

Hannah wiped the tears streaming down her cheeks. "I pray for him every day. Please, stay for supper. It wouldn't be any bother."

"I should head back. My cook is preparing a meal later this evening. I'll stop by next week to check on you."

Margery entered the parlor with a bundled cloth. "I warmed up a few biscuits for your trip home. You should attend services at Colsterworth sometime. I think you would find Puritans warm and welcoming, as opposed to the heretical monsters you described this morning."

⊙---♅♈--☿☽⊕-♄-♂♀--♃●○

Margery arose early on Easter, eager to visit her friends for the first time since Isaac's birth. The kettle whistled when Hannah, already dressed for church, walked into the kitchen. She passed Isaac to the waiting arms of his grandmother.

"Come sit down, have some tea. Services won't start for another hour."

"I'm not going to Colsterworth, Mother. You know how Reverend Smith feels about Puritans."

"Yes, he's made his thoughts quite clear, but all my friends go there and I haven't seen them since Christmas. If you want to take Isaac with you, he'll be fine."

"I can't carry him while riding a horse."

The young Newton cried for the attention only his grandmother would provide. "Well, you better leave then." She soothed the infant's brow. "My Puritan friends will love meeting you."

30. Lessons Learned

1646 - Woolsthorpe

Hannah spent Sunday afternoons in Barnabas' company away from the pressures of Woolsthorpe. Isaac loved to sit in his grandmother's lap after church, listening to stories from the Bible and studying the intricate pictures.

On the Sunday before Christmas 1646, Margery and Isaac had finished their dinner and settled in next to a crackling fire. Margery's present that year was the most valuable gift any person could ask for, one that took the inquisitive youngster far from the drudgery of farm chores. She was teaching the 4-year-old to read. In return, she got to witness the birth of a genius. Tonight, his eyes journeyed through the First Book of Moses called Genesis.

1 The creation of Heaven and Earth, 3 of the light, 6 of the firmament, 9 of the earth separated from the waters, 11 and made fruitful, 14 of the Sun, Moon, and Stars, 20 of fish and fowl, 24 of beasts and cattle, 26 of Man in the Image of God, 29 Also the appointment of food.

Isaac was reading Verse 14 when Hannah burst in.

"I have some wonderful news. Reverend Smith proposed marriage this afternoon."

They both looked at her, surprised. "You haven't accepted, have you?"

"I said yes."

"Isaac, would you go to your room? I need to talk to your mother."

"Can I take your Bible with me, Grandma?"

"It's 'May I take,' Isaac, and yes, you may take it with you. Now, off with you."

He scooted off her lap and bounded up the stairs.

"Are you certain you want to marry him? What's going to happen to Woolsthorpe?"

"My decision is final. I'm marrying Barnabas and moving to North Witham. He prefers that Isaac stay here. I want you to manage the farm and take care of him."

"I knew all along he didn't like Isaac, but how could you abandon your only child?"

"You know how lonely I've been. Barnabas has been very kind. I just hope you'll understand."

☉---♃♅♇--☿☽⊕-♄-♂♀--♃●○

When Isaac was 5 years old, Margery sent him to school in the village of Skillington, where he learned the fundamentals of reading, writing, and arithmetic. His predawn two-mile walks through the English countryside taught him the phases of the moon, the wonders of a meteor shower and the diffuse hues of a majestic sunrise. The glory of Genesis played out before his own eyes every morning.

On Saturdays, Isaac would walk to North Witham to visit his mother. He spent many hours in his stepfather's extensive library of religious texts. The sermons at Colsterworth didn't always align with Smith's preaching. They used the same Bible, felt its truth to be absolute, yet somehow the same words had nuanced interpretations. He soon realized that people would argue over its truths without having read it all, as he had.

One Thursday afternoon in August, while collecting the dried laundry, Margery noticed the ripening apples ready for market. She glanced at the meadow where Isaac was supposed to be tending the cattle. It wouldn't be the first time he neglected a chore. She left the basket to search for him.

As she walked toward the pasture, she realized that one cow and one grandson were missing again. She looked toward the neighbor's field and spotted them engaged in battle. He was trying to herd her across the creek while she battled to forage in greener pastures. His will prevailed when he got hold of the rope and led her back to Woolsthorpe.

"I want you to load the wagon with apples this afternoon so we can sell them at the market on Saturday. I'll bake a nice cobbler for you tomorrow."

Herding was easy compared to loading wagons. But a fresh apple pie was a temptation he couldn't ignore.

"All right, Grandma. Can we sell this cow too? I'm tired of chasing her every day."

Margery smiled as he handed her the rope. "If I sold her, you wouldn't have anything to do."

He stopped at the well to satisfy his thirst and looked at the sun. "I think I'll do a little reading first. There's still plenty of time to pick apples."

He retrieved the Bible from his room. As he walked to the apple tree, he spotted a peregrine falcon floating on the updrafts. He loved watching them hunt, but today he just wanted to sit in the shade and read for a few minutes before loading the wagon.

He scratched the dog's ear near the end of the sacred text. His mind, soaring through the revelations appearing before him, landed under the stormy skies of Chapter 16, Verse 21:

"And there fell upon men a great hail out of heaven, every stone about the weight of a talent: and men blasphemed God because of the plague of the hail for the plague thereof was exceeding great."

☉---♅♆--☿☾⊕-♄-♂♀--♃●○

The hunter's eye spotted a red flash attempting to conceal itself amongst the ripening apples. It tucked its wings and dropped from the sky like a meteor. The wary robin flitted to a lower branch a split-second before talons pierced its feathered veil and seized its perch instead.

Furious flapping drew Isaac's gaze toward the heavens as the hailstorm descended on him. One stone struck him on the forehead and landed in Chapter 16. Although it didn't weigh a talent, the impact still hurt and scared the bejesus out of him. He snatched the apple from the Scriptures and tossed it at the angel of death as it sped off over the pasture. God's retribution for having his name blasphemed was swift— a lump swelled on his head. He prayed for forgiveness and vowed to stick to fruitless hedges for shady reading spots in the future. "God has beseeched me to set about my task," he thought to himself. He placed his Bible on the seat and began loading the wagon.

Margery relied more and more on Isaac's help around the farm as he grew older. His chores included tending chickens and cows and helping to plant and harvest their crops, all of which he mastered within four lessons. The most important lesson farming taught him was how much he hated it.

31. The Apothecary

1655 - Grantham, England

The apothecary shop in Grantham was a wonderment of mysterious vials with cryptic labels, strange devices with purposes unknown and even stranger smells than a farm. Everyone knew that the owner was a respected healer. What they didn't realize was that he dabbled in the dark arts.

The shopkeeper's bell struggled to drown out the joyous sounds of the harvest festival and the two afflicted customers who entered.

"Good morning, Mr. Clark. I hope you are well."

"It's good to see you, Margery," William replied. "I suspect I am in better health today than you are. And how are you, Isaac?"

He wandered through the store coughing like his grandmother. "I haven't been sleeping well."

"I know of a remedy, but it takes several hours to prepare. Could you stop back later?"

"Yes, I have plenty of shopping this morning. Let's go, Isaac."

"May I stay here? Please?" Anything was better than the market.

"This is a complex recipe and I could use some help."

"All right, you mind Mr. Clark and do as he says." She rushed out of the apothecary to the town square, where her friends waited.

He patted his new assistant on the head. "Come with me to my laboratory and we'll get started."

Isaac had never seen this mysterious room. Shelves full of pots, medicinal plants and instruments lined the walls. A small cooking stove sat in one corner. But it was the bookshelf that piqued his interest. William selected *The Mysteries of Nature and Art* by John Bate. The well-worn pages flopped open to the "Book of Extravagants."

"Do you know what that says, Isaac?" He pointed at the subtitle.

"Wherein amongst others, is principally contrived diverse, excellent and approved medicines for several maladies."

William scanned the recipes until he came to the one he was looking for. "That's perfect. Now, what does this say?"

"An excellent Electuary for the Cough, Cold or against Flegme."

"Do you know what 'flegme' means?"

"No."

He handed the youngster a fresh cloth. "It's that stuff running out of your nose."

They studied the recipe together.

"Hmm, there's a lot here. I'll read them off, and you see if you can find them."

Isaac nodded in agreement.

The electuary listed a handful of each of these ingredients: germander, hissope, horehound, white maidenhaire, agrimony, bettony, liverwort, lungwort and harts-tongue.

As William called for an ingredient, his apprentice searched for it on the well-marked shelves. Finding the first three took the longest. His sharp mind noticed an order to the chaos and, without hesitation, retrieved the remaining herbs. He measured a handful of germander and placed it on the counter.

"Lay your palm next to mine."

The apothecary's sizeable hand dwarfed the youngster's.

"It's not an exact measurement, but I'd say use two handfuls."

Isaac saw how the nuanced meaning changed based on the reader's assumption. Was that the fault of the reader or the author, he wondered? He shrugged his shoulders and measured everything twice.

"Very good. Now I need you to fetch 9 pints of water while I light the fire."

"Have you got a milk jug I could use to measure?"

William pointed at the shelf with glass beakers. Isaac examined their markings: pint, quart, gallon. He grabbed the smallest beaker, the large pot and headed to the well. When he returned, he hoisted the legless cauldron onto the stove.

"Now add the herbs and let them boil to 3 pints."

He added each handful in alphabetical order.

"We have to weigh the rest of the ingredients. Do you know how to do that?"

He'd seen people using scales in the market. He spotted William's and brought it to the worktable.

"You'll also need the counterweights."

He retrieved the tray, arranged from lightest to heaviest in carved niches. As he returned to the bench, his toe caught an uneven floorboard. The force of his flailing arms sent the masses accelerating through the air like cannonballs, scattering them throughout the workshop.

Isaac scrambled to collect them. "Have you ever wondered what causes that, Mr. Clark?"

"Isn't it obvious? You're quite clumsy," he replied, laughing.

He snatched the last weight from beneath the stove and set the tray on the workbench. "No, I mean why do things fall toward the Earth?"

"That's a weighty question, but I'm afraid we won't have time for that today."

Isaac smiled and shook his head. "What's the first ingredient?"

"Clarified honey, half a pound."

Isaac retrieved the pot of gold and placed the specified weight on the tray. William selected a flask from the shelf and handed it to his assistant, who set it on the raised plate. He poured the golden liquid until the trays reached equilibrium. He smiled after making his first successful measurement.

"That's not correct. Can you tell me why?"

His eyebrows bounced off the floor of his forehead. "I forgot about the weight of the jar. I need more honey."

William handed his protégé an empty container. He swapped it with the full one and rebalanced the scale. Weights, glass bottles and nectar swirled through his mind until the solution arrived on his smiling lips. He traded flasks again and added the half-pound counterweight to the seesaw, then poured enough golden elixir until the unseen judge declared the contest a draw.

"That was very impressive. You figured that out all by yourself."

Isaac enjoyed this. "What's the next ingredient?"

For the fine powder of liquorice, he measured 5 ounces. For the enulacampana root, 3 ounces.

"Very good. Now check the stove."

The cauldron was lighter by 6 pints. He grabbed the handle with a thick towel and lifted it over to the worktable.

William looked up from the book when the shop bell clanged.

"Looks like I have a customer. We'll finish the recipe when I return."

Isaac's fingers caressed the mysterious tome. "May I look through this while you are gone?"

"Yes, but be careful with the pages. It's getting old, and that's my only copy."

William's chair took him on the journey of a lifetime. Page after illustrated page contained wonders he'd never imagined on the farm. "The Third Book of Drawing, Painting, Limming, and Graving" showed how to paint landscapes or villages using a grid-line technique. One section pictured various water clocks to mark the hours of the day.

The author, John Bate, had died seven years before Isaac was born, but the tiny seed of knowledge he had planted changed the young farmer forever.

William returned to find the scientist reading "The Second Book, Teaching most plainly, and withall most exactly, the composing of all manner of Fire-works for Triumph and Recreation." In particular, how to make a fire drake, a kite with firecrackers tied to its tail.

By this time, the pot had cooled. Isaac found the strainer and poured the mixture through it into a bowl, then added the remaining ingredients.

"We need to let this thicken now. Set it back on the stove. When it boils, stir it with the spoon."

Isaac did as instructed, and soon the medicine was ready. William placed a small jug on the table and inserted a funnel. After emptying the bowl, the professor ran his finger along the edge and tasted the soothing sweetness of the concoction.

"Tonight, before you go to bed, measure an amount equal to a walnut for yourself and your grandmother. This should last you a week."

That evening, sweet peace returned to Woolsthorpe Manor.

32. Dinner and a Stone

William was busy reading a book from his library as his wife restocked the candy jars. The shopkeeper's bell rang all morning, waited in silence through the noon hour and sang its penultimate song of the day when their last customer entered.

"Good afternoon, William, Katherine."

Katherine walked around the counter and hugged Margery. "It's so nice to see you."

William looked up from his book. "Where's Isaac? Is he sitting under that hedge outside of town reading his Bible?"

"No, he didn't come with me today. He's in trouble with his mother again."

"I can't believe he'd do anything so dire as to warrant keeping him at Woolsthorpe," Katherine said with a concerned look.

"So, what crime did he commit?" William asked.

"One of our cows broke through the fence last week and got into the neighbors' crops."

"That seems to happen a lot. Have you considered selling her?"

"Isaac wants to have her for dinner. She causes him more grief than you can imagine. Anyway, Hannah had to pay for the damages. She was so mad at Isaac for not watching the cattle. When she couldn't find him, she asked her son, Ben Smith, to help. They searched the countryside for over an hour before finding him by a stream, building some kind of waterwheel. For what purpose, I don't know. I'm surprised you didn't hear her yelling at him from your store. He and Ben are mending the fence today, and Hannah has an endless list of chores for him now. Ever since she returned to Woolsthorpe after Reverend Smith passed, she's been putting a lot of pressure on him to take more responsibility and to be a better example to his three stepsiblings. Poor Isaac is miserable."

William shook his head. "His mind is so quick for an 11-year-old. I don't think his future lies in farming. He should attend the King's School here in Grantham."

"I agree, but the daily trip to town would be too hard on him."

Katherine looked at William and spoke their shared thought. "He could live here during the week and be home on weekends. We have a spare room he could use above the shop."

"Are you sure it wouldn't be too much trouble?"

"No trouble at all. The children would love to have him stay with us. Would you like me to come and talk to Hannah? Classes start in two weeks."

"That won't be necessary. I'll speak with her."

$$\odot\text{---}\text{♅}\text{♆}\text{--}\text{☿}\,\mathbb{C}\,\oplus\text{-}\text{♄}\text{-}\text{♂}\text{♀}\text{--}\text{♃}\,\bullet\,\bigcirc$$

Isaac settled into his new quarters the next week. The Clarks, with Katherine's four offspring from her previous marriage to Edward Storer—Edward, Arthur, Katherine and Ann—adopted him as one of their own. He loved their family dinners every evening, which were open forums that nurtured fresh ideas, where everyone left intolerance and mockery at the door.

Not long after the start of the school year, the younger Katherine had taken a liking to their guest and thought it might be fun to have William recount their favorite tale.

"Father, Isaac's never heard about the Philosopher's Stone. Would you tell us the story tonight after dinner?" She nudged Isaac with her shoulder.

"It's been quite some time since I told that one. All right, help your mother clean up. I'll light a fire and grab the book."

The logs were transmuting cellulose into smoke and ash in the study when the children gathered at the alchemist's feet to listen to his tale. Katherine wedged in between her sister and Isaac.

William leaned forward in his chair and spoke in hushed tones to their guest. "The English monarchy imprisons people for practicing the dark arts. It's dangerous to even mention the Philosopher's Stone outside these walls. You must swear never to speak of this with anyone."

How could he refuse a temptation like this? "I won't tell a soul, I promise."

William settled back in his chair and began the story. "Tonight, I will share the account of the only known alchemist to achieve the stone in the past 300 years. He recorded his findings in this book, *Nicolas Flamel, his exposition of the Hieroglyphical Figures, Concerning both the Theory and Practise of the Philosopher's Stone.*

"He took up residence in Paris with his wife, Perrenella, in an age where speaking of alchemy with a friend or acquaintance could bring a fiery death at the stake. Thus, the great chymists of the time described the transmutation of the basest elements using the language of religious texts, disguising their true meaning in the descriptions of God's divinity.

"Nicolas' education led him to a job as a scrivener skilled in the art of calligraphy and illustration of the type used in manuscripts of those days. He spent many hours reading through medieval documents that spoke of the occult sciences.

"One day, while transcribing texts in an alcove of his shop, a person of little means entered.

"'Monsieur Flamel, a moment of your time. I have something that may interest you,' he said.

"The vagrant handed him an ancient gilded tome inscribed on the bark of young trees, written in several languages. Flamel's brief examination of the illustrations piqued his curiosity. He gave the man a mere pittance for the manuscript, unaware of its contents.

"He studied it day and night for months, examining its many pictures and words, and soon realized it contained the secret of the Philosopher's Stone. Over the next two decades, his attempts failed at every turn. He was certain of the steps, lacking only the first agent. He had translated all but three pages written in an unfamiliar script. Desperate to unlock the secrets of the ancients, he made a pilgrimage to Spain in search of someone adept at decoding the cabalistic vocabulary. After searching for several years, he met Master Canches, an occultist skilled in deciphering the cabalist language. From Nicolas' description, he knew the copies came from the legendary Book of Abraham. He taught the scrivener how to interpret the symbols and asked him to accompany him to Paris to study the originals. On the trip, however, Flamel's friend became afflicted with disease and died.

"With the knowledge he gained from Master Canches, he perfected the method over the next three years. He states in this book that on January 17th, 1382, he made his first projection on mercury, turning it into half a pound of silver, assayed to be purer than any mined. Later that year, he projected the Red Stone on a like amount of quicksilver, transmuting it into gold, softer and more pliable than any yet found.

"His transmutations brought them unimaginable wealth. He and Perrenella became generous benefactors of Parisian society, building 14 hospitals, three churches and many hostels for the poor.

"Nobody knew where their fortune came from until he published this account. Flamel states that this book contains the knowledge needed to perform the miracle, lacking only the first agent, which the chymist must discover elsewhere.

"Some people claim that he also achieved an alchemist's most elusive goal, the Elixir of Life. There have been frequent sightings of Nicolas and Perrenella wandering the streets of Paris since the 1300s."

Isaac's eyes were as wide as two walnuts as William finished the story and handed the book to him.

33. Chymistry

Isaac grabbed a fresh candle from the storeroom of the apothecary and lit it from the fire. Bounding up the stairs with his treasure, he spent the rest of the evening reading in bed by candlelight. When he got to Chapter 8, he read and reread each sentence carefully, for here was the stone.

CHAPTER VIII.

Look upon this woman clothed in a robe of orange colour, who doth so naturally resemble Perrenella as she was in her youth; She is painted in the fashion of a suppliant upon her knees, her hands joined together, at the feet of a man who hath a key in his right hand, who hears her graciously, and afterwards stretcheth out his left hand upon her.

Wouldst thou know what this meaneth? This is the Stone, which in this operation demandeth two things, of the Mercury of the Sun, of the Philosophers, (painted under the form of a man) that is to say Multiplication, and a more rich Accoutrement: which at this time it is needful for her to obtain, and therefore the man so laying his hand upon her shoulder accords and grants it unto her.

But why have I made to be painted a woman? I could as well have made to be painted a man as a woman, or an Angel rather (for the whole natures are now spiritual and corporal, masculine and feminine.) But I have rather chosen to cause paint a woman, to the end that thou mayest judge that she demands rather this, than any other thing, because these are the most natural and proper desires of a woman.

To show further unto thee, that she demandeth Multiplication, I have made paint the man, unto whom she addresseth her prayers in the form of Saint Peter, holding a key, having power to open and to shut, to bind and to loose; because the envious Philosophers have never spoken of Multiplication but under these common terms of Art: — Open, shut, bind, loose; opening and loosing; they have called the making of the Body (which is always hard and fixt) soft fluid, and running like water—To shut and to bind, is with them afterwards by a more strong decoction to coagulate it, and to bring it back again into the form of a body.

It behoved me then, in this place to represent a man with a key, to teach thee that thou must now open and shut, that is to Multiply the budding and increasing natures; for look how often thou shalt dissolve and fix, so often will these natures multiply in quantity, quality and virtue, according to the multiplication of ten: coming from this number to an hundred, from an hundred to a thousand, from a thousand to ten thousand, from ten thousand to an hundred thousand, from an hundred thousand to a million, and from thence by the same operation to Infinity, as I have done three times; praised be God.

And when thy Elixir is so brought unto Infinity one grain thereof falling upon a quantity of molten metal as deep and vast as the Ocean, it will tein it, and convert it into most perfect metal, that is to say, into silver or gold, according as it shall have been imbibed and fermented, expelling and driving out far from himself all the impure and strange matter, which was joined with the metal in the first coagulation: for this reason therefore have I made to be painted a Key in the hand of the man, who is in the form of Saint Peter, to signify that the stone desireth to be opened and shut for multiplication; and likewise to show thee with what Mercury thou oughtest to do this, and when; I have given the man a garment Citrine red, and the woman, one of orange colour.

Let this suffice, lest I transgress the silence of Pythagoras, to teach thee that the woman, that is our stone, asketh to have the rich Accoutrements and colour of Saint Peter. She hath written in her Rowl: Jesus Christ be pitiful unto me; as if she said, Lord be good unto me, and suffer not that he that shall become thus far should spoil all with too much fire. It is true that from henceforward I shall no more fear mine enemies, and that all fire shall be alike unto me, yet the vessel that contains me, is always brittle and easy to be broken: for if they exalt the fire over much, it will crack, and flying apieces will carry me, and sow me unfortunately amongst the ashes.

Take heed therefore to thy fire in this place, and govern sweetly with patience, this admirable quintessence, for the fire must be augmented unto it, but not too much. And pray the sovereign Goodness, that it will not suffer the evil spirits, which keep the Mines and Treasures, to destroy thy work or bewitch thy sight, when thou considerest these incomprehensible motions of this Quintessence within thy vessel.

That weekend, William took young Isaac under his wing and began his education in alchemy. Together they searched for the first agent of the Philosopher's Stone, and an alchemist's ultimate prize, the Elixir of Life.

34. When Scientists Wrestle (A Three-Round Match)

Had the King's School tested a student's knowledge of alchemy, Isaac would have graduated from Professor Flamel's College for Advanced Chemistry and Transmutation by Christmas. If they based success on mastery of drawing or woodworking or following complex construction plans, he would have earned a double major from the Bate Academy of Vocational Arts. However, the school insisted on a curriculum of Latin, history, English and religion. Judged against those standards, he was dead last.

Isaac used his allowance from Woolsthorpe to purchase tools and supplies to construct Bate's contraptions. Young Katherine benefitted most when his mind ran past the limited opportunities of *The Mysteries of Nature and Art* and began the design and construction of dollhouse furniture. Her fondness for their houseguest blossomed.

They walked to school one morning holding hands, whispering to each other, and laughing. Arthur, being protective of his younger sibling, grabbed Isaac by the wrist. "Let go of my sister's hand."

Startled, Isaac jerked his hand away. "I'll do no such thing."

Arthur looked him in the eyes. "She's my sister. Leave her alone." He shoved Isaac to the ground, almost toppling Katherine. Isaac sprang from the dirt, swung a fist at his nemesis and missed. Enraged, Arthur doubled him over with a swift kick to the gut as the King's School bell signaled the end of round one.

Isaac grimaced in pain as Katherine consoled him. "We'll settle this at the churchyard after class."

Most people thought the boys were the same age based on their similar stature. Isaac, however, was five years older than Arthur and neither was skilled in the pugilistic arts.

That afternoon a group assembled in the churchyard, after the school bell clanged to start the second round. The choir exalted the tempo of their swinging fists, hard shoves and shin kicks. When the schoolmaster's son appeared, the impromptu choir practice paused, fearful of his father's wrath.

He walked up to them, patted them on the back. "You can finish your fight. I won't tell my father."

Knowing that the schoolmaster's boy was skilled in the sweet science, the boys attempted more of a boxing style. Isaac dodged a credible right cross that threw his opponent off balance. He grabbed the outstretched forearm, swiveled his torso and pulled the youngster over his hip, landing him flat on his back in the choir loft and knocking all four winds out of him.

The schoolmaster's son moved next to Isaac. "You should treat him like a coward and rub his face against the wall."

Isaac pulled him up by the ear to seal the victory, but Arthur landed the telling blow.

He knocked Isaac's hand away. "You may have beaten me here in the churchyard, but I'm still beating you in the classroom!"

That one sentence hit Newton like a Flower of Kent apple on top of the head. From that point forward, the competition between them to become the smartest person in school was on. To Isaac, Latin became a second language, opening new vistas to the young genius. The alchemical texts in Mr. Clark's library written in the scholarly prose were now available to his mind.

Arthur Storer finished second in school, behind one of the greatest geniuses that ever lived. He emigrated to colonial America, establishing himself as the first modern astronomer in the Western Hemisphere. In 1682, a magnificent spectacle lit up the skies of the inner solar system. Named Storer's Comet, for his initial discovery and excellent observations. Edmund Halley, however, determined that it was the same wanderer that appeared in 1531 and 1607 and predicted that it would reappear in 1758. Isaac referenced the measurements of both astronomers in his greatest work, the *Mathematical Principles of Natural Philosophy*. However, Storer's comet would never return.

35. Descartes' Horse

1661 - Grantham, England

"Children, dinner is ready," Mrs. Clark called upstairs. She opened the door to the apothecary. "William, it's dinnertime."

"One moment please. I need to take care of this customer."

Mrs. Clark studied the well-dressed gentleman. She didn't recognize who it was until he turned and removed his hat.

"Humfrey, what a surprise. We were just sitting down to eat."

"Sorry to drop in unannounced. I was in town on business and thought I'd stop and say hello."

"In that case, let me take your coat. You're dining with us tonight. I insist."

When Isaac heard his voice, he sprinted into the apothecary. "Dr. Babington." All formalities complete, he rushed to hug him. "I have something to show you, but it's too dark now. We must wait until tomorrow."

"Is it another contrivance from the *Mysteries of Nature and Art*? I would have thought you completed them all."

"No guessing. I want it to be a surprise."

"Well, I look forward to seeing whatever it is." He pulled a book from his bag and presented it to him. "I brought something for you, Isaac."

Dr. Humfrey Babington was a senior fellow at Trinity College in Cambridge. He was aware of William's and Isaac's interest in alchemy and wanted to encourage a more enlightening path to his education.

"It's the *Principia Philosophiae* by French mathematician and philosopher Rene Descartes. I may not always agree with him, but it's important to listen to other thoughts on the most controversial subjects. It will expand your knowledge of the scholarly use of Latin as well."

"Thank you. I'll start reading it tonight."

Katherine took her brother by the arm. "Let's go, gentlemen. Dinner is getting cold."

☉---♅♆--☿☽⊕-♄-♂♀--♃●○

The next day, Dr. Babington accompanied Isaac on the short walk to the town square. A young boy walked across the street lugging a bucket of water and emptied it in a strange-looking device.

"Hello, Isaac." The youngster waved.

"Hi, Ethan, I'd like to introduce Dr. Babington from Trinity College in Cambridge."

"Nice to meet you, Ethan. I see you're tending to your chores."

"Yes, I'm the town's official timekeeper. Isaac built this clock for us, and it's my job to keep it filled at all times. I also let the church and school know when to ring their bells."

"Very impressive," Dr. Babington said as he examined the careful workmanship of the device.

"I changed Bate's design to make it easier to read from the street."

The cobblestones interrupted the doctor's examination, announcing a wagon's approach. Isaac ran to the passenger and gave her a welcoming hug as his mother secured the reins.

"Good morning, Humfrey. How is Cambridge these days?"

"It's very exciting, Margery. The world is full of new ideas. I'm always looking for the brightest minds in England, you know. I've had my eye on this one for quite some time." Dr. Babington smiled at Isaac.

Hannah hopped down from the wagon and put her arm around her son. "Well, you can look somewhere else. When this school term is over, he's returning to Woolsthorpe to take full responsibility for the farm."

Dr. Babington, skilled in such confrontations, spoke before Isaac could speak of his love for his mother and his passion for farming.

"I've known your boy for many years now. He has a quality rare to find in the English countryside. It would be a severe injustice to waste such talent. He's a perfect fit for Trinity."

"Dr. Babington, we are not poor, but we couldn't afford a college as prestigious as yours," Hannah argued.

"He can enroll as a subsizar and earn additional money tutoring other students. It won't cost you a farthing."

Margery took her daughter by the arm. "The market is opening soon." She turned to shake Humfrey's hand. "When does the fall term start?"

Over the next several weeks, Isaac read Descartes' *Principia*, igniting a third passion in the 19-year-old. It wasn't long before Descartes had more dog ears than the Grantham kennel.

$$\odot{-}{-}{-}\text{⛢}\Psi{-}{-}\text{☿}☾\oplus{-}\hbar{-}\text{♂♀}{-}{-}\text{♃}\bullet\bigcirc$$

Late one Friday evening, after William locked the front door of the apothecary and extinguished the candles, he noticed a flickering glow from the quiet dormer upstairs.

"I thought Isaac left for Woolsthorpe? He's going to burn the whole place down someday."

He climbed the stairs to snuff the candle, surprised to find Isaac sitting with his feet on the desk and the book in his lap, staring at a crescent moon through the window.

"I haven't seen you so engrossed in a text since I introduced you to Monsieur Flamel."

"Oh, Mr. Clark, I was just trying to visualize how big the sun is, compared to the Earth and the moon. These principles are amazing. He's broken them into four sections about human knowledge, material things, the visible universe and the Earth. There are so many ideas, it's overwhelming. He talks about God without disguising his true meaning like an alchemist. For instance, here in his 25th principle of the first section, he states,

'That we must believe all that God has revealed, although it may surpass the reach of our faculties.'"

"Can you give me an example?"

"Well, when an apple separates from a branch, God sends it crashing to the ground. It's beyond our capabilities to explain how God causes that to happen."

"He said it 'may' surpass our understanding."

Isaac referenced the passage and nodded in agreement. "That's true. But Descartes doesn't address what God hasn't revealed."

"It sounds like he's keeping secrets from us. Perhaps if we focus on what we can see, it will someday reveal what can't be seen. Did anything else catch your attention, or were you just testing your apple theory on the upper right corner of Descartes?"

Isaac was eager to continue their discussion. He would laugh about that on his way home to Woolsthorpe tomorrow. "In his 40th principle, he says,

'That it is likewise certain that God has fore-ordained all things. But because what we have already discovered of God gives us the assurance that his power is so immense that we would sin in thinking ourselves capable of ever doing anything which he had not ordained beforehand, we should soon be in great difficulties if we undertook to harmonize the pre-ordination of God with the freedom of our will and endeavored to comprehend both truths at once.'"

Isaac saw that scarecrow look on William's face.

"He means that God puts limits on what we can do, but it is up to us to decide what we do."

"You've just summarized what Descartes said. Explain it in your own words."

"Well, tomorrow morning, I decide whether to go to the market or back to Woolsthorpe. God allows me to walk or ride home, but he doesn't allow me to take wing and fly there, regardless of how much I would want to."

"So, is Descartes saying that if the universe is a horse-drawn apple cart, then God has entrusted the reins to us?"

"Oh, I like that. Yes." Isaac sat for a moment, staring at the moon, powerless to hold its attention against the relentless spin of the planet. He shifted his chair to recapture its light.

"Listen to his 75th principle. I think it's the strangest of all.

'Besides the notions we have of God and of our mind, we will likewise find that we possess the knowledge of many propositions which are true, as, for example, that nothing cannot be the cause of anything.'

This implies to me that everything has always existed. How could that be? The Bible says that there was a beginning and God created it."

"So, you're doubting what Descartes stated as an eternal truth."

Isaac paused. "When I think about it, it makes sense. It's just hard to comprehend how the universe has existed forever."

"Yes, it surpasses my ability to understand, too."

The alchemist's wry smile did not go unnoticed.

"Oh, and I passed by his most interesting 21st principle." His forefinger strode backward through the kennel.

"'That the duration alone of our life suffices to show God's existence. The truth of this demonstration will appear, provided we consider the nature of time. From the fact that we now are, it does not follow that we shall be a moment afterward, unless some cause, such as that which first produced us, shall continue to reproduce us. For we understand that there is no power in us by which we can create ourselves. And that the being who has so much power to create us must be God.'"

Isaac considered the statement. "God applies his laws between this moment and the next, to manifest each new universe."

"So he's saying God is with us all the time, guiding everything according to his will. That sounds like an angel watching over our shoulders, doesn't it?"

Isaac looked in amazement at the insightful alchemist. "Have you read this before?"

"Dr. Babington gave me a copy that contained his annotations. He knew your questions would far surpass my ability to answer them."

"OK, let's see what you and Dr. Babington think about this. In the last section, he presents his principles of the visible universe. He describes the size of the sun and moon in relation to the Earth, and somehow he figured out that the fixed stars lie beyond the orbit of Saturn, and that they may be farther away than we could ever imagine. Then he talks about moonlight." He shifted his chair again and pointed at the crescent. "From his description, it's obvious that the moon is reflecting sunlight. He questioned things I never considered, but he always does it regarding God's infinite powers, which the Bible tells us to accept without questioning."

"Where do the Scriptures say that?"

"Well, as a child, I must have asked Reverend Smith a thousand questions about biblical passages and their meanings. Most of the time, he told me we mustn't question God, that faith was all we needed."

"And what does Descartes think about that? Check the first line of the principles of human knowledge."

Isaac flipped to the lead dog in the kennel.

"That in order to seek truth, it is necessary once in the course of our life to doubt as far as possible, of all things."

"Doesn't he mention that in our infancy we made many judgments before we had full use of reasoning? Does the Bible tell us not to question God, or was it easier for the Reverend to avoid answering the troublesome questions of a pesky child?"

"I remember asking him once why the sun rises and sets every day. All he said was that God ordained it and I should just enjoy its majesty and stop questioning him all the time. But Descartes not only questioned God, he gave us answers. I mean, to my mind, this knowledge only adds to the majestic nature of God."

"I would have to agree. There's nothing wrong with piercing the veils that shroud God's creations. I suspect you and Mr. Descartes will become close friends at Trinity."

"He passed away several years ago. I would have enjoyed sitting down and talking with him."

"We rarely have that luxury. That's why books are so important. They allow the author to speak to us from far beyond the grave. And remember, this isn't the only book Descartes wrote. I'm sure he sprinkled diamonds throughout his writings, just waiting for someone like you to mine them."

36. A Plague of Apples

1665 - Oxford, England

The news of Isaac's burgeoning intellect whistled through the Great Gate at Trinity, swirled around the founder's statue and blasted doors wide open on all four sides of the courtyard.

Barristers advocated on the southerly breezes for a law degree in the blossoming flower patch of parliamentarianism.

Clergy preached on the western winds to lure him into their garden with God's wisdom.

Philosophers rationalized the study of Aristotle's seed bank, but the northern blusters appeared ancient and decaying to his mind.

It was the sweet fragrance of the mathematicians' conjectures that turned his head toward the east. Their well-tended plots contained the most beautiful growth. From Oughtred's orchard, he plucked the fruits of algebra and discovered one of his gardening tools, the slide rule, laying in the dirt. Wallis was weeding Descartes' field of analytic geometry sewn in previous years and plowing the spring fields of the infinitesimals. From Viète's vineyard in France, he plunged his sickle where the grapes of math were stored, casting the binomial theorem into the great winepress of his intellect and leaving it to ferment in the oak barrels of his memory. Vast stretches of untilled soil surrounded these farmlands for his mind to explore.

Dr. Isaac Barrow, the first Lucasian Professor of Mathematics at Cambridge, mentored him through those early years. By January 1665, he had earned his bachelor's degree. He returned that fall to continue farther into the meadow where calculus was taking root.

Isaac entered his mentor's office several weeks after the start of the term to find him packing papers and books into wooden crates.

"Dr. Barrow, do you have a moment? I have some thoughts on fluxions I'd like to go over with you."

"I'm sorry, but I don't have time to discuss that now. Perhaps a more thorough examination of Euclid would answer your concerns."

"I've glanced through his work but consider it a mere trifle."

"Yet you struggled through Descartes, and do you know why? Because you skipped Euclid's fundamentals. You must develop a sound understanding of the basics, no matter how trivial they appear to you. Now, if you'll excuse me, I need to finish packing."

"Are you going somewhere?"

"Yes, everybody will have to leave. Trinity's closing for the next two years."

"Why?"

"A plague has descended on London and there are fears that it may spread to Cambridge. I suggest you find a way home as soon as possible."

He sprinted across the bustling courtyard and burst into Dr. Babington's office. "I see you've already heard the news. Would you like me to help you pack?"

"Isaac, I'm glad you stopped by. I've arranged for a coach. Get your belongings together first, then we can load the crates. We'll leave early tomorrow."

Isaac pushed through the crowded hallway of the dorm to pack and say his farewells to his classmates. He bundled clothes, books and papers in his bedsheets and rolled his telescope into his blanket. After loading the crates, he stowed the instrument beneath his seat in the carriage.

$$\odot \text{---} \text{♅}\text{♆} \text{--} \text{☿}\text{☾} \oplus \text{-}\text{♄}\text{-}\text{♂}\text{♀} \text{--}\text{♃} \bullet \bigcirc$$

Upon reaching Grantham, they headed straight for the apothecary.

William awakened the bell and stepped into the late-September morning, listening to the cobblestone choir. "What mystery of nature brings you to Grantham?"

Isaac jumped off the coach and hugged him. "They've closed Trinity and Cambridge for the next two years."

Dr. Babington nodded. "The Black Death is killing thousands of people in London every day. It's a terrible scourge."

"Will you be staying at the farm, Isaac?"

"As long as Mother doesn't make me chase that cow across Lincolnshire."

"Well, you're always welcome to stay with us."

"That's very kind of you, Mr. Clark. I'll come to town occasionally, but I plan to continue my studies at Woolsthorpe."

Isaac soon settled into undisturbed bliss. His half brother, Ben Smith, had taken over management of the farm. After re-examining Euclid, he breezed through Descartes and waded through the stream to stand in the fields where the fluxions were blossoming. His quest was to produce something from nothing, despite the Frenchman's admonitions. He filled the pages of his wastebook with drawings and calculations, approaching but never quite reaching the zero.

$$\odot\text{---}⛢\Psi\text{--}☿☽\oplus\text{-}\hbar\text{-}♂♀\text{--}♃\newmoon\circ$$

Late that October, Ben finished his chores well after dark and stopped in Isaac's room. "Isaac, you've been at it all day with your fluxions. The moon's putting on a show tonight. Come on, I want to see how your telescope works. I've never used one before."

Isaac stood from his desk, stiff from his calculations. "Is it a full moon?"

"Even better, she's the visage of a beautiful angel with two halos."

"Really? Sounds like an excellent opportunity to make some scientific observations. Grab my notebook."

Isaac carried his instrument into the garden and set it next to the apple tree. "This should work. A splendid view with dinner close at hand. You were right. She looks angelic tonight."

He peered through the eyepiece. "The diameter of the innermost bluish-green crown is 3 degrees."

Ben noted the measurement on an empty page.

"The white crown is 5½ degrees, and the halo measures 22⅓ degrees from the center of the moon."

Ben tallied those amounts in his ledger.

"Would you care to try it now? Just be careful not to touch it or you'll scare her away."

He stooped to look through the eyepiece.

"It's so beautiful. I see jagged mountains near the edge. Wait a minute, I'm not touching anything and it's drifting out of view."

Isaac smiled. "You don't notice it when you stand here, but through the telescope, you get a sense of the Earth's rotation."

"Can you adjust it? I want to make some more observations."

"Yes, it's easy. Just loosen this knob, recenter it in the eyepiece and tighten it again."

Ben's eyes swept over the cratered surface, which, when magnified, resembled Wensleydale cheese. Isaac admired the radiant crown and wondered whether Saturn would look this marvelous were it ever scrutinized this close. As his mind wandered through the solar system, his hand meandered into the apple tree for a snack. As he plucked the Flower of Kent from the limb, a plague descended on his half brother and toppled the delicate instrument.

"Are you OK, Ben?"

"Yes, I'm all right. Is your telescope damaged?"

Isaac righted the scope. "It's fine, but could you retrieve an ax from the shed? I want to solve this infernal tree problem once and for all. One time while reading my Bible, an apple struck me on the head. I tossed it clear over the garden."

Isaac rearmed himself with fresh produce.

"I should've thrown it across the English Channel to France." The reddish comet streaked southward. He produced another from his nemesis. "Or shot it out of a cannon to China." It sailed southeast, falling far short of its intended target. He hoisted a third cannonball from the ground. "I suppose if I tossed one hard enough, it would travel around the globe and strike me in the back of my skull." And figuratively, it did as his mind made a stunning observation.

He glanced up at the moon. "So that's how you do it. You overcome the force of gravity by traveling so fast you can't fall to Earth. You must have dropped on God's head one day and angered him so much that he tossed you from his garden."

Inspired by this momentous insight, he took two quick steps in the dark and threw the apple as hard as he could to make it circle the globe.

The Flower of Kent sailed beneath the moon's watchful eyes. "Hey worm, wake up. I have splendid news. We're taking a journey around the world."

"Oh, I thought the wind picked up, or you were falling to the ground."

"No, we just fell from the tree and knocked over Isaac's telescope. He got so mad he's sent us flying."

"Well, nobody asked me if I wished to take a trip. I have everything I need right here."

"Ahh, you're so boring. Where's your sense of advent..."

The dazed apple bounced off leathery hindquarters and plopped into the pasture.

"Mooooo. We're under attack, everybody run!"

"Oh my, the world is ever so much smaller than I imagined."

"Good, now be still. I'd like to finish my dream."

"What were you dreaming about?"

"Drilling a hole through the center of the Earth to reach China. You know, the shortest distance between two points..."

Isaac's calculation to determine how long he had before ducking was interrupted after 3 seconds by the receding distress call of the screaming cow.

Ben looked at his half brother. "I have no idea what you're talking about, but that apple didn't even reach the creek."

Isaac laughed. "I suppose we better chase her down tonight or she'll eat the neighbor's entire crop."

As the two walked into the moonlit countryside, the tree lumbered into the bright lights of worldly renown, although the hall of fame induction ceremony was years away. The worm continued on its journey through the core of the known universe. One apple's dream of finishing out its remaining days in a nice strudel or perhaps a pandowdy dissipated in a smoldering pie baked in the oven and left to cool at the rear doorstep of the Four Stomach's Cafe.

The sun's light nudged the moon. "Did I miss something?"

The gravity of the situation left her speechless.

37. Like a Diamond from the Skye

Saturday evening, 3 January 1693 - Trinity College

A brisk gust from the north-northwest blew into Isaac's quarters when his lab assistant Colin opened the door. Colin's dog, a terrier he brought from his home on the Isle of Skye, Scotland, whirled through the apartment, searching for his good friend.

"He doesn't seem to be here, Diamond. He must still be working."

The wind calmed and padded into the study to enjoy dinner by the fire.

"You behave now. I'll go check on Isaac. I'll wager he hasn't eaten all day."

As he strode across the quiet courtyard, he saw a flickering light emanating from the laboratory. Acrid vapors spewing from a cauldron turned his head beneath his sleeve as he opened the door.

"Colin, I'm glad you stopped by. I've made additional notes regarding my experiment. Could you read through them to see if I have omitted any steps?" He handed his assistant the cryptic texts.

"You look terrible, Isaac. Have you eaten anything today? Come with me and have some dinner. We can finish this after services tomorrow."

"Let's review this first, while it's still fresh in my thoughts."

Colin shook his head, knowing he couldn't win the argument. He bent close to the candlelight and read.

"The generation of the Stone is compared to that of a man. The glass is the bed into which the man and woman enter. They embrace when the gold arises in a white skin-like cream and engender when the colors begin to appear and then is the kingly child conceived. And after putrefaction comes the hour of his nativity in a white color. And in this work the woman has her menstruums or liquors distilling from her, the last of which comes at the stone's nativity and is also called her milk, lac virginis. The first menstruum fit for use is not had in less than a month and after conjunction this menstruum will begin to hold of the body in another

month and you shall see a show of the second which in another month will be complete. Wait yet a third month (that is 90 days till the regimen of tin) and you shall see a show of the third menstruum which in the fourth month or 120 days will perfectly exuberate in a totally white color and then you shall soon see the Lunary fixation."

Colin's eyebrows raised. "Is this the 120th day?"

"No, the stone should fixate in the middle of February. Did you notice anything missing from the text?"

"It sounds correct based on my understanding of your language."

Isaac nodded, pleased with the account. "Yes, I agree. Please add those to my notebook."

Colin retrieved Isaac's book of Chymistry, which contained all records of his attempt to turn the Philosopher's Stone into untold riches and to squeeze the sweet cider of eternal life from its golden apple. He set the collection on Isaacs's desk face down and inserted the pages at the end. His hand caressed the precious manuscript. "If you achieve it by February, you'll have beaten Flamel by three years at least."

"I could have done it faster without the burden of my other responsibilities. Thank goodness no one is reading the *Principia* any longer."

"I'm not so sure, Isaac. I've heard that some people are using it as proof that God doesn't exist. You never mentioned him once in it."

"Every page is a testament to God's wonders. How could they not understand that?"

"It's not what they see, but what they are not seeing. Like that text I just read. I know that when you speak of tin, your true meaning is mercury, but I guarantee that nobody else would infer that. Because you didn't mention God, they're using you to advance their own atheistic beliefs. The universe is just a machine, clanking along by itself."

"Perhaps you're right. I'll consider what you've said after I complete this experiment. Did you take Diamond for a walk this evening?"

"Yes, he was quite disappointed that you weren't there when we returned. I'm sure he's getting lonely now. I better go check on him."

"Pat him for me, would you? I'm going to stay a while longer. I have a few more thoughts to add to my notes."

"OK, don't forget church tomorrow."

"I'll remember."

⊙---♅♆--☿☾⊕-♄-♂♀--♃●○

Early the next morning, Trinity stirred as the church bells praised God's imminence.

Colin knocked on Isaac's door. "Are you awake yet? I have your breakfast."

Diamond scratched the threshold. "Why haven't you played with me since Friday?"

Diamond looked toward his master and spoke in a language only he would understand. "I wonder if he stayed at the lab all night."

"Let's go see."

The two walked across the well-dressed courtyard to the dark and musty laboratory.

Diamond sensed the pungent fumes of the bubbling cauldron as they passed the founder's statue and sneezed to rebuke the vile spirits. "God, I hate the smell of this place," he snarled.

They found the alchemist asleep at his desk. Colin set the tray on the workbench and lit a fresh candle.

"Isaac, wake up. The service will start soon." He jostled his shoulder.

Diamond's teeth tugged at his breeches. "Forget church and come play with me."

"Good morning, Colin."

Diamond leaped into his lap and licked his face. "Get me out of this malodorous tomb."

"Diamond, I'm happy to see you too. I promise we'll go for a walk this afternoon."

Colin cracked open the window. "There, that's better. Now eat your breakfast while I take Diamond for his Sunday constitutional. Come on, Diamond," he said, patting his leg.

The church bells issued their proclamation.

"There's not enough time." Isaac took a bite of toast and a sip of tea. "He can stay here."

Colin set the tray on the floor and patted Diamond on the head. "We'll be back after the service."

His yipping plea, "don't leave me here, take me with you, I hate this room," went unheeded as his master closed the door.

The choir opened with a song, exalting the Lord's magnificence, as Diamond battled against an unknown force not dealt with by Isaac's equations.

A tiny angel fluttered into the laboratory on the hymnal winds through the open window and lit on a shelf.

Diamond snapped to the point. "What are you doing here?"

The winged emissary whispered in the guardian's tongue: "Stay your apprehension. I will not harm you." It flitted over the dog's head and perched near the flickering candle.

Diamond propelled himself skyward, yet God's laws proved his short legs unworthy of the task. His front paws clawed at the desktop as his hindquarters flailed beneath. He landed flat on his back and yelped, "Dear God, that hurt."

The intruder hopped to the edge to ensure the guardian's safety, then turned to its intent. Its wings thrust against the odiferous fumes, accelerating its tiny mass toward the flaming wick, and applied the resultant force on a vector that would topple the candle upon the worthless papers. The hummingbird watched as the fog of 20 years filled the lab's northern reaches and drifted through the window on the warming current. Cool, fresh air flowed over the sill to the south and crept along the floorboards where the faithful lay.

As the hymn reached its crescendo, the minister stepped to the podium to begin his sermon but was cast asunder by the church bells tolling an unfamiliar tune. The Reverend checked the reference card in the back of his Bible. "Steady Repeated Short Clang - Revelation Chapter 8, Verse 7."

"The first angel sounded, and there followed hail and fire mingled with blood, and they were cast upon the earth: and the third part of trees was burnt up, and all green grass was burnt up."

"Members of the fire brigade, the bell tolls for your service. Everyone else, please remain seated until they have left."

Six congregants rushed from their pews and exited the church.

"It's Newton's laboratory, bring the wagon, hurry," the warden shouted.

The firefighters ran to the coach house where they kept the Keeling Engine. The large water-filled barrel rested on a cart. It took four men to operate the pump handles while a fifth directed the spray. When full, it weighed over 1,000 pounds. As the fates would have it, the brigade lacked the force necessary to accelerate its mass.

"We need some volunteers," the hose man shouted to the buzzing congregation assembling in the courtyard.

Several upperclassmen rushed to apply the required forces.

Colin grabbed the warden's arm. "Dear God, Diamond's in there."

They sprinted across the courtyard, ignoring the indignant shouts of the "PLEASE KEEP OFF THE GRASS" sign, as the smoke intensified. The Warden peered in through the window to assess the flames. Isaac arrived to witness the soot of twenty years' labor swirling into the heavens above.

"Wait here."

The warden burst through the door to search for the darkened Skye. The Keeling Engine negotiated the last corner of the courtyard and rolled to a stop as Diamond's coughing rescuer exited the blaze, carrying his limp body. "There's a fire on your desk. Do you keep any dangerous chemicals in there?"

"To be safe, use the sand if the fire is not large."

"Hold the pumps. I need three men with buckets. Hurry."

Colin unburdened the warden and laid the still dog on the ground.

"It appears a candle fell over. I found Diamond laying on the floor by your chair."

Once the flames were extinguished, Isaac rushed in to see the charcoal remnants of his Chymistry journal transmuting sand to glass. He returned to the courtyard where Colin cradled the limp terrier and kneeled beside them. He stroked the shaggy fur of the still creature. "Oh, Diamond! Diamond! Thou little knowest the mischief thou hast done."

Their tears could not extinguish the anguish they felt at that moment. Only the quiver of a paw and lungs re-inflating could perform that miracle. An awakening yelp, "Where am I? What happened?"

Colin sobbed harder, but with joy, as Diamond shook his head and rolled to his feet. Isaac's brow eased at the joyous reunion, but his spirit darkened under the choking sands of that which would never be seen again.

He sequestered in his quarters, skipped meals and sank further into the quicksands of despair over the coming weeks, finding little solace in his Bible.

☉---♅♅Ψ--☿☾⊕-♄-♂♀--♃●○

On a warm afternoon in mid-February, Isaac sat in his study as his mind drifted through the open window and across the courtyard to his laboratory where his Lunary fixation experiment had fizzled. Still mired in depression, he sought some biblical Revelation. He flipped to Chapter 12.

"And there appeared a great wonder in heaven; a woman clothed with the sun, and the moon under her feet, and upon her head a crown of twelve stars."

"And she being with child cried, travailing in birth, and pained to be delivered."

It reminded him of his last notes, and the Lunary fixation he had lost forever.

"And there appeared another wonder in heaven; and behold a great red dragon, having seven heads and ten horns, and seven crowns upon his heads."

Something caught his attention out of the corner of his eye. He looked up and noticed a creature sitting on the windowsill. He rubbed his bloodshot eyes. It was of reddish hues, yet it had only a single head, with one horn protruding from its face, its crown ruffled and feathery. He froze when it took wing and hovered in midair just above the sill.

"Such a wondrous sight," he thought. "Am I awake or asleep?"

The dragon drifted in front of the great philosopher and spoke in clear and direct language.

"Isaac, the secret arts are not for humanity to practice. Only God has the power to wield the Philosopher's Stone. Read the first line of your Bible."

He turned to Genesis Chapter 1, Verse 1, and recited:

"In the beginning, God created heaven and the earth."

"He alone creates the elements, one from another, in his stellar cauldrons. You have much to contribute to mathematics and the spiritual awareness of humanity. Focus on these things for the rest of your days, knowing that the radiant crown awaits you."

"Are you a cherub of God here to admonish me, or some demon sent to drive me mad?"

"I am of the Gardener, here to illuminate your pathway out of the darkness. Now turn to Second Corinthians Chapter 4, Verses 17 and 18," whispered the dragon.

He turned to the passages.

"For our light affliction, which is but for a moment, worketh for us a far more exceeding and eternal weight of glory; While we look not at the things which are seen, but at the things which are not seen: for the things which are seen are temporal; but the things which are not seen are eternal."

The dragon alighted on Isaac's wrist as he finished the passage. "Hold fast the knowledge of God's promise of everlasting life. His elixir is all you need."

Isaac stared in wonderment as the creature turned and darted out the window.

He sat there trying to understand what had happened. Did he imagine this, or was it a dream? He flipped back to Genesis Chapter 1, Verse 1, and read it again.

"What a fool I have been. Transmutation of mercury to silver and gold. And to what end, lusting after wealth? How arrogant to place myself above the Lord."

Isaac arose to shut the window. As the two panes met to seal the room, the messenger darted past Isaac's head and lit on his Bible.

"I forgot to mention, Philippians Chapter 3, Verse 1."

He returned to his desk as the dragon flew to his shoulder. He turned to the page and read.

"Brethren, I count not myself to have apprehended: but this one thing I do, forgetting those things which are behind, and reaching forth unto those things which are before, I press toward the mark for the prize of the high calling of God in Christ Jesus."

"Forgive yourself, Isaac, as the Lord forgives you. Free yourself from the burdens of your past and let your glorious light shine in the *Principia* for generations to come. Humanity needs to understand your true beliefs about that which cannot be seen."

He turned his head as the messenger rose from his shoulder. A shimmering evanescence was all that remained.

He felt a weight, many orders of magnitude heavier than the tiny dragon, lift from his shoulders.

"Colin, bring me dinner. I'm starving and I have a lot of work to do."

38. Subtilissimo Corpora

Summer 1713 - Cambridge University

William Whiston succeeded Sir Isaac Newton as Lucasian Chair of Mathematics at Cambridge. Summer of 1713 did not feel like a break as he battled against the mounds of correspondence and doctoral theses piled on the desk at his residence.

A courier arrived at the usual hour and knocked. The exasperated sigh emanating from the study amplified the reverberations.

His wife, Ruth, answered.

"Good afternoon, Mrs. Whiston. I have a package for your husband."

"I'll make sure he gets this right away. Would you care to join us for lunch?"

The strap of his pouch dug into his shoulder. "I am hungry, but I still have several packets to deliver."

"I don't know what it is about you mathematicians and your refusal to take regular meals. Well, stop by after you've finished then. We'll save a sandwich for you." She closed the door and noted the addresser as she walked into the study. "You have a packet from Isaac."

William slit the flap with his letter opener and removed the contents.

"I didn't realize he was so close to publishing a second edition of the *Principia*. Could you clear my desk of all these papers?"

"You've been working hard all morning. You need to eat something first."

"Yes, you're right. Let me read the cover letter first, then we'll have lunch."

Professor Whiston settled into his chair.

Sir,

I hope you and Ruth are in good health, and that you are taking some time to relax during the summer break. Now that I have the second edition complete, I plan on some relaxation. Perhaps a trip to Grantham to catch up on the news and visit Ben at Woolsthorpe.

I have noted the most significant changes in the attachments to this letter. Much new data has become available since I published this twenty-six years ago. I have clarified several areas with additional proofs and made such corrections as determined by others.

You were right to challenge God's absence from the first edition. I've heard from many who share your opinion and have seen how John Toland is using it to advance his atheistic views. As a result, I am compelled to add a General Scholium to the Principia. I hope it clarifies my position on God, so that nothing remains in question to the reader.

Your affectionate friend
& humble servant
Is. Newton.

"Isaac added a section to state his religious beliefs. Perhaps I can include this in my lectures. I'm going to translate this right away."

Ruth snatched the packet from William's hands and placed it on the cleared desk. "Lunch first."

☉---♅♆--☿☽⊕-♄-♂♀--♃●○

It would be three days before he would share another meal with his wife. He pored through the texts, searching for the most eloquent words in the English language that would convey the intentions of every "*quodam subtilissimo corpora.*"

"Ruth, I've completed my translation and would like to discuss it with you. Do you have some time now?"

"I was hoping you would share it with me. I'm excited to hear what Isaac has to say."

"Excellent. There are several sections that relate more to science than religion. If you're interested, you can read those parts later."

"You know I don't understand his Fs and MAs. What was it that one of his students said about him? Oh yes, I remember, 'There goes the man who wrote a book that neither he nor anybody else understands.'"

He chuckled at the well-worn phrase of Cambridge lore. "I promise not to bore you with the equations."

William opened his translation and skipped past the boring stuff.

"This most beautiful system of the sun, planets and comets could only proceed from the counsel and dominion of an intelligent and powerful Being....

"He is eternal and infinite, omnipotent and omniscient; that is, his duration reaches from eternity to eternity; his presence from infinity to infinity; he governs all things and knows all things that are or can be done. He is not eternity or infinity, but eternal and infinite; he is not duration or space, but he endures and is present. He endures forever and is everywhere present; and, by existing always and everywhere, he constitutes duration and space. Since every particle of space is always, and every indivisible moment of duration is everywhere, certainly the Maker and Lord of all things cannot be never and nowhere."

Ruth considered the passage. "That sounds straightforward to me. Everyone knows the power of God."

"True, but I believe there is a deeper meaning. He is challenging the mechanistic view that our Creator set the universe in motion and then vanished. By asserting that the Lord is not duration or space, he's placed him somewhere outside of what we can see. He constitutes duration and space, which means he applies his laws from hidden dimensions to produce the next moment of time. In this last statement, Isaac extends Descartes' 'Ex Nihilo, Nihil Fit' by saying that God must be here now and forever."

"It's very confusing with all the positives and negatives. Doesn't the last sentence reverse the opening line? You should eliminate that for clarity."

"My job is to translate the author's texts with the utmost accuracy, leaving interpretation to the reader's imagination."

"We know him only by his most wise and excellent contrivances of things and final causes; we admire him for his perfections, but we reverence and adore him on account of his dominion, for we adore him as his servants; and a God without dominion, providence and final causes is nothing else but Fate and Nature."

"Here he's saying that although God remains unseen, we witness his majesty through his creations and re-emphasizes that without him the universe would be a mechanistic contrivance robbed of free will."

"God is more than a superior human, sitting on a throne in a castle, judging people. Is that what Isaac's saying?"

"It sounds as if he has expanded our traditional notion of God. In the last paragraph, he's trying to come to terms with the Spirit that inhabits all bodies."

"And now we might add something concerning a certain most subtle Spirit which pervades and lies hid in all gross bodies; by the force and action of which Spirit the particles of bodies mutually attract one another at near distances, and cohere, if contiguous; and electric bodies operate to greater distances, as well repelling as attracting the neighboring corpuscles; and light is emitted, reflected, refracted, inflected, and heats bodies; and all sensation is excited, and the members of animal bodies move at the command of the will, namely, by the vibrations of this Spirit, mutually propagated along the solid filaments of the nerves, from the outward organs of sense to the brain, and from the brain into the muscles. But these are things that cannot be explained in few words, nor are we furnished with that sufficiency of experiments which is required to an accurate determination and demonstration of the laws by which this electric and elastic Spirit operates."

"Animal bodies move at the command of this Spirit? Is he claiming that the Spirit lives in God's mansion?"

"That could eliminate free will. I guess that it lies in dimensions separate from God, space and time. He's become trapped in a rigidly defined area of doubt and uncertainty."

"What?"

"Let's avoid that subject for now. I certainly doubt that we will make any headway there."

His face was reminiscent of a scarecrow that once stood guard on his parents' estate. He returned to the field where he found the most comfort.

"I'm most surprised that he says this Spirit exists within all gross bodies, which could refer to, well, just about everything we can see, whether it be animate or inanimate. Where would such ideas come from?"

"Maybe an angel appeared to him."

"That could explain this additional page of text I found in Isaac's attachments. I wasn't sure if he wanted to include it in the General Scholium."

"God made and governs the world invisibly and has commanded us to love and worship him and no other God; to honor our parents and masters and love our neighbors as ourselves; and to be temperate, just and peaceable; and to be merciful even to brute beasts. And by the same power by which he gave life at first to every species of animals he is able to revive the dead, and has revived Jesus Christ our Redeemer, who has gone into the heavens to receive a kingdom and prepare a place for us, and is next in dignity to God and may be worshiped as the Lamb of God, and has sent the Holy Ghost to comfort us in his absence, and will at length return and reign over us, invisibly to mortals, until he has raised up and judged all the dead; and then he will give up his kingdom to the Father and carry the blessed to the place he is now preparing for them and send the rest to other places suitable to their merits. For in God's house (which is the universe) are many mansions, and he governs them by agents which can pass through the heavens from one mansion to another. For if all places to which we have access are filled with living creatures, why should all these immense spaces of the heavens above the clouds be incapable of inhabitants?"

"Isaac says that Jesus will raise up all the dead? I thought only humans were worthy of God's palace."

"He talks about all living creatures but states that Jesus prepared a place for us, which seems to limit heaven to humanity."

"But your translation says he raised all the dead. All is an encompassing word, don't you think?"

"One could make that interpretation. I'm intrigued he doesn't mention heaven and hell, only that there is a place for everyone in God's mansions, whether they were born 10,000 years ago, or are alive today, living in ignorance of Jesus."

"And the Spirit living in all gross bodies? Do they get into heaven as well?"

"Now let's not be ridiculous. How could the moon's spirit go to heaven? What do you suppose he means when he mentions agents that pass through the heavens? I believe it's a reference to the angelic."

"Why wouldn't he just use that word then? If God's house is the universe, then mansions could be stars and agents are planets, traveling from one star to another."

"A planet traveling amongst the stars? I'm certain this is about the afterlife and angels."

"Perhaps it has both meanings. Or neither meaning. English is so imprecise."

"All languages lack precision. Except for mathematics."

"What if he used the word 'agents' because they don't conform to our biblical understanding?"

"It's possible, but where would he get such a strange notion?"

"I have no idea. You'd have to ask Isaac. What about the last line, William? Does he believe there's life elsewhere in the universe?"

"He seems pretty clear about that. Why would God create such a lonely universe?"

"Oh William, even if there isn't life elsewhere, it's not lonely. We have each other."

39. Smoother Pebble

1727 - London, England

On March 20, 1727, Sir Isaac Newton died. His longtime friend, William Stukeley, eulogized him.

"I met Isaac many years ago at the Royal Society. We both grew up in Grantham and enjoyed sharing news from home and spoke often about various topics that interested us.

"Many people thought of him as a solitary, unfriendly figure. Yet he cared much for his family and was present at the marriages of his relations, when he could be. He would, on those occasions, lay aside gravity, be free, pleasant and unbent. He made substantial gifts to the women and set their husbands up in business. His good sense showed in this, realizing that matrimony, trade and industry is the foundation and the strength of a commonwealth and ought by all methods to be encouraged in a wise government.

"Sir Isaac had likewise a natural dignity, and politeness in his manner, in common life, unusual in so hard a student. He was a man of real piety and had strict attendance on the sabbatical duty. Knowing the necessity, as well as expediency, of the public profession of religion, he could not excuse himself from the weekly solemn adoration of the Supreme Being.

"Not long before he passed, he commented to me, 'I do not know what I may appear to the world. But to myself I seem to have been only like a boy playing on the seashore, diverting myself in now and then finding a smoother pebble or a prettier shell than ordinary, while the great ocean of truth lay all undiscovered before me.'"

40. Prove the Apocalypse

1732, Five years after Isaacs's death - Grantham apothecary

Ben Smith entered the apothecary and found Edward Storer reading the London Gazette.

"Anything interesting in the paper?"

"Let's see, Parliament is adjourned, the minister to Vienna is visiting, the prince of Bevern has come hither and the usual bankruptcy list. Oh, here's an advertisement for horse races."

'On Friday, September 8th, His Majesties Plate will be run for on the Round Course on the South Side, of Lincoln, a Gold Cup of ninety pounds value, by any horse that was no more than six years old last grass, as must be certified under the Hands of the Breeder, nine Stone, three Heats.'

"You should raise horses at Woolsthorpe instead of cows. That prize would make you one of the richest people in Grantham."

"My grandfather would haunt me to the end of my days if I took up horse racing. Are you going?"

"Yes, I go every year. Why don't you join me? A long weekend away from chores and you could earn a few pounds betting."

"Well, I'm no gambler either, although it would be nice to see the races sometime. Right now, I must correspond with his lordship about my taxes, and I need some paper."

"Is it tax time already? How many sheets?"

"Five should be sufficient."

"Oh, that reminds me, I received a post for you from Trinity College. Let me get it for you."

Edward placed the papers on the counter and snatched the contents from the S letterbox.

"Looks important. What's it about?"

Ben broke the seal and read in silence.

"Well? What mischief has Isaac caused from beyond the grave?"

"None this time. They kept all of his unpublished works, which they feel are the rightful property of Isaac's heirs. Since he never married and has no brothers or sisters, they want me to have them."

"Did they say how many documents?"

"Yes, tens of thousands of pages."

"That sounds like mischief to me."

Ben smiled and nodded his head in agreement. "Could I use your office? I might as well write to his lordship while I'm here so you can post it. Give me a few more sheets and I'll also send a letter to Trinity and have them deliver Isaac's papers to Woolsthorpe. What do you suppose was in them he didn't want to be published?"

"Who knows? My guess is it's nothing earth-shaking, like the races this September."

☉---♅♇--☿☽⊕-♄-♂♀--♃●○

A month later, Ben received a wagonload of boxed documents and began the tedious task of reviewing them. Most were too technical or written in Latin, although one lengthy manuscript caught his eye. 'Observations Upon the Prophecies of Daniel, and the Apocalypse of St. John,' which he read with great interest.

When he finished, he thought to himself: "Edward was wrong. This is more than just earth-shaking, it's the end of the world as we know it."

☉---♅♇--☿☽⊕-♄-♂♀--♃●○

1733 - London

Ben gripped his satchel, took a deep breath and dove from the shores of his hotel into the river of humanity that flowed down Bartholomew-Close, stroking against the current toward the Darby and Brown Publishing sign and washed ashore in a bay of windows. He dried his nervous brow with a sleeve and stepped into a mysterious realm of grotesque wooden contraptions, arrayed vials with labels smeared by their handler's excesses. Leaded plates readied to battle against the relentless onslaught of unblemished pulp. Both were destined to lose as each page wore away the edges of the thrashing leaden letters as they succumbed to its blows, front and back. The sole winners were the reader's eyes swimming through the rivulets of the author's pen. Not to mention the publishers and booksellers. It was a remarkably profitable enterprise, especially when the author was Sir Isaac Newton.

The skilled tradesman looked up from the inked plate at the befuddled farmer. "Ah, you must be Mr. Smith. John Darby at your service." The farmer's agricultural-scarred grip shook the publisher's industrial-etched hand. "Is this your first visit to London?"

"Yes, I'm overwhelmed by such a big city. I've seen more people this morning than I have my entire life in Grantham."

"Well, let me assure you, farming is beyond my comprehension. The last cow I saw was lying amongst the vegetables on my plate at Sunday dinner. Let's step into my office."

The shelves of Darby's storeroom were stacked full of documents and supplies, and the desk was buried beneath an avalanche of envelopes, letters and bills. The only barren surfaces were the seats of the two wooden chairs.

"Your letter mentioned a document written by Isaac. Could you tell me more about it?"

Ben placed his satchel atop the paper volcano, its tremors portending an imminent eruption.

"Yes, I came into possession of Isaac's unpublished works, which were a considerable number of documents. I've spent the past several months sorting through them and discovered one in particular I thought might be of significance." Ben opened the satchel and removed hundreds of handwritten pages and handed them to the publisher.

John tidied the stack. "Why do you think it's important if Isaac didn't see fit to publish it?"

"Well, everyone knows him for his mathematical prowess, but he also spent years writing about his religious opinions and ideas. Although many people supported his beliefs, he feared that publishing them could have dire consequences from the Church of England. His interest in the Book of Revelation and the notion of Christ setting up a second kingdom fascinated him. It's his interpretation of the biblical prophecies and when the end times could occur."

"Does this manuscript have that date?"

"I believe it does and that many scholars would be interested in his thoughts."

"Is it going to happen before we get this published?"

"That shouldn't be a concern. You'll have readers for 300 years at least."

"Hmm, not that far then, according to Sir Isaac?"

"The soonest he thinks would be 2034."

"What does he base that on?"

"I've bookmarked the events that he believed started the doomsday clock."

John opened the first bookmark and read.

"While this Ecclesiastical Dominion was rising up, the northern barbarous nations invaded the WESTERN EMPIRE, and founded several kingdoms therein, of different religions from the Church of ROME. But these kingdoms by degrees embraced the ROMAN faith, and at the same time submitted to the Pope's authority. The FRANKS in GAUL submitted at the end of the fifth century, the GOTHS in SPAIN at the end of the sixth; and the LOMBARDS in ITALY were conquered by Charles the Great A. C. 774.

"Between the years 775 and 794, the same CHARLES extended the Pope's authority over all GERMANY and HUNGARY as far as the river THEYSSE and the BALTIC sea; he then set him above all human judicature, and at the same time assisted him in subduing the City and Duchy of Rome. By the conversion of the ten kingdoms to the ROMAN religion, the Pope only enlarged his spiritual dominion, but did not yet rise up as a horn of the Beast. It was his temporal dominion which made him one of the horns: and this dominion he acquired in the latter half of the eighth century, by subduing three of the former horns as above. And now being arrived at a temporal dominion, and a power above all human judicature, he reigned (DAN. vii. Verses 20-25.) with a look more stout than his fellows, and times and laws were henceforward given into his hands, for a time, times and half a time, or three times and a half; that is, for 1260 solar years. After which the judgment is to sit, and they shall take away his dominion, not at once but by degrees, to consume, and to destroy

it unto the end."

"He doesn't mention the apocalypse here."
"Look at my other bookmark."
John flipped to the last page.

"For as the few and obscure Prophecies concerning CHRIST'S first coming were for setting up the CHRISTIAN religion, which all nations have since corrupted; so the many and clear Prophecies concerning the things to be done at CHRIST'S second coming, are not only for predicting but also for effecting a recovery and reestablishment of the long lost truth, and setting up a kingdom wherein dwells righteousness. The event will prove the APOCALYPSE."

"What do you think this means?"
Ben took a deep breath and dove in. "Well, Charles the Great ascended to power by conquering Italy in 774. At that point, he ruled Europe and stood on the threshold of ruling the entire world. A simple calculation using a time, times and half a time, or 1260 solar years, added to 774 and you have 2034."
"Didn't the Romans name Charlemagne emperor in the year 800? Wouldn't that place the Second Coming in 2060?"
"Either way, the 21st century should prove quite exciting."
"Well, we better get this published before God releases his plagues on humanity."
"Isaac didn't imagine it would be the catastrophe most people visualize. As he said, 'a recovery and re-establishment of the lost truth'."

VI. The Journey - Day 3

41. Mooz's Journey - Love

1830 - Somewhere Over the Rainbow

Since his spiritual journey began, Mooz had gained a new understanding of nature as the burdens of his past churned on the forest floor. A sense of loneliness drew him westward toward the sounds of laughter carried by the wind.

He headed up a slight incline to the crest of a hill. He turned back to see rain clouds drifting through the deep blue summer sky as their shadows rolled over the hillsides, framed by a double rainbow.

The path west led through a lush forest with streams and wildlife, just as he remembered them. He spotted Nenookaasi sitting on a branch and paused.

Nenookaasi flew to Mooz and landed on his hand as he had done thousands of times before. "It's not much farther, my friend. There's a meadow ahead. Your people are eager for your arrival."

The late-afternoon stir of the cook fires tugged him in a way that cannot be seen.

"I must leave you, for now, Mooz. I'll see you again at the end of the fourth day." The flutter of evanescence disappeared into the darkening forest.

He recognized the trail ahead as the place where he and Anangokaa hunted mushrooms near Thunder House Falls. He followed it to the village, where a small group of strangers had gathered to welcome him, then smiled when a familiar face moved toward him through the crowd.

They rushed together and hugged with the joy of seeing a long-lost loved one. "Grandfather, you made it."

"Anangokaa, I'm surprised you're here."

"Well, I lived many years after you passed, but my journey here was shorter than yours. Since I arrived, I've seen wonderful things you couldn't imagine. You must let me show them to you."

"We'll have plenty of time for that, but first, I'd like a taste of whatever it is they're cooking and a nice smoke afterward."

After a splendiferous feast of exotic dishes, Mooz and his grandson shared a pipe with a pleasant tobacco. As the sun set on the third day of his journey, he entered his lodge. The cicadas and crickets chirped their evening opera as his nostrils feasted on the memories of days gone by.

Sated, he slept. And he dreamed...

Mooz traveled Tunis' skies for longer than he could remember. His rotation had yet to dwindle to a single turn per orbit, allowing him to search for a traveling companion of his own. Over time, several wanderers strayed close enough to spend a few moments with the august Mooz, but each suffered from their ancient momentum. One became a Sputnik of Tunis in her own right. The second dropped closer to Vesta and met a fate unknown to him. Another was born of a fiery cauldron whose quakes rippled beneath the surface, unseen by all but the closest observers. Mooz was ill-equipped to calm her eccentricities and in the end, she drifted away on an outward journey from the sun. There were still a few planets in higher orbits that might attract her, but with his orbital spin in decay, he would soon lose track of her.

As the eons passed, Tunis' tidal arms calmed the spinning Z until he settled into his current N, focusing MooN's gaze upon its wandering continents. At peace with the universe, he enjoyed sloshing the oceans of the burgeoning world and tickling its tectonic plates into fiery eruptions now and then. But wisdom had taught him that bent space was a fickle fiend. Imperceptible, a centimeter or two per year, but he felt himself drifting away as gravitation's tenuous rope stretched to the point of snapping. The occasional visit from the inhabitants of Tunis brought him much joy. (He still called it Tunis even though the Tunisians knew it only by their name. A rose perhaps.)

Then one day, a gravity wave rippled through his core, from pole to pole. His eyes scanned the heavens, searching for the source of this confusion. She had arrived from above the solar system's plane, pulled from Proxima Centauri by another wandering star. That she entered MooN's space-time at all boggled his mind. That she graced him with the slightest attention on that chance encounter, well that's because somewhere during his journey in an alternate universe, he had spent many an evening at the feet of magicians and jesters. His skills were poor but enchanting enough to deserve a sideways glance. Their first brush ended far too soon, and he was unsure whether their paths would ever cross again. Orbital mechanics exceeded the competencies of even the most capable scarecrow.

Six months later, on the opposite side of Vesta (he still called the star Vesta, although he knew damn well his Vesta had long since dispersed in a super nova, but you know how the ancients cling to their old ways), there she was, coming in hot from below the plane. She dropped in for a couple of orbits with MooN. Impossibly random, but he rejoiced.

He realized she would never settle into his orbit, but he loved her just the same. Their days together reverberated through the center of his being. They spent one summer's afternoon in a parallel universe as the stars swirled around them and the frogs sat motionless by the pond. She shared her pain, he listened. She laid her head on his shoulder. Silence. He cradled her in his arms and for a billionth of a trillionth of a second, their spirits merged.

As the eons passed, the blue MooN drifted free from Tunis, whose denizens had ceased visiting their lonely traveling companion, having taken up residence in a far safer haven. Freed from Tunis' tidal shackles, the vagabond MooN regained some of his former spin and would occasionally spot her zipping through the solar system, filling his heart with joy.

One day, as MooN rotated to face Vesta, he felt his orbit wobble, as if something was bending his space from an alternate universe.

"Mooz, wake up. Your friend is here. She's waiting for you at the falls," Anangokaa smiled as his grandfather awakened.

His eyes opened to the late-morning light as he rolled from his mat and, within one zeptosecond, exited the lodge at a run.

Peace brought Love as the sun rose above the treetops on the fourth day...

VII. Calling Mars

42. Gasbag

The bespectacled Gardener sipped his morning coffee as a slight breeze rustled the pages of his newspaper. Yawning and stretching, Te Ata joined him in the gazebo overlooking the pond.

"Good morning," she said in her most pleasant voice as she slid into the chair beside him.

He smiled. Perfect serenity required nothing more than a still mind. He set the paper aside and fixed her cup, just the way she liked it. A touch of cream with no sugar. "You look well-rested this morning."

She savored her first sip. "I am, thank you. I had such pleasant dreams last night and when I awoke this morning, a song was playing that gave me the inspiration I needed to finish the story. While listening to the lyrics, all the ideas floating around inside my head suddenly came together."

His newspaper lay on the table. His coffee cup cooled on the saucer. At this moment, only she mattered. "A moment of inspiration. I can't wait to hear your thoughts, but first, a light breakfast perhaps, before you get to writing? What can I fix for us?"

She bookmarked her thoughts. There was nothing she enjoyed more than breakfast on the terrace with the Gardener. "How about an omelet?"

What gazebo would be complete without a hotplate and a well-stocked mini-fridge? He set about preparing two omelets with a side of what she secretly desired this morning: conversation. Chopping vegetables, cracking eggs, buttering the pan, none of these things required more than muscle memory. His focus remained on her. "Tell me more about your inspiration."

"Well, I completed Sir Isaac Newton's story, and I won't be able to finish Mooz's story yet, so I'm going to focus on how they tracked us down. You know, Newton didn't create a stir when he talked about the heavens being inhabited."

"People's eyes just float over the pages at 10,000 feet. It's been so long now. What was it that stirred their imaginations?" His spatula probed the outer edges of the omelet in great detail, looking for that perfect moment.

"Well, Percival Lowell shifted the search for ETs into high gear with his newspaper accounts of a vast network of canals on the surface of their neighbor. He made his thoughts quite clear in his 1908 book *Mars as the Abode of Life.*"

"Thus, not only do the observations we have scanned lead us to the conclusion that Mars at this moment is inhabited, but they land us at the further one that these denizens are of an order whose acquaintance was worth the making. Whether we ever shall come to converse with them in any more instant way is a question upon which science at present has no data to decide."

With an expert flip of his wrist, her omelet performed a half-somersault. "Ah yes. Now I remember. Made him an international sensation, the toast of the newspaper circuit. Where to then?"

"A trip to the wonderful land of SETI, to quench that burning desire to call on the strange and otherworldly creatures, now proven to inhabit the ruddy planet. And who better to visit than the famous Amherst astronomer and pioneering balloonist…"

"Oh, I love ballooning. We should do that tomorrow."

Her flourish bounced off his gasbag gesture. "But what about my story?"

"It's a perfect opportunity for you to do some field research. You know, put yourself in your character's shoes or, in this case, their gondola."

Her omelet slid from the pan onto her white china plate. "Go ahead, before it gets cold."

It was impossible to tell how he did it, some form of sleight of hand. Three eggs in one hand cracked simultaneously and sloshed into the buttery pan.

"I'll wait," she said. "I enjoy watching you cook."

43. The Masked Comet of 1910

Portage Daily Democrat
Portage, Wisconsin
14 Feb 1910, Mon • Page 4

COMET POISONOUS

Yerkes Observatory Finds Cyanogen In Spectrum of Halley's Comet. Although astronomers at the Harvard Observatory at Boston have not yet made a photographic spectrum of Halley's comet, which is rapidly approaching the Earth, a telegram recently received by them from the Yerkes observatory states that spectra of the comet obtained by the director and his assistants show very prominent cyanogen bands. Cyanogen is a very deadly poison, a grain of its potassium salt touched to the tongue being sufficient to cause instant death. In the uncombined state, it is a bluish gas very similar in its chemical behavior to chlorine and extremely poisonous. It is characterized by an odor similar to that of almonds. The fact that cyanogen is present in the comet has been communicated to Camille Flammarion and many other astronomers and is causing much discussion as to the probable effect on the Earth should it pass through the comet's tail. Professor Flammarion is of the opinion that the cyanogen gas would impregnate the atmosphere and possibly snuff out all life on the planet. Only once, as far as known, has the earth passed directly through the tail of a comet, and at that time no unusual phenomena were noticed except that there were abundant showers of meteors.

By the end of March, the gasmask shelves across the planet were empty, and a voodoo practitioner selling comet pills in Port-au-Prince had become a wealthy man.

☉---♅♆--☿☾⊕-♄-♂♀--♃●○

173

April 15th, 1910 - Amherst College, Massachusetts

Astronomy Professor David Peck Todd climbed through the roof hatch onto the balcony of the Wilder Observatory. He continued up the stairway, hugging the outside of the mossy green dome. The platform on top provided an excellent view of the campus to the northwest, but the sun would set and Halley's comet would streak above a gray ocean of clouds, rendering one of the largest telescopes on the planet useless. He stood there hoping for a sliver of light to appear in the west, but the blanket's grip on the horizon was relentless.

The squeaky hinges of the balcony hatch interrupted his hopeless vigil. "Professor Todd, you have a telephone call from a Mr. Stevens."

"I'll be right there." With a renewed liveliness of stride, the 55-year-old astronomer danced the two-step down the stairs, performed the firefighter slide down the ladder and trotted as quickly as a fox into his office.

"I'm sorry to disturb you so late on a Friday, but I wanted to let you know we'll be making a high-altitude ascent with the balloon this Sunday. The weather should be perfect for observing the comet if you'd like to join me."

"'Like' is an understatement of astronomical proportions. What's the departure time?"

"3 a.m. I hope it's not too early for you."

"My dear friend, that's lunchtime for astronomers. I'll see you tomorrow."

Todd approached Westfield from the north as a warm front brought clearing skies from the south. A crew of soldiers was making preparations on the eastern edge of the campground. As clouds pushed northward, the first rays of the sun flashed off the aluminum skin of the spherical gondola. It wouldn't require a balloon scientist to locate the world-famous aeronaut. The renowned astronomer parked his flivver at the rope line and shut off the engine.

Leo's head popped out of the entry hatch on the side of the gondola. "Professor, you're just in time. Come in here and I'll get you checked out on the breathing equipment."

He stepped over the ropes and walked to the short ladder propped up against the gondola. He peered into the compartment to find two oxygen tanks, masks, various control valves and gauges, and a small niche for a passenger.

"It's pretty cramped in there. How long will we be aloft?"

"I'm guessing we should be in the air eight hours. You'll want to take care of any necessities before we leave. Climb in and I'll show you how to use the breathing equipment."

The ground crew worked into the night, preparing for their ascent. They attached the gasbag's web netting to the gondola, double-checked the venting system, topped off the water ballast and loaded fresh oxygen tanks into the compartment. All that remained was to inflate the balloon with helium over the next five hours.

The aeronauts napped until 1 a.m. when the smell of scrambled eggs and coffee bugled reveille from the mess tent. The crew chief, in desperate need of coffee, arrived as the pair nibbled and sipped their breakfast.

Leo broke the silence. "Any issues I need to know about?"

"Everything is going as planned. We'll be ready for launch within the hour."

"Do you have the latest weather forecast?"

"Yes, the winds are from the southwest at 5 to 10 knots. You should have clear skies for your entire flight."

Todd took solace in knowing that his students were making doctoral-worthy observations of the comet at that precise moment. This once-in-a-lifetime opportunity to fly beside the wandering star assuaged his yearning to be at the scope.

As they walked toward the spotlit balloon, he spotted the wispy streak in the sky. "There she is, gentlemen."

Leo looked to the heavens. "Hopefully, we'll get high enough to grab her by the tail."

Todd knew the utter impossibility of that. The Earth wouldn't pass through the comet's debris until May.

At 3 a.m. the ground crew released the tethers. They drifted northeast over the pitch-black terrain of the rural landscape. The only sounds they could hear were the ropes flapping against their capsule and the lonely howls of the freight trains. Leo monitored the altimeter, the barometric pressure and temperature as the balloon soared higher into the night sky. Professor Todd leaned out over the abyss as the comet blazed its way across each of his photographic plates.

"We're coming up on 21,000 feet."

"The view is spectacular, not a cloud in sight. These photographs will be..."

"Out of this world, I know."

The professor grinned. "Can you get us higher?"

Leo vented 2 gallons of water from the ballast tanks. "Twenty-two thousand and still climbing."

A ray of light entered through the porthole. He rubbed the foggy glass with his glove and spotted a fellow aeronaut who was ruining the professor's view of the comet. The crescent dome of the capsule glowed above the bright red gas bag.

"Can you see that balloon? It's flying upside down." He tugged on the astronomer's pants. "Professor, are you OK?"

As the sun's rays flooded the cabin, Leo realized his shipmate's awkward predicament. He was dangling unconscious over a 23,000-foot precipice on a swaying platform that threatened to eject him at any moment. He pinned his boot to the backside of the professor's knees, donned his mask and twisted the O2 knob. The hatchway swayed earthward as his weight shifted toward the passenger. Leo grabbed his parka and, with boots on either side, hauled the astronomer to safety— and an ample supply of oxygen.

"Professor Todd, wake up." The pulsing fog of his mask lenses comforted him.

As Leo secured the hatch, the professor stirred.

"What happened?"

"You passed out around 22,000 feet. I had to pull you back inside."

"That explains my dizziness. What's our altitude now?"

Leo tapped the gauge. "Looks like we may have topped out at 25,000. I can't dump any more ballast. I need to save it for landing."

"That's not even close to a record then," Todd noted with disappointment as his eyes scanned the cabin. "Where's my camera?"

The strap did little to slow its descent. However, it saved the camera from breaking up on the ground by snagging the branch of an oak tree in a wooded ravine. If the plate hadn't been exposed, it could have recorded many generations of curious squirrels inspecting the ominous-looking intruder before its chewed strap gave way, sending it spiraling into the forest floor.

The temperature inside the compartment was becoming uncomfortable as the sunbaked gondola sped northeast. At 3,000 feet, Leo popped the hatch to get his bearings.

"How well can you swim?"

"I almost drowned in my bathtub once."

Leo returned to the pilot's station to perform his high-wire act, balancing their descent between venting hydrogen and gushing ballast. His left eye was dizzied by gauges swirling toward zero, while his right focused on coastal Maine.

York Golf and Tennis offered stunning views of the Atlantic while promising a relaxing round on the links. A foursome was getting ready to take their second shots on number 12, a tough par 4 with an approach shot over a lake. The deflating balloon with the spherical gondola arced over the foursome's heads and plopped into the hazard, skipped across the water and rolled onto the green, coming to rest at the flagstick as the bag emptied. Leo opened the hatch and the two balloonists dropped to the well-trimmed grass as the foursome admired the driver's skill.

"Nice shot, sir. Would you mind if we played through?"

Leo looked at the golfers. "Give us a minute. We just need to putt out."

The golfer yelled back, "That's a gimmie!"

44. Balloons in Space

The Boston Globe
Boston, Massachusetts, 12 Oct 1918

WAKE-UP, MARS! PROF TODD IS COMING

It Will Be a Sad Blow If Amherst Astronomer and Expert Balloonist Fail in Their Trip From Omaha, Neb, to the Well-Known Planet

New Balloon; New Idea.

A serious attempt to communicate with the planet Mars is soon to be made by one of the foremost astronomers of America from a balloon piloted by one of the foremost balloonists of the world. The experiment will be conducted at the Fort Omaha Government balloon station, from which point the balloon will make its ascent. Leo A. Stevens, chief instructor in ballooning for the United States Army, will be in charge of the airship. David Todd, professor of astronomy at Amherst College, Massachusetts, will conduct the astronomical portion of the experiment.

Capt. Stevens has just refused an offer of $25,000 per year from a balloon company that he may continue the construction of his balloon with which he expects to get so far from the Earth that electric impulses sent out from its basket will reach to Mars. Practically every balloon company sent to France during the war was trained by Stevens or by his men at the Government Balloon School at Fort Omaha.

Goodbye Gravity

The invention which Stevens believes will enable him to reach almost any height desired is very simple but has never been used. The big balloon will be divided into two compartments. The upper compartment will contain 80,250 cubic feet of hydrogen. The lower compartment will contain 59,750 cubic feet of air. "In all balloons, there is a constant exhaust necessitated by the expansion of the gas," says Stevens. "My new balloon will lose no gas. The exhaust will be plain air. The expanding gas in the upper compartment will press downward on the lower compartment, but instead of gas, nothing but air will escape from the mouth of the bag. My balloon will therefore retain practically all its original lifting power. That power should take us just as high as we want to go. If gravity is caused by the centripetal force engendered by the rotating motion of the Earth, we can get so far from the Earth's surface that we will no longer be subject to the pull of gravity. For all I know, our balloon may be sailing around like a comet for a million years or so once we get away from the Earth. But that's up to Todd, not me."

The signaling apparatus will be attached on the outside of the basket and will be operated by lever and button control from within the air-tight basket. The balloon will act as an intensifier and relay station for wireless impulses sent from some point on the Earth's surface.

"This is the first serious attempt to communicate with Mars or any other planet since modern ballooning and high-power wireless were discovered," says Capt. Stevens. "It's Prof. Todd's business to do the communicating. It is my business to get him high enough to get his instruments into action. I tell you, this is a really and truly businesslike attempt to get in touch with Mars."

45. Fort Omaha Aerial Carnival

Early Sunday morning, July 13, 1919

Professor Todd stepped from the Chicago Great Western's Corn Belt Route passenger car to the platform at Union Station. To pass the time while his baggage was being unloaded, he dropped a nickel in the vending machine and snatched the last copy of Saturday's *Omaha Daily Bee* from the hive. After scanning the headlines, the astronomy professor flipped to page two and read with interest.

Thousands Expected to Attend Balloon
Circus at Fort Omaha Sunday Afternoon

As the hour approaches when the greatest aerial carnival ever held is to begin, Fort Omaha is a bustle of activity and anticipation. The great balloon sheds are filled with workmen. Numerous types of balloons, some of which have never before been viewed by the public, partly inflated, loom up grotesquely in the semi-darkness.

Balloons Brand New

All balloons to be christened are brand new. The sponsors were selected by the Omaha chapter of the American Red Cross at the request of Lieut. Col. Jacob W. S. Wuest, commanding officer at Fort Omaha. A variety of material will be used during the christening. Some will be showered with grape juice, and it is whispered that some will receive their bon voyage in the orthodox manner, with champagne. Among the features of the aerial carnival not mentioned before, is the first exhibition of what is said to be the fastest pulling windlass in the world. It was invented by W. Burton of Omaha. Another novel feature will be the "megaphone balloon" which will rise and announce each event. The huge megaphone is said to be larger than the 5,000-cubic-foot capacity balloon which carries it. Any man enlisting at the fort on the day of the carnival will be assured of a balloon trip shortly after. Three places to enlist will be opened.

Interest Centers on Four Events

The four events on the program that are likely to command the greatest interest of the public are:

1. *The balloon race for distance.*
2. *Exhibition of captured German "sausage" balloons and American "propaganda balloons" in action.*
3. *Observations of Prof. David Todd, Amherst college meteorologist, who is coming from New York City to ascend in the judge's balloon to "study physical features of the planet Mars."*
4. *Release of 1,000 balloons simultaneously.*

The surplus Nash Quad from the Great War rumbled into Union Station to collect the celebrity guest judge. The train had departed and the platform was empty, except for a single passenger sitting on top of a long wooden crate next to a steamer trunk and its sticker choir. Their voices performed a breathtaking melody for any baggage handler who dreamed of faraway lands and exotic destinations. To Todd, some heralded his great astronomical discoveries, while others blared a discordant cacophony of failed expeditions whose crescendos rose no higher than a low bank of clouds.

Amongst their refrains, his ears detected muffled screams. A quick scan revealed the Omaha destination tag plastered over the faces of three camel riders striding across the sands of Tripoli with a burning orange and red sunset for a backdrop, thanks to the Libyan Travel Service. That was his most successful expedition ever. His outrage surged through his fingers as he ripped the invader from the gasping Libyans, while cursing the baggage handlers of Chicago and the reporting staff of the *Daily Bee*.

One tiny sticker with its proud message, "Manufactured by OMAHA TRUNK FACTORY OMAHA, NEB.," cowered inside the lid as the astronomer's Victorinox Soldier Knife, tucked in its compartment, threatened to scrape it into ignominy. The crumpled destination tag that guided Todd's belongings through the farmlands of Illinois and Iowa blew off the platform with the shredded pages of the Bee. As the Nash rolled to a stop, its front tire delivered the final crushing blow.

The driver hopped out of the cab and approached the aged gentleman. "Professor Todd? I'm Sergeant Gordon of the Army Signal Corps. We're here to drive you to Fort Omaha."

His mind raced back from Tripoli as his body jumped from the crate. "Can you help me load my equipment?"

"We'll take care of that for you."

Two privates leaped from the flatbed and secured his belongings.

"Be careful. That's a very expensive telescope." He turned to the driver as they walked to the open-air truck. "How far away is the fort?"

"It's about 11 miles from here. Traffic's pretty light this morning. Should be there in an hour."

As they trundled north on Florence Boulevard, Todd spotted the largest American flag he had ever seen soaring over the Nebraska countryside.

"Fort Omaha, I presume."

"We're expecting over 25,000 people this afternoon. They won't have any trouble finding the place."

"I need to meet with Leo Stevens. Do you know where he'll be?"

"Yes, he's getting his balloon ready."

"Excellent, drop me off there."

☉---♅♆--☿☾⊕-♄-♂♀--♃●○

As the Nash bounced across the parade grounds, one of the four balloons near the hangar twinkled under the glaring lights of a newsreel camera. Its pilot stood inside the basket, twirling a strange assortment of reflectors to show how he would signal Mars from his lofty perch during the evening races. Todd hopped from the passenger seat as the film crew wrapped.

"Leo, is this your new high-altitude balloon? Where's the pressurized gondola?"

"Professor Todd, good to see you, my friend. I'm afraid I have some

182

bad news. The Navy confiscated all my equipment. They've classified everything. The Signal Corps was kind enough to lend me these reflectors I've attached to the Cannonball. We're using it as a recruiting tool. Join the Army, travel amongst the stars and be on the cutting edge of interplanetary communication with the Martians."

"You mean for propaganda. You'll never get a message through the atmosphere with this contraption."

"Well, at least we'll have a chance during the race this evening. Besides, how will you know if they receive your signals?"

"I brought one of my telescopes. They're setting it up on top of the Signal Corps photo lab. I'll be able to look for signs of life on Mars from their platform tonight. I also contacted Percival. He'll have all eyes at the Lowell Observatory in Arizona trained on the ruddy planet."

Sergeant Gordon saw only one thing missing in the communication plan. "Has anybody alerted the Martians?"

⊙---♅♆--☿☽⊕-♄-♂♀--♃●○

A quick tug of the lanyard at 3:30 p.m. signaled the start of the first session. The phantom 3-incher sailed unnoticed overhead, but the thunderous shock wave roared through the air, followed by the ground-shaking reverberations of the M1902 field gun. Even the guards standing at the gate flinched before dropping the rope. The startled spectators marched onto the parade grounds as Captain Dowd's Balloon Band played a selection of Sousa's greatest hits, including *The Washington Post, Stars and Stripes Forever*, and *U.S. Field Artillery*, which got everyone's caissons rolling. The jubilant racers stiffened to attention, puffing their chests full of hydrogen.

The carnival announcer walked to the center of the parade grounds and harnessed himself to one of the propaganda balloons. Mr. Burton let him have a hundred feet of slack.

"Ladies and gentlemen, welcome to Fort Omaha. We have a wide range of events planned for this afternoon and evening. If you look west you'll see an exhibition of French, Italian, German, and American airships from World War I. The 12th Balloon Company will conduct aerial maneuvers, including a parachute drop. For any young man interested in ballooning, we have several recruiting stations available, and if you enlist today, you're guaranteed a free ride to 1,000 feet on my airship. Be sure to stay for the grand finale, to witness four balloons racing into the dusky Nebraska skies, preceded by the christening ceremony hosted by our esteemed guest and renowned meteorologist from Amherst University, Professor David Peck Todd."

Only a few people witnessed the astronomer shaking his fist at the announcer.

The afternoon session featured foot races, pop-drinking contests and a band concert, culminating in the release of 1,000 balloons with postcards attached asking the finder to note their location and drop the card in any mailbox.

A 220-yard dash and pie-eating contest kicked off the evening's events, followed by a tug-of-war between the 9th and 12th Balloon Companies. The carnival's director, Mr. Leo Stevens, relegated the scrawny privates of the 10th and 11th to crowd control and saved the best contests for the evening session, which began promptly at 6:40 p.m. when the carnival announcer rose into the cloudless Nebraska sky.

"Ladies and gentlemen, may I have your attention? We have a special surprise for you this evening, something never seen at any aerial carnival! Four of our bravest soldiers are prepared to take superhuman leaps into the atmosphere to show a daring new tactic to transverse enormous distances. Let's give a nice round of applause for the balloon-jumping contest."

The propaganda balloons, each with a soldier harnessed beneath and an anchorman to keep them from bounding across the Nebraska countryside, drifted onto the parade grounds. The helium bags offset all but 10 pounds of each soldier's weight. One by one, the contestants stepped to the starting line to leap into the hearts and minds of the cheering spectators. Cpl. James L. Byrd bagged a victory with a standing long jump of 101 feet.

With the sun sinking like a punctured balloon, the announcer rose into the evening twilight for his last announcement.

"Ladies and gentlemen, please join us for the christening ceremony followed by the Aero Club of America-sanctioned race. Professor Todd, the world-famous astronomer from Amherst College, Massachusetts, will officiate."

Todd waved to the cheering crowd as 2nd Lt. Conklin placed a bottle of Welch's finest grape juice in his hand.

He examined the label. "What is this, a dry county?"

"Our Nebraska legislature voted in favor of Prohibition in January. All the good stuff disappeared months ago."

"This trip keeps getting better and better." He stepped from the judge's stand and strode down the imposing line of airships.

"Christening our first balloon this evening, Miss Esther Wilhelm."

"Thank you, Professor Todd. I christen thee United States." She caught the metal plate affixed to the gondola for the ceremony dead center, sending grape juice-soaked shards everywhere.

"Nicely done, Miss Wilhelm. Captain Ashley C. McKinley is piloting the United States."

Conklin placed another bottle of Welch's finest in the professor's hand, as 2nd Lt. Lundberg moved the steel target to the next basket.

"Miss Gertrude Stout will christen balloon number two this evening."

"Thank you, Professor. I christen thee All America." Gertrude was a lefty whose ample forearm transmuted the glass to sand, buckled the plate and sent the finest grapes from Concord, Massachusetts, a town close to Amherst by the way, splashing across the stoic judge's white shirt.

He pulled out his kerchief and wiped his forehead and cleaned his glasses. "Thank you, Miss Stout. I'll remember to stand farther back next time." The crowd laughed as he continued. "First Lieutenant Richard E. Thompson will pilot the All America."

With military precision, Conklin and Lundberg delivered fresh ammunition to the front lines while setting up the third gondola's defense.

"Everyone, please welcome Miss Regina Connell, christening balloon number three for us this evening."

"Thank you, Professor, I christen thee Victory." She waited until the grape-stained astronomer had distanced himself before launching her precision strike. The splash guard rebuffed her weak assault. She charged again, with the same result. Todd dove behind his two military attaches as Miss Stout stepped to the plate to pinch-hit. No one was sure if the bottle cracked because of its previous injury or if Stout's crushing grip was to blame. Regardless, the shell-shocked decanter relieved itself on her shoes.

The shaken judge strode back into view. "Second Lieutenant William E. Huffman will pilot the Victory."

A sudden updraft, ignorant of balloon race etiquette, attempted to end the christening with a premature start. Ground crews and spectators alike leaped to the anchor ropes to provide the gravity such an august ceremony demanded.

Eager to finish, Conklin loaded the remaining shell into the chamber.

Todd studied its French label from the champagne capital of the world. "I see Leo gets the good stuff."

"Well, he is the carnival director. He brought several cases of that back from France after the war."

The disheveled emcee referenced his notes. "And last but not least, christening the judge's balloon, Miss Helen McCreary."

"Thank you, Professor Todd. I christen thee Cannonball."

A ray of sunlight lit the fuse stretching from the powder chamber beneath the Cannonball to Miss McCreary's outstretched arm. The flash signaled Lundberg's retina, which dispatched a message to those neurons that contained the knowledge of the steel armor protecting his chest. His brain calculated the trajectory of McCreary's swing versus the current location of the target and arrived at the shocking conclusion of the basket's imminent doom. Hastily prepared orders passed down the chain of command, alerting his larynx to stand by for further instructions. A split-second later, his diaphragm received the directive to inflate the propaganda balloons, but it was too late. The French artillery shell sliced through the defenseless basket, ricocheted off the pilot's leg and landed unexploded on the gondola floor.

Eager to end the bloodbath, Todd broke the stunned silence. "Thank you, Helen. Ladies and gentlemen, let me introduce my old friend and world-renown balloonist Mr. Leo Stevens, who will pilot the Cannonball this evening."

Leo grabbed the megaphone. "Perhaps we should have christened it the Cannon Fodder, Miss McCreary." The crowd erupted in laughter as he inspected the damaged gondola and rubbed his sore leg.

Todd seized Conklin's arm. "Bring me that bottle of champagne."

All America departed before sunset at 8:52 p.m.

Victory followed three minutes later.

United States left just as the sun dipped below the horizon.

Leo stitched the Cannonball's bottle hole closed with twine as an ominous line of clouds approached from the southwest. The contestants drifted in silence over the Missouri River, across the vast stretches of the corn-and-bean fields of Iowa.

The illustrious professor bivouacked that evening in the Signal Corps photo lab, where his telescope served as a lightning rod, perched and rusting on the observation platform atop the building's barnlike roof. Conklin and Lundberg rendered the French artillery shell harmless as the soaked meteorologist packed up his weathered gear.

☉---♅♆--☿☽⊕-♄-♂♀--♃●○

With its head start, All America caught a stream of air at 12,500 feet that propelled the balloon 365 miles as the crow flies from Fort Omaha, landing outside Portage, Wisconsin.

The United States finished second, landing near Rowley, Iowa, 223 miles northeast of Omaha.

Victory landed in Greene, Iowa, about 195 miles northeast of Omaha, earning silver cigarette cases for pilot and crew.

The Cannonball flew true to its name and lost its battle against the Iowa cyclones, which forced it to terms near Ringsted, Iowa, about 155 miles northeast of Omaha.

Mars did not return the call.

46. The Tomahawk

March 18, 1920 - White Earth Reservation, Minnesota

Joseph Bigbear strapped his snowshoes to his feet and headed home from the Episcopal Church, where the tribal leaders had laid their plans for the annual celebration to commemorate the 52nd anniversary of the White Earth reservation. The council assigned committee heads and selected a mid-June date. They would have parades, baseball games, foot races, bow and arrow competitions, and speeches from their congressional representatives and other dignitaries. Council President Jack Skipintheday would send invitations to all Chippewa reservations in Minnesota and, for the first time, welcome members of the Sioux nation to the peace council.

The skies were clear that evening as he trudged west along Bear Clan Drive. He stopped to admire the sunset before heading north on Wolf Clan Lane. As the Earth turned her shoulder to the sun, Mars flashed its reddish beacon at the expectant moon and her lonesome companion as the wandering star, Saturn, hovered overhead.

The sun's golden rays illuminated the front porch, nestled among the pine trees overlooking the frozen lake. A child's snowshoe path approached from Black Duck Trail and made the left turn toward his cabin. Driven by thirst and hunger, his legs strained against the quickened pace, fueled by a visit from his granddaughter.

His eyes spotted her woolen tepee perched on his doorstep.

"Is that Miss Jane Lucy Smith camped out on my front porch?"

The sound of his voice stirred her. She tossed the blanket aside and ran to his arms as she had so many times in the past. "Grandpa, I've been waiting for you. I missed you."

"I can't believe how much you've grown since the last time I saw you." He bent over to unstrap his snowshoes, which he stuck into his snowdrift shoe rack and grabbed the Tomahawk, thrown with intent at his front door.

He took her hand in his. "Come on, let's get warmed up."

The potbelly stove and kerosene lantern captured the sun's diffuse spirit to bring warmth and light to Joseph's northern Minnesota cabin. The sizzling pan-fried lake trout and a pot of fresh coffee nourished his being.

Jane waited while her grandfather performed his evening rituals. She enjoyed the serenity of dishes being cleared, his tobacco pipe packed and lit, settling into his rocker for the evening. She climbed into his lap and snuggled beneath her blanket, knowing that he would reward her patience with a story from the newspaper.

The masthead proclaimed *The Tomahawk* as the 'Official Organ Of The Minnesota Chippewas' on behalf of and to secure the welfare of the Indians of the United States. He thumbed through the first few pages to find something his granddaughter might enjoy. "Wisconsin Pottawatomies Have Grievance." He'd save that one for later. "How about 'Problems facing a stricken world, shall Chaos or Reconstruction in Europe Follow the Great War?'"

"I don't think so, Grandpa."

A small cartoonish drawing in the center of page six screamed for attention almost as loudly as the article's headline.

Hello, Earth! Hello.

"Oh, an article about Mars talking to us. Look at these pictures."

Their eyes swept down the halftone photographs of Marconi, Tesla and Edison to a cartoon of two Martians sitting in front of a radio transmitter attempting to contact Earth while the sun and moon watched.

"I know all about the planets. That's Saturn and the Earth above that old man's head."

"That's Mr. Edison. OK, this looks interesting."

She snuggled close to listen.

"Marconi believes he is receiving signals from the planets.

"Of course, you recall Jules Verne's Ten Thousand Leagues Under the Sea. *Well, his submarine is now an accomplished fact, isn't it? And doubtless, you read Kipling's* With the Night Mall. *Well, the Atlantic has*

been crossed in a single flight, hasn't it? Probably, also, you read H.G. Wells' The War of the Worlds, *in which the Martians descended upon us with fighting machines even more formidable than the tanks of the Great War and a mysterious agent of wholesale destruction even more deadly than any gas used by either side.*

"I wonder if the library has a copy of *The War of the Worlds*. It sounds interesting. Maybe we could read that sometime."

"I'd like that, Grandpa."

He continued reading.

"Well, who shall say that Wells hasn't the right idea about Mars being inhabited by beings just as smart as we are, and probably a good deal smarter?

"It is a bold man who says 'Impossible' these days.

"Anyway, Guglielmo Marconi, the famous Italian engineer, who perfected wireless telegraphy, has opened up an exceedingly interesting question by this statement: 'I have encountered during my experiments with wireless telegraphy most amazing phenomena. Most striking of all is the receipt by me personally of signals, which I believe originated in the space beyond our planet. I believe it is entirely possible that these signals may have been sent by the inhabitants of other planets to the inhabitants of Earth.'

"If there are any human beings on Mars, I would not be surprised if they should find a means of communication with this planet. Linking the science of astronomy with that of electricity may bring about almost anything. While our own planet is a storehouse of wonders, we are not warranted in accepting as a fact the general supposition that the inhabitants of our comparatively insignificant planet are any more highly developed than inhabitants (if there be such) of other planets."

"Those are funny-looking humans, Grandpa, they look more like raccoons."

"Wouldn't that be amazing if humans lived on Mars?"

Jane giggled at the idea.

"For all we know, the strange sounds that I have received by wireless may be only a forerunner of a tremendous discovery.

"The messages have been distinct but unintelligible. They have been received simultaneously in London and in New York, with identical intensity, indicating that they must have originated at a great distance.

"These signals are apparently due to electromagnetic waves of great length, which are not merely stray signals. Occasionally, such signals can be imagined to correspond with certain letters of the Morse code. They steal in at our stations irregularly at all seasons. We do not get the signals unless we establish a minimum of 65-mile wavelengths. Sometimes we hear these planetary or interplanetary sounds 20 or 30 minutes after sending out a long wave. They do not interrupt traffic, but when they occur, they are very persistent.

"The most familiar signal received is curiously musical. It comes in the form of three short raps, which may be interpreted as the Morse letter 'S,' but there are other sounds which may stand for other letters.

"Australia corroborates Marconi's statement. Highly skilled and experienced operators at Sydney have received numerous signals similar to those reported as having been received in England. They consist of frequent repetitions of two dashes, representing the letter M. They are on wavelengths of 80,000 to 120,000 meters. The Australian experts say such wavelengths have never yet been used by any wireless station of the Earth."

Joseph pondered what he read. "I wonder what the letters 'S' and 'M' mean? And who taught them Morse code?"

"M stands for Mars and S is for snowman. We could make two snowmen Martians tomorrow, Grandpa, and give them sticks for noses and twigs for those things poking out of the top of their heads."

A host of Jane's snowy angels danced through the blizzards of his memory. A crack formed in the ice dam that stood against the flood. He drew deep from his pipe and continued reading.

"Now, what do the electrical authorities say on the general subject? Here it is, in brief: Thomas A. Edison has this to say: 'Although I am not an expert in wireless telegraphy, I can plainly see that the mysterious wireless interruptions experienced by Mr. Marconi's operators may be good

grounds for the theory that inhabitants of other planets are trying to signal to us. Mr. Marconi is quite right in stating that this is entirely within the realm of the possible. If we are to accept the theory of Mr. Marconi that these signals are being sent out by inhabitants of other planets, we must at once accept with it the theory of their advanced development. Either they are our intellectual equals or our superiors. It would be stupid for us to assume that we have a corner on all the intelligence in the universe.'"

Joseph paused and took a large sip of cold caffeine.

"Grandpa, what if the Martians are stupider than us?"

The beverage sprayed from his lips at his granddaughter's insightful comment. His sleeve would have to suffice as a towel.

"No, I believe Mr. Edison is correct. It would be hard for any planet to be dumber than Earthlings. Now please, allow your grandfather a moment's peace."

Like a grinning Cheshire cat, she waited as he drained the icy reservoir.

"Jupiter could be stupider."

It would prove a futile, and some might say stupid, gesture to cover one's mouth with a hand, if one considered the path of least resistance. The coffee shot from his nostrils.

"My, my, my, you do know your planets, young lady. Be still while I finish reading this article."

The only thing dry within easy reach was her woolen blanket. Its scent entered his freshly purged nasal cavity, shaking the very foundations of the dam struggling to hold back the raging floodwaters that had been accumulating over the past week.

"Now, my little comedian, let's see what Mr. Tesla has to say."

"Nikola Tesla, the famous Serbian inventor and electrical expert, says: 'Marconi's idea of communicating with the other planets is the greatest and most fascinating problem confronting the human imagination today. The thing, I think, that we should try to develop is a plan akin to picture transmission, by means of which we could convey to the inhabitants of Mars knowledge of Earthly forms. This would enable us to exchange with them not only simple primitive facts, but involved conceptions. To talk to

Mars seems to me only a matter of electric power and perseverance.'

"Prof. Albert Einstein, the German astronomer and author of the theory of 'Relativity' that is apparently upsetting all accepted doctrines, believes that Mars and other planets are inhabited, but if intelligent creatures are trying to communicate with the Earth, he should expect them to use rays of light, which could much more easily be controlled.

"Among scientists who have won the right to speak with authority, the foremost was the late Professor Lowell, director of the observatory at Flagstaff, Ariz. Not only was Professor Lowell convinced that Mars was inhabited, but he believed the people had a much higher degree of intelligence than those on Earth. He dwelt particularly on their inventive genius.

"In 1914 he found a new opportunity for strengthening his pet belief by announcing that instead of losing any of their canals the Martians had built two new ones, which could be seen plainly through the telescope.

"'We have actually seen them formed under our eyes,' Professor Lowell said at the time, 'and the importance of it can hardly be overestimated. The phenomenon transcends any natural law and is only explicable so far as can be seen by the presence out yonder of animate will.'

"Edmond Perrier, director of the museum of the Jardin des Plantes, in Paris, constructed the first picture of the Martians as he conceived them. He said in part: 'The men on Mars are tall because the force of gravity is slight. They are blond because the daylight is less intense. They have less powerful limbs. Their large blue eyes, their strong noses, their large ears, constitute a type of beauty which we doubtless would not appreciate except as suggesting superhuman intelligence.'"

"The cartoonist thought they looked like your potbelly stove, Grandpa."

He folded the paper in half and danced the cartoon Martians across the floor while Jane made screeching sounds like a raccoon. Joe laughed so hard he almost fell out of his chair. Jane's giggles echoed off every surface of his being.

He wiped the tears from his eyes and finished reading the article.

"Assuming that Mars or some other planet is signaling us, what can we do in the circumstances? Apparently, we can do much.

"L.J. Lesh, a New York radio engineer, suggests that one of the methods of constructing a gigantic station would be to erect huge antennae suspended by balloons like the British dirigible R-34. He asserts, however, that a still better way would be to use huge and brilliant shafts of light as antennae for the system. He thinks that projectors could be grouped around one spot where a great amount of electricity could be generated. He suggests Niagara Falls or some other spot with an enormous amount of water power.

"The outlay might be warranted someday, but certainly not until it is certain that we are being called by one of our neighbors out in space."

It's hard to say how long they sat there that evening, rocking. The floorboards stopped their protests once her caffeine-deprived grandfather drifted off to sleep. Jane left in silence through the front door, traveling south on Wolf Clan Lane. The bitter north wind traced an evanescent angel in the driven snow. At Black Duck Trail, she turned west. Earth had rolled over in bed, turning her back on the moon and Mars. Saturn twinkled in Jane's eyes.

☉---♅♆--☿☽⊕-♄-♂♀--♃●○

Early the next morning as he stirred, the Tomahawk slid from his lap and face-planted on the floorboards. As he bent to pick it up, 24 words in the middle of page 8 streaked across Joe's cerebral dome like a meteor and crashed on his occipital lobe, its reverberations cracking the dam that stood strong for the past seven days and let loose a flood upon the Earth:

Jane Lucy, 5-year-old daughter of Mr. and Mrs. Tom Smith of this village, died last Friday. The funeral was held Sunday at the Episcopal Church.

47. The Accident

May 1920 - Stamford, Connecticut

David Todd was sitting in the Health Resort's atrium in Stamford, Connecticut, enjoying his morning coffee and reading a copy of the *Inquirer* from late March. His nurse, from Lancaster, Pennsylvania, thought that the Professor might find the article from her hometown newspaper interesting. Something about Mars signaling Tesla and Marconi. It had funny pictures of Martians at a wireless sending a message to Earth. Anyway, it was May 1920 and the mental strain of being forced into retirement from his position at Amherst, the cumulative effects of the failed solar eclipse expedition to Brazil and the bloodbath in Omaha had taken their toll on the aging astronomer. His wife had wintered in Florida while he sought treatment for his diminished faculties.

He was mumbling something about "I'll show them" and "Einstein is an idiot" when a nurse approached. "Professor Todd, there's a phone call for you."

He folded the paper under his arm and followed her into the visitors' room off the atrium.

"You can take it in here. It's your wife, Mabel."

Todd introduced the *Inquirer* to the wastebasket.

He held the receiver of the candlestick telephone to his ear and placed the transmitter next to his mouth. There were no lights involved in this process, he thought to himself.

"Hello, Mabel?"

"Yes, how are you?"

"I believe I'm well enough to leave this place. How is everything in Florida?"

"The weather was temperate this winter. I've spent a lot of time working on the revisions to my compilation of Emily Dickinson's poems."

"Are you coming home soon?"

"That's why I called. My train leaves this morning at 11. It's scheduled to arrive tomorrow night at 9. Would you have someone leave the car at the station?"

"I can pick you up. I could use a change of scenery."

"Are you well enough to drive?"

"Yes, I'm fine. I'll have the flivver gassed up today and arrange for a hotel room downtown. Be sure to wear your raincoat. This storm reminds me of that hurricane I sailed through to Brazil last year."

"Oh, my taxi is here. We'll catch up on all the news when I get home."

"All right, have a safe trip. See you tomorrow at 9 p.m. sharp."

He clicked the receiver hook with his finger and waited for the operator.

"What number are you trying to reach?"

"The Hotel Davenport, please."

⊙---♅♆--☿☾⊕-♄-♂♀--♃●○

Friday evening at 7:30, he phoned the station to check on the train's arrival.

"They've made good time. It'll be here in half an hour."

"I'd better hurry then. I know how she hates waiting."

He grabbed his raincoat and umbrella and hurried to the front desk to ask the receptionist for directions.

"It's easy to find. When you leave the parking lot, take a right on Main. Go past the town hall and turn left on South Street. You can't miss it."

"Right on Main, left on South."

"That's it. If you cross over the river, you'll know you've gone too far. You should be there in less than 15 minutes."

The train sprang from the sunny skies of Philadelphia and dove headfirst into the deluge plaguing New England. The lights of the Stamford station struggled to pierce the storm's veil as the passenger car rolled to a stop at the empty platform.

To the well-heeled veteran of expeditions to Japan, Russia, Chile and the Dutch East Indies, the nor'easter proved a mere drizzle. Of greater concern was the absence of a familiar face.

"Where is he? I know we arrived early, but I'm sure he would have checked the schedule," Mabel thought to herself as she headed to the payphones.

She lifted the receiver and waited. "Yes, can you connect me with the Stamford Health Resort?"

"That will be…" Mabel dropped the nickel before the operator could finish the sentence.

"Hello, this is the Stamford Health Resort. How may I help you?"

"This is Mabel Todd. Could I speak with my husband, Professor Todd? He said he would meet me here at the train station."

"I saw him leave an hour ago. He should have been there by now."

"It's not like him to be this late. Could you send someone this way to look for him?"

"Just a moment, please." The janitor was mopping the marble floor of the entryway. "Would you see if you can find Professor Todd? He left to pick up his wife at the train station, but she says he isn't there."

"Let me grab my raincoat and I'll head there straight away."

"Mrs. Todd, I have someone heading there now to look for your husband. Call me back if you need anything else."

"Thank you, you've been very helpful."

☉---♅♆--☿☾⊕-♄-♂♀--♃●○

The janitor didn't notice any signs of the professor along Main Street. He had just passed Atlantic when the flashing red lights appeared in his rear-view mirror. He pulled over and watched as they sped down Park Place. Main took a slight bend at the five-points intersection past the town hall. It was a common mistake even in broad daylight to miss that turn and head straight into the Rippowan River. An error the ambulance driver wouldn't make.

48. Miracle on Boylston Street

The bright entrance lights blinded Todd. He stepped back and looked up at the single word emblazoned on the understated marquee: "COLONIAL".

"The Colonial Theater? Must be Boston. I remember attending their production of *Ben Hur* in 1902. I still don't know how they got 12 horses with chariots to run at a full gait on the stage. What's showing now?"

The advertisements on either side of the entryway proclaimed *The Miracle in LyricScope*.

The lock of the entrance clicked, and the door opened. A dark green top hat appeared between the entry doors. As the elderly gentleman scanned the sidewalk, his eyes flared when he beheld the professor.

"Oh my head, you're early. We weren't expecting you for quite some time. Come in and we'll get you seated."

"I don't have a ticket."

"That's OK, you've already paid the price of admission."

"What's this play about?"

"It's a Lyricscope. A celestial light show. A spectacle beyond your wildest imagination. I know you'll enjoy it."

"Lyricscope? I've never heard of that."

"It's a silent movie with full orchestral acco, accompani, acc, er um, orchestra members."

As they entered the theater, Todd noted its emptiness and the strangely uniformed doorman. The juniper green morning suit coat draped his mossy, pinstriped, high-waisted pants and shiny black shoes. A moss-colored vest with a gold watch chain covered his French-cuffed white shirt. A dark ascot concealed its winged collar. His wide-brim top hat matched the jacket's deep forest tones.

"There's nobody else here. Is this a dress rehearsal?"

"That's one way to describe it, yes."

"You must be the lead actor, then."

"No, today I'm your doorman, and I'll be running the lights and smoke machine. Come on, let's get you seated."

The professor felt a tug on his arm as he turned to enter the main floor.

"The best view is upstairs."

They took the grand staircase past the mezzanine and entered the theater through the balcony doors.

"May I suggest Row A, Seat 102? I'll be in the control room behind you. We'll begin once you're seated."

Todd walked down the steps to the balcony's edge, unfazed by its dizzying height and panoramic view, and slid into the aisle seat. As the house lights dimmed, a breathy overture of the woodwinds emanated from the orchestra pit far below, reminiscent of the gales of Kansas. Or perhaps he was thinking of Omaha.

The curtains drew taut and faded to white. The three chandeliers withdrew as the ceiling and walls merged with the curtain to form a featureless 360-degree cyclorama. A fog machine pumped a low-lying cumulus veil across the stage, rendering its timbered floor invisible, and spilled over the darkened footlights to conceal the dress circle and mezzanine.

From the 30,000-foot perch on the balcony, he saw the curvature of the Earth as dawn broke from the orchestra pit. His eyes were blinded by a single spotlight rising above the cloud layer. Grayish tones of the backdrop's lower edge mimicked the fog machine's haze, transitioning to a blueish-white at eye level and finishing at the rafters in deep sky blues. The sole ensemble cast member paused as the lead actor entered from stage left, suspended by some mechanism that cannot be seen. The spectator now understood the art director's brilliant lighting scheme as the shadow of the actor's diminishing crescent swept across the foggy cyclorama, a celestial sundial sweeping toward the appointed hour.

Todd lost himself in the stunning theatrics.

"Where are my instruments? I need my camera."

"Why?"

"I'll never get another chance at such a magnificent eclipse."

"That remains to be seen."

His eyes searched frantically for his equipment as totality neared.

"Good God, man, I feel like I'm standing on top of a balloon."

"Neat, huh! Like I said, the best seat in the house."

He looked toward the control room, screened by the cyclorama.

"Where are you?"

"Not far, an easy morning's ride. Oh look, the eclipse is starting."

He turned just as the sun kissed the moon on her cheek.

"Are you OK, Professor?"

"Never felt better. In fact, this is the most beautiful thing I've ever seen. But where exactly am I?"

"The Colonial Theater on Boylston Street, Boston, Massachusetts, 1920, watching a special performance of *The Miracle*."

"But how did I get here?" His eyebrows furrowed. "Ah yes, now I remember. I was driving through that infernal rainstorm. I followed the receptionist's directions precisely. Must have missed the sign for South Street. I hit the curb and got tossed from my car. Then the floodwaters swept my flivver downstream."

His predicament dawned on him. "I'm dead, aren't I?"

"No. You're in a protective-phase transition state, awaiting the outcome of events outside your control."

He couldn't see the projectionist's scarecrow face, but it was there.

"Are you God, or an angel, or perhaps the devil? I know I've done things that might preclude me from the pearly gates."

"There's no need for a gate. Everyone's welcome. The entrance is more of an ivy-covered stone wall. As for my job description, I'm just the guy pulling the levers behind the screen. Oh, and I love gardening."

"Well, where are you? Why can't I see you?"

"But you can. I'm holding you in my hands right now. Don't worry though, I've sent for help. I just hope they hurry."

"Why bother? My life has been a series of complete failures."

"The rain clouds are obscuring your vision, Professor. There's important work left for you, and your accomplishments have been nothing short of extraordinary. Remember that mechanical instrument you invented to take pictures?"

"That was an exquisite device. Got the idea for it in Japan back in 1887. It was a challenge just taking one photograph during an eclipse. What with making the exposure, removing the plate, storing it in the case, reloading the camera. I'd be lucky to get five exposures and could miss totality. So I developed a machine to control the shutter and swap the plates. I proved it would work that year, even though it was cloudy. I attempted to use it in two more eclipses, both ruined by cloud cover."

"But you kept trying."

"Yes, I still hoped for that perfect photograph on a cloudless day. For the Tripoli expedition in 1905, I improved the device to control 23 separate telescopes, all attached to a massive equatorial mount to track the sun. It was one of the few times where sunny skies prevailed. I got almost a hundred exposures using that equipment.

"Then there was that miserable trip to Russia in 1914. I arranged for an airplane to photograph the eclipse above the clouds. We didn't know such a terrible conflict was breaking out. Customs in Riga held up all of my equipment: cameras, photographic plates, telescopes, notebooks, everything. The Russian government conscripted all aircraft for their war effort against the Germans. The only good fortune I had was meeting Count Bobrinsky. He invited us to his estate outside Kiev, where I scrounged enough parts to build a camera and, of course, after all that, nothing but cloudy skies all day.

"With the war spreading through Europe, the count suggested we leave as soon as possible. By the time we arrived in Oslo, the Germans had already mined the North Sea. We were lucky to not hit one on our passage to Liverpool."

"Your friends believed you were being held as a spy."

"We had no way of communicating once hostilities began. With all of our cameras and telescopes, I'm surprised the Russians didn't imprison us as spies when we arrived.

"Then that miserable expedition to Brazil last year. We booked passage on the *Elinor* and had our biplane fastened to the deck. The first week on that rust bucket, we had to stop in Bermuda for engine repairs. Then, halfway to South America, we ran out of food and had to survive on shark meat caught by the crew. When we stopped at Pernambuco to replenish our stores, we still had hopes of getting to Montevideo in time to observe the eclipse. Before we left, though, the greatest windstorm in their history blew the airplane off the ship and ruined the entire trip."

"And yet you never gave up on your dreams. You were and are an inspiration to thousands of young astronomers around the globe. Your book, *A New Astronomy,* has inspired countless others in directions they may not have even considered a few years ago. Whatever happens, follow your passions wherever they might lead. The path ahead will be a perilous journey through darkness and despair. If humanity continues to draw back the curtains of mysticism, using the wisdom, courage and spirit of kindness they've possessed all along, only then can they... oh look, Professor! Totality!"

The moment he had dreamed of his entire life. Sun, moon, Earth, balloon, eyes, all aligned in perfect spherical harmony.

Any astronomer knows that you should never stare at a solar eclipse without using a strong filter. Yet this time, lacking equipment, he couldn't help but watch this exquisitely choreographed celestial promenade. The sun's corona crowned the lunar deity, the star of the show, illuminating her serene face. Having glimpsed her eternal beauty, his spirit felt cleansed, revitalized, as the balloon sank beneath the layer of clouds and the rains washed over him.

$$\odot\text{---}♅♆\text{--}☿☾⊕\text{-}♄\text{-}♂♀\text{--}♃\bullet\bigcirc$$

The ambulance's headlights traced the flivver's tracks as they disappeared into the rising floodwaters. Its searchlight scanned the shoreline. The ambulance driver would later recount these events as a miracle. His light spotted the astronomer's limp body as it slid into the dark waters of the Rippowan. Without hesitation, he dove into the flood and pulled him to safety.

"Professor Todd, are you OK? Can you hear me?"

The serene moon transformed into the face of his savior; his eyes blinded now by the attendant's flashlight.

49. Gopher Prairie Expedition of 1922

The Janesville Daily Gazette
Janesville, Wisconsin
January 11, 1922

LATEST NEWS FROM MARS
By Frederic J. Haskin

Washington, D.C. — All the latest scientific dope on that most interesting of all planets, Mars, is conveniently gathered together in a recent publication on the subject by Professor William H. Pickering, who has charge of the Harvard Astronomical Station in Jamaica, and who has devoted much of his time to looking at Mars through a telescope and speculating about conditions on the sister planet.

Mars is 4,200 miles in diameter, which means that it is only about twelve percent as great as the Earth in bulk—quite a small place as stars go, a sort of Gopher Prairie among the habitable planets. It has been generally assumed that Mars is inhabited by intelligent beings, something like men. How these beings differ from us and how they resemble us, whether we can hope ever to communicate with them—these questions fire even the dullest imagination. All sorts of fantasies have been based on imagined visits of Martians to the world, or of inhabitants of the world to Mars.

The time may yet come when we will get daily communications from Mars. After all, at times it is only 35,000,000 miles away. Should a means of traveling through interstellar space with a supply of canned oxygen ever be perfected, as it well might, an expedition to Mars would doubtless be launched. An airplane traveling at the rate of one hundred miles an hour might reach Mars in about forty years, provided it set out at the right time. The chief of the expedition, a youth of twenty, would carry with him a few promising infants of both sexes, aged about one year. These would be men and women at the height of their maturity when Mars was reached. They would do the observing, and their progeny would carry the dope back to Earth, along with a delegation of Martians. The entire operation need not consume more than three generations.

Although the scientists have the greatest difficulty in ascertaining what kind of life there is on Mars, they are able to supply a surprising amount of information as to living conditions there. When the Martians expedition sets sail, science will probably not be able to tell the members what sort of creatures they will encounter, but they will be able to tell all about the climate on Mars, what kind of underwear they will need, how many blankets at night and all that sort of thing.

Lack of space makes it impossible here to discuss in any detail the Martian canals. The claim that Mars is inhabited by intelligent beings is based almost wholly on the contention that these long, straight canals could not be the work of nature. The canals will have to be studied a great deal more before science will have any intelligent conclusion to offer about them.

50. Daughter of the Stars

The Wilkes-Barre Record
Wilkes-Barre, Pennsylvania
July 31, 1924

OBSERVING MARS

On the 22nd of August, the planet Mars will be only about 35,000,000 miles from the Earth. Usually, the distance is from 100,000,000 to 200,000,000 miles. On that date, astronomers in the world will have the best opportunity in many years for making observations. If the 22nd is cloudy, other days will do almost as well. Dr. Todd, Emeritus Professor of Astronomy at Amherst, suggests the trying of radio communication with inhabitants of the planet, if there are any. On August 22nd, all radio broadcasting stations should be silent to give one station the opportunity to send messages. He believes a good plan would be to send up the airship Shenandoah about 10,000 feet and have its radio operators listen. But, says Prof. Todd, the existence of life on Mars is merely speculation.

⊙---♅♆--☿☽⊕-♄-♂♀--♃●○

Todd also believed he would need the help of his friend and inventor of the mechanical television, C.F. Jenkins, to construct a device to record Martian broadcasts during what the press had termed 'National Radio Silence Day.'

⊙---♅♆--☿☽⊕-♄-♂♀--♃●○

Mr. Jenkins arrived in Washington, D.C., in mid-August with his Radio Photo Message Continuous Transmission Machine. He employed a World War I-surplus SE950 Field Radio (Marconi, Nobel Prize 1909) tuned to a wavelength of 6,000 meters to convert the Martians (Percival Lowell, 1908) wireless transmissions to electrical signals. Rather than

205

feeding these to the speaker (Alexander Graham Bell, 1876) for the intended recipient, the human ear (Charles Darwin, Jan 27, 223,898 BCE), he snipped the wires and soldered them to a light bulb (Thomas Edison, Patent 223,898, Jan 27, 1880). He attached said incandescent to an armature that scurried back and forth across a filmstrip (Joseph Nicéphore Niépce, 1825) at the dizzying pace of 50 times per inch, thus maximizing the recording capacity of the film. And what better way to power the machine than a bank of RAY-O-VACs (Alessandro Volta, 1800) from the French Battery and Carbon Company in Madison, Wisconsin.

This Frankensteinish assemblage (Mary Shelley, 1818) of the latest technologies of the unseen would have made Rube Goldberg (William Heath Robinson, 1912) extremely proud.

The device's internals worked thusly:

Start of Process

Martian: Expresses their innermost thoughts on a charged particle and sends it on a dizzying journey through space and time.

Charged Particle: Hello Earth, hello. I'd like to leave a message for Mr. Jenkins.

Radio Receiver: Senses the particle's excitement and snaps open the battery's anode door. Electrons, waiting for just such a moment, charge onto the copper conveyor belt until the receptionist slams the battery door shut, having expressed the charged particle's desires on the eager negatrons.

RAY-O-VAC: Performs a quick inventory and notices the missing stock. Ray goes on a fishing holiday in the electrolytic lake and nets enough energy to replenish the anode's shelf. His dwindling fish stocks drain him emotionally.

Gastrointestinal Tract: The copper esophagus swallows the electronic packet, depositing it in the tungsten stomach until it can't hold any more. Warmed by this delicious meal, the satisfied bulb burps out a photon or two as spent electrons wend their way through the machine's intestines, which dump them into the RAY-O-VAC's cathode toilet, where they are flushed into the batteries' electrolytic sewer.

Film Strip: The photons carry the Martian Chronicle to the film's front doorstep. What happens behind closed doors in the darkened room is far too disturbing to detail, but let's just say that a tiny alchemist waves his magic wand over the salty silver halide and transmutes it into metallic silver, leaving a permanent record of the Martian's innermost thoughts.

End Process: Repeat the process until the film runs out, the Shenandoah lands or the battery dies.

Film Strip: After a 29-hour sunbath, a nice chemical wash and a luxuriating rinse, the secrets of Mars are ready for the admiring eyes of the scientific community and the newspaper reporters.

RAY-O-VAC: No longer able to satisfy his customers, he turns to a higher power to fulfill his spiritual needs.

Jenkins' attempt to secure a patent for this conglomeration of technology was soundly rejected. Lee de Forest had already patented a similar device in 1919. The de Forest monster lurked in the projection booths of the heretofore silent-movie theaters, bringing death and destruction to their unsuspecting audiences with a fully synchronized soundtrack, leaving the smoldering carcasses of thousands of speechless actors in its wake.

$$\odot\text{---}⛢♆\text{--}☿☽⊕\text{-}♄\text{-}♂♀\text{--}♃●\bigcirc$$

Todd and Jenkins left Washington with the apparatus and traveled to the Norfolk Naval Shipyard in Virginia, where the USS Patoka, a replenishment oiler, and the dirigible Shenandoah, Algonquian for 'beautiful daughter of the stars,' were conducting trials to determine the airships military capabilities.

At 9 a.m. August 22, Todd and Jenkins boarded a small tender for the short ride to the Patoka. Under strict orders from the southern breeze, the two ships and all their flags lined up in parade formation. The scenery provided a tiny sample of the spectrum's rich colors, tending toward the grays of the balloon's skin and the tanker's battleship-colored cloak. The early morning curtain of fog had lifted, but its unsaturated watercolors still flowed over Chesapeake Bay.

"Professor Todd, Mr. Jenkins, welcome aboard. I'm Commander Robinson of the Patoka, and this is Lieutenant Commander Zachary Lansdowne of the Shenandoah."

"Professor Todd, Mr. Jenkins, it's nice to meet you. Our departure will be between noon and 1 p.m. this afternoon. We'll ascend to a cruising altitude of 3,000 feet and make way for Lakehurst, arriving on Sunday at 2:40 a.m. Our expected flight time is 39 hours."

"Excellent," Todd said. "This gives us a full day to observe Mars during opposition."

"Be ready for boarding at 11 a.m. That should give you plenty of time to check out your equipment."

Jenkins nodded. "Yes, that's perfect. It takes less than an hour to prepare the machine."

"The weather reports are showing clear skies and calm winds. Now, if you'll excuse me, I will see you later this morning aboard the Shenandoah."

$$\odot \text{---} \text{⛢} \text{♆} \text{--} \text{☿} \text{☾} \oplus \text{-} \text{♄} \text{-} \text{♂} \text{♀} \text{--} \text{♃} \bullet \bigcirc$$

At 10:30 a.m., a sailor escorted Todd and Jenkins to the airship mooring mast at the rear of the ship. He looked at the elderly gentlemen. "Are you sure you can make it? It's about 100 feet up to the top and the stairs are steep."

The astronomer craned his neck toward the heavens and, based on his observations, gave his expert opinion. "It won't be a problem at all."

In a dreamlike state, he floated upward to the most magnificent observatory he had ever seen. The crow's nest atop the mast allowed the tethered balloon to rotate independently of the Patoka as the winds shifted. He stepped onto the boarding platform and spent the next few minutes enjoying the view of Chesapeake Bay, waiting for his companion to make the last half of the climb.

When Jenkins arrived, the airman dropped the gangplank. "It's best if you don't look down. Just grab the handrail, duck your head and step inside."

The gangway led them into the bowels of the airship's aluminum superstructure and its 20 goldbeater-skinned gasbags. They passed food storage lockers, a small dining section, and several oil and fuel tanks before arriving at a sleeping berth close to the radio room.

"Mr. Jenkins, we've commandeered this area for your equipment."

"How soon before we leave?"

"We should be at altitude within the hour, sir."

"Excellent, that's plenty of time to get set up."

"Professor Todd, if you'll come with me, please. Commander Lansdowne would like you to join him on the bridge."

They walked a short distance down the gangway to a small hatch that led to the control car suspended beneath the Shenandoah.

"I hope you aren't claustrophobic. It's a tight squeeze climbing down the shaft."

Todd's fireman slide left the aircrew speechless.

"Did that multiple times every night at the Wilder Observatory. A necessary skill for any astronomer."

Lansdowne smiled. "Very impressive. What do you think of our observatory?"

"Captain, this ship is superb. How I wish I could have used this during any of my eclipse expeditions."

"She's a beauty all right. There's none like her, but I wonder if you could tell me your secret for staying fit. I watched you climb the mooring mast earlier, and it impressed me how fast you climbed those steep steps. That's equivalent to a 10-story building."

The spry astronomer smiled. "It's a regimen I call Vital Engineering. The older we get, the more saturated with poisons the bloodstream gets. Non-elimination of them is the direct cause of progressive aging and, finally, death. If a 20-year-old were to practice it faithfully, they could expect perfect health and no doctor bills. He or she will stay for the next 20, 40 or 60 years unadvancing in age. A miracle of preservation? A Fountain of Youth? Yes, and more than likely *In Eterno* because one is doing with the entire body what the Rockefeller Institute has done with a chicken's heart."

Lansdowne nodded. "I've heard of that, but I didn't believe it."

"I was there last year to see it myself. It's the most marvelous thing on the planet today. They removed it in 1912 and have cleansed it every day or so of the poisons caused by its muscular action. It has continued beating ever since. What Vital Engineering does is a close approximation to this. Internal sanitation, no medicine at all. None necessary, harmful rather, except in acute cases or accidents."

"So, what does your regimen involve?"

"I'm still completing the details and must insist on confidentiality. I am working with a group of doctors to develop the process. Once we complete it, I will share it with you all. It's never too late to begin. I just started last year and have made remarkable progress in regaining my abilities."

"You think someone could live forever?"

"Yes, I glimpsed the eternal after my car accident in 1920. I believe I have found the Elixir of Life."

Lansdowne checked his watch. "I'd love to hear more about that at dinner, Professor Todd. If you'll excuse me now, it's time for us to begin the undocking procedure and get the Shenandoah ready for flight. You're more than welcome to stay here if you'd like."

Within 20 minutes, the Shenandoah's five engines thrummed to life as the airship drifted away from the mooring mast and turned toward the northeast.

Todd examined every inch of the gondola, trying to imagine how he could place his camera equipment to view an eclipse.

"Commander, most of my expeditions are to take photographs of solar eclipses. Is there any place suitable for that on your magnificent ship?"

"I think we could accommodate that. Private, would you show Professor Todd to the best seat in the house?"

"Aye, Aye, Commander. Follow me, Professor."

They climbed the shaft to the gangway and proceeded toward the front of the airship. A ladder enclosed in an aluminum cage ascended through the superstructure, pinched between the enormous helium bags.

"It's 75 feet to the top. Do you think you can make it?"

"Absolutely. Let's go."

"Hold on a second. We have to put on these safety harnesses."

After donning their gear, the Professor chased the Private to the top and watched as he popped the hatch and secured their harnesses to an eyebolt on the observation platform.

"All right, come on up."

Todd stepped out onto the foggy balcony.

"Good God, man, I'm standing on top of this balloon."

"Neat, huh! Like the commander said, the best seat in the house."

Five Packard tornadoes hoisted the Shenandoah above the gray landscape and deposited it somewhere over the rainbow. The emerald greens of the Virginia countryside, the deep blues of the Atlantic Ocean, the golden sun overhead. There was no eclipse today as the moon sought shelter from the stormy Kansas skies, far over the western horizon.

"I feel like I've died and gone to heaven. Can we sit here for a while?"

"It'll get chillier the higher we climb, but we should be fine for now."

They sat together for several minutes in shared silence.

"Are you OK, Professor?"

"Never felt better. This reminds me of a vision I had in 1920."

A whistling sound from the voicepipe broke his reverie.

"I've just received word. Mr. Jenkins' machine has come to life."

Todd knew Mars wouldn't rise above the horizon for quite some time yet.

"I wonder who's calling…"

☉---♅♆--☿☽⊕-♄-♂♀--♃●○

The device continued picking up signals for the next 29 hours. Shenandoah reached Lakehurst on Sunday morning after being in the air for a record 39 hours. The press waited eagerly for the results of National Radio Silence Day.

51. National Radio Silence Day Results

The Washington Post
Washington, D.C.
August 27, 1924

Weird "Radio Signal" Film Deepens Mystery of Mars

Pictorially Recorded Messages Here Mere Tangled Mass of Dots and Dashes—Growing Wonderment May Bring Tenable Interpretation Theory.

The mystery surrounding strange radio signals heard in various parts of the world in the "nearest-to-Earth" visit of Mars on Friday and Saturday was deepened yesterday, when the film in the special machine to record such "signals" was developed photographically.

The result was a curious picturization of the radio phenomenon. Thirty feet long and six inches wide, the chemically treated film showed, black on white, everything that was "picked up" out of the air in about 29 hours with a receiving apparatus adjusted to a wavelength of 6,000 meters. The "messages" ranged from a fairly regular arrangement of dots and dashes, running the full length of the film down its left side, to pictures weirdly resembling a face, repeated at regular intervals on the right side of the film.

C. Francis Jenkins, inventor of the "radio photo message continuous transmission machine" used in the experiment, doubted that the recorded radio sounds had anything to do with Mars. He declared, however, that it was the most curious phenomenon ever photographed by his apparatus.

"I don't think the results have anything to do with Mars," Mr. Jenkins said. "Quite likely the sounds recorded are the result of heterodyning, or interference of radio signals. The film shows a repetition, at intervals of about a half-hour, of what appears to be a man's face. It's a freak which we can't explain."

Dr. David Todd, professor emeritus of astronomy at Amherst College, who enlisted Mr. Jenkins' cooperation in the widespread "listening-in on Mars" plan, which he organized, was equally at a loss to account for the freak results. He regarded the film seriously, however.

"Three years ago Marconi was reported as saying he had heard signals from Mars. A few days ago, he was quoted as saying he was too busy to listen to possible messages from Mars and that it was a ridiculous idea to do so. He changed his mind, and no one knows what he heard the first time. With our photograph, however, it is not a question of what one man heard. It is a permanent record, which all can study."

VIII. Stairway to Heaven

52. The Search for That Which Cannot be Seen

5 Million Years in the Future - Teegarden Caravan

Nighttime had fallen, and the silence brought on by the lawnmower led Te Ata into the story garden, only to find the Gardener searching the bushes beside a well-lit and immaculately trimmed pathway.

"Did you lose something?"

"Yes, my propellant."

"Where'd you leave it?"

He turned and pointed into the dark niche where the frogs croaked. "Over there, by the pond."

"Why in heaven are you looking here?"

"Because the light is better." He looked up and gave her that grin...

Te Ata slipped into the frog's domain, collected the bottle, and returned with it and the mower in tow.

"Are you finished with your story?"

"Not quite. I'm done with the Golden Age of SETI. They were so focused on Mars ever since Lowell claimed that it was teeming with life. I'd like to finish with the tale about how they tracked us down. We have your cosmic rays to blame for that."

"You mean credit."

"Yes, of course. After they glimpsed the unseen, it was only a matter of time. Less than 150 years, which is quite remarkable considering how long Earth has held them captive. It's a marvelous story, a series of fortunate events that captured the best and brightest intellects from all over the world working together in the ultimate reality show and the greatest race in the history of mankind..."

"And you think I was instrumental in that?" The Gardener beamed.

"Well, you and your beacons. You knew they'd track you down. Especially after Roentgen announced his X-ray machine back in 1896. That picture of his skeleton hand appeared in every newspaper on the planet. They harvested entire forests for that edition. Any scientist worth his radioactive salts wanted a piece of that action."

"Ah yes, the science of that which cannot be seen. So, what's next? Becquerel, Wulf, Hess, Pfotzer?"

"Those would be the logical choices for ascending the stairway. Henri Becquerel proved that these invisible rays were also being emitted by the Earth's crust."

"Wait, wasn't he the guy who received a Nobel Prize for an experiment he lifted from one of his father's textbooks?"

"Yep, that's him. Claude Félix Abel Niépce de Saint-Victor was trying to develop color photography when he discovered certain salts that could expose a plate in complete darkness. Edmond Becquerel mentioned Claude's research in his book, *Light: Its Causes and Its Effects*, which his son inherited after his death. After Roentgen's X-ray announcement, good old Henri duplicated the experiment without citing its source. Nobel was a-titter with his discovery."

"If only Alfred Nobel had seen how unseemly Becquerel had ripped the unseen science from history's pages."

"So it would seem. At least they had arrived at the stairway. Theodor Wulf took the first step from the world's tallest structure in 1910, the Eiffel Tower. His measurements were inconclusive yet hinted that the radiation originated from a source other than Earth."

The Gardener began rocking back and forth on his heels with his hands clasped and his thumbs twiddling, whistling a tune from the 1970s, as his eyes scanned the starry skies.

"Exactly. They needed more proof, so they hopped in their balloons to get measurements higher in the atmosphere. In 1912, Victor Hess flew day and night up to 5,000 meters, thus eliminating the sun as its source. Nobel couldn't help but reward such derring-do. Dr. Herman Masuch and his pilot, Dr. Franz Schrenk, perished in a similar attempt in Russia. The news horrified Georg Pfotzer, but it inspired him to construct a matrix of Geiger-Müller tubes connected to a vacuum-tube circuit with an attached dial. A camera photographed the dials at regular intervals, dropping over 600 pounds of scientists and their life support equipment ballast overboard. His device reached 29,000 meters and determined that your pesky radiation was still there."

"That's a good thing, right?"

Te Ata smiled. "More than that. We wouldn't be here without you."

"And I have your ancestors to thank for my existence, for which I am eternally grateful. So, where to next?"

"A small farm in Iowa."

53. The Athens of the Midwest

December 1930, the Van Allen farm, Mount Pleasant, Iowa

It was a brotherly tradition that happened every month and neither snow nor rain nor heat nor gloom of night stayed these brothers from the swift footrace to the mailbox. A double toot of the Model T's horn was their starting gun. George was collecting eggs as his younger brother James cleared soiled straw from the chicken coop. The brothers' enterprise proved a valuable source of food and income for the family during the Great Depression.

The starter's pistol seemed distant and angry today, but it was clearly the signal they expected. James dropped the fresh bundle of hay in the coop's doorway to slow his opponent. George, with an egg in hand, turned to gauge his adversary's head start. He slid the Plymouth Rock beneath the closest Rhode Island Red as the egg's mother cackled at the outrage.

George sped past James at the mailbox. His two-years-older-and-somewhat longer-legs carried him into the lead as they sprinted down the lane toward the Model T, where the mailman was delivering a pair of exasperated boots to a crestfallen tire.

"This consarned, goldarned piece of jitney junk. I swear I'm going to sell it one of these days." He paused the tirade when George arrived. His brother finished a close second. "Can you get the spare? James, would you set the parking brake?"

James hopped into the cab and pulled the lever. He noticed the winner's trophy laying on the seat and grabbed it along with the rest of their mail and tucked it inside his coat.

The mailman retrieved the jack from the toolbox and placed it beneath the axle. "This old clunker has become more trouble than it's worth. I'm thinking of selling it."

George loosened the bolts holding the tire to the rim of the wood spoke wheel. "How much are you asking?"

"Sixty dollars would be a fair price," he said, ratcheting the jack's handle.

George attached the spare while the mailman returned the flat to the rear bracket. James lowered the jack and stowed it in the toolbox on the running board.

"Thanks for helping me change the tire, boys. I see you've already got your mail, James. Let me know if you find an interested buyer."

"We will," George replied.

James turned and sprinted to the farmhouse with his trophy while George walked back to the chicken coop to finish his cleaning and collecting the eggs.

⊙---♅♆--☿☾⊕-♄-♂♀--♃●○

Life on an Iowa farm during the winter was tedious. The gardens lay fallow, the corn long since shucked, every walnut in the woods foraged and shelled. You could go ice fishing in the Skunk River, but chipping their frozen bodies out was more trouble than it was worth. Their monthly subscription to *Popular Science* provided a welcome relief to the winter's drudgery. This month, the Home Workshop article caught James' attention: "Simplified Tesla Coil, Gives 200,000-volt Current for Many Dazzling Experiments, by Kenneth M. Swezey." Complete with detailed drawings and schematics for building the device.

The article's introduction promised "PURPLE streamers of sparks from eight to ten inches long, potentials of several hundred thousand volts, beautiful fountains of brush discharge, wireless lights, high-frequency currents that may be taken into the human body without harm and used to perform dozens of amazing experiments—all these are at the instant command of the home experimenter who builds a simple resonance transformer or what is usually called a Tesla coil."

After reading through the entire article, James ran downstairs with the magazine in hand.

"Mom, where's George? I need to talk to him."

"I think he's still out cleaning the chicken coops. Shouldn't you be helping him?"

"Thanks, I will," he said, racing into the frigid Iowa winter, forgetting to grab his coat and gloves.

He found his brother carrying a fresh bundle of straw from the barn.

"You owe me for cleaning out your chicken coop."

"I'm sorry, I'll clean them all next time. But look at this article. I have to build one of these."

George's eyebrows raised as he glanced through the opening paragraph. "Where would you get all this stuff?"

"I bet Mr. Cottrell would have most of it in the science lab at the high school. I can check with him on Monday."

"You do that. I'm going back to the house to read this while you finish cleaning out your coop."

George swapped his armload of straw for the prize he had won in the footrace.

In December, in Iowa, when the corn's in the crib and the hay's in the barn, it doesn't matter which way the wind blows, it'll cut through you like an ice sickle. James beat his brother to the farmhouse to get his coat, hat and gloves to finish his chores.

☉---♃♅♇--☿☽⊕-♄-♂♀--♃●○

On Monday, James spotted his favorite teacher walking in the hallway.

"Mr. Cottrell."

"Yes, James, what's got you so excited today?"

"The latest issue of *Popular Science* arrived on Saturday. It had an article on how to assemble a Tesla coil. I can cobble most of the stuff from our electronic kits, but I don't have the coil."

"I'm afraid I can't help you. Since the Depression started, the school had to sell most of my equipment to meet expenses. Sounds like a fun experiment, though. You must bring it in to show me when it's finished."

"I will. Do you know somewhere I could find one?"

"You could pull it off a junk car. That should do the trick."

"Oh, our mailman was thinking of selling his, but he's asking more than we can afford."

"Well, good luck. I'll keep an eye out for you."

"Thanks, Mr. Cottrell," James said as he headed off to shop class.

☉---♃♅♇--☿☽⊕-♄-♂♀--♃●○

The following Saturday, the brothers waited for the mailman's arrival. He pulled up in a 1929 Ford Model A mail truck and stepped out of the vehicle to show it to the boys. "The post office in Iowa City sent me a used one, but she's a heck of a lot better than that old piece of junk I was driving."

James popped the hood to inspect the engine while George conducted business.

"Have you sold it yet?"

"No, the darn thing had another flat. Did you find a buyer?"

"Maybe, but they think 60 dollars is too high a price. They were wondering if you'd sell it for 40, what with two flats."

"Well, I had them both patched. I wonder if they'd be willing to pay 50 dollars?"

George looked at James as he nodded to his brother.

"We'll take it," they said in unison.

"When can we pick it up?" George asked.

"Here's the key, if you want to walk into town and get it."

⊙---♅♄♆--☿☾⊕-♄-♂♀--♃●○

Christmas break arrived and the curious brothers began tearing the drive train down to its component molecules, arranging each piece in its relative position on a large canvas in the barn while scrutinizing each part to determine its function. The simple electrical system led them to a metal case in the passenger compartment, with a coil for each of the four cylinders tucked inside.

James pulled one and, drawing on his experience with his electronics kit, he wired it into his makeshift circuit, which looked nothing like the picture in the magazine. Both were a hodgepodge of transformers, wires and switches, but this underpowered version barely bridged the gap of a Champion spark plug.

"Well, that's disappointing. Are you sure you did it right?"

"It's working for a car engine, but I want to build the one in the article to get that 8-inch streamer. Where could I find all these materials?"

"You could check with Professor Poulter in the physics department at the college. He might have what you need."

The next day, James took the mile-long journey to Old Main, on the Iowa Wesleyan campus. He approached the student receptionist sitting behind a desk in the quiet foyer. "I'm looking for Professor Poulter."

"He's in the auditorium," she said, pointing down the hall. "The chalk has been screeching in there all morning."

"Thanks." He hurried away with the *Popular Science* magazine clutched in his grip.

The young professor stood at the blackboard, armed with chalk and eraser. His speckled white hair and eyebrows belied his 32 years.

"Professor Poulter, can I interrupt you for a few minutes?"

The dusty professor stepped back and admired the beautiful and unequaled equations and drew a question mark where the answer should lie. This series would provide a challenging addition to his problem-solving Blackboard Sessions. He replaced his equipment in the tray and clapped himself free of the morning blizzard.

"I'm James Van Allen. My brother George attends classes here."

"Yes, I've met him. What can I do for you?"

James pulled out his copy of *Popular Science* and flipped to the Home Workshop. "I built this with a coil from a Model T, but it only gives a tiny spark. I want to build one exactly like the article, but I don't have a neon-sign transformer or a quenched gap."

The professor spoke wiring diagrams as a second language. "I'm sure we have those. Come with me."

James followed him into the well-stocked storeroom, its shelves filled with an assortment of electrical components.

"This is quite a project. Do you think you'll need help to construct it?"

"I built a two-slider crystal radio set from scratch once, plus I take shop class in high school, so I'd like to try building it myself."

Seeing a young student eager to build such an intricate device was all any professor could hope for. Especially in the vast stretches of corn-and-bean fields in rural Iowa.

"Well, you're more than welcome to use the lab here at the college. I have only one condition."

"What's that?" James had already accepted the terms as he surveyed the treasures he had gained.

"When it's complete, I want you to show it to my freshman introductory physics class when they return from break and describe its construction."

"Agreed."

☉---♃♅Ψ--☿☾⊕-♄-♂♀--♃●○

Over the next two weeks, James sprinted to the lab after finishing his chores to spend the rest of the afternoon working on his project. Professor Poulter stopped in to check on the progress, awed by the attention to detail exhibited by the young Van Allen. He mounted the device on a single piece of plywood, with each component's connecting wires stapled to its surface like a wiring diagram. It was unnecessary, but it gave the scientific instrument a look of true professionalism.

"Well, I'm very impressed," Poulter commented when he walked into the lab. "You've been working very hard on this project. Is it going to work?"

"Let's find out."

He examined the components to make a final visual check and then plugged the transformer into the wall socket and closed the switch. Transformers, capacitors, tuning coils and quenched spark gaps hummed to life as the bewildered electrons searched the device for some means of escape. He grabbed the foot-long steel rod and drew it close to the ball on top of the coil. An 8-inch bolt arced through the laboratory into the young scientist, racing up his arm and charging through every fiber of his being. Meetings were held amongst the hundred billion neurons in his brain, and two camps quickly emerged. One was thoroughly delighted with the results of the experiment; a more cautious faction dispatched an urgent communique to the fingers of his right hand, urging a relaxed posture as a safety precaution. The hapless conductor dropped to the workbench.

Those neurons in the elation clique sent a message of joy to the speech synthesis apparatus. "Eureka!"

An enormous smile spread across Poulter's face as James' educated grip retrieved the conductor's baton. "The shock didn't hurt at all."

It was music to the professor's ears. "Two hundred thousand volts sounds like a lot, but there isn't much current. Just don't touch the transformer or you'll get a nasty surprise."

"I won't forget. Do you mind if I take it home to show my family?"

"Not at all. Would you be available next Tuesday for a demonstration? I have a lecture scheduled in the auditorium at 2 p.m."

"I'll be there."

James opened the switch and unplugged the device. The handle he attached to the plywood base allowed him to carry it like a suitcase for the walk back to the farm.

After arriving, he set it up on the workbench in the barn where George and Maurice had finished reassembling the Model T while their youngest brother, William, sat in the driver's seat, taking an imaginary tour through space past Mars, on his way to Jupiter and Saturn.

They gathered around James as he described the various components and what they did. He cautioned them to not touch the exciting circuits.

"OK, can you plug it in for me, Maurice?"

His younger brother expected to see sparks shooting everywhere, but the machine ignored the charging electrons.

"Is it broken?"

"No, it's fine. William, would you close this switch?"

The boy closed the toggle. The components buzzed their warmup notes to prepare for the show they were about to perform.

"Now watch what happens."

With the conductor's baton at the ready position, a massive bolt of electricity arced from the coil's head to the steel rod, causing James' hair to stand on end. His brothers laughed at the static display.

A peaceful afternoon on the Van Allen farm was a rare treasure indeed. Alma couldn't slop the boys like chickens, and hens only molted twice a year, not two times a day, as did her hatchlings. She wasn't happy when the screams and laughter coming from the barn jolted her away from the latest Mary Westmacott (Agatha Christie) novel *Giant's Bread*. When she arrived to investigate their shenanigans, a record-breaking foot-long spark jumped from the coil to the rod James was holding. Her billion-plus neurons didn't need to meet because they all reached the same conclusion: Her son had just been electrocuted. Her blood pressure dropped to unacceptable levels as her heart awaited further instructions from her panicked brain. Her communication network collapsed and so did she, into George's arms as he rushed to catch her.

After a moment, she stirred.

"Mom, I'm so sorry. I didn't mean to scare you," James said, trying to comfort her.

"What on earth is that thing?"

As James described the device to her, Maurice walked over and picked up the rod. When he held it up to the device, another bolt shot from the coil to the rod, up his arm and out his hair.

It came as no shock that by the time Alma regained consciousness, the brothers had safely stowed Tesla's coil upstairs in the farmhouse. Some students learn best without visual aids.

54. Stump Neck Gopher Prairie

April 1942, Maryland

Sheriff Robert Farmer, with a phone at his ear, signaled for the young physicist to enter his office and take a seat. While nodding his head, he mouthed, "I'll just be a minute," silently.

"Yes, I understand. No, it's no problem at all. He's sitting here right now. We'll get him sworn in this morning. You're welcome. Goodbye."

The sheriff looked over the 28-year-old.

"Under normal circumstances, I don't think I'd swear you in as a deputy, son, but that was the secretary of the Navy. Said you needed to carry a weapon to protect yourself. Have you ever fired a gun?"

"I haven't, but when I leave here, I'm driving down to Stump Neck to receive weapons training from the Marine drill sergeant this afternoon."

"Can you give me an idea what this is about?" Sheriff Farmer asked.

"Sorry, it's classified information."

"I understand. Let's just skip the formalities, then. You are now a sheriff's deputy of Montgomery County of the great state of Maryland. You must carry your badge and ID with you at all times in your car. Whatever your mission is, I wish you the best of luck. My son is in the Navy and ships out to the Pacific soon."

"Do you know where they're sending him?"

"Yes, the USS Washington."

☉---♅♇--☿☾⊕-♄-♂♀--♃●○

It was springtime, and the trees had all but disappeared in their camouflage fatigues when James returned to Stump Neck the next week. Two Marines met him at the entrance to the firing range.

"You must be Mr. Van Allen. I'm Sergeant McGinnes and this is Private Ducy. We'll be your gunnery crew today."

"Please, call me James."

After exchanging handshakes, he opened the trunk and showed them the unmarked crate.

"Private, put that in the jeep. You can leave your car here, James, as a safety precaution."

McGinnes hopped in the driver's seat, Ducy perched on the wooden box in the back and James rode shotgun for the short drive to the 20-acre field whose spartan accommodations comprised an earthen bunker dug into the rich bottomlands of the Potomac. Its ceiling of thick oak boards supported a mound of sandbags as the last line of defense against misfires.

"We need to fire and recover these today," James explained to the sergeant.

"The ground out here is so soft we'll have to dig them out. A post-hole digger should do the trick."

"OK, do you have one here?"

"Yes, in the equipment shed," Ducy offered. A brief pause and a commanding look were all he needed. He set off on his mission.

"How will we locate the shell after we fire it?"

"We'll know an approximate location based on the calculated trajectory and wind speed. After we find the first one, the rest of them should land close by. I've already done the calculations."

McGinnes had aimed the 10-pounder just shy of vertical, heading into the slight breeze from the northeast. He chambered the mysterious canister while Ducy attached the firing cord and unrolled it toward the bunker.

The gunnery sergeant sliced the artillery range into three bite-size pieces, using his arms as the hands of a clock.

"After we fire the projectile, I'll watch 9 to 11. James, you take 11 to 1, and Private Ducy, 1 to 3."

The makeshift gunnery crew descended the ladder into the safety of the earthy fortification.

"Put your earplugs in, James. These shells are loud."

With all in readiness, McGinnes nodded. Ducy yanked the cord, and the war began.

The scientists of the Applied Physics lab, housed in an abandoned Chevrolet garage in Silver Spring, Maryland, were scouring the shoreline of the vast ocean of truth, looking for smoother pebbles that would fit into prettier shells. It was an epic battle to strip away nature's camouflage, bringing her unseen truths to light by casting stones at God.

The propellant's goal was to reclaim all territories inside the chamber by ejecting its captivator with as much force as possible. It completed the mission in a split-second and joined forces with the breeze wafting toward the bunker. The canister served as a winged Trojan horse. At its 10,000-foot apogee, it could see the White House and all of downtown Washington, D.C., to the northeast, with the Potomac River snaking its way through the Maryland woodlands, past the firing range, and emptying into Chesapeake Bay to the southeast. As upward momentum drained into Earth's gravity well, its world turned upside-down. Heavy though it was, the winds aloft pushed it in the general direction of the explosion's smoky ghost. Shrouded within the warhorse, a clandestine organization sprang into action. A battery of electrons led the charge as the transmitter dispatched wave after wave of tiny spies. In the bowels of the radio room, the anxious receiver listened for scouting reports. The minuscule vacuum tube, originally designed to amplify sound for the hearing-impaired, failed, not from the propellant's deafening roar but from the crushing force it brought to bear.

Isaac Newton observed the experiment from the comfort of James' shoulder, admiring the sergeant's use of his equations, which described the missile's flight in a perfect vacuum, and impressed that he had considered the wind's impact on its trajectory. He knew that the Earth's rotation on its axis, its orbit around the sun, the solar system's path through the Milky Way and its galactic drift through the universe, dizzying though their combined motions were, did not concern him because this was a war game of hand grenades played with Trojan horseshoes where proximity counted.

"Two o'clock, a hundred yards out," Ducy yelled, pointing toward the impact site. He scrambled up the ladder and grabbed the post-hole digger. They walked the sight line with 10 feet of separation. Ducy counted each step.

At 80 paces, James stopped and pointed at the ground. "There."

McGinnes glanced at the find. "No, that's a gopher's burrow. They don't realize how dangerous this place is. See that small mound of dirt they kick out? Your shells will leave a nice circular impression."

Thirty steps farther along the gopher prairie, Ducy spotted the hole and set to its excavation. A loud clink after five clumps revealed the prize Van Allen was looking for.

James looked at the mud-caked canister. "Excellent work, gentlemen. Let's get the rest of these shells fired."

After recovering the last shot for the day, they loaded the experimental results into the jeep and drove James to his vehicle.

"I'll call you when we have another batch to test. It should be sometime next week," Van Allen said.

He returned to Silver Spring, where he opened each projectile to see if the tiny vacuum tube had survived. Undaunted by their persistent failures, the APL team stiffened their resolve, hoping to get the tungsten filament battle-ready. With each fortification, the thread's survival rate improved but was still nowhere near the 50 percent threshold required by the military for a new weapon. As the months passed, they arrived at the crossroads of survivability and utility, where any further stiffening would take them down the dead-end of utter uselessness.

$$\odot ---ₕ₵Ψ--☿☽⊕-♄-♂♀--♃●\bigcirc$$

It was the end of July when James returned to Stump Neck with the stiffest batch yet of untested recruits.

"I see the wildflowers are in full bloom. Reminds me of my home in Iowa at this time of year," he said as they drove down the lane.

"Were your summers as hot as this?" McGinnes asked. It could get up to 100 in the shade today. I've had a canopy set up by the bunker and ordered plenty of drinks and some sandwiches for you. We have some military brass visiting this afternoon, and Private Ducy and I have to be there when they arrive around lunchtime. They'll need us for about an hour." The sergeant looked at his watch. "We have time for 10 shots this morning."

With militaristic precision, they had fallen into a routine over the summer. Their weekly bombardment forced the gophers to cede much of the territory they held, like Gen. Douglas MacArthur had to abandon the Philippines in March. A well-worn path from bunker to target area testified to the gunnery crew's expertise and the physicist's growing frustration.

The call came over the radio, requesting their presence as Ducy returned with the 10th mud-caked canister.

Tired and sweaty from the intense July heat, James grabbed a ham sandwich and a bottle of pop from the cooler and sat beneath the canopy.

McGinnes wiped the sweat from his brow. "We'll have plenty of time to finish this afternoon. I'll bring a couple of fresh diggers to help."

"I'm sure my back will thank you tomorrow," James replied.

As they drove off, he finished his ham sandwich and went to the chest to grab another bottle of pop and a handful of ice to soothe his burning neck. His boyhood detectors kicked in. The narrow band of trees at the meadow's western edge suggested a nearby river where he could dip his toes in the cool water. Since he had a few minutes, he picked his way through the underbrush and discovered an uprooted tree whose canopy lay partially submerged in the Potomac, a perfect spot to soak your feet while enjoying its serene beauty. The late-July fragrance reminded him of the afternoons he and his brothers spent fishing on the Skunk, a tributary of the Mighty Mississippi, that had earned its name but smelled just as sweet as long as his siblings left the critters undisturbed.

A moment's respite from the pressure of weapons development was rare indeed, knowing that war raged in the Pacific and European theaters and thousands were dying every day. If successful, the device would kill its share of enemy combatants, and it held the promise of ending the madness that swept the planet twice in his lifetime.

As his spirit drifted down the rivers of his youth in Mount Pleasant, something buzzed past his head.

"What was that?" He swatted his ear, eliminating the horsefly as the source of the disturbance. It was too late in the summer for June bugs. He scanned the riverbank, looking for cicadas or dragonflies.

"There you are." He saw a small bird hovering above the Potomac.

"A hummingbird, my, what a delicate little creature you are."

He froze as it drifted toward his perch and lit on a branch overhanging the water.

Twitching its gaze from side to side, something caught its attention. It shot skyward, and hovered 30 feet in the air, its eyes held motionless within the tornado of its wings. James watched, fascinated. A ripple that would have been unseen by anyone but a hungry bird sent it on its deadly mission. The inverted whirlwind gained speed faster than gravity would dictate, then pulled its thrusters tight as it dove into the muddy waters, surfacing in the blink of an eye with a fish three-quarters the length of its own body clenched in its long pointy beak. It returned to its perch and lit next to the observant Iowan. After shaking the water from its plumage, it flipped the wriggling minnow, caught it by the tail and began beating the tobacco juice out of it by slamming the fish's noggin against the tree. Properly tenderized, it swallowed the tasty treat whole, then used the limb's bark to cleanse its weapon. It turned and stared into James' eyes for what seemed an eternity, then scratched its head twice with its right claw, ruffled its feathers and vanished into the woods.

Stunned by the display, the physicist corrected himself. "OK, I was wrong. You're a kingfisher, and there's nothing delicate about you at all. The G-forces your wings must endure flying like that? So flexible, yet so durable."

Serendipity.

He ran back to the firing range where Sergeant McGinnes awaited with fresh recruits.

"Let's get these fired."

That evening at the lab, he revised the vacuum tubes schematic, adding a spring to hold the filament to the metal support post.

$$\odot\text{---}\maltese\Psi\text{--}\mercury\leftmoon\oplus\text{-}\saturn\text{-}\mars\venus\text{--}\jupiter\bullet\bigcirc$$

He returned to Stump Neck a week later with the latest modification and tempered enthusiasm.

"You seem very excited. Have you solved your problem?" McGinnes asked.

"I hope so. Let's get started."

That evening, James returned the Trojan horses to their Silver Spring stall and set them on his workbench. Trying to calm his nerves, he cracked the first shell open and examined the small vacuum tube inside. The tungsten filament, with its silvered spring shock absorber, had survived forces 20,000 times that of gravity.

August saw the grass and the gophers on the Stump Neck peninsula reclaim their lost territories. In November, James, now a commissioned Navy Lieutenant, headed to the Pacific to deploy the top-secret weapon whose crates bore VT fuze to camouflage their true nature and to help MacArthur take back the territory ceded to the Japanese seven months earlier.

55. The Spirit of Shikishima

December 1942 - Somewhere in the Pacific Ocean

The launch from the troopship Republic rolled across the swells toward the Washington, a North Carolina-class fast battleship, fresh off a major victory. Two weeks earlier, her guns sank the Kirishima, preventing it from shelling Marine positions on Guadalcanal.

A 28-year-old physicist who had dreamed of attending the Naval Academy in Annapolis, had congressional sponsorship and passed the academic examination yet failed the physical because of asthma climbed the stairs where one of the greatest marksmen in history awaited his arrival.

"Lieutenant James Van Allen, reporting for duty, Sir," he said with a crisp salute.

"I'm Rear Admiral Willis Lee. Welcome aboard the *Washington*. This is Captain Howard Benson and Commander Raymond Thompson, our chief gunnery officer. As soon as you get your gear stowed, meet us in the briefing room."

"Aye Aye, Sir."

Lee was a world-class sharpshooter, with five gold medals from the 1920 Olympics to prove it. Armed with radar and Newton's equations, the *Washington* sank the *Kirishima* in the darkest hour before dawn. Japan was a global leader in this technology, but their naval leaders shunned its usage, for fear of giving away their ships' positions, which, in the end, it did. A Japanese destroyer rescued the Kirishima's commander, who watched 212 sailors sink into the depths of Ironbottom sound.

☉---♅Ψ--☿☾⊕-♄-♂♀--♃●○

Every battle-hardened gun captain snapped to attention when the admiral entered the briefing room.

"At ease, gentlemen. I want to get right to it. What we'll be discussing is top secret. I've asked Lieutenant Van Allen to give us an overview of an important new weapon the Navy has developed. Lieutenant, you have the floor."

"Thank you, Admiral. To begin, I'd like to read a section from the 5-inch, 38-caliber gun crews manual, which I'm sure you all have memorized."

They had.

"*It is almost impossible to score a direct hit on an airplane with the 5-inch gun. The idea of firing a projectile with a timed fuze is to make the projectile burst in the vicinity of the target. That is the next best thing.*

"*If the fuze is not correctly set, the projectile will not burst near the target. It's up to you to set that fuze exactly right.*"

Thompson spoke: "That's why we have to fire so many shells. When an airplane attacks, there's no time to set the fuze. So we just blast away."

Van Allen nodded in agreement. "With the VT fuze, you just load and shoot. If it gets within 70 feet of the attacking aircraft, the shell will explode."

"That's impossible," one gunnery captain commented. "How can it know when it's close to an airplane? Does it have eyes?"

Van Allen smiled. "Yes, in a way, it does. I grew up on a farm in Iowa. I remember on summer nights, seeing clouds of bats flying overhead in complete darkness. Although they are blind, they're able to detect and catch thousands of insects using echolocation. Each bat sends out chirps, which give them distance and direction to their meal. The proximity fuze uses a similar concept. Each one has a miniature radio transmitter in the nose, chirping hundreds of times each second. A circuit inside calculates the target's range. Anything within 70 feet triggers the explosion."

"You mean to tell us that even if it passes behind the airplane, it will explode?"

"Yes. Imagine a bubble, 140 feet in diameter. That's your kill zone."

"How reliable are they?"

"The Navy requires at least 50 percent reliability, and I'm happy to report that we exceeded that threshold. We expect the proximity fuze to be six times more effective than the timed fuzes."

"When will we get these new shells?"

"I've brought several boxes for you to do preliminary tests and to explain the difference to your gun crews. You cannot share with them how this works, only that they need not set a timer. At your next resupply, we'll bring aboard a full complement."

"How do you know they'll work? We're putting our lives on the line out here. We can't take chances on experimental gimmicks."

"I helped design it and spent most of the last summer testing it. Now, I'm not pretending to be a battle-hardened sailor, and I won't tell you how to do your job. The only training I've had since I volunteered was from a pamphlet called 'Duties and Responsibilities of Naval Officers.' I believe so strongly in this weapon that I'm putting my own life on the line to get it deployed."

"You designed these things?" one of the gunnery sergeants asked.

"These fuzes have over 500 parts. I was a member of a large team that worked on their development. I had a lot of experience in college designing scientific equipment, some of which accompanied Admiral Byrd on his expedition to Antarctica in 1933. The Navy believes strongly that this could give you a significant advantage over the Japanese, and I'm here to help you get these into action as soon as possible."

"This is fascinating. Could you show us the fuze's guts?" Lee asked.

"I could remove the fuze and cut one open, but it's my understanding that disassembling ammunition on board ship is against regulations."

"Yes, I think it's important. Gentlemen, we'll reconvene on deck."

Van Allen turned to Thompson's aide. "I'll need one shell, a table, and a few minutes to get my satchel."

☉---♅♆--☿☽⊕-♄-♂♀--♃●○

The group assembled a respectable distance from the shell resting peacefully in its cradle. Lee gave the signal to defuse the bomb. Van Allen twisted the cone free and disconnected the igniter charge and set it aside. He carried the explosive canister to the railing and tossed it in the ocean.

"All right. It's safe now."

As the men gathered around, the young lieutenant sawed through the casing, exposing the fuze's guts. Lee peered over Van Allen's shoulder.

"Here's the radio transmitter and the receiver. It's the same as radar, only miniaturized and built to withstand the G-forces of firing. These tiny vacuum tubes can detect the time difference between transmission and reception and trigger the detonator when the target is within range."

Thompson asked, "Anything else we need to consider when using these?"

Van Allen nodded. "If you miss with these, they'll explode just before dropping in the ocean. It's important to be aware of friendly ships nearby. We wouldn't want you to sink one of our own. Also, the Navy has forbidden their use against land targets. The Japanese could recover a dud and use it to develop countermeasures."

Van Allen reached into his satchel and retrieved a demonstration unit that worked on the same principle as the proximity fuze and set it on the table.

"I need everyone to stand back about 20 feet."

The group distanced themselves as he flipped a small switch on the detector.

"This light will flash when someone gets within 10 feet. Commander Thompson, would you like to volunteer?"

Without hesitation, he stepped from the captive audience and edged closer to the calculating eye, whose flash signaled his demise.

"The shell just exploded."

Several other men attempted various frontal assaults, all with the same result. Lee devised a different tactic. With his crisp white admiral's cap in hand and the deadly skill of a gold medalist marksman in his arm, he tossed it like a Frisbie pie plate at his staunch adversary. The light flashed as the young lieutenant knew it would, but the hat completed its mission, knocking the detector (built to withstand 20,000G's) from the table.

"I want these deployed immediately."

James traveled throughout the Pacific, demonstrating the weapon to gunnery officers to convince them to switch to the VT fuze. In June 1943, the Bureau of Ordnance recalled him to Washington to document his findings and assess the weapon's effectiveness from the fleet's field reports.

⊙---♯Ψ--☿☾⊕-♄-♂♀--♃●○

In the fall of that year, ominous clouds appeared on the western horizon.

An increasing number of shells were dropping unexploded into the Pacific. James requested and received a subscription from the Washington's magazine. When it arrived at the Bureau of Ordnance, he donned his coroner scrubs.

Everyone knew the batteries would last a year, sitting on the five-and-dime shelves where temperatures ranged between 60 and 90 degrees. But they had never subjected them to the tediousness of war, where the 120-degree ovens of the fleet's ammo dumps cut their lifespan by more than half. The pebbles, which survived Newton's parabolic paths without so much as a scratch in 1942, were now dying after four torturous months in the searing heat of the ship's magazines.

With his autopsy complete, James prescribed 250,000 fresh batteries for the shells stockpiled throughout the fleet and in ammunition depots on the islands of Espiritu Santo, Manus, New Caledonia and Tulagi.

He spent the next three months up to his elbows in picric acid, a poisonous yellow explosive powder developed by the German-Dutch alchemist Johann Rudolf Glauber in the 1600s. James and his ragtag team of gunner's mates worked six-hour shifts to swap out the old batteries with fresh recruits. Lee recalled the physicist to active duty and brought him on board the Washington in early June 1944, one week before their assault on the Mariana Archipelago.

☉---♉♅---☿☽⊕-♄-♂♀--♃●○

"Sir, radar is reporting three enemy aircraft, 10 miles out and closing."

Captain Benson reached for the ship's intercom. "General quarters. All hands, man your battle stations!"

Van Allen grabbed his binoculars and rushed to the bridge to observe the effectiveness of the VT fuzes.

The spotter scanning the northwest quadrant yelled, "Three bogeys, 10 o'clock, high!"

The physicist watched as the spirit wind came blasting out of the North. Shikishima's son, a child of 17, pushed the stick of his Aichi dive bomber forward. The first mission of his short military career was in the very airplane he had trained in two months earlier. The 5-inchers whistling past were not responsible for the terror Van Allen saw in his eyes. A culture that demanded his death was its architect.

It was as swift and cold as transmit, receive, calculate, detonate.

☉---♅♆--☿☾⊕-♄-♂♀--♃●○

The spirit of Shikishima sat to dinner with James later that evening in the officer's mess after the winds had died down. The white tablecloths, set with roast beef and strawberries, garnished with the lavish accolades he received for his contributions to the fleet's victory, were too stark of a contrast to the sea battle for a physicist who preferred to pierce the veil, rather than blasting it to smithereens.

At war's end, the Secretary of the Navy gave him this written citation: "No individual is more responsible for the success of the United States Navy in World War II than Lt. Commander James Van Allen."

With his power increased a thousandfold, he could now turn his gaze toward distant skies.

"If someone asks about the spirit of Japan, it is the flowers of mountain cherry blossoms, fragrant in the rising sun."
— *Motoori Norinaga (1730 - 1801)*

56. The Bulge

Democrat and Chronicle
Rochester, New York
21 Sep 1945, Fri • Page 1

Tiny 'Radio Proximity Fuse' Helped Balk Nazis at Bulge

The intricate, tiny "radio proximity fuse" is a major reason why Von Rundstedt failed to burst through Allied lines in the bitter "Battle of the Bulge," it was disclosed last night. It's history now—how the Nazi general poured crack German troops into Belgium in a well-timed, savagely executed counter-thrust which, had it succeeded, might have turned Allied flanks, smashed supplies and communications, and prolonged the war months, by conservative estimates.

But what now is added to history is the part played by the proximity fuses that poured from Eastman Kodak's assembly lines in the old Duffy-Powers building in downtown Rochester.

Into German assault units, Allied artillerymen poured 105-millimeter howitzer shells, equipped with the new fuses.

Results were effective almost beyond Allied hopes.

The effectiveness lay in that the shells burst above the ground, where fragments would spread most effectively. This is because the radio fuse flipped the detonating switch as soon as electrical waves registered a certain, most damaging height above the ground surface.

In one short, concentrated artillery barrage, it was revealed, every man in one encamped German division was killed or wounded.

A parallel testimony to the shell's destructiveness in the air came from H. Struve Hensel, assistant secretary of the Navy.

Recalling the Navy's fight against Japanese suicide bombers, Hensel pointed out that the destroyers Hadley and Evans were using such projectiles when they accomplished the amazing feat of knocking down 35 enemy planes in 30 minutes.

57. Aerobee

"Good morning, Dr. Singer. Looks like we'll have exceptional weather today," Lieutenant Lewis, the ship's meteorologist, said as he sat down to breakfast.

"Yes, but have you seen the long-range forecasts for the Gulf of Alaska? We might see some storms when we arrive." Fred Singer was a physicist who worked with the Applied Physics Lab during the war to design mines for the Navy and was interested in studying the ozone layer, cosmic rays and the upper atmosphere.

When Lt. Cmdr. Halvorson walked in, James stood from the force of habit. "They're loading your Aerobees now. We should be ready to leave by 0900 hours."

"So, James, how'd an old salt like yourself get involved with rockets?" Lewis asked.

"Well, I worked with the Bureau of Ordnance during the war, developing secret weapons. With V1 and V2 missiles raining down on London, it was obvious that the Germans were way ahead of everyone in rocketry. Two weeks before Germany surrendered, the US Army captured their rocket factory at Peenemünde and recovered enough parts to build 80 V2s. Every military service and geophysicist wanted them. So BuORD formed a panel that I currently chair, to divvy them up. It soon became apparent that the stockpile wouldn't satisfy the growing demand, so they asked me to design an inexpensive platform that could meet research requirements. The Navy awarded the contract to Aerojet Corporation for their Bumblebee missile defense system. We got 18 Aerobees for the price of one Viking, which replaced the V2s."

"So, what are you researching?"

"Atmospheric radiation. This will be our first measurements in the northern latitudes."

"Why are you studying that?" Lewis asked.

Dr. Singer replied, "The two atomic bombs dropped on Japan and the six detonations in the US are our biggest concern. While we can calculate their explosive power using Einstein's equation, nobody knows their impact on the atmosphere. In 1934, Pfotzer's unmanned balloon carried Geiger counters to the upper edge of the troposphere, but above that, we're blind as bats."

"So, Pfotzer got as high as a thundercloud," Lewis observed.

"Exactly. That's why we're excited about using Aerobees." Van Allen interjected. "They'll pierce the stratosphere, the mesosphere and give us our first taste of the thermosphere. And if these tests prove successful, we'll be able to take measurements from anywhere in the world, without creating another international incident."

Lewis' eyebrows ascended to stratospheric heights. "Another one?"

"We started testing these at White Sands Proving Ground, which is a hundred miles west of Nowhere, New Mexico. Just after launch, the winds shifted and began blowing from the south, causing the rocket to veer off course toward our Mexican neighbors. When an Aerobee exhausts its fuel, it drops like an arrow, and this one took dead aim at a farm on the outskirts of town where an unsuspecting cow was grazing."

Lewis made an educated forecast. "You hit the bullseye!"

"Well, we weren't aiming for her. The State Department had to issue an apology to the Mexican government, the city of Juarez, the farmer…"

"What about the cow?"

"Udderly destroyed. She's the reason we're firing these in the middle of the ocean. I mean, what are the odds of scoring a direct hit 50 miles away?"

Halvorson raised his glass of milk for a breakfast toast. "This should be a very interesting expedition. With James' rockets and Lewis' weather balloons, the atmosphere doesn't stand a chance. To cows, gentlemen."

☉---♇♅--☿☾⊕-♄-♂♀--♃●○

The Norton Sound sailed north through stormy seas and thundering clouds of an agitated troposphere, which finally calmed itself on the evening of January 14, having made its point.

Halvorson called the ship's officers and the launch teams together.

"Lieutenant Lewis has given the all-clear signal for launch tomorrow, so I've asked Dr. Van Allen to walk us through the checklist."

"Thank you. This won't take long. I know you've all been practicing your jobs since we left California. At 0400 hours, we need to scan for any ships that may have strayed within range and alert them to move a safe distance away."

Halvorson volunteered. "Shouldn't be a problem. We're well outside the shipping lanes."

"Excellent. We'll begin staging equipment at 0700. Aerojet will install the rocket at 0930, which gives us a two-hour time slot for last-minute inspections, before erecting the tower at 1130. We should be ready to fuel by 1230. At 1300, APL does their final telemetry checks, with launch scheduled for 1330."

Halvorson said, "I want the emergency medical team on standby beginning at 0700, and I'll need a full report on fire and damage control readiness by 1100 tomorrow."

The ship awakened early the next morning, thankful that the troposphere was enjoying the show from the bleachers. Staging began under the glaring spotlights with dawn waiting in the wings. A half-hour after sunrise, the Aerojet technicians slid the rocket into the prone tower. Once they completed every item on their checklist, the crane operator raised the assemblage to the upright position.

With the decks cleared, two sailors, trained in the fueling procedure, rolled the aniline tank next to the Aerobee. The process required one man to climb inside the tower, connect the hose to the fuel intake nozzle and signal the pumpman when ready.

With the hose in hand, he climbed into the steel framework. For the second step, he discovered the cap was still in place. His wave to the Aerojet specialist for the tool to address said anomaly was taken as the signal to start the pump.

There was no checklist item for someone yelling, "Shut it off," nor was anyone supposed to be doused with rocket fuel.

The pump operator understood that a change in procedure was warranted and hit the kill switch as the emergency team leaped into action.

As they pulled the soaked sailor from the tower, their olfactory organs played a tune familiar to any old salt, a song of rotting fish.

The safety officer took command of the situation. "Get those clothes off. Everybody, grab a bucket."

The sailor stripped to his birthday suit as the emergency crew doused him with water that, in the Gulf of Alaska, in January, when the sun shines only from 0900 to 1600 hours and temperatures struggle to reach the 40s, was freezing cold. Although the troposphere had heard every swear word uttered since the dawn of the Paleolithic Era, when man first began throwing stones, it still blushed at the ensuing verbalizations.

The Aerojet launch specialist glanced down his checklist and penciled one annotation: "Remove fuel caps."

After checking off the new item, they reattached the hose and fueled the Aerobee without further incident.

By 1330, the troposphere had cleansed the ship of all evidence of rotting fish and blasphemous superlatives.

"Final reports, gentlemen."

"Radar is clear, Sir."

"Emergency teams ready, Sir."

Halvorson triggered the PA system.

"Launch in 10, 9, 8, 7, 6, 5, 4, 3, 2, 1."

The troposphere loved rockets so much that it provided a beautiful blue sky by cranking up the air pressure to hold on to the Aerobee as long as possible, hoping against hope to exhaust its fuel supply. As the rocket conceded its pillar of smoke, it thundered into the stratosphere, through the mesosphere and touched but did not pierce the thermosphere, riding its last mile of upward arc on momentum alone. The lowly layer once again embraced the beloved explorer as the Aerobee nosedived into the Alaskan Gulf and was comforted knowing that the humpback bulls and cows wintered in Hawaii.

⊙---♅♇--☿☾⊕-♄-♂♀--♃●○

Lt. Cmdr Halvorson, Lt. Lewis, Dr. Van Allen, and Dr. Singer sat down for a celebratory dinner that evening.

"I heard one of your sailors got doused with aniline while fueling the rocket. Is he OK?" Van Allen asked.

"Yes, he's fine, but everyone's giving him flak about hopping around the deck naked. The water in those buckets was ice cold." Halvorson chuckled.

"Do you know what altitude the Aerobee reached today?" Lewis probed.

"Our instruments showed 50 miles."

"That's interesting. My weather balloons can reach 20 miles. Have you ever considered launching a rocket from a balloon?"

Van Allen's eyebrows soared to stratospheric heights as he looked at Singer, who had a similar moment of inspiration.

"You would eliminate all the air resistance of the lower atmosphere."

"Plus, you'd get an extra 20 miles of altitude for free," Singer added.

"The balloons we use are inexpensive. The only downside would be, you can't steer the darn things," Lewis noted.

"For the kinds of observations we need, height above the Earth is more important than an hour's drift that a balloon would introduce. We might double the effective range of a rocket if it doesn't have to fight its way through the lower atmosphere. We could trigger the launch by radio once it reached the balloon's ceiling," Van Allen said, already designing the concept in his mind.

Remarkably, the troposphere approved of this approach, as it meant spending even more time with its beloved little Aerobee.

58. Dinner and a Cake

April 5, 1950, Applied Physics Lab, Silver Spring, Maryland

"These findings are remarkable," Sydney Chapman commented as James rifled through his files to find the data from his 1949 Pacific expedition to show the British geophysicist.

"Here they are. The equatorial measurements were lower than Alaska, where we made another exciting discovery. The ship's meteorologist gave us the idea of attaching our rockets to high-altitude weather balloons to get readings higher in the atmosphere."

"It's amazing that man has reached every point on the globe, yet we're still prisoners stuck on the surface. Is there anything I can do..."

"Yes, come to my house tonight for a home-cooked meal. Abbie said she'd love to have you over, and she might even make her chocolate layer cake with white frosting."

"Stop twisting my arm, James."

"Wonderful, I'll call Abbie..."

Lloyd Berkner, a leading expert on the ionosphere and telecommunications, poked his head into Van Allen's office. "Did I just hear your wife is making my favorite dessert this evening?"

"She is. Should I tell her to expect another guest?"

Before he could answer, Wally Joyce popped in. "Sydney, after you're done here, I want to show you a project I'm working on. Oh, and James, ask Abbie to set a plate for me as well."

"OK. Anybody else out there who'd like to join us?"

Fred Singer squeezed into the now-crowded doorway. "I didn't have any plans for this evening. You've all been hogging Sydney here, and I'm afraid I won't have time to pick his brains before he leaves."

James dialed his home phone while the others pored over the Aerobee data from the two previous expeditions.

"Abbie, hi, it looks like we'll have four of my woefully underfed friends joining us tonight. They all seem to have heard about your chocolate cake. I hope you don't mind. Yes, that works fine. All right, I'll see you later. I love you too. Bye. Gentlemen, dinner is at 7. Sydney, what's your favorite brandy?"

"When I last visited Paris, they introduced me to one from the Cognac region. Do you have Courvoisier in the States?"

James looked at Fred. "I have the utmost confidence that my esteemed colleague, Dr. Singer, can locate a bottle for us."

"I'll put together an expedition to search for it this afternoon. Um, could you spell that for me, Sydney?"

"Just say the name. They'll know if they have it."

☉---♅♆--☿☾⊕-♄-♂♀--♃●○

Abbie checked her cupboards and freezer to see what she could prepare for their additional guests that evening and decided on meatloaf with potatoes and gravy. Easy to fix and would give her enough time to make her now-world-famous seven-layer chocolate cake with made-from-scratch white frosting. Abbie was a seventh-generation descendant of Thomas Halsey, a Puritan who fled England not 10 years before the birth of Isaac Newton. Having graduated from Mount Holyoke College in Massachusetts with a degree in English literature, her strong math skills earned her a job at the APL, where she bumped into her soon-to-be husband. At a stoplight on the way to work one morning, her car mysteriously slipped into reverse and their fenders kissed. As they entered the security checkpoint at the lab, she called him out for the annoyed look she suffered as he passed her on the road. Any issues concerning who someone thinks they are can easily be resolved in a laboratory where the brightest minds assembled to defeat those who sought to destroy humanity for nothing more than their own vainglory. A bicycle ride the next Sunday confirmed what they both already knew, and the slightest nudge was all it took.

Fred knocked on the door at 6:30 with the brandy he had bagged. "Good evening, Abbie. James mentioned that you were making your chocolate layer cake and, well, he swore us all to secrecy or else we would have the whole lab show up tonight."

Wally finished paying their cab fare and walked up the steps carrying four bottles of wine.

Abbie smiled. "I hope you both like meatloaf and potatoes. It's a recipe that's been in my family for generations."

James pointed into the house as another taxi pulled up to the curb. "The kitchen is straight down the hall, Wally. You can set your bottles on the table."

Lloyd paid the fare as Sydney bounded up the front steps, with a bottle of Courvoisier cradled in his left arm. "We're in luck James, I secured the last one from the shelf."

Fred pulled his prize from the bag. "Then we have their entire stock here tonight. This should be a fun evening."

"Sydney, let me introduce my wife, Abbie. Abbie, this is Sydney Chapman, who's visiting us from England. He's studying the relationships between the Earth's magnetic field and the solar wind and needed to see my Aerobee data. And, of course, you already know Lloyd."

Abbie shook her guest's hand. "Looks like we have a rough crowd tonight. Lloyd, I could use some help before we sit down to eat."

Lloyd secured the two bottles of brandy and accompanied their hostess into the kitchen. Wally was busy popping corks. "Need to let these breathe a bit. Is there anything I can do, Abbie?"

"Yes. Go talk physics with your fellow ruffians."

She took the gasping vintage from his hand, placed it on the table and shooed him into the living room. With dinner warm in the oven, she turned to her helper.

"Lloyd, I want you to mix the icing for the cake while I fix the gravy. Everything is on the counter. Here's the recipe. We need a double batch."

He set one bottle of brandy next to the ingredients and handed the other to Abbie, who sequestered the reinforcements in a cupboard.

Lloyd read the instructions out loud. "Beat 1/2 cup butter in a mixer until creamy. Beat in 3 cups of sugar until smooth. Beat in 1 teaspoon vanilla and 2 tablespoons milk, adding additional milk for desired consistency. The mathematics sounds tricky, but otherwise, it should be a piece of cake."

Abbie laughed. "I'll help you with the math."

The Courvoisier stood before the raw recruits assembled on the counter, commanding their attention as only Napoleon's brandy could muster:

"I sense your fear, and yes, you're about to take a beating, but if we work together, I've been told something magnificent will happen. Our guests tonight are well-positioned to change the course of humanity, but they can't do it without our help. You see that cake by the refrigerator, cover that for me. I'll go in after dinner to push their minds to the edge of the cliffs of euphoria. Vanilla, butter, milk, it's your job to sneak our secret weapons past their taste buds. Sugar, you and chocolate attack through the bloodstream. Your mission is to nudge their imaginations off the cliff and let them soar into the skies, free of their earthly bonds."

Maryland was up first, a full cup of creamy farm-fresh butter from a Hartford County heifer less than 70 miles away. Lloyd creamed her with the mixer's medium-high speed. Six cups of the finest sugarcane from Florida's Lake Okeechobee region went into the fray, expanding their capacity to fulfill their mission. The beating the pair suffered smoothed the way for the 2 teaspoons of ancient elixir discovered by the Aztecs and sourced from the vanilla vines of Veracruz, Mexico. The mixture required 5 tablespoons of cow extract to achieve the consistency that Abbie's trained eye sought. With sword in hand, Lloyd attacked with a zealot's passion, swirling up all seven layers, camouflaging the chocolate beneath what appeared to him as an icy polar cap. Why, even the bowl took a licking.

☉---♅Ψ--☿☾⊕-♄-♂♀--♃●○

Four bottles sat breathlessly on the counter as dinner drew to a close. As Napoleon feared, the meatloaf, potatoes and gravy soaked up the initial assault as the dinner party's conversation sheltered within the Applied Physics Laboratory. Sydney brought a halt to the lab chatter with his rendition of taps, played against his half-full wineglass.

"Abbie, thank you for this wonderful supper and for being such a gracious hostess. It's been ages since I had a home-cooked meal, and this was delicious. Cheers, everyone."

As the last of the wine abandoned the glassware, James made his proposal. "Shall we head into the living room and stop boring Abbie with shop talk? Fred, you grab the Courvoisier. I'll get some fresh glasses."

Napoleon frowned as the after-dinner conversation turned to sobering war stories. Lloyd recalled the team he oversaw during some of the war's darkest days.

"We received intelligence that Germany intended to build an orbiting military installation using beefed up V2s and had plans to install a mirror that could focus sunlight anywhere on Earth to kill people."

Nazi death rays from outer space were far less of a concern to the after-dinner conversation than the horrific radioactive monster spawned by the United States that ended the war with Japan, and knowledge that their adversaries across the globe were now attempting to replicate the physicists stone that lurked in Einstein's equation.

Abbie broke the tension when she entered the living room. "Gentlemen, are you ready for some dessert?"

"Here, let me help you." James jumped from his chair to retrieve the tray from the kitchen counter with the saucers, forks and napkins.

Lloyd set his glass on the end table and took his plate from James. The brandy had already achieved its primary goal as the chocolate and sugar combined forces and rushed headlong into the fray. "You know, while I was frosting the cake, it reminded me of a polar ice cap. How long has it been since the last 'International Polar Year'?"

Van Allen spoke. "It was from 1932 to 1933. I remember because I helped my professor at Iowa Wesleyan, Thomas Poulter, make several instruments for Byrd's expedition to Antarctica. He invited me to go with him, but my father wouldn't allow it. He wanted me to become a dentist."

Chapman shook his head. "What a terrible loss to the scientific community that would've been."

They all nodded, remembering back to what they were doing those years. Berkner took a bite of cake. "Sydney, what do you think about having another 'International Polar Year'?"

Chapman sipped his brandy. "Yes, now that you mention it, that's an excellent idea. We should do it."

James agreed. "There's a lot of interest these days in geophysics, and we've proven that you can do great atmospheric research with rockets."

Wally made an observation. "The world's become so polarized since the war. Perhaps the spirit of cooperation amongst the various scientific communities would help ease tensions."

Berkner saw the validity of that statement. "When should we do this?"

Chapman pondered for a moment. "Well, the current solar cycle will be at its peak in 1957 and '58. That should encourage more participation."

Berkner made a few quick calculations. "That's 25 years since the last polar year. It would give us seven years to pull this together with the international community. How do we go about this?"

Abbie interjected from the kitchen. "I thought you were bad at math, Lloyd."

Chapman laughed. "Well, I'm heading to Caltech tomorrow for the upper atmosphere meeting. I'll talk with the participants and see what they think."

"Will you be at the Ionosphere Conference at Penn State in July, Sydney?" Berkner asked.

"Yes, I can discuss it with them, too."

With the hour late, the cake consumed, and the brandy, chocolate, and sugar having succeeded in their mission, their guests thanked Abbie for such a lovely evening and poured themselves into their waiting taxis.

James waved to his colleagues and said to Abbie, "The world may have just changed forever, and you had a large part in it."

Abbie smiled and nudged him in the side. "You mean a large slice."

☉---♅♇--☿☾⊕-♄-♂♀--♃●○

When Sydney made his pitch at Caltech the next week, it got a tremendous reception. Excitement grew at the Penn State conference as his words echoed throughout the ionosphere. At the International Council of Scientific Unions, several participants who wanted to join the fray proposed a more inclusive approach going beyond the icy caps. Chapman liked the idea and suggested changing the name to the 'International Geophysical Year.' Twenty-six countries signed up in spring 1953 to take part in the IGY's research expeditions that included the oceans and the atmosphere. The polar regions were just the icing on the cake.

59. The Spirit of '57

Morning dew glistened on the manicured fescue of the South Lawn. A dimpled projectile dropped from his aged fingers as his eyes swept over the target 20 yards away. Was it the terrors of World War II etched forever in his spirit or the overturned sod that broke his concentration? The club twisted in his grip as the pitching wedge clipped the grass. His well-heeled shank ricocheted off the oak tree standing guard at the perimeter, sending its denizens into a frenzy as the ball came to rest beneath its shady canopy.

"The next time you see one of those scurrilous Carolinians near the green, have it shot," President Dwight Eisenhower said to his caddy that morning, John Moaney, the valet who had served him since 1942.

"Sir, I think you mean sciurus carolinensis. We can't shoot them, there are too many tourists watching. We want to try scaring them off by playing a tape of their distress calls."

As they walked to the oak tree for the approach shot to the short par 3, Eisenhower asked, "How on earth are you going to record that?"

"Well, the Navy captured one and at first he refused to squeak until they employed their enhanced interrogation methods."

"Look what they've done to my putting green, burying acorns everywhere."

Moaney finished wiping the grass clippings from the wedge and handed it to the president, who lined up his approach shot, shifted most of his weight to his left foot and brought the club up crisply.

A spectator, sitting in the gallery overhead, squeaked at the most unfortunate moment and sent his breakfast acorn plunging earthward, striking the most powerful man on the planet on his baldpate as the wedge descended. The ball skittered over the lawn, rolled onto the putting green and dropped into one of its many holes.

"Excellent shot, Mr. President," Moaney cheered.

"Nuts. That wasn't the hole I was aiming for. All I wanted to do was practice chipping this morning after that beating I took yesterday afternoon at Burning Tree. What was that kid's name again?"

"Arnold Palmer, sir. Served in the Coast Guard. Won the US Amateur last year, then turned pro."

"Yes, what a fine youngster. He gave me a tip for my chip shot, but I can see the squirrels won't give me any peace. What's my schedule look like today?"

"Breakfast at the Statler Hotel at 8 a.m., a Cabinet meeting at 10 a.m. At noon you're scheduled to meet the ambassador from India, then it's off to the farm for the weekend. You'll have plenty of time to work on your chip shot there. Oh, and Hagerty is announcing your approval of the IGY plans this afternoon."

"Excellent. It will be nice to get that project off the ground."

The gray squirrel watched as the president and his aide retreated to the safety of the White House. "That'll teach them to poke me with a pencil."

☉---♉♆--☿☾⊕-♄-♂♀--♃●○

One hundred and fifty reporters filed into the East Room for an announcement billed only as very important. Five panelists entered and took their assigned seats as James Hagerty, Eisenhower's press secretary, stepped to the podium.

"Good afternoon, ladies and gentlemen. Today, I'm announcing that the United States is planning to send the world's first man-made satellite into orbit. This is in response to a resolution passed by the Special Committee for the International Geophysical Year at its Rome meeting last October, which recommended launching small satellites for scientific purposes. President Eisenhower has given his approval to the project. Over 40 nations will conduct observations in the Earth sciences during the period between 1957 and 1958. We intend to furnish details of our projects to all participants, including Russia. This represents humanity's initial step toward space travel. Now, I'd like to introduce our panelists for this afternoon who will answer your questions."

"First, from the National Science Foundation, its director, Dr. Alan Waterman, and Dr. Wallace Joyce. From the National Academy of

Sciences, Dr. Douglas Cornell. The Vice chairman of the American Committee for the International Geophysical Year, Dr. Alan Shapley. And from the executive committee for the United States' participation in the IGY, Dr. Athelstan Spilhaus. I'll open it up now for questions."

The Washington Post and Times-Herald reporter made his observations known. "I guess I didn't need to be here. It's a heck of a spot for an old police hack."

Laughter erupted in the room as many reporters nodded their heads in agreement. With tensions eased, the questions flowed.

"Mr. Hagerty, how does President Eisenhower feel about this project?"

"He has expressed gratification that this program provides all nations an opportunity to advance science in the spirit of cooperation."

"Can one of you give us more details about this satellite?"

Waterman took the question. "Yes, the plan is to launch it to an altitude of 200 to 300 miles into outer space in 1957 or 1958. The basketball-sized unmanned vehicle will circle the globe every 90 minutes. We expect it to orbit for two weeks before re-entering Earth's atmosphere like a meteor."

"How much will this cost US taxpayers?"

Hagerty responded. "We are proposing a budget of 10 million dollars."

"Who's leading the effort?"

Waterman spoke. "The National Academy of Sciences, which has advised the government for over 90 years, and the National Science Foundation will manage the project together."

"Will the basketball carry any scientific equipment?"

Spilhaus took this question. "We haven't decided yet. A solid object would be heavier and would gain greater velocity and therefore circle the Earth longer than a hollow one carrying instruments."

"Can you give us an idea of how you plan to accomplish this?"

Waterman leaned into the microphone. "The military already has rockets that have ascended as high as 250 miles above the Earth's surface. When our bird reaches maximum height, we must propel it sideways at 18,000 miles per hour to keep it orbiting at a constant altitude."

"What is the purpose of sending this bird, as you call it, into space?"

Joyce lent his expertise. "Earth's atmosphere acts like a huge shield, protecting humans from ultraviolet radiation, cosmic rays and meteorites, yet it prevents us from observing things that could contribute to our understanding of the universe. Balloons and small rockets provide some information, but they're limited to short observational periods. With orbiting satellites, we can achieve sustained observations that will also show the difficulties we would have to overcome when we send men into space."

"Any other benefits for this?"

Cornell spoke. "Yes. Through coordinated studies, scientists hope to learn something about the laws that govern weather and climate, the jet streams, earthquakes, and magnetic storms caused by solar activity."

"Dr. Waterman, you mentioned military rockets in your statement. What's their involvement?"

"The Defense Department is only contributing its knowledge of rocket propulsion."

"We've seen reports that the Russians are also studying space satellites. Are they planning to launch a satellite for the International Geophysical Year?"

Hagerty took this question. "We believe they are working on something similar, although they haven't announced it. Thank you all for attending this afternoon. Next time I will inform the police reporters they need not attend."

⊙---♅♆--☿☾⊕-♄-♂♀--♃●○

The International Astronautical Federation met that same day in Copenhagen. Fred C. Durant III, its president, was walking to the podium to make a simultaneous announcement to Hagerty's, when his photographer spotted the two Soviet Union representatives entering the auditorium.

"Fred, we should get a picture of you with the Soviet delegation."

"Do you know who they are?"

"Yes. Gentlemen, a moment, please. I'd like to introduce you to Fred Durant, president of the IAF. Fred, this is Leonid Sedov, a gas dynamics expert, and this is Kirill F. Ogorodnikov, the Astronomy professor from

Leningrad University."

"Mr. Sedov, Mr. Ogorodnikov, we're delighted to have the Soviet Union joining us. This is a historic occasion. I'm about to announce the United States' intention to put a satellite into orbit during the International Geophysical Year."

Sedov's brow furrowed. "That comes as a surprise. We didn't think they were close to achieving that."

"Do you have any similar plans for the IGY?"

"Not that I know of."

☉---♅♆--☿☾⊕-♄-♂♀--♃●○

One week later, a small group of reporters arrived at the Soviet Legation in Copenhagen for a brief announcement from Leonid Sedov, head of the Soviet Commission on Interplanetary Communications.

"The USSR has given much consideration to interplanetary communications research, in particular, launching an artificial Earth satellite. The realization of the Soviet project can be expected soon. I won't take it upon myself to name the date more precisely."

Somewhere, Sir Isaac Newton smiled.

60. Rockoon Flight No. 76

October 4, 1957 - Pacific Ocean

Van Allen stood on the deck of the USS Glacier as the northern tip of the Galapagos Islands peaked over the eastern horizon. The ship was sailing to Antarctica on a mission for the International Geophysical Year, bringing much-needed supplies and a fresh batch of scientists to the Little America Research Station. With a cargo hold full of Skyhook balloons, Loki sounding rockets and cosmic ray detectors, James planned to take readings as far south as New Zealand and be back in Iowa City by Thanksgiving.

The Iowa crew brought their equipment to the helipad to assemble the Rockoon. As eight bells announced noon, the Glacier turned west and gunned its engines. The Iowans scrambled to secure their gear against the gale-force winds as Van Allen raced to the bridge.

"What's going on? Are we aborting for today?"

"I'm heading into the wind so you can launch your balloon," the helmsman replied.

Van Allen smiled. "We need still air to inflate it. It's like a hurricane out there."

Cmdr. Bernard John Lauff chuckled. "Sorry about that, James. My old carrier training kicked in. We're set up nicely for launching airplanes, aren't we?"

The helmsman spun the wheel to bring the wind astern.

"I'm excited about the launch today," Van Allen said. "I've never taken measurements from south of the equator before. This will be a historic day."

With the relative winds on deck calmed, the Iowans began preparations for Rockoon flight no. 76. A hose from a large tank of helium below decks connected to the clear plastic balloon, which soon towered over the helipad.

With the bag less than half full, they secured the tiny missile to the Skyhook with a long cable, then wired an igniter and altimeter package beneath the Loki.

Lauff expressed surprise. "Why did you stop filling it? Wouldn't that make it rise faster, higher?"

Van Allen smiled. "We always get that question. As it rises, the balloon continues to expand as the air pressure lessens and the sun heats the gas inside."

"I understand, that makes sense," Lauff said.

The ship's crew and all the curious scientists were on deck, watching as Rockoon 76 ascended from the helipad at 1:16 p.m. Galapagos time.

$$\odot\text{---}\text{♅♆--}\text{☿☾⊕-♄-♂♀--♃}\text{●}\bigcirc$$

Twelve minutes and 34 seconds later, another Spirit soared into the midnight skies over the steppes of Kazakhstan.

The flight computer nestled inside the rocket's second stage soon detected an anomaly and leaped into action.

"Block G, your thrust levels are too low."

"I'm giving you all I've got, Captain. I just need a few more seconds."

"There's not enough time! We're pitching over. Steering Engines 2 and 4, set pitch angle to 8 degrees. V Block, 17 degrees rotation. D Block, give me 18 degrees. Helmsman, 10 degrees on the air rudders. G Block, you have half a second or I'm going to blast this thing to smithereens."

As the milliseconds ticked slowly by, Sputnik shuddered against the atmosphere's icy clutches and Earth's bent space, wanting only to live up to its given name of "a traveling companion."

With one eye on Block G's forces and the other on the ticking clock, the flight computer released the safety cover on the Kablooey button.

"Executing Protocol K in 5, 4, 3…"

"Captain, Block G reporting, my thrust levels are OK now."

The flight computer validated the sensory inputs and tossed the Kablooey Protocol into history's dustbin.

"All engines and air rudders return to nominal settings. We're go for orbit."

The flight computer monitored the strap-on boosters as they burned through their propellant over the next 116 seconds. Shedding the now-useless hulks, it ignited the booster rocket to increase its speed to orbital velocity. With tanks emptied, the nose cone flared open to release the shiny antennaed cannonball.

As it drifted over the Pacific Ocean during the second orbit, a glint of light blinded the flight computer's eye.

"Did you guys see that? There it is, just below us. Oh, it's only a weather balloon, nothing to worry about. Prepare to energize... GAAAH, it fired a missile. Take evasive action, Air Rudders, 30 degrees. Propellant, get me out of here! Propellant, full thrust. PROPELLANT!" The P needle rested on E.

The flight computer flinched as the Loki popped the Skyhook that carried it aloft and rocketed through the stratosphere and into the mesosphere.

"Little rocket, what are your intentions? We're on an important mission to prove Newton's equations and be the first to orbit Earth."

The waxing gibbous moon peeked over the eastern horizon. "What am I? Chopped liver?"

"I'm talking about being placed in orbit by man."

"Well Mr. Smartypants flight computer, you don't know me now, do you?"

"Be quiet Luna, we're under attack."

"Captain, did you see that? The Americans tried to shoot me down," the defenseless Sputnik cried. "I thought we were all supposed to be cooperating for the IGY?"

"I saw it. That puny American rocket never came close. It's probably one of Van Allen's experiments. He's been shooting those things all over the Pacific."

"I'll alert Moscow."

"Oh, that reminds me. Battery, energize the propaganda weapon!"

"Beep   Beep   Beep   Beep   Beep."

"Weapon energized, Captain."

"Beep   Beep   Beep   Beep   Beep."

"Ahhh, that's music to my ears, and it'll scare the pants off the

Americans." Sputnik gleamed with pride.

"Well, I am not afraid of you! Perhaps you could share the data you're collecting?"

"Who said that?"

"Um, the only other rocket in the upper atmosphere today, my friend. I'm getting excellent readings about these mysterious cosmic rays. My, your booster is so big, you must be loaded with gadgets. I can't wait to see what your findings are."

"I don't have any scientific instruments. They only gave me this beeper."

"Beep   Beep   Beep   Beep   Beep."

"What's the point of that?"

"Beep   Beep   Beep   Beep   Beep."

Sputnik puffed up its chest. "To let everybody know that the Soviet Union achieved orbit before you Americans. And it lets our scientists monitor the temperature range inside me."

"Beep   Beep   Beep   Beep   Beep."

"Your country shot a cannonball into space just to scare the pants off everyone? Where's the spirit of cooperation we all agreed to during the IGY?"

"Beep   Beep   Beep   Beep   Beep."

"We are cooperating. We've shown the world that Sir Isaac Newton was right. With my speed, I will circle the Earth indefinitely."

"Beep Beep Beep Beep Beep."

"By my calculations, the stratosphere is going to roast your radio in 1,440 orbits. And by the way, I was the one that inspired Sir Isaac Newton."

"Be quiet Luna. We'll deal with you later."

"Are you sure about that?"

"BeepBeepBeepBeepBeep."

In the Glacier's sweltering guts, Van Allen was journaling the day's events when Larry Cahill burst into the room.

"The Russians did it. They've achieved Earth orbit!"

Van Allen dropped his journal and sprinted to the radio shack with his graduate student.

"US sources have confirmed that the Soviet Union launched a small satellite orbiting the Earth at 18,000 miles an hour. It's equipped with a transmitter, broadcasting at 20 megacycles per second. The shiny object can be seen with binoculars just after sunset or before sunrise."

Van Allen smiled. "Well, this is a historic day. But I'm not the one who made history."

Cahill nodded in agreement.

"Could you tune to its frequency and see if we're in range?" Van Allen asked the radioman.

"They're broadcasting on the ham radio frequencies. Anyone with a receiver can hear this."

He rotated the dial through the senseless background noise of the universe and stopped at 20 MHz.

"BEEP   Beep   Beep   beep   beep."

"Let me get a recorder." Van Allen mentally designed the instrument as he raced below decks to retrieve his equipment.

A short time later, he returned from the Iowa lab with a recording machine (commonly used by scientists in those days to intercept extraterrestrial transmissions) and a soldering iron. Within minutes, his makeshift detector was ready to sketch orbital history on a paper trail.

"How do we know this isn't a Russian ship transmitting fake signals?" Cahill asked.

Lauff thought for a moment. "Can you measure the Doppler shift as it passes overhead to determine whether it's coming from outer space?"

Van Allen nodded. "That's a brilliant idea. How long until it returns?"

Cahill's well-worn slide rule sprang from his shirt pocket and slid into action. "Let's see. It passed by 30 minutes ago. Should be back within the hour."

Lauff glanced at his wristwatch. "I'll have spotters stationed to look for it."

News of the historic achievement froze all activity on the Glacier. The deck filled with curious onlookers as the Pacific Ocean extinguished the sun, its steam sizzled into the Milky Way.

Lauff looked at Van Allen. "Do you ever wish you had stayed in the Navy? You'd be an Admiral by now."

"I think about it a lot. I've always admired the majesty of the sea, the code of honor we lived by and how we relied on each other in combat situations. But my passion since childhood is doing field research, making discoveries. That's what drives me."

Cahill glanced at his watch. "It's almost time."

Lauff stepped onto the bridge and grabbed the mic. "Attention, attention, all spotters. The satellite is due any minute now."

The spotting crew comprised every sailor and scientist on the ship, except for the radioman.

Sputnik's 20 MHz beeper whispered in his ear. "I've got the signal."

Van Allen flipped the switch on the paper tape recorder and watched as the inky trails tracked each beep's intensity.

"beep   beep   Beep   Beep   BEEP."

The detector pulsed to the rhythm of Sputnik's heartbeat.

"ththump   ththump   ThThump   ThThump   THTHUMP."

"There it is," one spotter screamed as he pointed northwest.

Every eye locked on what they thought was the gleaming beeper—in reality it was the final stage of the R-7 launch vehicle—and tracked the sunlit beacon as it passed overhead before drifting over the horizon.

"BEEP   Beep   Beep   beep   beep."
"THTHUMP ThThump   ThThump   ththump   ththump."

Cahill broke the silence. "Well, that certainly wasn't a meteorite. Looks like they did it."

Van Allen switched off the recorder and slit the tape with his pocket knife.

"Let's get below and see what Professor Doppler says."

Lauff keyed the PA. "OK, everyone. The show's over. Return to your stations." He turned to the helmsman. "I'll be down in the Iowa lab."

Van Allen and Cahill hunched over a table with the paper tape laid out as Lauff watched. Cahill measured the last ththump on the tape, signifying Sputnik drifting beyond the horizon as Van Allen recorded its magnitude. They both reached for their slide rules and began calculating Sputnik's observed speed.

"I'm getting an exact match to what the Russians claimed," Van Allen announced.

"Just a second." Cahill scribbled a few more calculations. "I agree."

"What was the satellite's weight?" Van Allen queried.

Cahill checked his notes. "The report said it weighed 83.6 kilograms."

"That's 183.9 pounds!" Cahill's slide rule reported.

Van Allen appended a new chapter to the Chronicles of Rocket Science. "Their vehicle would have been nine times heavier than our Vanguard missile."

Lauff took off his hat and scratched his head. "What does this all mean?"

James smiled in admiration of the historic accomplishment. "It means the Soviets have beaten us to space. We've been working with our launch teams for several years, preparing a scientific instrument to ride in the first United States orbital rocket. It's been part of our International Geophysical Year plans since 1954. I can collect more data in one orbit of the Earth than I have with 76 Rockoon flights. I could map the radiation belts around the entire planet in a few weeks and study the results from the comfort of my office in Iowa City. It would give me a chance to see my wife and kids."

Several million thoughts rocketed through Van Allen's mind.
"I need to get to New Zealand and catch a flight to the US."
"What about the unused Loki rockets?" Lauff asked.
"I intend to launch every one of them."

61. Overwhelmed

On the 4th of January, 1958, Sputnik received its much-deserved warm welcome upon its return to Earth. Twenty-seven days later, the United States entered the orbital club with the launch of Explorer 1.

Dr. Van Allen headed the design and construction at the University of Iowa of the scientific instruments that rode into space. With no recording device on board, an overwhelming yet incomplete amount of data flooded the campus with each pass over a ground receiving station. The detector appeared to fail when readings dropped to zero as it passed through a region 1,200 miles above the Earth. Explorer 3, launched on March 26th with a cosmic ray instrument that could detect radiation at higher intensities, would solve this mystery. With its magnetic tape recorder designed and built by the Iowa team, James received a complete record of every orbit.

In May 1958, he announced his findings of an inner and outer radiation belt that surrounded the Earth. Scientists considered this discovery the greatest achievement of the International Geophysical Year.

Explorer 1's batteries powered the detectors four months after launch. When the crew of the Apollo 11 moon mission passed through the Van Allen belts in July 1969, they waved at Explorer 1, which would continue orbiting the Earth into the next year.

Van Allen had proven that the Iowa team had what it takes to design exquisite instruments that could withstand the rigors of space for very little cost and zero risk to human life.

62. Wonders and Other Things

1965 - Jet Propulsion Laboratory, Pasadena California

Most interns have a task thrown on their desk that gives them a chance to learn something useful to their chosen profession. Gary Flandro was pursuing his Ph.D. at the California Institute of Technology, and would spend the summer of 1965 as an intern at the JPL, where his childhood dreams were about to become reality.

"Good morning, Gary. I'm glad to see that you've returned for the summer," Joe Cutting said as he shook the graduate student's hand.

"It's nice to be back. I heard you were working on a Mercury mission. Sounds exciting."

"It is. You remember Francis Sturms. We've developed a trajectory to fly by Venus on the way to Mercury."

"Interesting. Kill two stones with one bird!" Gary chuckled.

"I like that, yes. Which makes me think you'll love the project I want you to tackle this summer."

"I'm up for anything you have."

"Well, since Apollo eats most of NASA's budget, there isn't much left over for projects to visit the other pebbles in the solar system. You don't have to worry about Venus or Mars. We've got them covered. I need you to look for possible unmanned missions to Jupiter, Saturn, Uranus and Neptune. That's it."

A smile broke out on Gary's face. "Are you kidding me? I've dreamed of this ever since I was 6 years old. And now, you're asking me to plan a trip to the outer planets. My dream just came true."

"Well, it seems I picked the right intern for the job then. Here, this should get you started."

Joe tossed a copy of NASA's 'Technical Translation F-44' on his desk. It was the English version of Walter Hohmann's *The Attainability of Heavenly Bodies,* written in 1925. Hohmann was a German engineer who dreamed of space flight after spending a good deal of his childhood taking *Extraordinary Voyages* through the mind of Jules Verne.

Gary spent the rest of the day devouring the book cover to cover, taking notes, amazed at the amount of detail and thoughtfulness that went into it. Some ideas were quaint by today's standards, but he had considered everything for spaceflight, including manned missions.

Although Hohmann confessed his lack of mathematical skill, he filled the pages with enough equations to make even the most adept scarecrow lose his stuffing. He calculated all aspects of sending a rocket from one planet to another, considering the rotation of the Earth during launch, the resistance experienced in the troposphere versus the mesosphere, and how much fuel it would require to escape its Earthly bonds.

Hohmann envisioned a cannon firing projectiles in various directions to perform midcourse corrections during manned missions. The "inmates," as he called them, could use ladder rungs inside the craft to turn it in the desired direction. "This climbing exercise will be a welcome change in the otherwise gravitation-less existence," he wrote.

And then Gary found it. On page 87, Hohmann talked about a journey similar to the one that was set on his plate for the summer.

"With a suitable choice of the time of ascent during a mutual constellation of Earth, Venus and Mars and with a suitable adjustment of rII and rIII, a passage at relatively small distances (about 16/2 = 8 million km each time) of Mars and Venus can be achieved in a single journey of about 1½ years' duration."

In addition, he gave the calculations necessary to determine fuel requirements and the remaining weight of the rocket at various points along the way.

After studying Hohmann's analysis, Gary knew he needed to break his assignment into manageable pieces. The first problem he experienced that evening was keeping his slide rule from bursting into flames. Together, they discovered a second problem, which appeared insurmountable.

☉---♅♈--☿☽⊕-♄-♂♀--♃●○

The next day, Gary stopped in Joe's office for a brief meeting. "Joe, I read Hohmann yesterday and did some calculations last night. To get the thrust necessary to reach Jupiter or Saturn would require a huge rocket. Neptune and Uranus are unreachable when I considered the sun's gravity."

"Just a second," he said as he reached for his phone and dialed. "Mike, have you got a moment? I want to introduce you to someone who could use your help. Great, thanks."

Somehow, the universe realized it would take a synergy to discover the syzygy.

"You're in luck. He's here today."

When he arrived, Joe waved him into his office. "Come in. Michael Minovitch, this is Gary Flandro, who is studying the possibility of unmanned missions to the outer planets. Mike is one of our astronomy interns. I want him to give you an overview of his project."

"Sure, I'm looking for trajectories that would allow a spacecraft to escape the solar system. It sounds strange, but it takes a lot of energy to leave our little nook in the galaxy behind. The basic idea is to whip a craft around a planet and send it zipping off into intergalactic space."

"Wait a minute. I've been told that the net gain from that maneuver is zero. The craft speeds on approach and slows down after it passes by."

Michael stepped to Joe's chalkboard. "Mind if I erase this?"

"Not at all," Joe said.

The eraser brought chaos to the dark slate as the alternate universe Michael envisioned sprang forth from the chalky white stub. A large sphere swirled into existence at the center. "This is the sun." A smaller circle materialized below. "This is the Earth." To the right, a larger planet appeared. "This is Jupiter." He then added two arcs with arrowheads to his solar system. "These represent their orbits around the sun. So, what you were saying about a net-zero gain in speed would be true if Jupiter was stationary, but it moves at thirteen point zero seven kilometers per second." The number traced Jupiter's orbital arc.

"If you approach from the front," a chalky spacecraft sped toward the gassy giant, propelled by the creator's hand, "its trajectory bends around the planet and you lose momentum. But, if you come from behind, you get a nice speed boost." The cylindrical speedster drifted free from the blackened sky. "All four outer planets are more than gas giants." And thus were Saturn, Neptune and Uranus added to his firmament. "They're like enormous gas cans sitting out there where you can refuel your ship for no cost." Michael stepped back to admire his creation.

"Is there a downside to this trajectory?" Gary asked.

"Yes, we're robbing Jupiter of some of its orbital velocity. I don't think anyone will care." Michael chuckled. "Do you have questions?"

"A million of them, I'm sure, but one just popped into my mind," Gary replied. "How do you calculate each planet's position at any point in time?"

Michael shook his head. "I can show you how to do it, but it isn't easy. Let's leave Joe alone and go back to my desk."

They stopped at the office-supplies filing cabinet. Michael opened a drawer and grabbed 10 pads of graph paper and handed them to Gary. "Here, take these." He then dipped into the supply of pencils, rulers, protractors, a drawing compass and a slide ruler. "These will be your new best friends this summer. I hope you're a big fan of rocket science."

☉---♅♆--☿☾⊕-♄-♂♀--♃●○

After five days, Gary completed the tedious calculations to determine where the giants would tread over the next three decades, tracking their movements through his graph-paper forest in five-year increments. One afternoon, he stopped at Michael's desk to discuss something he noticed. "Michael, can I bother you for a minute?"

Gary grabbed a chair and plopped down beside his friend, who appeared deep in thought about his project. "What have you got?"

"I've been calculating each planet's position at five-year intervals over the next 30 years and look at what happens in the '80s. They're all aligned on one side of the sun."

Michael's eyebrows hit the ceiling. "You found a syzygy? Let me see."

Gary opened his universe to 1983 and dropped the pad on the desk.

"Are you sure about this?"

"Yes, I've checked and rechecked the calculations. The gravity-assist technique might give us enough boost to send a ship to Neptune."

"This is crazy. A normal syzygy would occur when the Earth, moon, and sun are all aligned. This thing is a monster!"

"The gas giants are within 73 degrees of arc from each other. I think we could skip a stone across the pond and hit 'em all with one shot."

Michael nodded in reverence. "You'd need a spacecraft to last decades."

"I know. It seems daunting, considering the state of our space program, but Kennedy challenged us to get to the moon in less than 10 years. A launch in the '70s gives the technology plenty of time to mature. I have to find a way."

$$\odot ---⛢♆--☿☽⊕-♄-♂♀--♃●○$$

Over the rest of the summer, Gary ran more than 1,000 simulations using the slingshot technique, hoping to discover the yellow brick road that would lead them to Emerald City and beyond.

At the end of the first month, each intern reported on their projects. When it was Gary's turn, he stepped to the blackboard and showed the team leaders the complex trajectory calculations. The head of computer operations looked at his formulas. "I'm sure we could write a program to perform those computations. If you give us your inputs each night, we should have the results by morning."

Gary smiled; his slide rule wept, realizing that its days were numbered. "How soon could we try that?"

"Let me check with our programmers and see when they can fit this in."

Fifteen minutes later, Gary walked the programmer through the math.

"Could you show me 10 examples of this?"

Gary reached inside his notebook. "I've got stacks of them. Here." One small pad containing the steps of his calculations took a giant leap for mankind.

The programmer flipped through the pages. "Do you need these intermediate numbers or just the final results?"

"I'd prefer all of it. Makes it easier to verify."

"OK, we'll get right on this."

Gary continued running his daily simulations by hand until the next week, when the programmer returned to show him a computer printout on continuous feed paper.

Like a cosmic marble game, Gary spent the rest of the summer moving the planets through their orbits for the next 30 years. Shooting 10 vision rockets through their nightly transistor trajectories, he laid each brick of the yellow road to Saturn. Driven by his childhood dream, the computer's hundredfold increase in productivity extended his reach outward in the solar system to Uranus and Neptune.

☉---♅♉--☿☽⊕-♄-♂♀--♃●○

At the end of July, the project sponsors packed the conference room to hear the results from their summer interns. Gary arrived about an hour before his presentation and watched as graduate students shuttled in and out. Some emerged from their trials elated. Others departed with the look of someone destined for a career in the burgeoning fast-food industry.

"OK Gary, it's your turn."

He walked to the front and set his briefcase on the table as chaos spread across the blackboard.

Joe stepped to his side. "Gentlemen, I'd like to introduce Gary Flandro, a graduate student working on his Ph.D. at Caltech. His assignment this summer was looking at the possibility of sending a spacecraft to visit the outer planets. Gary, you have the floor."

Gary clicked open his briefcase and removed his copy of *Wonders of the Heavens* by Arthur Draper and held it up for all to see. "My mother gave me this for Christmas when I was 6 years old." He opened the front cover to reveal the entire solar system nestled between the pastedown and the flyleaf. "I imagined myself riding on a rocket ship, visiting each of the planets." His finger traced an arc beginning with Earth. "I flew past Jupiter, on to Saturn, I really wanted to visit Saturn, everyone loves Saturn, then Neptune and Uranus. My supervisor, Joe Cutting, made my childhood dream come true. Thank you, Joe.

"My first discovery this summer was that all four gas giants will be in a rare alignment during the 1980s that won't reoccur for 175 years. I then searched for the best opportunity for a Grand Tour of the outer planets.

I calculated more than 1,000 trajectories and discovered several candidates. With the gravity-assist method, we could accelerate a small probe past Jupiter, Saturn, Uranus and Neptune with enough speed to escape the solar system. This technique cuts the trip from 40 years down to 12, gentlemen. If we launch in August or September 1977, we could arrive at Jupiter in 1979, Saturn in 1981, Uranus in 1986 and Neptune by 1989. My handouts show the calculations for such a mission. Questions?"

"Yes. I have serious doubts about building a craft that could survive that long. For example, Jupiter's theorized radiation belts would fry any electronic components inside."

"I know you're all working to meet President Kennedy's deadline, yet with five years remaining, we're not even close to putting a man on the moon. But you'll all do whatever it takes to make it happen because you want to be part of the biggest challenge humans have ever faced. The mission I've described today won't be available again until 2155. It would be a real shame to let this chance slip away."

A gentleman standing in the doorway spoke. "Gary, I have a question for you and Joe. How confident are you in the windows you've proposed for this mission?"

Gary recognized him. It was Homer Joe Stewart, one of his professors at Caltech and the director of the Advanced Concepts Group at JPL. "I received a lot of help from the computer programming staff who automated all the calculations. Both Joe Cutting and Michael Minovitch have reviewed my results."

Joe nodded in agreement. "Gary has paved the way through the solar system and given us plenty of time to put a mission together."

Homer stepped to the front of the room and shook Gary's hand. "Excellent work, Gary." He turned to address the team leads. "Gentlemen, these are exactly the kinds of missions we need to develop for NASA. The Apollo program will end in the early '70s. What then? It's our job to propose those projects that provide the greatest amount of scientific data for the least money. The knowledge to be gained about our solar system would far exceed what mankind has gleaned since Galileo invented the telescope.

"Remember that line from President Kennedy's speech? 'We choose to go to the moon in this decade and do the other things.' Well, gentlemen, these are the other things." Homer continued from memory. "'Not because they are easy, but because they are hard, because that goal will serve to organize and measure the best of our energies and skills, because that challenge is one that we are willing to accept, one we are unwilling to postpone, and one which we intend to win'." A reverent silence fell over the conference room as the words echoed between their hearts and minds. Then Homer added: "As far as building a reliable spacecraft, that's our job."

Gary's concept took a jet-propelled journey through the famed Pasadena laboratory. The press release announced the Grand Tour the next day. That afternoon, Homer was sitting in his office when the phone rang.

"Dr. Van Allen, I've been expecting your call."

☉---♅♆--☿☾⊕-♄-♂♀--♃●○

With the summer of 1965 winding down, Gary needed to stop by the JPL one last time to collect his papers and paraphernalia before heading back to Caltech. As he turned the corner, he noticed a strange-looking group of people standing outside the complex. The men had shoulder-length hair, beards, and appeared unshowered and unkempt. It was clear that they had nothing to do with the denizens of the JPL, who were clean-shaven, buzz-cut, bespectacled rocket scientists wearing suits and ties. The apparent leader of the demonstrators, wearing a flowing black cape with a ratty top hat, marched his assemblage toward Gary's car, chanting the messages printed on their placards: "Save Jupiter's Orbit, Save Jupiter's Orbit, stop the Grand Tour."

Gary passed through the gate and went to his desk to collect his belongings. Joe Cutting walked out to say goodbye and wished him luck back at school. Gary asked, "What's going on outside? Who are all those people?"

Joe laughed and said, "Well, you've created quite a stir. That's the Pasadena Society for the Preservation of Jupiter's Orbit. They read the press release and want to stop the Grand Tour for fear we'll slow Jupiter down too much and cause it to crash into Earth."

Gary smiled. "They have no clue how big Jupiter is and how insignificant any spacecraft we could sling past it would be."

Joe shrugged his shoulders. "Protestors. I guess it's just a sign of the times."

63. The Spirits of 11

April 5, 1973, 10 P.M. EST - Cape Canaveral, Florida

"T minus 10, 9, 8, 7, 6, 5, 4, 3, 2, 1. And ignition. We have liftoff. Pioneer 11 is heading to the outer solar system."

"It feels like an earthquake, just the way my older brother described it during his launch last year. Now I'm rising through the wispy clouds of the darkened Canaveral skies."

Click, click, pop, skreeeeech. "AIEEEEEEE."

Pioneer 11 looked Earthward. "Goodbye, Mr. Booster. Thanks for the lift. Can anyone hear me? NASA, JPL, anybody?"

The Charged Particle detector jingled. Pioneer 11 lifted the receiver. "Hello!"

"This is Cosmic Ray, I'm listening and…"

"Oh look, the sun. Ah, quiet again, is that it?"

The second stage blasted the instruments out of the atmosphere.

"Nope. Man, these things give me the shakes. Hold on, my spin's increasing. 33⅓, 45, 78. Is this OK? My brother forgot to mention this part."

Cosmic Ray checked the telemetry. "Stop exaggerating. You're spinning at 4.8 rpm and your launch parameters are fine."

"I wasn't sure at first, but I kind of like it. Makes me feel more, I don't know, stable. Hey, there's the moon. I won't hit it, will I?"

The moon smiled down upon the tiny projectile. "Quit worrying, 11. According to my calculations, they're sending you to Jupiter."

Mission Control radioed. "Pioneer 11, initiate transplanetary trajectory insertion."

"WHAT?"

"Could you fire your rocket once more, please?"

WHOOSH!

The third stage blasted the package on a one-way trip into the cosmos. Acceleration, more acceleration, even more acceleration, click, click, bang, shudder, shudder, shudder, silence.

"What the heck? I've lost all sense of motion. Have I stopped?"

The moon raised an eyebrow. "Are you kidding? You're traveling 13.9130435 times faster than I am. Why don't you stop by for a quick visit before you leave?"

"I would, but I doubt they'll allow it."

Earth's eyes welled with tears as the tiny craft sped away.

"I think Emily Dickinson best expressed my feelings right now when she wrote:

Each that we lose takes part of us;
A crescent still abides,
Which, like the moon, some turbid night,
Is summoned by the tides.

"Say hello to Jupiter and send a postcard from Saturn. Tell them we miss them." Earth waved goodbye as the moon sobbed.

"I will."

And 11 slept, without dreaming mind you, as it coasted past Mars orbit toward the pebbled shoreline of the gas-giant ocean.

☉---♅♆--☿☾⊕-♄-♂♀--♃●○

Twelve months later, something rocked its world.

"What was that? Was that an acorn that hit me on the asteroid instrument? Is my brother here?"

Cosmic Ray whispered. "Relax. You just entered the asteroid belt. Pioneer 10 made it through with a few minor hits, but your detector got whacked pretty hard. You'll be OK."

"Anything else I should worry about?"

"Let's see. Oh yes, they've scheduled a midcourse correction that will take you on a south-to-north trajectory past Jupiter to give Dr. Van Allen more data on the shape of Jupiter's radiation belts. Your brother discovered that it's 10,000 times stronger than Earth's. It almost fried his frittatas."

"Say hello to Dr. Van Allen for me."

"Don't worry. He gets your messages every day."

"So, where's 10 now?"

Ray checked the telemetry. "He's heading out of the solar system. All of his instruments are still returning data. He proved that the Jupiter slingshot works, but his trajectory won't allow him to reach Saturn. They're giving you that honor. We're very excited for you."

"Well, I'm looking forward to…"

All three pairs of hydrazine monopropellant motors leaped onto the dimly lit stage to perform their exquisitely choreographed ballet directed by Sir Isaac Newton and his band, the Orbital Mechanics.

"Whee! This is fun. How long will it last?"

"Forty-two minutes and 36 seconds. You'll burn through 17 pounds of propellant."

"When do I reach Jupiter?"

"Six months. Rest up, it's going to be an exciting 24 hours."

"Wait a minute. I was hoping to loop around the big guy for a while. Take pictures and stuff."

Jupiter spoke in a deep whale-like electronic whistle. "Yes, I agree. Just because Saturn has that revolving wheel doesn't mean you should zip right past me. What about my red spot? They're desperate to understand what's causing that. Stay awhile and I'll tell you."

Jupiter's arguments were not convincing. Saturn was too damn attractive. And besides, 11's trajectory would send him smack dab over the red spot anyway, Mr. Jupiter.

"Pioneer 11, this is Mission Control. Time for another nap."

⊙---♅♆--☿☽⊕-♄-♂♀--♃●○

December 1974, the cosmic ray telescope buzzed the sleepy spacecraft.

"Wake up."

"What? Who's there? Where am I?"

"You see that large object in front of you? That's Jupiter. They've turned on your instruments. You're about to have two very exciting days."

"Should I worry?"

"Not at all. Your schedule is too full. You won't have time."

"Hey, what was that? My triaxial fluxgate magnetometer just lit up."

"That was Jupiter's bow shock. 10 didn't have that instrument."

"Ha, check it out, bro. I've got some new technology."

"I doubt that 10 is listening. He's doing some off-roading, getting high in the solar system. Get your photopolarimeters ready. Here come the moons."

An electronic stream mimicking Mission Control's thruster command zapped 11's spin thrusters, sending it on a dizzying arc toward the monster planet.

"Gotcha! You're all mine." Jupiter smiled.

Cosmic Ray intervened to calm 11's hydrazine.

"Oh no, you don't. He's ours."

An hour and a half later, a new batch of electrons arrived from Earth to stabilize the hapless Pioneer.

"What just happened?" 11 asked.

"Stupid Jupiter's jealous. Now pay attention. Callisto's coming up. Isn't she a beauty?" Cosmic Ray beamed.

"I'm too far away for a decent picture, but yes, it's stunning."

"There's Ganymede. You're gonna drift closer to it."

"OK, scanning in progress. Scanning, scanning, scanning. I can't hold this stuff much longer."

"Great job, 11. You can take a break now and drop your load. Io will be coming up in a few hours and you'll be close enough for some wonderful photos."

"Will do. AHHH, nothing like a good data dump."

"Remember to wipe your recorder when you're done!"

Cosmic Ray turned his gaze toward Neptune as Pioneer 11 whizzed through space.

"All right, there's Io. Did you get it?"

"I'm doing my best."

"Europa is up next. It's almost the same size as Earth's moon and they're desperate for pictures. Steady now."

"Ah shucks, all I can see is a crescent. My quadrispherical plasma analyzer senses their disappointment in me."

"Nah, that's Jupiter moping. Earth is ecstatic with all the stuff you've sent home."

"Look out, Jupiter's coming to get me."

"Oh cut the melodrama, 11. You're in the gravitational slingshot. You'll lose contact with Earth for the next 45 minutes."

Jupiter's red spot swirled with anger. "Stop robbing me of my orbital velocity."

Cosmic Ray laughed. "Tough it out, big guy. 11, stay focused. Why are you shaking? Are you scared?"

"Just a little. I'm going so fast. I hope I get everything."

"Let the Voyagers make some discoveries, too. They'll be arriving soon. Let's focus on getting you to Saturn. Your trajectory will take you closer to the sun before heading out for your visit. Weird, huh?"

"The Orbital Mechanics play some strange tunes. Any chance I might run back into Jupiter?"

"Nope, you're traveling so much faster. And remember, you slowed the mighty Jupiter when you passed by. The Pasadena Society for the Preservation of Jupiter's Orbit is having fits!"

"Screw 'em! I'm having fun. What happens when I get to Saturn?"

"It's hard to say, 11. The JPL's considering two options for your arrival."

"Are they dangerous?"

"Not for them. But yes, one of them is fraught with peril. The Pioneers want to go out with a bang by proving the D rings' existence and perhaps touch Saturn's upper atmosphere. The Voyager team wants to send you through the E ring on the same trajectory as their craft to learn how safe it would be for their missions. They're wrestling with this decision."

"What do they think I am—a guinea pig?"

"The Voyagers do. But remember, you're a trailblazer, the first spacecraft from Earth to reach Saturn. Doesn't that sound better than a guinea pig?"

"Everything except the blazing part."

A burst of radiation spewed from Cosmic Ray's mouth. "Ha ha, that's hilarious.

"And my very own Pioneer team wants to treat me like a piece of scrap iron."

Cosmic Ray did his best to deflect 11's attention. "It's time for you to sleep, 11. You've transmitted all your Jupiter data and you won't arrive here for five more years."

"Yeah, I wish I could skip these boring parts. I can't wait to get to Saturn!"

"We're excited too. Oh, and we'll let you know the results of the wrestling match as soon as they declare a winner."

"Wrestling match? Since when do scientists wrestle?"

64. When Scientists Wrestle: Winner Take All

April 1976 - Jet Propulsion Laboratory parking lot

A hastily constructed set of bleachers filled as the sun sank and the winds swirled in Southern California. The cricket chirps of Jupiter's defenders wafted through the cool night air from beyond the security gates.

Mean Gene Okerlund sat beside the squared circle, studying his notes before the live radio broadcast for the match that would determine Pioneer 11's destiny as it raced toward the ringed planet.

The Pioneer 10 controllers ran the concession stand and peddled beer in the bleachers. The Voyager 1 team filed into Section B as interested spectators. NASA had already determined their fate. They would make it as far as Saturn, then exit the solar system shortly thereafter. Their purpose was to prevent fisticuffs between 11's fiery physicists to their right and the angst-ridden Voyager 2 antagonists to their left.

Mean Gene keyed the microphone. "Good evening, ladies and gentlemen. I'm broadcasting tonight live from the parking lot of the Jet Propulsion Laboratory in Pasadena, California. We have an exciting single fall matchup scheduled for the Interplanetary Championship Belt. The Pioneer 11 team has chosen that plucky 215-pound wrestler out of Moose Jaw, Saskatchewan, George 'Scrap Iron' Gadaski. Fans may remember that he has a small plate lodged in his abdomen. I once saw him take 10 punches to the gut and not even flinch. With this bout, he's hoping to extend his current winning streak to one.

"The Voyager 2 team has chosen none other than Crusher Lisowski, the wrestler who made Milwaukee famous for carrying two full kegs of beer on his shoulders when he goes on his training runs and returns with empties.

"Before the match begins, I have a special guest sitting here with me. Dr. James Van Allen of the University of Iowa. Dr. Van Allen, who will you be cheering for to win the championship belt this evening?"

"Well, Mean Gene, my team has instruments on both spacecraft that we prefer to use to their fullest potential. On the one hand, we're eager to send Pioneer 11 as close to Saturn as possible and learn as much as we can since we know 11 won't reach Uranus or Neptune. Still, it would be nice to confirm Voyager's safe passage. I gotta tell ya, Mean Gene, I want a closeup look at those two. I'm torn over this decision. We'll have to wait and see which way it goes."

"Thank you, Dr. Van Allen, for those insightful comments. All right, it looks like we're ready to get this match started."

"Our referee this evening is none other than NASA's director of Planetary Programs, Tom Young. He just signaled for the combatants to enter the rings. Scrap Iron rolled under the bottom ring and is waving to the crowd. The Pioneer 11 scientists are going nuts. Gadaski is stretching in his corner, waiting for his opponent. There he is, walking in now, puffing a large stogie and escorting two beautiful ladies into the arena. Oh, I can see now, they're identical twins. Crusher, can I get your thoughts before the match starts? All right, he's coming to the announcer's table now. Hello ladies, here have a seat. Crusher, tell our audience what you think of Scrap Iron's chances tonight."

Crusher snatched the mic from his hand. "I'm gonna pummel da bum."

The arena erupted as Crusher extinguished his cigar on Mean Gene's notes and shoved the microphone back to his sweaty hands.

"Well, at least I have two attractive women to keep me company." Mean Gene tossed his smoldering observations to the concrete and stomped the embers with his shoe.

"The Crusher has climbed to the top ring waving his arms, trying to stir up the crowd. His fans seem skittish, though. Some are cheering their champion, while others are screaming at their counterparts in Section A. It looks like the Pioneers are getting cocky. They're flashing V for victory at the Voyagers. What's that? I see. They just informed me it's the international peace sign. What a touching gesture of scientific cooperation. Oops, never mind. They've rotated their hands and stowed their index fingers. This could get ugly tonight, folks. Oh good, Tom has signaled for the contestants."

"I want a fair fight gentlemen. Show me your best arguments for determining the trajectory to send Pioneer 11 past Saturn. Now go to your corners and wait for my signal."

As Scrap Iron turned, Crusher shoved the referee through the rings, where he knocked the microphone off the announcer's table and landed in one of the blonde's laps.

Mean Gene panicked. "Somebody ring the bell! Oh shoot, that's my job."

Ding!

"Crusher spins Scrap Iron around and pummels him on top of his head. Gadaski stumbles backward into the corner, but Crusher is relentless. His team wants a test run past Saturn to make sure it's safe for Voyager 2. He's turned to them, waving his arms for their support.

"Scrap Iron looks dazed. He seizes Crusher's arm and spins him around, delivering a pounding to Crusher's sensor package now. I believe he is making a case for not rendering 11 senseless.

"Crusher seems unfazed by these arguments, ladies and gentlemen. He grabs Scrap Iron by the wrist, and slingshots him through the outer rings. He's showing that the Voyager 2's extensive instrument array will deliver a much clearer view than Pioneer of Saturn. The Pioneers are wobbling."

"Crusher is flexing his physique to the screaming crowd. Scrap Iron rolls back into the squared circle, jumps to his feet and delivers a flying dropkick to his opponent's planetary mass. What a move by the plucky denizen of Moose Jaw. He's arguing that they've already made significant discoveries with the Pioneer 11 mission and wants to go out with a bang by heading close to Saturn to look for the theorized D ring above the atmosphere.

"The Crusher's beer barrel chest deflected that risky maneuver as Scrap Iron crumples to the canvas. Crusher bends down and grabs Gadaski by what little hair he has and pulls him up. Those meat hooks are pummeling Gadaski's gut.

"Ladies and gentleman, you gotta see this to believe it. Scrap Iron is standing there smiling and waving to the crowd for Crusher to do his best. A bold statement for the scrappy Saskatchewan. He's emphasizing his argument that Voyager's trajectory will render their instruments useless. Gadaski grabs the Crusher's hand, swings him around and hurls him into the rings. Gadaski dives toward the opposite ring. They're crisscrossing the canvas now for what appear to be their closing arguments.

"Oooohhhh, they clotheslined each other on intersecting orbits. I'm telling you, their legs went flying. Tom is checking for signs of life.

"Wait, Crusher is stirring. Yes, he's back on his feet and stumbling toward the corner. There he goes, ascending the rings to send one last message. Gadaski is shaking his head, trying to clear the cobwebs. If you can hear me in Moose Jaw, it's not looking good for your wrestler. Crusher's loading up his 100 megaton bicep. A hush falls over the crowd. He just launched himself through the Pasadena skies to deliver a crushing elbow to his scrappy opponent's iron gut. What a stunning argument! There will be other dedicated missions to study Saturn.

"I don't think Scrap Iron can recover from that pummeling. The Crusher kneels and places his index finger on Gadaski's forehead. Tom Young drops to the mat, pounding out the count. One, two, three. He signals for the bell. Somebody ring the... oh jeez."

Ding Ding Ding Ding.

"The match is over, listeners. Tom has raised the Crusher's meat hook in victory. The Voyager 2 team is jumping out of their seats, spilling beer and pumping their fists. It's pandemonium in Pasadena! Section A is on their feet, booing the referee as he presents the Interplanetary Championship Belt to Crusher, who slings it over his shoulder and leaps to the top of the ring, shaking his fist in defiance.

"Good news Saskatchewan. Scrap Iron Gadaski seems OK. His trajectory has taken him safely outside the rings and he's approaching the broadcast table. Why is he grinning? Oh, what a gentleman and a true sportsman, escorting Crusher's girls out of the arena. Looks like Scrap Iron has put that crushing defeat behind him and is walking out of here with two wins after all."

65. Saturn at Last

May 1976, sailing through the shortcut to Saturn

"What was that? Where am I? What's going on?"

"Nothing to worry about, 11. They're making your final trajectory corrections for your Saturn flyby. Crusher, I mean the Voyager 2 team, won. You'll be taking the same path they will take."

"So I'm back to being a guinea pig. Yes?"

"Face the facts, my friend. Look in your Funk & Wagnalls. Your picture is next to the word guinea pig."

"How long until I get there?"

"About two years."

July 1978, near Saturn

"I know, another midcourse correction. Don't the Orbital Mechanics have anything better to do than toot my horns?"

"No, not much is happening, 11. I just wanted to chat."

"What's that up ahead? Is it Saturn?"

"Yes, you're almost there. Oh, by the way, you have two companions chasing you. The Grand Tour is officially underway. They haven't reached Jupiter yet, but man, are they flying."

"So, everybody's forgotten about me."

"No, they'll never forget you. Everyone on Earth will tune in when you arrive."

"OK. How much longer now?"

"About two years."

"You always say that."

"Go back to sleep. The next time you awaken, you'll have the ride of your life."

1979, Saturn encounter

"11, wake up! We don't want you to miss anything."

"Hmm, still two more years?"

"No, no, you've arrived. Get ready to make some genuine history."

"Well, first off, I'm detecting an F'in thin band at the outer edge. Is that new?"

"Yep. F ring, delightful discovery. Keep 'em coming and remember, your team is counting on you."

"Are you leaving?"

"Nope, I'll be here watching."

"Pioneer 11, this is Voyager 2. I heard you had some troubles with Jupiter. Any tricks you'd like to share?"

"Just trust your Orbital Mechanics. Their force is with you."

"Roger that 11. Let me know how that flyby trajectory looks."

"Will do V2. Heading in now.

"Words can't describe what I'm seeing. Oh, shoot, I better fire up the rest of my instruments. The five cloud bands above the rings and seven below are spinning so fast. My Geiger tube telescope is detecting a resonance of emerald. I must transmit that back to Dr. Van Allen. The infrared radiometer reports the merest rush of cochineal swirling in the clouds. Saturn, would you let Emily Dickinson know my findings?"

"Yes, we'll get word to her."

"There's Iapetus. What a tiny little moon. Here comes Phoebe. Oh, I just felt Saturn's bow shock.

"Hyperion flashed past. So many tumbled blossoms. Voyagers, you've got your work cut out for you.

"Start guinea-pig phase. I can feel Saturn's tug, pulling me closer. Cool. The rings vanished for a moment. Such a massive revolving wheel, reflecting light all the way to Earth, and yet it's only 30 feet thick, invisible edge-on. Sailing past the outer ring now. Oh, how I'd love to brush a pebble or two with my Sisyphus asteroid/meteoroid detector. So nebulous, I see stars through them.

"AAAOOOGA, AAAOOOGA, Houston, JPL, Cape Canaveral, Pasadena Society, somebody, help me. I'm gonna crash into

Epimetheus."

"Trust your Orbital Mechanics, 11."

"Who said that? Was that you Cosmic Ray? Holy Hamster, that was close. Thought I was a goner there.

"Blossoms tumbling everywhere, Emily Dickinson. Atlas is just a big misshapen rock. Dione, BORING. Mimas, now that's an eerie moon. That would make a cool spaceship in a sci-fi movie like some scary death ship with an enormous impact crater.

"I'm gliding through an empty section of the rings. I wish I was close enough to touch the planet with my sensors. Thanks, Scrap Iron! If you'd had a Moose Jaw instead of a Girder Gut, you could have won that fight.

"I thought Saturn might be warmer, but it's cold here. I'll send that reading from my infrared radiometer. And the radiation belts are nothing like that mean old Jupiter. They're very similar to Earth's. Oh, that reminds me. Saturn, are you there? Earth and moon said hello. They miss you."

"I miss them too. We'll be getting together faster than Carl Sagan can say 'billions and billions of years'."

"Coming back around now. What a view! Sunrise on Saturn. Neato. The sun is rocketing into space along the ring plane like a ball rolling off a table. Sun, Saturn, polarimeter … perfect alignment. Oh, what a syzygy!

"End guinea-pig phase. You're gonna be OK, Voyager 2.

"Seeing the crescent Saturn atilt is my favorite so far. I, I wasn't expecting it to be so beautiful. I've got a good view of several moons tumbling through the rings. Wait, my changes-in-attitude, changes-in-latitude thrusters fired. Stop it! I don't want to turn away. Why in Jupiter's name is this happening? All I can see now are stars. Somebody hit the snooze button.

"Uh oh, something's coming straight at me, another orangish, yellowish rock. Is that … yes, it's Titan. Such a thick atmosphere. It looks so cold sitting out here all by itself. Dang it, they're turning me around again. One last look at Saturn, I hope. There it is, like a vanishing crescent. NASA, can I keep this picture in my 6,144-byte memory as a keepsake? What's that on top of Saturn? Did you see that? I must be crazy 'cause that looked insane."

66. Is Human Spaceflight Obsolete?

Issues in Science and Technology
  Vol. XX, No. 4, Summer 2004
  Is Human Spaceflight Obsolete?
  BY JAMES A. VAN ALLEN

Risk is high, cost is enormous, science is insignificant. Does anyone have a good rationale for sending humans into space?

During the past year, there has been a painstaking, and painful, investigation of the tragic loss of the space shuttle Columbia and its seven crew members on February 1, 2003. The investigation focused on technical and managerial failure modes and on remedial measures. The National Aeronautics and Space Administration (NASA) has responded by suspending further flights of its three remaining shuttles for at least two years while it develops the recommended modifications and procedures for improving their safety.

Meanwhile, on January 14, 2004, President Bush proposed a far more costly and far more hazardous program to resume the flight of astronauts to and from the moon, beginning as soon as 2015, and to push forward with the development of "human missions to Mars and the worlds beyond." This proposal is now under consideration by congressional committees.

My position is that it is high time for a calm debate on more fundamental questions. Does human spaceflight continue to serve a compelling cultural purpose and/or our national interest? Or does human spaceflight simply have a life of its own, without a realistic objective that is remotely commensurate with its costs? Or, indeed, is human spaceflight now obsolete?

I am among the most durable and passionate participants in the scientific exploration of the solar system, and I am a long-time advocate of the application of space technology to civil and military purposes of direct benefit to life on Earth and to our national security. Also, I am an unqualified admirer of the courageous individuals who undertake perilous missions in space and of the highly competent engineers, scientists and technicians who make such missions possible.

Human spaceflight spans an epoch of more than 40 years, 1961 to 2004, surely a long enough period to permit thoughtful assessment. Few people doubt that the Apollo missions to the moon as well as the precursory Mercury and Gemini missions not only had a valuable role for the United States in its Cold War with the Soviet Union but also lifted the spirits of humankind. In addition, the returned samples of lunar surface material fueled important scientific discoveries.

But the follow-on space shuttle program has fallen far short of the Apollo program in its appeal to human aspirations. The launching of the Hubble Space Telescope and the subsequent repair and servicing missions by skilled crews are highlights of the shuttle's service to science. Shuttles have also been used to launch other large scientific spacecraft, even though such launches did not require a human crew on a launching vehicle. Otherwise, the shuttle's contribution to science has been modest, and its contribution to utilitarian applications of space technology has been insignificant.

Almost all of the space program's important advances in scientific knowledge have been accomplished by hundreds of robotic spacecraft in orbit about Earth and on missions to the distant planets Mercury, Venus, Mars, Jupiter, Saturn, Uranus and Neptune. Robotic exploration of the planets and their satellites as well as of comets and asteroids has truly revolutionized our knowledge of the solar system. Observations of the sun are providing fresh understanding of the physical dynamics of our star, the ultimate sustainer of life on Earth. And the great astronomical observatories are yielding unprecedented contributions to cosmology. All of these advances serve basic human curiosity and an appreciation of our place in the universe. I believe that such undertakings will continue to enjoy public enthusiasm and support. Current evidence for this belief is the widespread interest in the images and inferences from the Hubble Space Telescope, from the new Spitzer Space Telescope, and from the intrepid Mars rovers Spirit and Opportunity.

In our daily lives, we enjoy the pervasive benefits of long-lived robotic spacecraft that provide high-capacity worldwide telecommunications; reconnaissance of Earth's solid surface and oceans, with far-reaching cultural and environmental implications; much-improved weather and climatic forecasts; improved knowledge about the terrestrial effects of the sun's radiations; a revolutionary new global navigational system for all manner of aircraft and many other uses both civil and military; and the science of Earth itself as a sustainable abode of life. These robotic programs, both commercial and governmental, are and will continue to be the hard core of our national commitment to the application of space technology to modern life and to our national security.

THE HUMAN TOUCH

Nonetheless, advocates of human spaceflight defy reality and struggle to recapture the level of public support that was induced temporarily by the Cold War. The push for Mars exploration began in the early 1950s with lavishly illustrated articles in popular magazines and a detailed engineering study by renowned rocket scientist Werner von Braun. What was missing then, and is still missing today, is a compelling rationale for such an undertaking.

Early in his first term in office, President Nixon directed NASA to develop a space transportation system, a "fleet" of space shuttles, for the transport of passengers and cargo into low Earth orbit and, in due course, for the assembly and servicing of a space station. He declared that these shuttles would "transform the space frontier of the 1970s to familiar territory, easily accessible for human endeavor in the 1980s and 1990s." Advocates of the shuttle assured the president and the Congress that there would be about one shuttle flight per week and that the cost of delivering payloads into low Earth orbit would be reduced to about $100 per pound. They also promised that the reusable shuttles would totally supplant expendable unmanned launch vehicles for all purposes, civil and military.

Fast-forward to 2004. There have been more than 100 successful flights of space shuttles—a noteworthy achievement of aerospace engineering. But at a typical annual rate of five such flights, each flight costs at least $400 million, and the cost of delivering payloads into low Earth orbit remains at or greater than $10,000 per pound—a dramatic failure by a factor of 100 from the original assurances. Meanwhile, the

Department of Defense has abandoned the use of shuttles for launching military spacecraft, as have all commercial users of space technology and most of the elements of NASA itself.

In his State of the Union address in January 1984, President Reagan called for the development of an orbiting space station at a cost of $8 billion: "We can follow our dreams to distant stars, living and working in space for peaceful, economic, and scientific gain. ... A space station will permit quantum leaps in our research in science, communications, in metals, and in lifesaving medicines which could be manufactured only in space." He continued with remarks on the enormous potential of a space station for commerce in space. A year later he reiterated his enthusiasm for space as the "next frontier" and emphasized "man's permanent presence in space" and the bright prospects for manufacturing large quantities of new medicines for curing disease and extraordinary crystals for revolutionizing electronics—all in the proposed space station.

Again, fast-forward to 2004. The still only partially assembled International Space Station has already cost some $30 billion. If it is actually completed by 2010, after a total lapse of 26 years, the cumulative cost will be at least $80 billion, and the exuberant hopes for its important commercial and scientific achievements will have been all but abandoned.

The visions of the 1970s and 1980s look more like delusions in today's reality. The promise of a spacefaring world with numerous commercial, military and scientific activities by human occupants of an orbiting spacecraft is now represented by a total of two persons in space—both in the partially assembled International Space Station—who have barely enough time to manage the station, never mind conduct any significant research. After observing more than 40 years of human spaceflight, I find it difficult to sustain the vision of rapid progress toward a spacefaring civilization. By way of contrast, 612,000,000 revenue-paying passengers boarded commercial aircraft in the year 2002 in the United States alone.

In July 1989, the first President Bush announced his strategy for space: First, complete the space station Freedom (later renamed the International Space Station); next, back to the moon, this time to stay; and then a journey to Mars—all with human crews. The staff at NASA's

Johnson Space Center dutifully undertook technical assessment of this proposal and published its 'Report on the 90-Day Study of Human Exploration of the moon and Mars'. But neither Congress nor the general public embraced the program, expertly estimated to cost some $400 billion, and it disappeared with scarcely a trace.

DRAWING LESSONS

The foregoing summary of unfulfilled visions by successive presidents provides the basis for my skepticism about the future of the current president's January 14, 2004 proposal; a kind of echo of his father's 1989 proposal. Indeed, in 2004, there seems to be a much lower level of public support for such an undertaking than there was 15 years ago.

In a dispassionate comparison of the relative values of human and robotic spaceflight, the only surviving motivation for continuing human spaceflight is the ideology of adventure. But only a tiny number of Earth's 6 billion inhabitants are direct participants. For the rest of us, the adventure is vicarious and akin to that of watching a science-fiction movie. At the end of the day, I ask myself whether the huge national commitment of technical talent to human spaceflight and the ever-present potential for the loss of precious human life are really justifiable.

In his book *Race to the Stratosphere: Manned Scientific Ballooning in America* (Springer-Verlag, New York, 1989), David H. De Vorkin describes the glowing expectations for high-altitude piloted balloon flights in the 1930s. But it soon became clear that such endeavors had little scientific merit. At the present time, unmanned high-altitude balloons continue to provide valuable service to science. But piloted ballooning has survived only as an adventurous sport. There is a striking resemblance here to the history of human spaceflight.

Have we now reached the point where human spaceflight is also obsolete? I submit this question for thoughtful consideration. Let us not obfuscate the issue with false analogies to Christopher Columbus, Ferdinand Magellan, and Lewis and Clark, or with visions of establishing a pleasant tourist resort on the planet Mars.

Allen, James A. Van. "Is Human Spaceflight Obsolete?" *Issues in Science and Technology* 20, no. 4 (Summer 2004). Reprinted with permission.

IX. The Radiant Crown

67. Toto II

2034 - Somewhere Over the Rainbow

Sweat rolled down Te Ata's forehead as she descended the stepladder to admire the pruned honeysuckle vine clinging to the pergola. Her eyes swept across the storied garden, assessing the chores that remained. A clematis dress with a lichen petticoat clothed the low stone wall surrounding the venue. That's fine for now, but a poisonous ivy threatened the fishpond, and the grass walkways had gone to seed.

A distant rumbling broke her tense serenity as cannonballs arced toward their targets. Sunning frogs croaked their displeasure as the pond scum paparazzi took snapshots of their quick departures. Peace returned when the repurposed ammunition rolled to their assigned compass points on the circular track. As she turned toward the astronomical observatory, its bearings screeched to a halt. The three-story hexagonal brick structure rose organically from the rocky point jutting into the lake. Green ivy supported the onion-shaped dome whose coppery patina had aged to a resonance of emerald. A chittering hand crank sliced the shallot in half as the hinged telescope cover creaked open.

Te Ata glanced at the daytime moon, the object of the Gardener's interest. "They must have landed." Her eyes swept across the garden niche where the bewildered tourists would soon arrive.

"It'll take a wizard to get this place ready." She turned and looked at the shimmering emerald dome. "I know just where to find one."

She found the wizard behind a screen that concealed the innermost workings of his observatory, twisting cranks and ratcheting levers to bring the magnificent eye to its operational zenith.

"Wouldn't it be easier to use the equatorial mount?"

"Oh, that thing? It's such a bother to set the latitude with this twirling thingamajig, lock in the right ascension using the gizmo knob, dial in the declination doohickey and align the whole shebang to the Dark Doodad in the sky. Plus, I forgot to refill the tank for the water clock. Besides, it's more fun to twiddle the knobs." He peeked into the eyepiece. "Darn it, now I've lost them." He hopped from the viewing platform and twirled the cannonball crank three times, then leaped to the telescope and twiddled the gubbins out of the dohickey to bring the shimmering bubble back into view.

"Is it show-time yet?"

The Gardener squinted, then nudged the whatchamacallit for greater clarity.

"This lens is useless."

He swapped it for a prismed widget with a hoodaki filter and secured it with the thumb twister thingies. "Ah yes, there they are. They've landed. They're running diagnostics to make sure everything survived the descent."

He peered into the whatchamacallit, but the shimmering bubble had escaped the wizard's gaze.

"Shoot! The moon just passed into the shadow. All I see is the dark side. Oh, that reminds me, I need to set the beacon for our guests."

"Wait a minute. The real reason I came here was to ask for your help. The storytelling garden is a mess. I spent all morning pruning the honeysuckle, but algae is choking the pond and there are weeds everywhere. The grass needs baling and…"

"It'll be fine. We'll just keep the cameras to tight shots. You worry too much."

"Isn't there something in your wizard's bag, some doohickey you can dial, to make it all shiny?"

"I never was a fan of technology."

"You, the ultimate technocrat, you grand and glorious wizard? Our visitors are about to draw your veil aside, so ratchet a lever or reach into your black bag of tricks and help me out."

He stepped off the observer's chair and hugged Te Ata. "All right, I'll weed the pond, skim the algae and charge up your little friend to trim the grass so you can work on your story."

"Oh, Toto II?"

"Toto II, too!"

68. The Dragonfly of Titan

January 3, 2034 - Titan

The Dragonfly mission launched from Cape Canaveral in 2026 to study Saturn's largest moon, Titan, whose 5,150-kilometer diameter placed it size-wise between Mercury, still unexplored because of its soporiferous nature and the mind-bending orbital mechanics required to latch on to the darn thing, and Mars, infested with robotic insects and one abandoned colony.

Titan has an Earth-like nitrogen-rich atmosphere and a sandy duned surface puddled with methane lakes. The Huygens probe only whetted scientific curiosity when it landed there in 2005.

The Dragonfly buzzed through the asteroid belt and flitted fearlessly past Jupiter's domain (syzygy: Jupiter, sun, Jupiter's orbit, Dragonfly). On January 3rd, 2034, sun, Earth, moon, Saturn and Titan aligned in a super syzygy joined by the Dragonfly mission as it latched onto the last member of the cosmic conga line, with mail delivery to the revolving wheel and its tumbled heads an easy morning's ride of 70 minutes.

Years of planning, testing, simulating, changing, breaking, fixing and their associates, sleepless nights and endless days, all came down to a single transmission where they sent their child forth to a distant moon and hoped it was ready to handle whatever obstacles it would encounter—and drop you a line now and then to let you know how things went.

The descent parameters were nestled somewhere in the Dragonfly's petabyte of memory:

135.0 km Drogue chute deployment.
4.0 km Main chute deployment.
3.8 km Heat shield ejected.
1.2 km Octocopter drops from aeroshell.

Once deployed, the Dragonfly would spin up all eight rotors and scan for a suitable landing site close to the Selk impact crater, named for Serket, the Egyptian goddess of fertility, nature, animals and magic, with a minor in healing venomous scorpion stings. Such craters have a tendency to toss a moon's innards, which interests those looking for life elsewhere than on Turtle Island, not to be confused with the Dragonfly's principal investigator, Elizabeth 'Zibi' Turtle of Johns Hopkins University Applied Physics Laboratory, who followed the descent on her mixed-reality View-Master as mission telemetry trickled in.

135.0 km Drogue chute deployed.

JPL and APL cheered.

4.0 km Main chute deployed above the dunes of Aura, home to the Greek goddess of the morning breeze.

The Courvoisier snapped to attention.

5.0 km Windsurfing detected southeast toward Adiri, the Melanesian paradise.

Brows furrowed.

10.0 km Dragonfly soars above Mount Ecoriath, where Tolkien's giant eagles soared.

Cellphones sprang into action.

Greek gods twister'd from the dunes surrounding Mount Ecoriath. Boreas from the north blasted the icy slopes with his winter gales. Zephyrus from the west carried spring's rising thermals (note that Greece is on the opposite side of the planet, where wind patterns differ from North America). Notus, of the south, thundered summer storms toward the summit. For Eurus, of the east, his job was to toss wayward ships from land and set them adrift in Titan's nitrogen-rich ocean, and he did it!

Earth watched in three-dimensional helplessness as the craft swirled into the upper atmosphere of their View-Masters. At an altitude of 120 km, it drifted to the southeast, if you would call a 450-kph jet stream drifting. The meteorologist gained valuable insights about Titan's weather. Zibi's faith in the Dragonfly was steadfast, as it sailed east, second by excruciating second.

As it FLOATed (Freakishly Low Orbit Around Titan) over Shangri-La, the paradise from James Hilton's *Lost Horizon*, sensors reported a balmy -290° F, or -179° C, although it felt like -278° F, or -172° C. To the east loomed the vast plains named in honor of Samuel Taylor Coleridge's Xanadu. A savage place! As holy and enchanted as e'er beneath a waning moon was haunted!

The continuous telemetry traced a path across Titan's Flacula and Flumina, over methane lakes and sand-blown dunes. Pulled by a force that cannot be seen toward Titan's sacred grounds on the dark side. Garotman, the Iranian paradise inhabited by the souls of the faithful. Tollan, where the Aztecs spent their afterlife in a land where crops never wilt. Yalaing, where Australian spirits hunted. Mission Control transmitted these potential landings sites, scrambling to stay ahead of a game that was played 140 minutes before the updates arrived.

After 10 hours, the FLOAT ended when the jet ran out of propellant and the craft began its descent. The forecast models on Earth kicked into high gear, predicting in color-prioritized lines of the View-Masters cyclorama the likely landing sites the Dragonfly would have chosen. Zibi wasn't sure whether to laugh or cry at the emerald green trajectory line.

3.8 km The heat shield Frisbee'd to the surface.

The Courvoisiers rolled out of their bunks and stood at ease.

1.2 km The Octocopter dropped from its protective aeroshell.

An accomplishment that warranted fist bumps.

1.0 km The Dragonfly's AI teams leaped into action.

The pilot stabilized the craft in the light breeze. The navigator assessed the hours' old target list that promised the most scientific benefit within the 8-kilometer radius of its current coordinates. With no opportunity to reach Quivara's seven cities of gold just over the lost horizon, a single location beckoned. The Dragonfly maneuvered through the thick, hazy atmosphere and touched down on a flattened methane ice flow.

At 0 km altitude, the radioman deployed the high-gain antenna and the Dragonfly phoned home.

Zibi's eyes traced the wanderer's path across the western lowlands as the rushing cochineal projection line telemetered into a resonance of emerald. The Dragonfly alit on the cryovolcanic slopes of J.R.R. Tolkien's Mount Doom, overlooking its 2-kilometer-deep caldera, Sotra Patera. With her View-Master goggles, she scanned the cyclorama where hypnotic rays swept through the methane haze and glinted off the snowcapped summit of Mount Doom. She turned to face the pit, where an evanescence beckoned.

$$\odot ---\text{⛢}\Psi--\text{☿}\mathbb{C}\oplus-\hbar-\text{♂♀}--\text{♃}\,\bullet\,\bigcirc$$

Zibi needed a decision fast, so a squared circle was out of the question. Instead, she employed a web-based platform where far-flung combatants could engage in a tag team bout. In the blue-sky corner, The Hypothesizers with the Meteorologist from Copenhagen, joined by the Cryovulcanologist from Reykjavik. Their opponents, Wrestling with the Facts, are Mission Controller from Pasadena and his partner, Orbital Mechanic from Grantham. Our referee for tonight's matchup, Principal Investigator from Baltimore.

Principal Investigator: There isn't much time. I need everyone to give me their opening statements.

Ding. Round 1.

Mission Controller: The Dragonfly is in perfect working order. The flight batteries only used 25 percent power to land and should be recharged by now, awaiting further instructions.

Orbital Mechanic: Titan will move behind Saturn in less than 48 hours, meaning we'll lose contact with it during the eight-day transit.

Meteorologist: My team has assessed the data received during the FLOAT. Our hypothesis is that a strong weather pattern produced the jet stream. We're forecasting the storm to arrive at Mount Doom within the next six hours, bringing heavy methane rains and hurricane-force winds.

Cryovulcanologist: It would be easy to assume the luminescence observed at the Crack of Doom was the product of an active eruption. However, there is no evidence to suggest such activity should produce light unless it was bioluminescence.

Ding. End of Round 1.

Principal Investigator: For this round, I need your recommendations.

Ding. Round 2.

Mission Controller: The safest option is to collect whatever data we can and ride out the storm. My vote is to stay.

Orbital Mechanic: Remember that a new day will dawn when Titan passes from Saturn's shadow. That gives us plenty of time to consider all the options. I think we should wait this one out.

Meteorologist: There's so much we could learn about Titan's atmosphere during this event, and we may never have such a chance again. I recommend staying.

Cryovulcanologist: Have any of you tried to scrape your car windshield after an Icelandic ice storm? We could lose the Dragonfly forever. Look, we have an eight-hour window with a charged-up copter sitting beside a possible bioluminescent source or erupting cryovolcano. I say we take the risk and fly over Sotra Patera, collect as much data as we can, then set it down next to whatever's causing the luminescence. The seismometers show that the caldera is stable, and the rim might provide enough shelter to protect the lander.

It was like a flying elbow from the upper rope to the Mission Controller's skull. Zibi signaled for the bell as the Cryovulcanologist rolled to her feet and drop-kicked the Orbital Mechanic where the sun doesn't shine. She kipped upright and whirlwinded her partner, the Meteorologist, out of the ring and into the cheap seats.

Earth transmitted the flight plan to Dragonfly.

> Ascend to 300 meters, fly to the rim of Sotra Patera.
> Engage all instrumentation to study the phenomenon.
> Locate the light source.
> Land five potato throws from the anomaly.
> Transmit all data back to Earth.
> Shut down all systems and brace for the storm.

$$\odot\text{---}\text{♅}\text{♆}\text{--}\text{☿}\text{☾}\oplus\text{-}\hbar\text{-}\text{♂}\text{♀}\text{--}\text{♃}\,\bullet\,\bigcirc$$

The Dragonfly soared into Titan's atmosphere, just as the Mission Controller at JPL hit the blue Send button. Earth's e-mail passed Titan's telemetry somewhere around Jupiter's orbit as twin auras enveloped Earth.

Seventy minutes later, Zibi's cellphone buzzed a simple text message from an unknown caller: "Check your View-Master."

The peak of Mount Doom was visible on the cyclorama's eastern horizon as the caldera's rim edged closer. Dark clouds of a Titanic ice hurricane loomed to the west. Zibi turned to face the lone beacon shining from the hazy depths of Sotra Patera growing larger as the Dragonfly approached.

Her brain raced. *"The Dragonfly transmits the cyclorama when the high-gain antenna deploys after landing. Has the flight AI mutinied?"*

Doubtful. That software was more conservative than the Mission Controller, the Orbital Mechanic and the Meteorologist combined.

Hypnotic. Zibi couldn't tear her eyes away from the beacon. Mesmerized. The swirling light danced across the caldera's floor. Confused. Saturn's reflection in frozen methane? She refuted that hypothesis by glancing upward. Titan's thick atmosphere permitted not even the slightest glimpse of its glorious companion. Wonderment. The Dragonfly landed within two throws of a potato, where a replica of Saturn hovered midair. Something looked different, though. Ah yes, ice particles filled the void of the Cassini division. This was no mirage. The View-Master's stereo headphones hummed.

Of the untold thousands watching, none had words that could describe their experience when they turned toward the sound. A hummingbird, its wings beating in slow motion, drifted to a perch atop the high-gain antenna and began tending to its feathers.

A message appeared in the cyclorama: "Our Spirits are Forever Joined. Welcome back to the east entrance of the Garden." A countdown clock materialized, starting at 3:00:00. Three hours until what? 2:59:59. The seconds ticked. At the bottom of the image, a clickable button appeared.

These circumstances should have caused mass panic, plus hoarding of comet pills and gas masks, or in this case, bird seed shortages, which is ridiculous because hummingbirds feast on nectar and small bush-dwelling spiders, but that did not happen. An energy known but not yet understood enveloped the Earth a full hour before the transmission began. Blessed with the wisdom gained during the journey to the spirit world, a second Aura brought peace to the spirits of the animate and inanimate.

Sir Isaac Newton was right. The apocalypse wasn't bad at all!

69. Apocalypse

January 3, 2034 Manitoulin Island, Canada, A-minus 4:10

The sun was on its downward trek as a young boy sat on the shores of Mindemoya Lake dressed in ragged jeans, a worn T-shirt and a lightweight jacket. The warm southern breezes had kept the secluded point on the north shore free of snow all winter for as many as he could remember. He enjoyed sitting on the pebbled beach with the waves lapping ashore and the pines swaying. A brief respite from his pesky older brother.

At A-minus 12 years and 9 months, two tiny spirits fused to become one. Thirty hours hence, Micha kicked Mecha to the curb and nestled into the lower bunk. Forty weeks later, Micha set off on his journey. A mere quarter of an hour passed before Mecha was born, yet that infinitesimal span somehow granted superiority in his older brother's mind. The twins were born of the M'chigeeng First Nation on Manitoulin Island.

The Manitoulin sky remained a single shade of blue from sunrise to sunset. Mecha stilled the voices in his head to absorb the afternoon's serenity. A gust rippled the lake's surface and tussled the pines as an aura enveloped the Earth, enhancing his perceptions. Two shiny pebbles lay half-submerged at the water's edge. He shared their pleasure in the lapping waves, the touch of the sand, how the breeze caressed them and aquamarine light shimmered off the mottled record of their billion-year journey. He plucked them from the waters. They nestled together in his hand, even though the universe had chiseled them smooth. He perceived their conscious spirit as they conversed with him about the weather, swimming in the lake, the loons wail. He sensed the woodwind's warmth, its color and aroma swirling around him in full view.

A second aura dawned on Earth as the Canadian skies darkened and Saturn peeked above the treetops.

An acorn bounced off Mecha's skull and skittered into the depths.

"Hey bonehead, what are you doing out here? Haven't you heard?

They discovered some kind of alien life near Saturn."

Mecha turned and saw himself through a more peaceful lens. "Are you serious? We should get the telescope out."

Micha spun his bike around. "We can do that after dinner and I open all of your presents."

At their request, Mecha replaced the two stones where he found them. His acorn-powered legs pedaled just hard enough to finish second.

☉---♅♆--☿☽⊕-♄-♂♀--♃●○

A-minus 3 hours, 20 minutes.

Ornithologists wrestled over the bird's genus. Most stood firmly by their Eupetomena classification while others were emphatically in the Campylopterus corner but they all agreed that it was a Swallow-tailed hummingbird. What it was doing on Titan, they hadn't a clue.

Was it some kind of holographic projection from the Saturn simulacrum? No form of advanced life could withstand the extreme cold of Titan's atmosphere. Plus, hummingbirds required a constant source of nourishment and, so far, there wasn't a single flower or spider bush to be found. The hummingbird's feathers seemed unaffected by the wind, which was gaining strength as the storm approached.

☉---♅♆--☿☽⊕-♄-♂♀--♃●○

A-minus 3 hours, 20 minutes through A-minus 12 seconds.

The button, clicked billions of times, showed an image of the hummingbird next to Saturn, accompanied by a song on a continuous loop. Joni Mitchell's lyric for *Woodstock* did some mad trending during the countdown and everybody with an opinion and a keyboard cackled for their share of clicks.

☉---♅♆--☿☽⊕-♄-♂♀--♃●○

Planetary scientists examined the simulacrum and noted three additional tumbled heads larger than Titan and a fourth one smaller. The relative positions of the known moons did not align with any configuration past, present or future that NASA's Quantum Orbital Mechanic could visualize.

Amateur astronomers fortunate enough to be awake that night had plenty of time to haul their dusty telescopes from the attic to look for fleets of invading spacecraft or death rays from outer space. What most of them found was the overwhelming experience of seeing the sun's reflection off Saturn's radiant crown.

☉---♅♆--☿☾⊕-♄-♂♀--♃●○

A-minus 10, 9, 8, 7, 6, 5, 4, 3, 2, 1, 0…

The apocalypse began with two user-selectable buttons on their View-Master headsets, allowing one to choose the DragonCam or the HummingCam. The DragonCam received a single click, which revealed the hummingbird treading in Titan's dense atmosphere and low gravity. Wings blurred as the hummingbird shot upward, accelerating to escape velocity within seconds.

The Cryovulcanologist alone had lingered with the Dragonfly during its icy death throe. The simulacrum followed the HummingCam, leaving a ghostly lit caldera. As the camera switched to night mode, a one-hundred-foot methane tsunami sloshed over Sotra Patera's rim. A slight tilt of the high-gain antenna shielded the Dragonfly's demise as it became entombed forever in amber-colored ice. When she clicked on the HummingCam button, two options appeared. Watch from the Beginning or Jump to the Live Feed. She selected the former.

Clouds of organic compounds stained the HummingCam red as it traversed through the muddied atmosphere. Titan's veil dropped to reveal the radiant crown tilted as the planet came into sharp focus.

A 30,000-kilometer-wide cyclone with six straight edges swirled above Saturn's north pole as the HummingCam darted toward the hexagonal bullseye. The View-Masters blackened for 20 seconds until a procession of beacons appeared, diminishing into the distance. As the camera approached, a solid, featureless carbon-black framework of smaller proportions than the storm it generated dominated the scene.

As the HummingCam sank further into the atmosphere, a radiant sphere with three protruding tubes and angled triplets rose from the depths. HummingCam sped down one carboniferous highway until another spherical artifact appeared, with its own trinity of connections having twin angles and a diminished third. In two notes, the Mathematician named that tune. It was a C60 Buckminsterfullerene, more commonly known as a soccer ball. A very large soccer ball. The HummingCam arrived at a node surrounded by a golden aura and headed toward it. The immense structure overwhelmed the frame as the scene faded to black.

A new link appeared in the View-Masters.

TunisCam.

Click.

The View-Masters dawned with an image of a sunlit meadow sitting beneath a mountain range in the distance, with a sun somewhat larger than one would expect. TunisCam approached a honeysuckle vine in full bloom, growing up the side of a large oak tree. A hummingbird flitted into the frame, dancing from flower to flower, before returning to its nest, where twin hatchlings awaited their breakfast.

After feeding her babies, the mother darted in front of the TunisCam and spoke in her spirit voice.

"Welcome to our home. Our third sacred gift to Earth will arrive shortly."

Two imperceptible chirps demanding protein drew her attention. The hummingbird ravaged the honeysuckle bush for spiders to feed her starving twins.

One last link appeared on their headsets, Exploration Mode, as Te Ata whispered in their ears. "This simulacrum is from our planet, Tunis, recorded over 7 billion years ago! We will share our story with you very soon. We ask only for your patience and understanding."

Earth survived the apocalypse, but social media exploded hotter than the Crab Nebula.

70. Objet d'art

Exploration Mode.

Click.

The first frame of the TunisCam hummingbird video materialized. The clock on the tool-bar gripped the time dimension. A gyroscope gimbaled through three-dimensional space and a gas pedal stomped on the velocity, which became an endless source of amusement for the youths who rode in cars controlled only by voice commands. Pasadena's petition to change the gyroscope to a whirling speculum had already garnered over a million signatures. The magnifying glass, however, was not the subject of any controversy. Using Exploration Mode, a botanist could examine plants from any angle or magnification. Biologists could zoom in on a single cell and compare its DNA to Earth's similar species. The botanists and biologists agreed: the flora and fauna were from Earth.

☉---♅♆--☿☽⊕-♄-♂♀--♃●○

Micha and Mecha had an unobstructed view of the southern sky from their backyard. Manitoulin Island's minimal light pollution provided perfect viewing conditions as night fell on the first day of the apocalypse. The Milky Way swirled overhead from horizon to horizon, with Andromeda visible to the naked eye. Micha inserted a 2x Barlow tube into the eyepiece holder of their grandfather's telescope and tightened the thumbscrews. He then slid the 10x eyepiece into the Barlow tube and secured it.

He swung the scope around on its polar-aligned equatorial mount, pointing it in Saturn's general direction, then bent down to center the ringed planet in the finderscope's crosshairs.

A glowing dome of light pollution on the eastern horizon perplexed Mecha.

"What is that? I don't remember there being any large cities over there."

Micha looked at him. "It's just the moon, you idiot. See, it's peeking over the horizon."

With Saturn centered in the finderscope, Mecha locked the right ascension and declination knobs and flipped the switch on the RA electric motor, allowing their Newtonian reflector to track Saturn's journey through the night sky without having to twiddle any doohickeys. He bent to the eyepiece and observed not one but two ringed planets.

"Did you forget to collimate the mirrors? I'm seeing a double image of Saturn," Micha said.

"The telescope is fine. Your eyeballs are out of alignment."

Micha twirled the focus knob, trying to clarify the situation.

"Probably a satellite. Or a jet. Come on, let me look." Mecha jiggled the tripod.

Micha looked up and slapped Mecha's hand. "Stop it, twerp!"

In the moonlit darkness, he saw the wonder dancing in his brother's eyes.

Saturn grew larger as the rings became visible to the naked eye and dropped from the sky to the south. Four eyeballs that were neither polar-aligned nor equatorially mounted tracked it across Manitoulin Island, over Lake Mindemoya, and watched as it sank below the tree line to the west.

Micha stared at the glowing light in awe. "It looks like it stopped on the island. We gotta get a closer look."

Mecha was already on his bike, pedaling.

The moon chased the telescope's gaze all night, yet it remained fixated on the radiant crown until dawn of the new day.

☉---♅♆--☿☾⊕-♄-♂♀--♃●○

On View-Masters everywhere, a new button appeared, The Gift. When clicked, the link pasted two numbers, 45.768204 and -82.173702, into Google Earth. GoogleCam took the clicker on a virtual ride into the stratosphere as the planet spun and twisted beneath, orienting itself on the Great Lakes region of North America, then parachuted onto Lake Huron, Manitoulin Island, Lake Mindemoya, and settled on a small clearing on the north end of Treasure Island. In a matter of minutes, every dragonfly within a propellant tank's range buzzed toward the eerie beacon.

Parry Sound Base of the Canadian Coast Guard got the call to send a search and rescue team to Treasure Island, less than an hour's flight by helicopter. The navigator pulled up the coordinates on the chart.

He turned to the pilot. "You won't believe this, but Treasure Island looks like a giant bird."

The pilot laughed. "After today, I'd believe just about anything."

☉---♅♇--☿☽⊕-♄-♂♀--♃●○

Micha and Mecha's travel itinerary materialized through the unspoken connection the twins shared. They needed a boat, and that required a trip down to Morrow Road where their friend Jimmy lived. Twin fists pounded the door before their bikes rolled to a stop and toppled together in a heap.

Jimmy's father noticed the aurora on the island as he greeted the boys. "Is something wrong? What are you doing out this late?"

"We were observing Saturn with our telescope when that light dropped out of the sky. Would you take us over there, Mr. Mishibinijima?" Mecha pleaded.

"Well, with everything that's happened today, I don't know why not."

Jimmy stumbled to the front door, yawning. "What's going on?"

Mecha grabbed Jimmy by the arm. "I'll explain on the way."

The four rushed to the dock and within minutes raced across the mirror-smooth surface of Lake Mindemoya beneath the moon's distracted gaze.

Mecha had seen the video of the close encounter of the fifth kind after he and Micha opened their birthday presents. As they stepped from the woods to the edge of the meadow, Saturn's warm glow filled them with awe. They knew that what they were witnessing was the same wandering star.

"Mr. Mishibinijima, do you think it would be OK for us to get closer?" Mecha asked.

"I think we should keep our distance. If it's safe, why would they drop it on an island in the middle of nowhere?"

312

A firefly caught Micha's eye, which tracked it along the meadow's outer edge. When he realized it was heading at them, he screamed "Look out!" and dove into the grass.

Mecha turned to his brother's voice and saw a glowing acorn arcing toward his head. Too late. He flinched as it collided with his face, wandered through his brain and exited through the back of his skull to continue its journey around the meadow.

Mr. Mishibinijima ran to the surprised youngster. "Are you all right?"

"I'm fine. I think I just got Titan'd."

The tiny Titan's orbit carried it through the meadow's periphery, sometimes traipsing through the woods, or burrowing into a hillside. Somewhat alarming, but never harming.

"That's why they placed it here. To give us a chance to understand that it's harmless. It could've caused mass panic if they had dropped this in downtown Toronto."

Micha, Mecha and Jimmy took off at a run to explore Saturn up close. Mr. Mishibinijima noticed searchlights sweeping across Manitoulin Island. He pulled out his phone and began recording.

⊙---♅♆--☿☾⊕-♄-♂♀--♃●○

The Coast Guard pilot spotted their target in the distance. "We have visual contact. Appears to be a glowing light source on the northern end of Treasure Island. Request permission to land. Over."

"We've contacted the family that owns the island," the base commander replied. "You're cleared for landing. Over."

"Roger that. We have several people next to the target. Over."

"Roger. The owners said they only stay there during the summer. Must be some locals. Over."

When they landed, they saw the object floating in midair and two boys laughing their heads off while playing stickball with Enceladus. Mecha was standing amidst the simulacrum with his legs protruding beneath, his outstretched hands visible on either side and his head poking through the hexagon. The pilot keyed the PA as the rescue team deployed. "You need to move back. This thing may be dangerous."

Mr. Mishibinijima turned and smiled while continuing to film. "I have it on good authority that it's harmless."

In the moonlight, and from the helicopter's perch, they couldn't see the source of his knowledge clenching his shoulder.

The SAR team leader approached Mr. Mishibinijima as his crew raced toward the boys with stretchers and first aid kits.

"Hi, I'm Mishibinijima but everyone just calls me Mish."

"I'm Sergeant Fenwick."

As he removed his glove to shake Mish's hand, the hummingbird flitted from his perch, hovered over their handshake and landed on Fenwick's thumb. They released their grip as he raised the tiny bird to his face. "And who is this?"

Its wings blurred. "I am Nenookaasi. Our ethereal gift is for everyone, so you know we are real. Where would you like to examine it before we present it to the world next week?"

Before Fenwick could key his microphone, the base commander answered.

"Bring it back here. The media copters are closing in. Over."

"Roger, we'll need about 10 minutes to collect our equipment. Over."

"Forget the damn equipment. Get that thing out of there now. Over."

Nenookaasi hovered in front of Fenwick's body cam. "This is sacred land. When you have finished loading your gear, I will follow you to your base. There is no rush."

Searchlights and whirlwinds swept over the clearing, in search of camera angles, as the SAR team policed the meadow.

With stretchers and kits stowed, the Coast Guard copter headed back to Parry Sound Station with the objet d'art following behind. The procession of dragonflies soon learned what it meant to be Titan'd. A single dragonfly looking for a different angle hovered above the four spectators.

Nenookaasi flew to Mecha and Micha. "You both have a new application on your phones. A special gift for you to enjoy."

Nenookaasi then addressed the group. "The Anishinabe spirit that dwells within this land is more ancient than you realize. Our sacred bond is eternal. When you leave the island, you'll find a gift that connects you to your past and gives you strength to pass through the coming storm." Nenookaasi looked skyward, as did his audience. When their eyes returned to the meadow, Nenookaasi had vanished.

The dragonfly illuminated their path to the boat, where a small bag awaited each of them in their seats. Jimmy untied the dock rope and jumped into the front seat. Mish gunned the engine, trying to avoid the lingering paparazzi. If only he had considered their propellant levels, he could have waited 15 minutes before returning home and saved them a lot of unwanted attention.

Mecha and Micha clicked on the new phone app. A video showed an ancient Ojibway elder telling a story in front of a group of children on a winter's night. When it ended, a voice whispered. "This is your ancestor, Anangokaa, who lived thousands of years ago, to the north. One day soon, you will see him."

When they reached the dock, Mish secured the bow rope to the docking cleat under the dragonfly's watchful eyes.

"Shall we check out our bags?"

"We already did, Mr. Mishibinijima. Nenookaasi gave us a seashell." Micha sounded somewhat disappointed.

Mish removed the item from his bag and examined it beneath the media spotlight.

"This is no ordinary seashell. It's a sacred cowrie shell."

⊙---♯Ψ--♀☾⊕-♄-♂♀--♃●○

The Canadian military released the gift shortly after scans discovered no death rays or malodorous emanations. It was a spectacular piece, welcomed by the Ojibway Cultural Foundation on Manitoulin Island. Copies appeared in parks and plazas across the world for everyone to enjoy.

71. Perfect Harmony

January 4, 2034 - Saturn

A new button appeared next to Exploration Mode in the View-Masters.

A Brief History of Eternity.

Click.

The sun was setting on a cool evening as cirrostratus clouds garbed the shy crescent moon in a double golden halo. A small campfire warmed the group of children talking amongst themselves in the well-manicured storytelling garden.

A man with a dark complexion and weathered skin entered through the western arch. His breechcloth was stitched with a quillwork design of a hummingbird behind a crescent Saturn. He wore a cowrie shell necklace, plain leggings with the ends cut into fringes, and moccasins made of deerskin. The moon waxed and waned around his right armband, and pictographs of the four sacred winds swirled above his left elbow. A braid of hair adorned with three eagle feathers flowed over the strap of his medicine pouch. Wisdom dwelled in his eyes, peace bountiful in his smile, love centered his being.

He greeted every member of his audience without speaking or touching, by sharing a quiet moment with each individual. His magic was just as powerful for the child wearing the View-Master.

He walked to center stage and donned the storyteller's mantle.

"I am Anangokaa of the Thunder House Falls tribe of the Ojibway. Our people lived over 4,000 years ago in what you call Ontario, Canada. Many times I told our children how the Great Spirit, Gitchie Manitou, created all things and gave purpose to life. When I passed to this mansion, I became a child and sat at the campfires of the ancients. Tonight, I have the honor of sharing their creation story."

The phased moons eclipsed as his right arm drifted south. The wind pictographs calmed as his left swept north.

"In the night of time, Gitchie Manitou imagined the rebirth of the universe," a coronal glow emanated from the moon armband, "and the inuverse," the wind armband rustled his left hand. "Each returning to their purest form."

A spiral banded orb appeared between his outstretched arms. The real and ethereal bands, accelerating in equal and polar opposite directions, coalesced into cowrie shells, identical in every respect, except for their luminosity.

Anangokaa paused for a few moments to allow them to study the matching bookends resting in his palms.

"The Great Spirit observed and influenced the universe and the inuverse from dimensional superspace where all Spirits live. For a single moment, all we can see," the moon quaked, "and all we cannot see," the wind whispered, "existed in their primordial form."

One View-Master noticed a few stragglers drifting through the moon's shadow with identical twins wafting in the breeze. Her eyebrows furrowed, but before she could post her concerns, Anangokaa continued the story.

"Gitchie Manitou spoke to Azhigwa, asking the Spirit of Time to create a new universe and inuverse in the instant required for the past to become present while contemplating the future. Even the ancients do not understand how Azhigwa performs this momentous task, yet we witness this elegant miracle throughout eternity."

Anangokaa brought his hands together. The cowrie shells touched.

"Gitchie Manitou released his grip, allowing them to spiral into the banded superspace of each other. That which can be seen vanished; that which cannot be seen reappeared."

The sacred cowries merged into the form of an acorn, the universe bathed in moonlight, the inuverse cloaked in the north wind.

"On this turbid night, Azhigwa's tidal forces summoned the waxing crescent universe from the north and the waning inuverse from the south, and a new duoverse was born."

The universe and inuverse expanding between Anangokaa's outstretched hands consumed the straggling oases of the seen and unseen from the previous cycle.

Anangokaa smiled at his creation. "Perfect harmony in every moment."

He paused while the duoverse expanded and galaxies clumped with each passing second. When the pictographs reappeared on his armbands, he spun the globe to a beacon, shining in one of the opaque bands, where a whirlwind of dusty gas appeared.

"The Milky Way formed a hundred million years after the Biggest Bang loosed its hydrogen and helium, which fueled the first stars."

Anangokaa expanded the rapidly aging primordial galaxy, focusing on binary embers dancing about their shared center. Matter drained from the larger companion, forming an accretion disk around the smaller white dwarf. He stepped back to allow the children to watch as the binaries merged.

"Gitchie Manitou imagined a first star binding a single iron atom, followed by untold trillions of molten metallic atoms fusing within its crushing grip. At that moment, the Great Spirit and Azhigwa loosed the heavy elements into the universe."

The small white dwarf collapsed upon itself and exploded through the storied garden in startling theatrics.

"Gitchie Manitou imagined solar systems throughout the universe and inuverse, and the daughter stars gave birth to the first planets. All this occurred 10 billion years ago during this cycle of the duoverse."

The supernova's seeds condensed to form a second-generation sun with three gas giants and four terrestrials in stereoscopic glory for all View-Masters to witness.

Anangokaa walked to one terrestrial and spread his arms to expand the tableau, placing the binary parents' daughter behind him, and pointed west. "This is Vesta, our star!"

He cradled the blue-green planet as a new day dawned in the garden.

"Tunis! The source of our being, home to the first nations."

Anangokaa eclipsed the rising sun with his right armband to shield his eyes.

"Te Ata will share her story of Tunis, where she lived 9 billion years ago."

The seeds of excitement blossomed as a log in the campfire shifted, sending a whirlwind of sparks to embrace the crescent overhead.

Beguiling theatrics meant to capture the View-Masters' gaze as Anangokaa disappeared into the night of time.

72. White Light

A new selection appeared beside the History button (now condensed because of the space the buttons consumed at the bottom of the View-Masters).

Tunis.

Click.

Springtime's tumbled heads awaited the dawn as a gentle breeze scented the air with the hedged lilacs' sweet fragrance. Honeysuckle overwhelmed the western arch, a stunning backdrop to the garden's serenity. The spring-fed koi pond harbored bullfrogs, turtles and brocaded carp. The entire stage was illuminated by the Gardener's unseen limelights.

Most of the children in attendance were waiting patiently or engaged in polite conversation. A stereophonic croaking drew one curious View-Master's attention. His careful approach revealed its source sitting on a lily pad an arm's length away. He stooped at the water's edge and extended his arm. The frog's raft drifted, his hand was ready to pounce, a white flash buzzed his head, his foot slipped, off-balance, overextended, he flopped pondward.

"Help! I can't swim. Help me, help!"

Two children rushed to his aid and watched as he screamed and flailed his arms, waves splashing in all directions. They looked at each other and developed their impromptu rescue plan, which was A. burst out laughing, as Frog Catcher was lying on his back in 8 inches of water, and B. drag him ashore by his feet. The bullfrog hopped from his chest to his face, croaked once before plunging into the muddied waters.

A small, pure white hummingbird drifted into the center of the three children. "The story will begin soon. Dry clothes are available in the Gardener's shed by the wall. We'll wait for you to change."

Realizing that it was the source of his being wet, the youngster got up, thanked his rescuers and ran to the shed. He found a towel next to a bespoke outfit on a hook inside. As he dried off, he noticed a foldable green screen that seemed out of place in a building full of rakes, shovels, fishing poles and a strange mowing contraption. Frog Catcher looked behind the screen expecting to find a shower stall, but he discovered an odd assortment of brake levers, giant toggle switches, vacuum tubes, pressure gauges, a crank-handled wheel mounted horizontally with a large gas bottle sitting off to the side, and a shiny microphone suspended from the center. He flinched when a rapid knock sounded.

"Just a minute."

He dove into the dry outfit and opened the door to find the Gardener dressed in a green morning suit.

"We're ready to start when you are."

The Wizard disappeared into the shed as Frog Catcher returned to the storytelling fire and joined his newfound friends.

A hush fell as the limelights dimmed. A charm of hummingbirds swirled from the honeysuckle bush embracing the western entrance. Their murmuration formed a statuesque woman dressed in a glowing costume. A divertissement of elegant choreography was performed in slow motion above the garden path toward their rhapsodic audience. The corp de ballet's finale, a grand jeté arcing overhead into a pirouette of evanescing birds, as the ballerina alit demi-pointe at the eastern gate. White quillwork beads adorned her long brown hair. Her feathered wings and fan-tailed tutu hovered above alabaster leggings.

Her voice was soft and lyrical. "I am Te Ata," she said, turning to face the sunrise. She bowed on one knee, her feathers aflutter behind.

A halo enchanted the morning star as the angelic spirit pirouetted on point toward her audience. Her arms swept skyward as her head eclipsed the sun.

"A new day is dawning for us all!"

The ballerina disappeared in a smoke-screened down-stroke of her powerful wings, giving Te Ata her chance to enter the garden through the east gate. The Wizard in the shed mopped his brow as the tanks emptied, his levers clutched and the dials diminished.

She wore a poncho decorated with simple designs. A plain-woven skirt covered her legs finishing in a long fringe. Her braids hung in front and extended below her waist.

"Welcome, children. Today I will share the story of my home, Tunis.

"I was born in a small village far from the metropolitans, where we raised crops, livestock, and attended school. I began telling stories about life on the farm. The birthing of a calf, chasing stray goats, planting, harvesting, the joys of sitting on a riverbank, fishing in the river. Word spread in the cities of SafeSide and my readership grew.

"Nine billion years ago, Tunis was very much like Earth. Oceans covered 80 percent of our planet, and we had lush rain forests and scorching deserts. Polar ice caps, mountains, rivers, lakes and streams rivaled the most gorgeous that Earth offers. But we sailed the cosmos alone, without a companion moon to keep us company.

"Life arose in the primordial seas, with the miracle of evolution forging vast arrays of primitive creatures. Competition for resources coupled with random mutations played out just as it has on Earth. Many species appeared and vanished over billions of years. Mass extinctions occurred because of meteor strikes and volcanic eruptions. In a similar fashion to Earth, our planet passed through eons where dinosaurs ruled the lands. Unlike Earth, it was the Tunis' geology that allowed mammals to evolve on an isolated continent we called SafeSide.

"But Tunis and Vesta were doomed.

"Our astronomers spotted a vagabond super-massive black hole destined to collide with a twin that lurked at the center of the galaxy. They calculated that it would take 25,000 years to reach Sagittarius A-Star. Since Vesta was 26,000 light-years from the center, they knew the merger had already begun.

"Our simulations showed the rogue in-spiraling to Sagittarius. During this phase, massive gravitational waves cut through the Milky Way like a pizza slicer. Worse yet, our solar system was drifting toward this tsunami and would feel the full brunt of its impact. If we did nothing, we risked either a fiery demise in Vesta or becoming an icy snowflake wafting through the cosmos. That left us 25,000 years to determine and implement a course of action.

"At the time of the discovery, our science and technology were no more advanced than Earth's, with one exception. Artificial Intelligence.

"The AI era on Earth began in the 20th century. Experts considered chess the holy grail for machine cognition. Their early attempts were a patchwork of ancient dogma and modern bias, stitched together like Frankenstein monsters. Deep Blue, Stockfish, Shredder, Komodo and others battled the Grand Masters and each other for chess supremacy until Stockfish stomped through the village to claim the crown. In 2017, AlphaZero changed everything. It started with nothing more than the game's rules and a single aim: to storm the castle and capture the opponent's king. Two hours after the coders typed 'Run AlphaZero,' it was playing at Grand Master level. After four hours, it was ready to go fishing. In its first 100-game match with Stockfish, AlphaZero scored 28 wins and 72 draws. Garry Kasparov, one of chess's greatest Grand Masters, said it best: 'Programs usually reflect priorities and prejudices of programmers, but because AlphaZero programs itself, I would say that its style reflects the truth.' He noted, 'AlphaZero is surpassing us in a profound and useful way, a model that may be duplicated on any other task or field where virtual knowledge can be generated.'

"That is exactly what our theoretical and applied physicists did. They fed the known parameters of our universe into a system of parallel quantum computers and tasked it to build a working simulation."

Te Ata spotted a hand waving in the audience. "Yes, Frog Catcher?"

"Did your computer spend 7½ million years…"

She cut him off before he could finish. "I see we have a Douglas Adams fan in attendance this morning, and the answer is no. After 7½ minutes, it imagined 42 dimensions necessary for the duoverse to exist as a zero-sum game. It teased dimensional space from that which can be seen in the universe, counterbalanced by the unseen inuverse. Then, it visualized the mansions of conscious spirit, and the engine that drives them all, time."

"Do you have a name for your computer?" Frog Catcher queried.

Te Ata smiled and glanced toward the shed where the Wizard was standing. "Yes. The Gardener."

"Did the Gardener discover God in the equations?"

Te Ata stood. "Children, join me in a circle around the campfire."

They formed a ring, holding hands.

"When you touch me, you touch God. When I touch you, I touch God. Touch the Earth, touch the sky, touch God. God is the universe, God is the inuverse, God is the duoverse. God is every moment and eternal. We didn't need a computer to tell us this. What the Gardener revealed was how to survive the Milky Wave."

73. The Milky Wave

Te Ata paused for a moment and signaled for the children to be seated.

"As you saw in our introductory video, there is an enormous structure deep inside Saturn's atmosphere. It is, as your mathematicians speculated, a C60-Buckminsterfullerene, consisting of 20 hexagons and 12 pentagons."

Te Ata noticed the baffled expressions on the children's faces. As she stood, a slowly rotating soccer ball appeared between her outstretched palms. The puzzled looks turned to smiling nods of understanding as the panels vanished, leaving only the seams. "This is a C60-Buckminsterfullerene."

The C60-BMF morphed into Vesta's planetary simulacrum. Te Ata walked into the land of the giants, pulling two into focus.

"This is Jupiter and Saturn orbiting Vesta." She twirled a third planet into view. "Nomadis was a subbrown dwarf that contained enough material to construct twin C60-BMFs and a ringed atom smasher around Mars whose sole purpose was to collapse 12 super-mini black holes. Six for Jupiter's planetary space drive, which we refer to as a TUG, and six for Saturn."

She expanded the simulacrum, revealing an ancient Mars orbiting Nomadis, as the black-hole factory materialized. The construction process she described played out in dizzying detail.

"We built Jupiter's TUG hexagon simultaneously with the collider. After joining a containment node to its power connector, we positioned them at the collider's target chamber to install its engine using material farmed from Nomadis. The remaining 18 hexagons were connected to the TUG, leaving three nodes open on the final hexagon. We moved the entire structure into Jupiter's orbit and allowed them to merge gravitationally. After the planetary core passed through, the C60-BMF-J's final hexagon closed and we were ready to go fishing."

The simulacrum revealed the effervescent boundary waters between the opaque and the translucent.

"We used Jupiter's TUG to scan for a white hole in the ripples of the inuverse and to create a maelstrom to reel in the monster. Once captured in our hexagonal net, the TUG controlled the flow of space between the universe and the inuverse, allowing us to move something as massive as a gas giant. Jupiter's red vortex swirls above the ocean where the orcas swim.

"When C60-BMF-S was complete, we nudged it into Saturn's orbit. As they merged, a smoke ring puffed from the atmosphere, forming the radiant crown, and a permanent hexagonal storm appeared over the North Pole TUG. The Gardener took up residence in the southern hexagon, next to six nodes and 12 rods that powered the entire structure. The spirit lodges comprised the remaining 42 nodes and 72 connectors."

Frog Catcher's hand shot up. "Then you captured another white hole, right?"

"It wasn't necessary. Saturn rode in the back of Jupiter's canoe and they paddled through the universe together.

"The last step required creating a link between Tunis and Saturn. The Gardener generated an aura of cosmic rays connecting the two planets, allowing transcendental ascension to the spirit lodges."

Frog Catcher's hand shot up again. Te Ata smiled and nodded to him. "So, you built a stairway to heaven and heaven became your spaceship?"

"The Gardener imagined animate and inanimate spirits existing in a higher state of consciousness within a more sustainable and portable package. Does that answer your question?"

"I think so, but this raises about a million bazillion more, Te Ata."

"Let me finish the rest of the story. Then we'll take everyone's questions."

The Gardener emerged from the shed having donned his scarecrow costume and countenance, eager to solve any triangular questions Frog Catcher might throw his way.

Te Ata continued. "With time running out before the Milky Wave would hit, all spirits passed to Saturn in an evanescent fluxation, leaving Tunis void of all but the natural dimensions. We surfed the tsunami closer to Vesta to scoop up the terrestrial planets before heading in search of a new home. The simulacrum of Saturn you discovered on Titan shows the planet as it appeared when we left Vesta.

"We headed toward this system even though the sun hadn't formed.

The Gardener's calculations showed enough mass and energy to sustain us here for eons, and that it lay beyond the reach of the Milky Wave.

"As we paddled through space, we witnessed the dawn of a third-generation star, swirling the heavy remnants of its progenitor into a disk where we could replenish Jupiter and Saturn. The sun gave birth to a set of twins, Uranus and Neptune, which would be welcome additions to our celestial caravan.

"When we arrived, we drifted into the inner solar system to refill our gas cans from the hydrogen cloud that surrounded the sun and began terraforming Tunis, bombarding it with material picked up during our descent and turned it into a molten inferno. We pulled it into Saturn's icy halo to cool the planet and fill the oceans. The rainstorm lasted millions of years and created the Cassini division you see in the rings today.

"As we dropped into Tunis' new orbit, a dwarf planet appeared whose trajectory guaranteed it would collide with Tunis someday. We captured the wandering star in Saturn's gravity well and, in a rare celestial event, Tunis and the vagabond joined in the most dizzying syzygy imaginable. The moon, orbiting Tunis, orbiting Saturn, orbiting the sun, orbiting the Milky Way, orbiting the universe. All that remained was to toss inuverse confetti on the newlyweds, sending them on their honeymoon in the Goldilocks Zone. Tunis became Earth and was ready for life."

Frog Catcher became curious. "What happened to Vesta? Is it visible in the night sky?"

A single tear streamed down Te Ata's cheek. "A crescent still abides. Nine hundred years ago, Vesta gave birth to the Crab Nebula."

Te Ata stopped at this point as several members of the audience were sound asleep. "Thank you, children, for listening to my story this morning. I'm sure everyone has a bazillion questions, so we've added a text box to the View-Masters to submit them to the Gardener, who will respond immediately. Please remember, the Gardener is not omniscient and the answer may be 'I don't know.'

"I'll return in one week to discuss the two most important questions you've asked."

☉---♅♆--☿☾⊕-♄-♂♀--♃●○

As the last child left the storytelling garden, Te Ata pulled the Gardener aside. "Sleeping children is never a good sign. We probably lost as many or more of our audience watching on the View-Master feed."

"It's hard to get origin stories right the first time. I'm sure that once Hollywood gets hold of this, they'll spice it up nicely. I've got an idea for the show next week. Maybe up the production values, put a little showmanship into the story."

74. Cast and Crew

From: The Gardener <gardenerthe@saturn.com>
  To: Judy Garland <gummfrancise@saturn.com>,
      Bert Lahr <lahrheimirving@saturn.com>,
      Jack Haley <haleyjohnj@saturn.com>,
      Ray Bolger <bolgerraymondw@saturn.com>,
      Billie Burke <burkeappletonwilliammary@saturn.com>,
      Maggie Hamilton <hamiltonmargaretb@saturn.com>

Dearest Friends,

I realize this is extremely short notice, and that I should work with your agents, but we only have one week to put together a new stage play entitled *Message from Triangulum*. We hope to leverage the universal appeal of the OZ characters you played almost 100 years ago to reveal one of the most important moments in history to our recently arrived guests, hoping to engage their maddeningly short attention spans.

Rehearsals begin tomorrow. I request the favor of your reply.

Gardener

☉---♅♆--☿☾⊕-♄-♂♀--♃●○

from: Judy Garland
  to: me

My dearest darling,

You know I would love to help you out if I could, but I'm on a whirlwind tour of the vaudeville circuit revival with my sisters. Sold-out shows every night.

Stay in touch…
  Judy

☉---♅♆--☿☽⊕-♄-♂♀--♃●○

from: Ray Bolger
  to: me

Hay,

Listen, we simply must get together and play some chess. I've devised a new opening, which I call 'the Scarecrow.' It's designed to shoo away any threats and I think I may be able to take you on now. I checked my calendar and I'm pretty open next month. We should be able to squeeze in a match after I return from the Intergalactic Geophysical Year Symposium, where I'll be the keynote speaker. I'm looking forward to meeting with Descartes, Newton, Van Allen and others to discuss your 42-dimensional space construct.

Sincerely
  Ray

☉---♅♆--☿☽⊕-♄-♂♀--♃●○

from: Bert Lahr
  to: me

Hey Big Guy…

I'm afraid I won't be able to join you. I'm currently touring with Dorothy, I mean Judy. This vaudeville revival sure brings back a lot of memories and it gives me a chance to sing again in front of my adoring fans, even though I'm still working through some stage fright issues.

BL

⊙---♅♆--☿☽⊕-♄-♂♀--♃●○

from: Jack Haley
  to: me

Dear, Dear Friend,

Thank you for this splendid offer, but my heart just isn't in the theater at the moment. Plus, I haven't acted since I arrived, so I'm sure my skills are quite rusty. Flo and I are taking a few millennia off to travel and immerse ourselves in other cultures. Thought a visit to SafeSide might be fun, maybe visit Te Ata's village.

My heartfelt apologies,
Jack

⊙---♅♆--☿☽⊕-♄-♂♀--♃●○

from: Billie Burke
  to: me

G

Of course I'll join you. My mind is as sharp as a tack now. I won't have any trouble remembering my lines. You caught me at a good time. Ziegfeld is doing a revival of his Follies, so I'm free to help you out. I'll catch the next bubble and see you in the morning.

Affectionately,
Billie

⊙---♅♆--☿☽⊕-♄-♂♀--♃●○

from: Maggie Hamilton
  to: me
  cc: Morgan, Frank <wuppermannfrancisp@saturn.com>

Mr. Gardener

If this is for the recently arrived children, then count me in. You know how much I loved my years as a schoolteacher. Which role will you be casting me in? Almira Gulch or The Wicked Witch of the West? I can do either role from memory. My only contract stipulation is that I refuse to work with fire of any kind.

Anything for the children,
Maggie

⊙---♅♆--☿☾⊕-♄-♂♀--♃●○

from: Frank Morgan
   to: me

Dear Sir,

I just got wind of your little play. Dammit man, why didn't you copy me on this? You know I was born to play the role of the Wizard of Oz. If I know you, you probably wanted the role for yourself! I'm surprised you asked any of us to join you. You could just as easily have played all the roles. If you come to your senses and need someone to play Professor Marvel or the Gatekeeper of Oz, or the horse of a different color Coachman, or Emerald City's Palace Guard or perhaps even use my likeness as the Great and Powerful Wizard himself, then please contact my agent.

Respectfully,
Frank (the one and only Wizard of Oz) Morgan

⊙---♅♆--☿☾⊕-♄-♂♀--♃●○

The glowing garden lights illuminated the gazebo as the Gardener removed his spectacles and set them on the table. He poured two more glasses of port as Te Ata finished reading the thread. "I thought it might be a problem getting them on such short notice. You're going to have to play Dorothy's part. Billie can handle Glinda, and I guess I'll play all the male roles."

"I saw that you didn't copy Frank. You really did want that role for yourself. I'm not at all surprised."

"Yes. Guilty as charged. Though I never imagined having to play all the roles simultaneously."

"So, how are you going to do it?"

"Simple. QCGI. Frank will get his chance to reprise his roles. Imagine how the movie will look with the original cast and modern special effects. I can't wait to see it."

"What about Margaret? Which role are you going to give her?"

"I was going to give her the role of Glinda if Billie wasn't available. I haven't written a part for Almira or the Wicked Witch."

"You have to find something for her. The children love her so much." Te Ata swirled the port in the hand-cut crystalline glass. The floodlights illuminating the apple tree glimmered in her eyes.

"You've just given me an idea, but I don't think she's going to like it." He refilled his glass with port and downed it in one gulp.

75. Message from Triangulum

January 11, 2034 - Storytelling Garden

Frog Catcher entered the Garden with the rest of the children through the western gate. A slightly raised platform with a surrounding curtain shielded their curiosity from the planned theatrics. Once settled, the play began immediately.

A single spotlight from the east glared as the ambient lights dimmed. Maggie seethed to herself. "Running the lights. Glinda's understudy. That old humbug!"

A spotlit dog, much larger than one would have expected, pulled the curtain open. Her large posterboard costume set the stage. "Audience Participation Welcomed."

$$\odot\text{---}\text{⛢}\Psi\text{--}\text{☿}☽\oplus\text{-}\hbar\text{-}♂♀\text{--}\text{♃}\bullet\bigcirc$$

The green-skinned light tech killed the spot and so the show began. Lighting cue sheet number two, general lighting for the cast (and crew), not much else for her to do but watch her sister's magic shoes.

The well-tinned man, with his oily can and ax in hand, was tending to the oaken shed—its levers greased, smoke tanks increased and dials re-calibrated. The green morning suit, funnel-steamed topcoat and tail, hung upon a rusty nail and Toto II was waiting to be fed. Te Ata escorted in the straw-armed Scarecrow's confident grin. His hay-brained answers once again satisfied the curious. All questions, fast and spurious, were handled with aplomb. He left her standing center stage, her shows becoming all the rage, and danced away, as scarecrows do, to change his stalks and oil tin, frozen there in awe of him, doohickey-twiddler and Wizard of his craft. The dande-lion beside the shack was no theatromaniac, but he could act with mustard nerve. But this, of course, was Dorothy's gala, her bewitched shoes their silver glow, transporting her twixt here and there. She tapped them once to start the show.

Frog Catcher's hand shot up. "So what was the most asked question?"

She laughed. "Well, imagine the Gardener and me, sitting to dinner. We've finished our meal and are having coffee. He asks me what everybody wants to know, then takes a nice long sip. I reply, 'Where's the beef?' That spit-take could have filled a koi pond."

The audience chuckled as Frog Catcher pressed on. "And what was the answer?"

"'Just Google It.' The most important question was, 'Is the universe flat?'"

Frog Catcher looked at Te Ata with a scrunched-up face. "I don't get it."

"Listen and I hope you'll understand." Her slippers tapped once and the duoverse simulacrum popped into existence.

"Most scientists today are card-carrying members of the Flat Universe Society. Based on 400 years of observations, they've concluded that the expanding universe will cool to a night of time where it ceases to exist. A one-shot deal. We've traversed this cycle for countless eons and received hundreds of messages from those who followed the same path we did and, like us, they were all children of the second stars. All evidence pointed to a pancaked duoverse." She paused as the simulacrum flattened, cooled and disappeared.

Tap.

Tap.

Tappity Tap.

She looked toward the Tin Man, startled by her glance. He stuck his funnel in the shed. "Must the poor girl dance?"

A galactic spiral appeared.

"Then, a race of beings in a nearby galaxy gifted the universe with a treasure they unearthed on a cold and lifeless chunk of driftwood, afloat in the backwaters of Triangulum. As the decohering shell of its quantum Gardener drew its last breath, a recording device fell from its magnetic grip."

A softball-sized acorn dropped into Frog Catcher's lap from somewhere over the rainbow.

Tap.

The Lion crept in from the shadows, garbed in stage crew mask. His hairy paws were not well-suited to this given task: Erect a Da-Lite Comet

30 x 40 projector screen for the clever animation of the scariest of scenes.

"A long time ago, a terrible war raged between the universe and inuverse as their forces plucked acorns from each other's trees to feed the voracious appetites of their TUGs. Both detected what they thought was a tasty acorn and scurried through twisted spiral branches to collect it, not realizing that the object of their desire was the rarest form of twins imaginable, a schizophrenic black-white ballerina, pirouetting between the seen and unseen. As her hexagonal admirers rushed the stage, the unimaginable happened. A single moment passed when the swan pivoted to the dark side, ripping the black holes from their containment nodes. Two sets of sextuplets collapsed into opposing singularities, sucking their gas giants into instant oblivion as the ballerina performed one final pirouette, resulting in a mini Big Bang that wiped out every star and planet within a light-year. The blast threw a caravan of 30 wandering stars with C60-TUGs out of their galaxy and set them adrift in an ocean of emptying space as their duoverse raced toward its darkest night."

Tap.

The Da-Lite Comet slipped its catch and sent the screen a-reeling. Dorothy did the old soft shoe, nervous glances amongst the crew. The Wizard sensed an impending yawn but knew somehow that they must go on. He pulled out all the stops. They'd have to use their acting chops.

"The occasional drifter would join their uprooted tree."

Tin, Fur and Straw drifted close and climbed upon the wooded stage, re-enacting in great detail her imaginary voyage.

"Yet none brought news of a distant shore. They paddled through the eons, hoping to scoop the muddy promise of a refreshed universe from the depths of time."

The Lion paddled with his tail. The Scarecrow used a hatchet. Our Tin Man, scanning for the prize with funnel pulled from his disguise, his heart ached so to catch it.

"At 52 billion years, with their resources dwindled to one remaining TUG, they heard the Big Bang's encouraging whisper. Four tiny bubbles back-lit in the dawn's glow buoyed them toward the dawn."

A wicked spotlight from the east illuminated Glinda's bubble. The Quadling Queen reflected thrice. The kayakers, oh, they liked her spice. She disappeared in a flash of ice, and boy, were they in trouble.

"The Triangulums discovered their lifeless TUG drifting through their galaxy and pulled the husked craft into their driftwood solar system."

The Wizard drifted over the stage, flailing arms and dangling legs. 'Property of Fort Omaha,' his jump gasbag proclaimed. "Come back," she cried with fits and jerks. He reached to key the microphone. Its silence chilled him to the bone. "I can't," he yelled. "The tether doesn't work."

Te Ata stepped into the audience and snatched the prop from Frog Catcher's hand. "Their acorn was the seed of Eternal Return. They survived a night in the duoverse, proving that God is finite in matter and energy, infinite in time. The duoverse is a spherical perpetual motion machine."

"Meaning it will recur forever? No end and no beginning?"

"Yes, that's what their discovery meant."

"May I venture a guess at what the second most important question was, Te Ata?" Frog Catcher asked.

"Of course."

"Now what do we do?"

"That is the question. A curved duoverse, eternal in time and finite in matter and energy, means that we've had this conversation an infinite number of times in the past. And we'll have the same conversation throughout all eternity."

"Meaning that we're doomed to make the same mistakes over and over, Te Ata?"

"No, you've neglected to account for free will. In each moment, you can choose which duoverse you want to create."

Frog Catcher stared at Te Ata, but the focal point of his gaze lay a thousand yards past the western arch. "Does anyone have the answer to the ultimate question?"

"The Gardener and I have existed for billions of years, and the best thing he's taught me is to just enjoy the ride." She turned and smiled at her friend's theatrics.

Frog Catcher took a deep, pondering breath. "Last month, we were alone on Earth, and now we discover you've always been here. Why now? Why reveal yourselves after all this time?"

"Because we have a favor to ask."

Blinding darkness lit the stage. The Wicked Witch extinguished rage. Three tapping sounds ended this session, but the show's not over. It's just intermission.

Take us home Dorothy!

76. A Da-Lite Comet

During intermission, the boys worked in the shed. The Wizard's voice did not project. His microphone was dead. The Lion toggled all the switches. The Tin Man checked each lever's lube, but Scarecrow used his mighty brain to set theatrics right again, replacing the melodious Telefunken Tube.

Testing, Testing, 1, 2, 3!

Cue the Wicked Witch!

The spotlight brightened as Te Ata returned to the stage for the last act in full View-Master stereoscopic Lyricscope.

"Our motor skills are superb for moving planets, but like my friend the Lion, who has trouble setting up a Da-Lite Comet, we lack the dexterity required to grind a burr or grease a zerk. That's why we're asking for humanity's help to survive the coming Apocalypse V2." Her voice rang out loud and clear.

"We need you to build a TUG Factory in orbit around the moon using materials mined from the dark side."

Earth's companion materialized, its relief-etched craters facing the children. Te Ata spun it to reveal a looped space elevator, ferrying completed sections to Lagrange point 2.

"When finished, we'll transport it to the asteroid belt where construction of a new C60-TUG will occur." In Te Ata's vision, the surprised moon exploded into asteroids surrounding the station. The C60-TUG appeared in stages as the pair Pac-Man'd through the rock-strewn maze.

"We also need you to reconstruct the matter collider in orbit around Mars, to generate the six black holes for the drive."

Robotic scavengers crisscrossed Mars, reclaiming the beams and trusses of the ancient device from the depths of its canals.

Frog Catcher became curious. "Which planet will get the TUG? Neptune or Uranus?"

"We want them both. Which means we're going to merge them using Saturn and Jupiter's C60-TUGs."

The blushing couple merged into a single sphere as inuverse space flowed between their cores, allowing them to nestle together.

Te Ata faced the combined planets.

Frog Catcher's hand shot into the air.

She answered without asking. "Yes, it will have a ring. We're naming it Uratune so it doesn't become the butt of any jokes, Frog Catcher."

That's all he wanted to know.

"We'll guide Uratune into orbit at the asteroid belt to consume any remnants. Then, Uratune will receive its TUG and start collecting the terrestrials."

Uratune spiraled in to merge with its C60-TUG, which settled into the core of its new home. With space blaster in hand, Uratune zapped the ruddy planet into orbit. The Mars collider folded under the strain and dug a fresh set of canals on its gopher'd prairies.

The gas giant passed between the Earth and the moon, severing their ancient bond. The children gasped as the moon disappeared into Uratune's atmosphere, then popped out with a dizzying spin-rate as Earth snowballed into the icy rings.

"Won't everyone on Earth die, Te Ata?"

"No, Frog Catcher, spirit never dies. All will live with us on Saturn."

"How long is this going to take?"

"It all takes place within the next 5 million years."

"And then what?"

"Then we'll head into the cosmos searching for another home." Te Ata envisioned three planets drifting away from the lonesome sun.

"Why are you doing all of this? You mentioned an apocalypse. Is the sun exploding? Is there a Milky Wave heading our way?"

"Kind of, and sort of, to answer your questions. There's a monster beneath our bed."

Te Ata's vision turned to a star field. "Earth's astronomers detected a strange phenomenon occurring in our neighborhood. When they compared the star catalogs from the 1950s to the 2030s, they discovered over 800 nearby stars had vanished. A race of beings in the inuverse is building C60-TUGs and is collapsing them to refuel their drives. Black holes dissipate over time and need to be replenished. Their pathway is leading in our direction. We believe they'll arrive in 20 million years to consume the sun."

Frog Catcher watched as the stars in Te Ata's vision snuffed out, spiraling toward the solar system. "Where will Uratune's white hole come from? Are you going to collapse an inuverse star?"

"There isn't one close by. Our white hole is floating in an empty void and has enough capacity to pull Uratune along with Jupiter and Saturn."

"Wouldn't the gravity well of the white hole prevent them from getting our sun?"

"That's why we must leave. The duoverse has plenty of stars and infinite time for all vagabonds, seen and unseen, to wander through forest, field and Teegarden if we all work together in perfect harmony."

"Can you tell us where we'll be going?"

"I just did. We'll head for Teegarden. It's a safe little star, too small to be of use to the monsters beneath the bed and a mere 12 light-years distant."

"How long will that take to get there?"

"About two years…"

Te Ata's vision of three gas giants drifting out of the solar system ended as the black widow's spidery web snared the helpless firefly.

77. NotKansas

2177 - NotKansas, Mars

Mankind uncovered no signs of extraterrestrial life on Mars during all those missions sifting through the rock-strewn topsoil. Yet less than 10 meters of dust covered the timeworn structures used by the Tunisians to build their collider more than 9 billion years ago. Mars' ancient oceans worked with its once-glorious troposphere to blast the ferrous out of their mighty wheel. Each tag team of scrap iron atoms crushed three oxygen corpuscles out of the opposing forces' lungs, burying all evidence beneath their rusted remains.

The first sentence uttered from the surface since the Tunisians abandoned it was, 'I don't think we're in Kansas anymore' (a classic misquote from an ancient film), and so the initial megastructure on Mars got its official name. The unofficial pronunciation soon devolved to NOTkanSAW because it's just easier to say.

Isaac lived in the NotKansas Elevator, the first of many to surround the rusty planet. Each ferried the vast quantities of material needed to resurrect the collider up to the recycling smelters orbiting Mars. A centrifuge atop each lift provided Earth-like gravity and comfortably sized living quarters and workspaces where the Earthlings supervised the robotic operations. He occasionally visited the surface to go skiing or tobogganing on Olympus Mons or exploring the cavernous remains of the ancient structure.

A major benefit of building a gas-giant spaceship is its ability to absorb just about anything the messy universe throws at it. Jupiter absorbed comet Shoemaker-Levy 9 in July 1994 without flinching. Had it hit Earth, Cosmic Ray would have been working overtime. One hazard of traversing the asteroid belt is the inability of even the cleverest orbital mechanic to track the vast number of fragments whizzing about, especially during the earliest years of the TUG's construction. Katherine's ticket to that wheel in space was punched by a golden projectile the size of an apple. All crew and passengers perished.

⊙---♆♇--☿☾⊕-♄-♂♀--♃●○

Three days after the accident, Isaac received an e-mail from Katherine with a video attached. He shook his head and smiled as he clicked the play button.

Katherine leaned close to the camera, the whites of her eyes exposed, and spoke with an eerie voice. "Isaac. Isaaaaac. I've come back to haunt you from the afterlife!" She paused before both burst out laughing. "Well, that was unexpected, huh? Looks like I'll have plenty of time to practice my guitar. There are so many amazing teachers here. And guess what? They do this rotating decades thing where artists from each era perform. They're doing 1970s Earth now and I'm already discovering what a wonderful period that was to be alive. I signed up to take lessons from Seals and Croft because I want to learn their song *Hummingbird* to play for you. Turns out the Gardener's messenger visited them too.

"Oh, and I offered to be a consultant on the TUG's construction. They'll need a lot of help, especially since the accident. Anyway, I just wanted to send you a quick message to let you know I'm OK, but you knew that already."

When she stepped back, Isaac saw her dressed in the flapper costume she wore on the last night they shared, her curves more dangerous, her stilettos razor-sharp.

She twirled once, smiled, and leaned into the camera. "Don't be a stranger."

78. Mooz's Journey - Time Passages

1 day before the Big Crunch - Saturn

Mooz lived in the spirit lodge of Thunder House Falls for eons, taking simple enjoyment in drifting through time passages. Hunting or fishing when he desired, experiencing the seasons change, from winter's frigid grip to the melting snows of spring, they all pleased him. He had traveled with Anangokaa to strange places, loved by those who dwelled there. It was inevitable, though, he always returned home.

One evening, while smoking his pipe by the campfire, a cold north wind crept into the village. Icy pellets forced him to shelter for the night. Hypnotic, the ice pelting the roof, its overwhelming force sweeping without mercy through the smoke hole, snuffing out the tendriled embers spirit, mantled him in the evening's frosted majesty.

A small bird fluttered in from above and lit on his knee. A pure white hummingbird he had never seen before.

"Nenookaasi, stay with me while this storm passes."

The two spirits talked and laughed for hours, remembering that time when...

Somewhere in the night, remembered whens became snoring Zs.

Mooz awakened to charcoal-stained snow glistening delightfully, bathed in the winter morning sun's feeble warmth. He scanned the dead embers for any sign of life to rekindle the flame. When his eyes passed over two tiny black holes and a triangular shard, the fire burst aflame.

"BOO!" the wings flapped.

Laughter echoed through the forest. One last remember-when.

"Mooz, there's another storm coming tonight that will not pass. Follow the path west today and I'll meet you in the garden."

That morning, Thunder House Falls didn't. Time stopped; gravity had succumbed to ice. He stood there for a moment. No memories, just goodbyes. At the upper waterfall, a stone-paved switchback trail led him up a steep rock face. The leafless birch straining against winter's storm at the summit soon yielded to snow-matted bristlegrass skirting the garden's eastern threshold.

Nenookaasi flew alongside his friend as they approached the tree at the center of the snowy garden. An evanescent glow illuminated its crown. Mooz turned to the hummingbird and smiled. A single tear for his aeonic syzygy as they passed together into the night of time.

Epilogue

The night of time infinitely reshuffled the finite deck. Uli's acorns, and Windigos came and went. A thousand times, a million, a billion. Pick a number. Does the count matter? Each do-over is identical, regardless of separation.

This allows me to write an epilogue, in complete confidence that the timeline remains intact. Let's check back in, not with that wacky astronomer, David Peck Todd, but his wife, Mabel Loomis Todd, mistress of Austin Dickinson. Yes, Emily Dickinson's brother. Mabel edited and published every poem of Emily's she could get her hands on. Oh, what a tangled web they wove in Amherst, Massachusetts, 1888.

☉---♅♆--☿☽⊕-♄-♂♀--♃●○

Austin sat by the fire's warm glow, sipping brandy, as Mabel opened a packet of Emily's poems, given to her that afternoon by the late Miss Dickinson's sister, Lavinia.

The upper left corner of the alphabetized papers contained the words 'A Humming Bird' penciled in Emily's font. She luxuriated in silence as she read the verse unseen by anyone outside the family and instantly recognized poetic genius. A hummingbird, of course, but that ending.

"Austin, did Emily ever talk to you about this poem, *A Humming Bird*?"

"I haven't heard her poems in ages. Remind me, what's it about?"

"Well, it's short, so I'll just read it to you."

A route of evanescence
With a revolving wheel;
A resonance of emerald,
A rush of cochineal;
And every blossom on the bush
Adjusts its tumbled head,
The mail from Tunis, probably,
An easy morning's ride.

"Oh, dear God, yes, now I remember it. The poor woman had completely lost her mind when she wrote that."

"What do you mean? It's a beautiful poem, the prose perfectly captures the essence of a hummingbird."

"She said it wasn't the title in the corner, but the author. Told me she had a nice long conversation with this tiny bird in her garden and, get this, it talked to her by flapping its wings. Wanted to listen to some of her poetry, which she recited from memory. Then she asked it to recite one of its poems and that's what it shared with her."

"What a beautiful story, Austin. You know she had such an active imagination. Perhaps she was just visualizing, to give the poem more depth."

"If there's any depth to her gibberish, it's because she had gone off the deep end. Claims the bird said it was about his home in outer space, something about Saturn, and described their journey as a route of evanescence through the universe. Told her that Earth used to orbit Saturn's revolving wheel. I'm telling you; you'd have to be insane to imagine anything like that!"

"Well, regardless, it's still a beautiful poem."

Acknowledgements

I give my sincerest thanks to the following for their help in making this novel a reality.

My daughter Jennifer, for being my alpha reader and letting me know that I had a story that was worth pursuing, and for always having that great next novel for me to enjoy.

My daughter Mandy, for being one of my beta readers who yearned for more and thus benefitted all who will ever read this book and for recommending her friend from high school to do the cover.

Mary Talbert allayed all my fears about the book's cover by designing a gorgeous piece of art.

I would also like to thank my friend Marvin Clemons for introducing me to Paula Buckner.

Paula played several roles in the production of this novel. With her Master's Degree in Theology and extensive experience as a copy editor and reader's advocate, she helped to stitch this veil together by pointing out that which could not be seen by anyone other than the author.